DEVDUTT PATTANAIK

SITA

AN ILLUSTRATED RETELLING OF THE

RAMAYANA

Illustrations by the author

PENGUIN BOOKS
An imprint of Penguin Random House

PENGUIN BOOKS

USA | Canada | UK | Ireland | Australia
New Zealand | India | South Africa | China

Penguin Books is part of the Penguin Random House group of companies
whose addresses can be found at global.penguinrandomhouse.com

Published by Penguin Random House India Pvt. Ltd
4th Floor, Capital Tower 1, MG Road,
Gurugram 122 002, Haryana, India

Penguin
Random House
India

First published by Penguin Books India 2013

40 39 38 37 36 35

ISBN 9780143064329

Typeset in Garamond by R. Ajith Kumar, New Delhi
Printed at Replika Press Pvt. Ltd, India

www.penguin.co.in

To all those who believe that the *Mahabharata* is more realistic
and complex than the *Ramayana*:

May they realize that both epics speak of dharma,
which means human potential,
not righteous conduct:
the best of what we can do
in continuously changing social contexts,
with no guarantees or certainties,
as we are being constantly and differently judged
by the subject, the object and innumerable witnesses.

In one, the protagonist is a kingmaker who can move around rules,
while in the other the protagonist is a king who must uphold rules,
howsoever distasteful they may be.

Contents

AUTHOR'S NOTE

What Shiva Told Shakti

Shakti, who is Goddess, asks Shiva, who is God, to narrate a tale that will comfort all in turbulent times. Shiva narrates the *Ramayana*, the story of Sita and Ram.

The story pours out in different ways, in different tongues, different words, different nuances and different emotions. Sometimes it is poetry, sometimes prose and sometimes just a gesture. Characters emerge, transform and then disappear in a blink. It tells of plants that talk and animals that think; gods who fail and demons who triumph; heroic villains and villainous heroes; sages and hunters; victims and seducers. Time twists and space unfolds as the narration proceeds.

A curious crow called Kakabhusandi overhears this narration and shares what he can remember with Narada, the travelling sage who loves to gossip and exchange ideas between heaven and earth. Narada narrates what he recollects to Valmiki, who turns the story into a song and teaches it to the twins Luv and Kush.

Luv and Kush sing it before the king of Ayodhya, not realizing that he is the protagonist of the tale, and their father. Ram does not recognize his sons either, and finds it hard to believe that the song they sing so beautifully is all about him. The Ram they describe is so perfect. The Sita he remembers is even better. But the song is incomplete. There is more to the story.

The song of Luv and Kush is Purva-Ramayana, the early section. It describes Ram as *eka-bani* (he whose arrows always strike the target), *eka-vachani* (he who always keeps his word) and *eka-patni* (he who is devoted to a single wife). He is *maryada purushottam*, supreme upholder of rules. It ends happily after six chapters with the triumph of Ram over the rakshasa-king Ravana, and his eventual coronation as king of Ayodhya with his wife, Sita, by his side.

But the tale continues into Uttara-Ramayana, the latter section, with the seventh chapter describing the separation of Sita and Ram, the fight between father and sons, the reconciliation ending with her disappearing into the earth and with him walking into the river Sarayu, never to rise again.

So where does the *Ramayana* actually end, with the happy sixth or the unhappy seventh chapter?

Neither, says the sage Vyasa, he who collected and classified the hymns of the Vedas. He informs us that after shedding his body that was Ram, Vishnu ascends to Vaikuntha, his celestial abode on the ocean of milk, and then returns with a new body, that of Krishna, who is very different from Ram.

Neither king nor faithful to a single wife, Krishna is a cowherd and charioteer lovingly reviled as *makkhan-chor* (one who steals butter), *chitta-chor* (one who steals hearts) and *rana-chhor* (one who runs away from battle and lives to fight another day). He is *leela purushottam*, the supreme game changer. His story is told in the *Mahabharata*. That makes the *Mahabharata* an extension of the *Ramayana*.

Does the *Mahabharata* then mark the end of the story that begins as the *Ramayana*?

Not quite. In the chronicles known as Puranas, we are informed that after Krishna, Vishnu takes many more forms before descending as Kalki, who rides a horse,

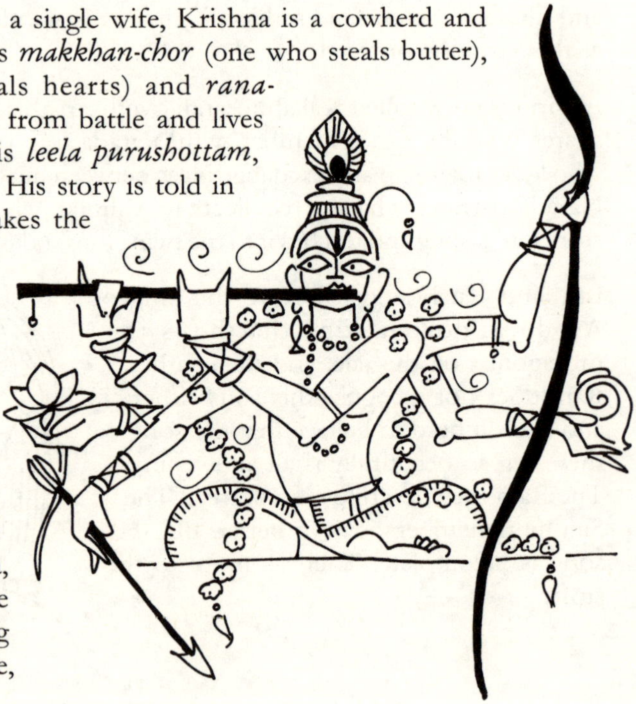

brandishes a sword, very much like an invading plunderer, and heralds pralaya, the end of society as we know it.

Is pralaya then the end of the *Ramayana*?

No, for just when the sea is about to rise and submerge all the lands, Vishnu takes the form of a small fish and begs humanity to save him from bigger fish. The man who responds to his cries becomes Manu, the founder of a new social order, for he demonstrates the uniquely human potential to help the helpless, defying nature's law that favours the strong.

Vishnu then turns into a turtle and helps churn Lakshmi, the goddess of wealth, out of the ocean of milk. He then turns into a boar and raises the earth from under the sea upon which humans can establish society.

This is when Brahma conducts the ritual of yagna. With fire, he domesticates nature and establishes culture. He declares himself creator and master. But Brahma is creator only of culture, not nature. Culture may be his daughter, but nature is his mother. Culture is the domesticated Gauri; but nature is the sovereign Kali. Both are forms of Shakti, the Goddess. Brahma ignores Kali and exerts his authority over Gauri: a father does what a father is not supposed to do! The Goddess resists. But when Brahma persists, an annoyed Shiva wrenches off the creator's head. Shiva mocks Brahma for seeking value through culture. He proposes the path of tapasya, meditation and contemplation that ignites inner fire, tapa, to burn all fears, and hence the desire for domination and dominion. Brahma does not understand. He declares Shiva, the hermit, to be the destroyer.

Vishnu intervenes. He realizes the value of both Brahma's yagna and Shiva's tapasya. He recognizes the fear in Brahma that makes him shun Kali and control Gauri. He recognizes the wisdom of Shiva that enables him to outgrow all fear. It is to bring the two together that he descends from his heavenly abode, Vaikuntha, taking various forms, the avatars.

As Vamana and Parashurama he supports the yagna, as Ram and Krishna he questions the yagna, as Buddha and Kalki he withdraws from the yagna. He also coaxes Shiva to open his eyes that are always shut in tapasya: to engage with culture, marry Brahma's daughter, father children, transform into a householder and see the world from the other's point of view. This Vishnu does again and again, in era after era, from pralaya to pralaya, in a cycle of life that knows neither beginning nor end.

In the eternal turbulence of his household, only the *Ramayana* gives Shiva reprieve. For in every cosmic cycle, Sita and Ram are always at peace in the palace and in the forest; neither is overawed by culture or intimidated by nature. Tapasya makes them wise; yagna enables them to convey love. Together, they establish dharma, the best a human can do, in continuously changing contexts, despite being judged differently by different people whose view of the same situation is very different.

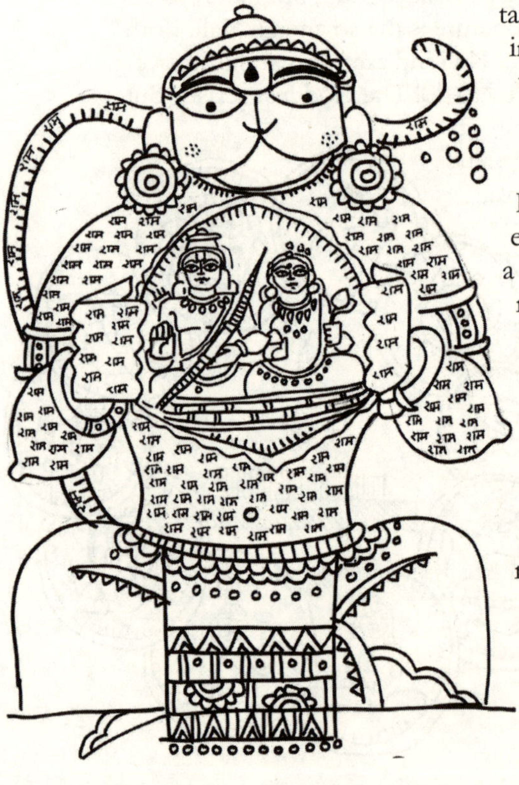

Thus the *Ramayana* is a segment of a vast cyclical tale, one piece of a complex jigsaw puzzle. Events in the tale are a consequence of the past and the cause of the future. It cannot be seen in isolation, at least not in a Hindu context. To do so is to see the stars and miss the sky.

Further, the *Ramayana* is not a single text, or even multiple texts. It is a belief, a tradition, a subjective truth, a thought materialized, ritualized and celebrated through narrations, songs, dances, sculptures, plays, paintings and puppets across hundreds of locations, over hundreds of years. Each retelling has many tributaries and many branches. Each has its own tilt, focusing on different plots, on different characters, on different aspects of the human condition, each one innovatively recreating as well as contributing to the plots and the themes. What makes a Ram-katha, Ram-leela, Ram-akhyan, Ram-charita, Ram-kirti or Ram-kavya venerable is its ability to uplift the spirits, despite, or even because of, the disturbing aspects of the tale.

There are other *Ramayana*s, of course. There are the ancient Sanskrit plays where Ram is a mighty yet lovelorn hero, not quite God. There is Bhatti's *Ramayana* that has more to do with the rules of Sanskrit grammar than the telling of Ram's story. There is the *Ramayana* of the Jains where Ram subscribes to the Jain doctrine of non-violence and leaves the killing of Ravana to Lakshman. There is the *Ramayana* of the Buddhists where Ram is the Bodhisattva who keeps his word by staying in the forest for the stipulated period of time, even though he can return home early. There are the *Ramayana*s of South-East Asia such as the Thai *Ramakien* and the Khmer *Reamker* where Ram is a popular cultural icon, even a model for kings, but not divine. Then there are the modern retellings that are more political and less reverent, more judgemental and less enquiring. In spirit, they are very different from the *Ramayana*s that nourish the Indian soul. They share the same literary narrative (*shabda-artha*) but not the same emotional narrative (*bhaava-artha*).

Valmiki identifies Shiva's *Ramayana* as Ananda Ramayana; Vyasa calls it Adhyatma Ramayana. Here Ram is not a hero, he is God. Sita is not a victim, she is the Goddess. And Ravana is not a villain, he is a brahmin (offspring of Brahma) who despite his vast knowledge is unable to expand (brah, in Sanskrit) his mind (manas) to appreciate the Goddess, hence is unable to find God (brahman).

The Goddess in Hindu scriptures is not the female version of God favoured by feminists, nor is God the all-powerful, judgemental external agency described in the Bible, who sets down codes of conduct and determines what is right and wrong. God is not even the deified hero of Greek mythology, which greatly informs the modern rational and atheist discourse. Goddess and God have very particular meanings in the Hindu understanding of the universe.

Indic thought, particularly Hindu thought, starts with an observation: the human ability to imagine that enables us to position ourselves outside nature. We alone, of all living creatures, can refuse to submit to nature's laws. This human mind (manas/purusha) is potentially God while nature (prakriti/maya/shakti) is always the Goddess.

The male form *represents* the mind, the world of thoughts. The female form *represents* nature, the world of things. This gendering of gender-neutral ideas is done to communicate ideas through the powerful medium of stories. It is based on the observation that a man's body can create new life only through a woman's body just as formless thoughts can only be expressed through things.

- A mind that is self-indulgent and dominating is the creator Brahma, God who shall not be worshipped. For him, nature is the patient Saraswati, source of wisdom, awaiting his enlightenment.

- A mind that is indifferent to the other's point of view is the destroyer Shiva, the hermit. For him nature is the alluring Shakti, source of power, awaiting his engagement.

- A mind that cares for the other's point of view is the preserver Vishnu, the householder. For him, nature is the playful Lakshmi, source of enrichment and abundance. When Vishnu is Krishna, Lakshmi is Radha, Rukmini, Satyabhama and Draupadi. When Vishnu is Ram, she is Sita.

The notions of creation, preservation and destruction in Hindu mythology thus deal with culture, not nature. Of course, this subtle interplay of word and meaning can easily be misunderstood, and often is, especially since we live in a world that is dominated by the Western discourse shaped by Greek and biblical mythology that are more comfortable with tangible, measurable and categorizable actions and things than abstract thoughts.

This book seeks to rediscover the *Ramayana* as one of the many maps of the human mind, an open-source document evolved by generations of thinkers, a narration that evokes empathy and affection for the human condition. I hope I succeed. If I don't, indulge me, for:

Within infinite myths lies an eternal truth
Who sees it all?
Varuna has but a thousand eyes
Indra, a hundred
You and I, only two.

- The traditional belief is that whatever *Ramayana* we know is incomplete. Of the millions of *Ramayana* narrations available, Shiva narrates the story in a hundred thousand verses, Hanuman narrates 60,000 of these, Valmiki narrates 24,000 and all other poets narrate fewer than that.
- Academicians often distinguish the informal story of Ram or Ram-katha from the *Ramayana*, the more formal written retellings attributed to a poet or an author. There are many Ram-kathas and many *Ramayana*s, each influencing the other.
- For the past two centuries, European and American scholarship with its methodologies and academic funding has played a significant role in the study of the *Ramayana*. It has

allowed for meticulous translations and documentation of rare *Ramayana*s and Ramkathas that would otherwise have stayed inaccessible.

- European scholars in colonial times preferred the conqueror's gaze and so interpreted the *Ramayana* along racial terms (Aryans versus Dravidians, North versus South, Vishnu-worshippers versus Shiva-worshippers, priests versus kings).
- American scholars in postcolonial times have preferred the saviour's gaze and so interpret the *Ramayana* in terms of gender and caste conflict, which inadvertently leads to demonizing men, especially brahmins, and viewing devotion only in feudal terms.
- Indian scholars tend to be defensive or apologetic as they are expected to carry the burden of justifying the actions of their heroes and gods.
- Modern scholarship values the outsider's gaze, as it is deemed more objective, scientific and less sentimental. Writings that flow from this often come across as rather irreverent and judgemental to most Hindus. For while modern scholarship demands that the enquirer distance himself from the object of enquiry, traditional scholarship from India demands the enquirer be transformed by the enquiry.
- Modern scholarship has been unable to classify the *Ramayana*. Is it actually history, as right-wing scholars insist? Is it propaganda literature serving the interests of particular social groups, as left-wing scholars insist? Is it the story of God, as the devotees believe it is? Or is it the map of the human mind, an attempt to explain the human condition?
- There are three dominant trends of approaching the various retellings of the *Ramayana*: first, the modern gaze ('only the *Ramayana* of Valmiki in Sanskrit is valid'); second, the postmodern gaze ('all *Ramayana* retellings are equally valid'); third, the post-postmodern gaze ('respect the gaze of the believer').
- Few have been able to fathom the hold of this 2500-year-old narrative over the Indian psyche, especially those who see the epic as irrational but modern education as a tool to make people rational. In 1987 the first teleserial based on the *Ramayana*, made by Ramanand Sagar, brought the country to a standstill every Sunday morning when it was being telecast. In 1992 dispute over the location of the birthplace of Ram led to a political crisis that ripped the secular heart of the nation. In 2013 the *Ramayana* continues to be referred to in articles that speak of the unsatisfactory status of women in India. Appropriated by politicians, criticized by feminists, deconstructed by academicians, the epic stands serene in its majesty giving joy, hope and meaning to millions.

A Few *Ramayana* Beacons across History

Before 2nd century BCE: Oral tellings by travelling bards
2nd century BCE: Valmiki's Sanskrit *Ramayana*
1st century CE: Vyasa's Ramopakhyan in his *Mahabharata*
2nd century CE: Bhasa's Sanskrit play *Pratima-nataka*
3rd century CE: Sanskrit Vishnu Purana
4th century CE: Vimalasuri's Prakrit *Paumachariya* (Jain)
5th century CE: Kalidasa's Sanskrit *Raghuvamsa*
6th century CE: Pali *Dashratha Jataka* (Buddhist)
6th century CE: First images of Ram on Deogarh temple walls
7th century CE: Sanskrit *Bhattikavya*
8th century CE: Bhavabhuti's Sanskrit play *Mahavira-charita*
9th century CE: Sanskrit Bhagavat Purana
10th century CE: Murari's Sanskrit play *Anargha-Raghava*
11th century: Bhoja's Sanskrit *Champu Ramayana*
12th century: Kamban's Tamil *Iramavataram*
13th century: Sanskrit *Adhyatma Ramayana*
13th century: Buddha Reddy's Telugu *Ranganath Ramayana*
14th century: Sanskrit *Adbhut Ramayana*
15th century: Krittivasa's Bengali *Ramayana*
15th century: Kandali's Assamese *Ramayana*
15th century: Balaram Das's Odia *Dandi Ramayana*
15th century: Sanskrit *Ananda Ramayana*
16th century: Tulsidas's Avadhi *Ram-charit-manas*
16th century: Akbar's collection of *Ramayana* paintings
16th century: Eknath's Marathi *Bhavarth Ramayana*
16th century: Torave's Kannada *Ramayana*
16th century: Ezhuthachan's Malayalam *Ramayana*
17th century: Guru Govind Singh's Braj *Gobind Ramayana*, as part of *Dasam Granth*
18th century: Giridhar's Gujarati *Ramayana*
18th century: Divakara Prakasa Bhatta's Kashmiri *Ramayana*
19th century: Bhanubhakta's Nepali *Ramayana*
1921: Cinema, silent film *Sati Sulochana*
1943: Cinema, *Ram Rajya* (only film seen by Mahatma Gandhi)
1955: Radio, Marathi *Geet Ramayana*
1970: Comic book, Amar Chitra Katha's *Rama*
1987: Television, Ramanand Sagar's Hindi *Ramayana*
2003: Novel, Ashok Banker's *Ramayana* series

**Dating is approximate and highly speculative, especially of the earlier works.*

- The *Ramayana* literature can be studied in four phases. The first phase, till the second century CE, is when the Valmiki *Ramayana* takes final shape. In the second phase, between the second and tenth centuries CE, many Sanskrit and Prakrit plays and poems are written on the *Ramayana*. Here we see an attempt to locate Ram in Buddhist and Jain traditions as well, but he is most successfully located as the royal form of Vishnu on earth through Puranic literature. In the third phase, after the tenth century, against the backdrop of the rising tide of Islam, the *Ramayana* becomes the epic of choice to be put down in local tongues. Here the trend is to be devotional, with Ram as God and Hanuman as his much-venerated devotee and servant. Finally, in the fourth phase, since the nineteenth century, strongly influenced by the European and American gaze, the *Ramayana* is decoded, deconstructed and reimagined based on modern political theories of justice and fairness.
- The story of Ram was transmitted orally for centuries, from 500 BCE onwards, reaching its final form in Sanskrit by 200 BCE. The author of this work is identified as one Valmiki. The poetry, all scholars agree, is outstanding. It has traditionally been qualified as adi kavya, the first poem. All later poets keep referring to Valmiki as the fountainhead of Ram's tale.
- Valmiki's work was transmitted orally by travelling bards. It was put down in writing much later. As a result, there are two major collections of this original work – northern and southern – with about half the verses in common. The general agreement is that of the seven chapters the first (Ram's childhood) and last (Ram's rejection of Sita) sections are much later works.
- The brahmins resisted putting down Sanskrit in writing and preferred the oral tradition (shruti). It was the Buddhist and Jain scholars who chose the written word over the oral word, leading to speculation that the Jain and Buddhist retellings of Ram's story were the first to be put down in writing in Pali and Prakrit.
- Regional *Ramayana*s were put down in writing only after 1000 CE, first in the south by the twelfth century, then in the east by the fifteenth century and finally in the north by the sixteenth century.
- Most women's *Ramayana*s are oral. Songs sung in the courtyards across India refer more to domestic rituals and household issues rather than to the grand ideas of epic narratives. However, in the sixteenth century, two women did write the *Ramayana*: Molla in Telugu and Chandrabati in Bengali.
- Men who wrote the *Ramayana* belonged to different communities. Buddha Reddy belonged to the landed gentry, Balaram Das and Sarala Das belonged to the community of scribes and bureaucrats and Kamban belonged to the community of temple musicians.
- Keen to appreciate the culture of his people, the Mughal emperor Akbar, in the sixteenth century, ordered the translation of the *Ramayana* from Sanskrit to Persian, and got his court painters to illustrate the epic using Persian techniques. This led to a proliferation of miniature paintings based on the *Ramayana* patronized by kings of Rajasthan, Punjab, Himachal and the Deccan in the seventeenth, eighteenth and nineteenth centuries.

A Few *Ramayana* Anchors across Geography

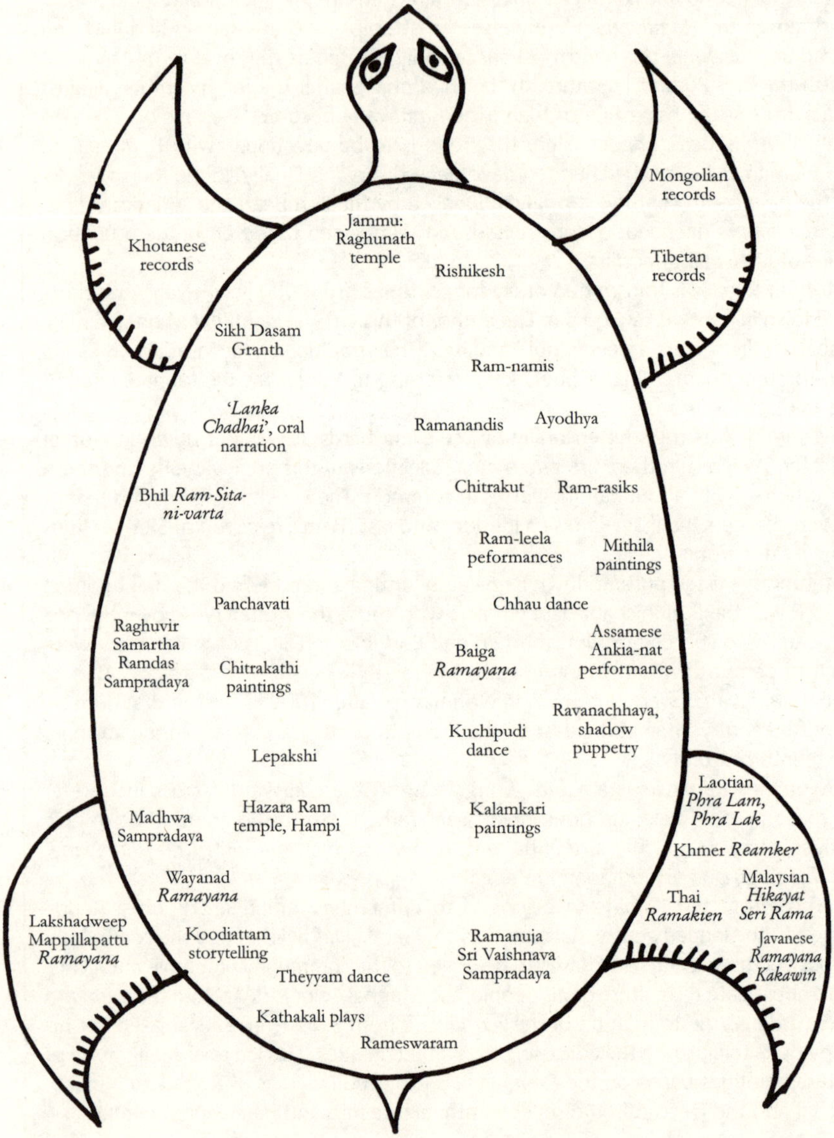

* *Locations not drawn to scale*

- Across India there are villages and towns that associate themselves with an event in the *Ramayana*. In Mumbai, for example, there is a water tank called 'Banaganga' created by the bana (arrow) of Ram.
- Most Indians have heard songs and stories of the *Ramayana* or seen it being performed as a play or painted on cloth or sculpted on temple walls; few have read it. Each art form has its own unique narration, expression and point of view.
- The earliest iconography of Ram is found in the sixth-century Deogarh temple in Uttar Pradesh established during the Gupta period. Here he is identified as an avatar of Vishnu, who in turn is associated with royalty.
- The Alvars of Tamil Nadu wrote the earliest bhakti songs that refer to Ram in devotional terms as early as the seventh century.
- In the twelfth century, Ramanuja gave bhakti (devotion) in general and Ram-bhakti in particular (devotion to God embodied as Ram) validity through Sanskrit commentaries based on the Vedanta philosophy. In the fourteenth century, Ramanand spread Ram-bhakti to North India. Ramdas did this in the Maharashtra region in the seventeenth century. The names Ramanuja (younger brother of Ram), Ramanand (bliss of Ram) and Ramdas (servant of Ram) indicate the value they placed on Ram.
- Tibetan scholars have recorded stories from the *Ramayana* in Tibet since the eighth century. Similar records have been found in Mongolia in the east and Central Asia (Khotan) in the west. These probably spread via the Silk Route.
- The story of Ram did spread beyond the subcontinent but had its most powerful impact in South-East Asia, where it spread via seafaring merchants who traded in fabrics and spices. These South-East Asian *Ramayana*s lack elements that are typically associated with the bhakti movement of India, suggesting that transmission probably took place before the tenth century CE, after which Ram became a major figure in the bhakti movement.
- The *Ramayana* of Laos is very clearly related to Buddhism but the Thai *Ramakien* identifies itself as Hindu, even though it embellishes the temple walls of the Emerald Buddha in Bangkok.
- From the fourteenth to the eighteenth centuries, the capital of the Thai royalty (until it was sacked) was called Ayutthaya (Ayodhya) and its kings were named after Ram.
- The *Ramayana* continues to be part of the heritage of many South-East Asian countries such as Indonesia and Malaysia, even after they embraced Islam. So now there are stories of Adam encountering Ravana in their *Ramayana*s.
- While it is common to refer to one *Ramayana* in each regional language, for example, Kamban's in Tamil or Eknath's in Marathi, there are in fact several dozen works in each Indian language. For example, in Odia, besides Balaram Das's *Dandi Ramayana*, we have the *Ramayana*s of Sarala Das (*Bilanka Ramayana*), Upendra Bhanja (*Baidehi-bilasa*) and Bishwanath Kuntiya (*Bichitra Ramayana*).
- There is a saying in Kannada that Adi Sesha, the serpent who holds the earth on its hood, is groaning under the weight of the numerous authors and poets who have retold the *Ramayana*.

Ram's Name in Different Scripts

Kharoshti script 300 BCE	𐨪𐨨
Ashokan Brahmi 300 BCE	𑀭𑀸𑀫
Gupta Brahmi 300 CE	𑀭𑀸𑀫
Kashmiri Sharada 800 CE	𑆫𑆳𑆩
Kannada (Kadamba)	ರಾಮ್
Telugu	రామ్
Tamil	ராம்
Malayalam	രാം
Odiya	ରାମ
Bengali	রাম
Devanagari (Hindi/Marathi)	राम
Gurmukhi	ਰਾਮ
Gujarati	રામ
Urdu	رام

**Dating is approximate*

- Most scripts in India emerged from the script that we now call Brahmi.
- In Jain traditions, the first Tirthankara of this era, Rishabha, passed on the first script to his daughter Brahmi.
- Writing Ram's name is a popular expression of devotion. In fact, there is a 'Ram Ram Bank' in Ayodhya where people even today deposit booklets of Ram's name (Ram nam).
- Though a highly evolved language, Sanskrit has no script of its own. It was written down after Prakrit, first in the Brahmi script and then in scripts such as Siddham, Sharada, Grantha which were eventually supplanted by modern scripts, most prominently Devanagari since the nineteenth century.

PROLOGUE

Descent from Ayodhya

Blades of grass!

Ends of her hair sticking out!

That is all that was left of Sita after she had plunged into the earth. No more would she be seen walking above the ground.

The people of Ayodhya watched their king caress the grass for a long time, stoic and serene as ever, not a teardrop in his eyes. They wanted to fall at his feet and ask his forgiveness. They wanted to hug and comfort him. They had broken his heart and wanted to apologize, but they knew he neither blamed them nor judged them. They were his children, and he, their father, lord of the Raghu clan, ruler of Ayodhya, was Sita's Ram.

'Come, it is time to go home,' said Ram, placing his hands on the shoulders of Luv and Kush, his twin sons.

Home? Was not the forest their home? That was where they had lived all their lives. But they did not argue with the king, this stranger, this man who they now had to call their father, who until recently had been their enemy. But their mother's last instruction to them was very clear: 'Do as your father says.' They would not disobey. They too would be sons worthy of the Raghu clan.

As the royal elephant carrying the king and his two sons passed through the city gates, Hanuman, the monkey-servant of Ram, caught sight of Yama, the god of death, hiding behind the trees, looking intently at Ram. Hanuman immediately lashed his tail on the ground: a warning to the god of death not to come anywhere near the king or his family.

A frightened Yama stayed away from Ayodhya.

But Ram's brother Lakshman did not stay away from Yama: a few days later, for some mysterious reason, Lakshman left the city and walked deep into the forest, and beheaded himself.

Hanuman did not understand. His world was crumbling: first Sita, then Lakshman. Who next? Ram? He could not let that happen. He *would* not let that happen. He refused to budge from the gates of Ayodhya. No one would go in, or out.

Shortly thereafter Ram lost his ring. It slipped from his finger and fell into a crack in the palace floor. 'Will you fetch it for me, Hanuman?' requested Ram.

Ever willing to please his master, Hanuman reduced himself to the size of a bee and slipped into the crack in the floor.

To his surprise, it was no ordinary crack. It was a tunnel, one that went deep into the bowels of the earth. It led him to Naga-loka, the abode of snakes.

As soon as he entered, he found two serpents coiling around his feet. He flicked them away. They returned with a couple more serpents. Hanuman flicked them away too. Before long, Hanuman found himself enwrapped by a thousand serpents, determined to pin him down. He gave in, and allowed them to drag him to their king, Vasuki, a serpent with seven hoods, each displaying a magnificent jewel.

'What brings you to Naga-loka?' hissed Vasuki.

'I seek a ring.'

'Oh, that! I will tell you where it is, if you tell me something first.'

'What?' asked Hanuman.

'The root of every tree that enters the earth whispers a name: Sita. Who is she? Do you know?'

'She is the beloved of the man whose ring I seek.'

'Then tell me all about her. And tell me about her beloved. And I will point you to the ring.'

'Nothing will give me greater joy that narrating the story of Sita and her Ram. Much of what I will tell you I experienced myself. Some I have heard from others. Within all these stories is the truth. Who knows it all? Varuna had but a thousand eyes; Indra, a hundred; and I, only two.'

All the serpents of Naga-loka gathered around Hanuman, eager to hear his tale. There is no sun or moon in Naga-loka, nor is there fire. The only light came from the seven luminous jewels on the seven hoods of Vasuki. But that was enough.

- Sita has always been associated with vegetation, especially grass.
- Kusha grass is a long, sharp grass that is an essential ingredient of Vedic rituals. Those performing the yagna sit on mats made of this grass and tie a ring of the grass around their finger. It is used as a torch to carry fire and as a broom to sweep the precincts. The Puranas link it to Brahma's hair, Vishnu's hair (when he took the form of a turtle) and Sita's hair.
- Ram belongs to the Raghu-kula or the Raghu clan. He is therefore called Raghava, he who is a Raghu, or Raghavendra, best amongst Raghus. Raghu was Ram's great-great-grandfather and belonged to the grand Suryavamsa or the solar dynasty of kings, established by Ikshavaku and known for their moral uprightness.
- Yama, the Hindu god of death, is described as a dispassionate being who does not distinguish between king and beggar when it comes to taking their life when their time on earth is up. He fears no one but Hanuman, in popular imagination.

- Hanuman is a monkey or vanara. The monkey is also a symbol of the restless human mind. He is the remover of problems (sankat mochan), feared even by death, hence the most popular guardian god of the Hindu pantheon.
- Broadly, the Hindu mythic world has three layers: the sky inhabited by devas, apsaras and gandharvas; the nether regions inhabited by asuras and nagas; the earth inhabited by humans (manavas), rakshasas and yakshas. These are the lokas, or realms: Swarga-loka above, Patal-loka and Naga-loka below, and Bhu-loka – that is, earth – in the middle.
- Nagas or hooded serpent beings who can take human shape are known to have jewels in their hoods. These jewels have many magical properties that enable them to grant a wish, resurrect the dead, heal the sick and attract fortune.
- Traditionally, the *Ramayana* was always narrated in a ritual context. For example, Bhavabhuti's eighth-century play *Mahavira-charita* was performed either in the temple or during the festival of Shiva.
- The idea of Hanuman narrating the *Ramayana* is popular in folklore. It is sometimes called Hanuman Nataka.
- Hanuman, the celibate monkey, is considered in many traditions to be either a form of Shiva, a son of Shiva, or Shiva himself. The nagas embody fertility, hence they are closely associated with the Goddess.
- Western thought prefers to locate the *Ramayana* in a historical and geographical context: who wrote it, when, where? Traditional Indian thought prefers to liberate the *Ramayana* from the limits imposed by time and space. Ram of academics is bound to a period and place. Ram of devotees is in the human mind, hence timeless. Politicians, of course, have a different agenda.

BOOK ONE

Birth

'She was born of the earth and raised amongst sages.'

Foundling in the Furrow

It was the start of the sowing season. The fences separated the farm from the jungle. Outside the blackbuck roamed free; within the farmer would decide what was crop and what was weed.

The farmers invited their king Janaka to be the first to plough the land with a golden hoe. To the sound of bells and drums and conch-shell trumpets, the king shoved the hoe into the ground and began to till the land. Soft, moist earth, dark as the night sky, was pushed away on either side to reveal a furrow. As the furrow extended itself, firmly and fast, the king felt confident and the farmers were pleased.

Suddenly the king stopped. The furrow revealed a golden hand: tiny fingers rising up like grass, as if drawn by the sunshine. Janaka moved the dirt away, and found hidden within the soft, moist earth a baby, a girl, healthy and radiant, smiling joyfully, as if waiting to be found.

Was it an abandoned child? No, said the farmers, convinced it was a gift from the earth-goddess to their childless king. But this was not fruit of his seed – how could she be his daughter? Fatherhood, said Janaka, springs in the heart, not from a seed.

Janaka picked up the infant, who gurgled happily in his arms. Placing her close to his heart, he declared, 'This is Bhumija, daughter of the earth. You may call her Maithili, princess of Mithila, or Vaidehi, lady from Videha, or Janaki, she who chose Janaka. I will call her Sita, she who was found in a furrow, she who chose me to be her father.'

Everyone felt gladness in their hearts. The ceremony was truly successful. The childless king had returned to the palace a father. No harvest could be better.

- Videha is located in modern-day Bihar (Mithila region) suggesting the narrative has the Gangetic plains as its base.
- Vedic hymns refer both to herding and agricultural activities. The ritual of tilling the soil was closely associated with the Vedic yagna Vajapeya that was meant for 'vaja' or food.
- Furrows do not exist in nature. Furrows indicate agriculture, the birth of human civilization. Sita then embodies the fruit of nature's domestication and the rise of human culture.
- In the Vedas, there is reference to Sita, goddess of fertility.
- Janaka is a family name. The first Janaka was Nimi. His son was Mithi, who founded the city of Mithila.
- In the *Mahabharata*'s Ramopakhyan, Sita is Janaka's biological daughter. In many regional versions, Sita is found in a box or the earth-goddess, Bhudevi, appears and gifts the child to Janaka. There are even versions such as the Jain *Vasudevahindi* and the Kashmiri *Ramavatara-charita* where Sita is actually a child of Ravana's, cast away into the sea and passed from the sea through the earth to Janaka.
- In the *Ananda Ramayana*, Vishnu gives a king called Padmaksha a fruit that contains a baby, who is Lakshmi incarnate. She is named Padmavati who eventually becomes Sita.
- That Sita is not born from a mother's womb makes her 'ayonija'. Children born so are considered special. They defy death.
- A rationalist would say that Sita was perhaps a foundling, a girl child abandoned.
- The district of Sitamarhi in Bihar is associated with the field where Sita was ploughed out by Janaka.

A Daughter Called Shanta

Dashratha, king of Ayodhya in the land of Kosala, also had a daughter. Her name was Shanta, she who is peaceful. But she did not bring Dashratha peace, for he wanted sons.

So Dashratha went north to Kekaya and asked King Ashwapati for his daughter's hand in marriage. It was foretold the princess would bear an illustrious son. The

king objected, 'Kaushalya is already your wife, and has given you a daughter. If my Kaikeyi marries you she will just be a junior queen.'

'But if she bears me a son, he will be king and she will be queen mother,' argued Dashratha, to convince Ashwapati, who let him marry Kaikeyi.

Unfortunately, Kaikeyi gave birth to neither son nor daughter. So Dashratha married a third time, a woman named Sumitra, but even she failed to produce a child.

Dashratha was filled with despair. Who would he pass on the crown to? And how would he face his ancestors, in the land of the dead, across the river Vaitarni, for they would ask him if he had left behind sons who would help them be reborn?

That is when Rompada, king of Anga, came to him and said, 'My kingdom is struck with drought because Indra, ruler of the sky, god of rain, is afraid of one of my subjects, Rishyashringa, son of Vibhandaka, a mighty hermit. This same Rishyashringa, who causes drought in my kingdom, is, I am sure, the cause of your childlessness. The crisis will end only if my daughter succeeds in seducing this hermit and turns him into a householder, thus tempering his powers to Indra's satisfaction. But I have no daughter, Dashratha. Let me adopt yours. And if she succeeds in bringing rain to Anga, I will make sure that Rishyashringa compels Indra to give you sons.'

Suddenly, the daughter became the answer to Dashratha's problem.

- The story of Shanta is elaborated in the *Mahabharata* and in many Puranas. In some versions, like the southern manuscript of the Valmiki *Ramayana*, she is the daughter of Dashratha adopted by Rompada and in other versions she is Rompada's daughter with no association with Dashratha. The narratives are not clear if Kaushalya is the mother.
- In Upendra Bhanja's Odia *Baidehi-bilasa*, courtesans led by Jarata seduce Rishyashringa and bring him on a boat to perform the yagna that brings rain to Anga. Mighty pleased, Dashratha offers his daughter, Shanta, and brings him to Kosala to perform a yagna

that will give him sons. The story reveals a comfort with eroticism and courtesans who were part of the temple devadasi culture that thrived in coastal Odisha, especially in the Jagannath temple in Puri. Tulsidas in his Avadhi *Ram-charit-manas*, which was meant to serve as devotional literature, does not mention Rishyashringa at all. In the Sanskrit *Adhyatma Ramayana*, which focuses on metaphysics, Rishyashringa makes an appearance, but the tale of seduction is kept out.

- In a male-dominated society, when a couple does not bear a child, the problem is first attributed to the wife, and only then to the husband.
- In Hindu mythology, fertility of the land is closely linked with the fertility of the people who reside on the land, especially the king. Thus the story connects the failure of the rains with the failure of the king's ability to father sons.
- The tale correlates drought with monastic practices. Celibacy affects the rains adversely. This reflects the discomfort with rising monastic orders. Even the hermit Shiva is turned into a householder, Shankara, by the Goddess, to ensure that the snow of the mountains melts to create a river - Ganga - on whose banks civilization can thrive.

The Abduction of Rishyashringa

Vibhandaka was called a rishi, a seer, because he saw what others did not. He knew that food turns into sap, then blood, then flesh, then nerve, then bone, then marrow and finally seed. When seed is shed, new life comes into being. No living creature has control over the shedding of their seed, except humans, especially men.

When seed is retained in the body it turns into ojas. Ojas can be turned into tapa through the practice of tapasya. Tapa is fire of the mind, generated through meditation and contemplation. With tapa comes siddha, the power to control nature: the power to compel gods to bring down rain, make barren women fertile, sterile men virile, to walk on water and fly without wings. Vibhandaka was determined to perform tapasya, churn tapa, acquire siddha, control nature and make her dance to his tune.

Fearful that Vibhandaka would succeed and use siddha against him, Indra sent an apsara, a damsel from his paradise, to seduce him. The mere sight of this apsara caused Vibhandaka to lose control of his senses. Semen squirted out of his body – much against his will – and fell on the grass. A doe ate this. So powerful was the semen that it made the doe pregnant. She gave birth to a human male child with antlers, who came to be known as Rishyashringa.

Vibhandaka saw Rishyashringa as a symbol of his personal failure, and so raised him with rage and ambition, without any knowledge of women. He drew a line around his hermitage; nothing feminine could cross this line and approach his son: neither a cow nor a mare, neither goose, ewe, doe nor sow. No flowers bloomed here, there was no nectar or fragrance; it was a barren land. Any woman who dared cross the line around Vibhandaka's hermitage instantly burst into flames, which is why Indra could not send his apsaras to seduce Rishyashringa.

Furious, Indra had refused to come anywhere near Anga, where the hermitage was located, until the ruler of Anga resolved this problem. The resulting drought compelled Rompada to seek out the women of his land. But no man was willing to risk the life of his wife or sister or daughter. Even the king's queens, concubines and courtesans refused to help. That is why Rompada needed Shanta, renowned not just for her beauty but also for her intelligence and her courage.

Shanta waited for the few hours in the day when Vibhandaka left the hermitage to gather food from the forest. During that window of opportunity, she stood outside the gates and sang songs of love and passion, drawing Rishyashringa towards her. The young, innocent ascetic wondered what kind of a creature she was. At first he feared her sight, then he allowed himself to enjoy her song, and finally he had the courage to talk to her.

'I am a woman,' revealed Shanta, 'a different kind of a human. You can create life outside your body but I can create life inside mine.' Rishyashringa did not understand. 'If you step out,' said Shanta, 'I will show you.' Rishyashringa was too afraid to cross the threshold. So from afar he watched Shanta reveal the secrets of her body, arousing in him emotions and desires and a deep sense of loneliness he had never known before.

When Rishyashringa told his father about this creature, Vibhandaka warned him, 'She is a monster who seeks to enslave you. Stay away from her.'

But try as he might, Rishyashringa could not stop thinking about her. After days and nights of suffering, he could not hold back any more. When his father was away, he found the courage to cross the boundary of Vibhandaka's hermitage, and offered himself freely to Shanta. She returned triumphant to Anga with Rishyashringa in her arms.

- While the story of the 'Lakshman-rekha' fired popular imagination, the story of the 'Vibhandaka-rekha' did not. Lakshman's line seeks to secure a woman's chastity. Vibhandaka's line seeks to secure a man's celibacy. The former is necessary for social order. The latter threatens the very order of nature and culture.
- The tension between the hermit's way and the householder's way is made explicit in this story. The hermit's way threatens the world by not producing children and not allowing rain to fall. The solution lies with sex and marriage.
- The Puranas are full of stories about how a beautiful nymph seduces the celibate hermit. Tapasvi means fire (tapa) ascetic, and apsara means water (apsa) nymph.
- The association of women with fertility is one reason that in later times women were viewed as temptresses and distractions from spiritual activities that came to be increasingly associated with celibacy.
- Hindu temples are incomplete unless they are embellished with images of happy couples making love. Marriage is critical for both the deity and the devotee. Celibacy as the route to divinity was initially viewed rather suspiciously, but later it became the dominant mode of religious expression because of monastic orders such as Buddhism, Jainism and Vedanta acharyas, as well as the global spread of Catholic and Victorian values in colonial times.
- The Rishyashringa story is also found in the Buddhist Jataka tales such as the Nalini Jataka and Alambusha Jataka indicating this struggle between monastic celibacy, popularized by Buddhist monks, and the need for children in society. In these stories, Vibhandaka is the Bodhisattva (Buddha in a former life) and Shanta is identified as Nalini. In the Mahavastu scripture, Rishyashringa is identified as Ekashringa, the Bodhisattva, and Nalini is Yashodhara (Buddha's wife) in her previous life.
- Until the rise of Buddhism, the hermit was clearly someone who stayed outside the city, in the forest. The Buddha brought the monastic way into the city, creating a tension. The resolution of this tension manifests itself in the number of fertility images of trees, pots overflowing with vegetation, fat men and bejewelled women in Buddhist shrines.
- Rishyashringa is linked to the sacred city of Shringeri in Karnataka.
- It is significant that the great epics of India, the *Ramayana* and the *Mahabharata*, reached their final form in the centuries that followed the rise of Buddhism, whose founder, born a prince, abandoned his wife and infant son, to start a monastic order. The *Ramayana* and the *Mahabharata* are all about family; they strive to show how it is possible for a hermit to live a householder's life; there is no need to become a monk. The struggle between the hermit's way and the householder's way forms the cornerstone of Indian thought. They manifest as Shiva's way and Vishnu's way.

Dashratha Gets Four Sons

The rains poured. Flowers bloomed and beckoned the bees. The bull sought the cow, and the buck sought the doe. All was well in Anga. Rompada kept his promise and requested Rishyashringa to help Dashratha father sons. Rishyashringa readily agreed. Well versed in the secrets of nature, he decided to conduct a yagna.

Rishyashringa declared Dashratha as the yajaman, initiator of the yagna, and prepared the altar, lit the fire and chanted potent hymns to invoke the devas. He instructed Dashratha to feed the devas who were being invoked with offerings of clarified butter. Each time Dashratha poured ghee into the fire, he was asked to say 'svaha', reminding the gods it was he who was feeding them. As the devas burped in satisfaction, Rishyashringa requested the gods to satisfy Dashratha's hunger, in exchange. The invocation, the offerings and the requests continued, until the devas were so pleased that from the yagna emerged a potion, the havis. This when consumed by Dashratha's wives would enable them to bear sons.

Dashratha gave half the potion to Kaushalya, the wife he respected, and half to Kaikeyi, the wife he loved. Kaushalya gave a quarter of her potion to Sumitra, as she felt she should not be overlooked. Kaikeyi did the same. As a result, Kaushalya gave birth to Ram, Kaikeyi to Bharata, and Sumitra to the twins Lakshman and Shatrughna.

Thus, Dashratha's three wives could become mothers of four sons all because of his daughter, Shanta.

- The birth of Ram is celebrated as Ram Navami, the ninth day of the waxing moon in spring. On this day, images of Ram are placed on a swing and worshipped. He is the ideal son, the obedient son that mothers crave for.
- Based on astrological calculation, Ram's date of birth has been identified as 10 January 5114 BCE, nearly seven thousand years ago.
- Village songs in the Gangetic plains say that Ram was born after sunset but there was no need for a lamp as Ram's radiance filled the room. There are songs where Dashratha thanks Ram for saving him from the humiliation of being a king who cannot father an heir. We also have songs where a delighted Kaushalya lists the prayers and invocations that led to the birth of Ram.
- Valmiki's *Ramayana* does not refer to Rishyashringa as a son-in-law. Later versions turn Rishyashringa into the son-in-law perhaps to dismiss allusions that Rishyashringa was brought in to perform niyoga, an ancient practice of getting a hermit to make childless women pregnant, which is elaborated in the *Mahabharata*.
- When the European Orientalists were first exposed to the Vedic scriptures and read about the yagna, they called it the 'fire sacrifice' based on their understanding of ritual. But in a sacrifice, the one who sacrifices loses something to appease a demanding deity. In a yagna, the beneficiary is the yajaman who initiates the yagna. He gives in order to receive. It is therefore best defined as an 'exchange'. The fire is the medium through which the exchange takes place. Fire is the 'middleman', much like the priest.
- That Kaushalya and Kaikeyi share their portions with Sumitra becomes significant when compared to the three main queens of the *Mahabharata* – Gandhari, Kunti and Madri – who compete with each other as to who can have the most children. The *Ramayana* thus presents a happy household where the co-wives are not rivals, at least not initially.
- In the *Ananda Ramayana*, a portion of what is given to Kaushalya is taken by a crow and dropped into Anjana's mouth. Thus is Hanuman born. In another retelling, a portion of what is given to Kaushalya is taken by a crow and dropped into Kaikesi's mouth. Thus is Vibhishana born.
- For centuries, pilgrims have travelled to Ayodhya identifying it as the birthplace of Ram. But the exact location of the birthplace of Ram, in Ayodhya, is the subject of great dispute and political turmoil in India. Ever since colonial times, Hinduism has felt under siege, forced to explain itself using European templates, make itself more tangible, more concrete, more structured, more homogeneous, more historical, more geographical, less psychological, less emotional, to render itself as valid as the major religions of the Eurocentric world like Christianity, Judaism and Islam. The fallout of this pressure is the need to locate matters of faith in a particular spot. The timeless thus becomes time-bound and the universal becomes particular. What used to once be a matter of faith becomes a territorial war zone where courts now have to intervene. Everyone wants to be right in a world where adjustment, allowance, accommodation and affection are seen as signs of weakness, even corruption.
- The Valmiki *Ramayana* describes the sacrifice of a horse as part of the yagna conducted by Rishyashringa. Descriptions of such practices are found in ancient Vedic ritual texts but are absent in later texts.
- In the Jain *Ramayana*s, Ram is called Padma.

Sulabha and Janaka

'Maybe you should consider calling Rishyashringa to Mithila' was the advice Janaka received often enough. Since the arrival of Sita, his wife, Sunaina, had given birth to a daughter who was named Urmila, and Janaka's brother, Kushadhvaja, had fathered two daughters, Mandavi and Shrutakirti. Four daughters to two brothers in the land of Videha, but no sons!

Janaka would respond, 'The earth grants Janaka what he deserves. The fire grants Dashratha what he wants. I choose the destiny of daughters. He submits to the desire of sons.'

Word of this reached a woman called Sulabha. In beautiful attire and beautiful form, she approached the king and demanded a private audience with him. Everyone wondered why.

Sulabha noticed the king's awkwardness and asked, 'This land is called Videha, meaning "beyond the body". I assumed the king of this land would value my mind more than my body. But I assumed wrong.'

Janaka felt acutely embarrassed at being chastised so.

Sulabha continued, 'Humans are special. We have a mind that can imagine. With imagination we can, without moving, travel through space and time, conjure up situations that do not exist in reality. It is what separates humanity from the rest of nature. Such a mind is called manas, which is why humans are called manavas. You are a manava with male flesh and I am a manava with female flesh. We both see the world differently, not because we have different bodies, but because we have different minds. You see the world from one point of view and I see the world from another point of view. But our minds can expand. I can see the world from your point of view and you can see it from mine. Some, like Vibhandaka and Rishyashringa, instead of expanding the mind, use it to control nature through tapasya and yagna. They do not accept

the world as it is. Why? Enquire into the human mind, Janaka, and you will better understand the flesh and the world around this flesh. That is veda, wisdom.'

Inspired by these words, Janaka invited to his land all the rishis of Aryavarta to share the knowledge of the Vedas. They emerged from caves, from mountaintops, from riverbanks and seashores and travelled to Janaka's court to exchange ideas and discover other ways of seeing the world. This conference of intimate conversations that would eventually broaden the gaze of humanity came to be known as the Upanishad.

- The Valmiki *Ramayana* does not name Sita's mother. In Vimalasuri's Jain *Paumachariya*, her name is Videha. In the Jain *Vasudevahindi*, her name is Dharini. The name Sunaina or Sunetra comes from later regional works.
- Sita's father is identified as Siradhvaja Janaka in the Valmiki *Ramayana* to distinguish him from other Janakas. Siradhvaja means 'he whose banner is a plough'. Kushadhvaja means 'he whose banner is grass'. The Janaka kings of Videha were closely associated with agriculture.
- In the Jain *Paumachariya*, Sita has a twin brother called Bhamandala, while in the Vishnu and Vayu Puranas, she has a brother called Bhanuman, a name that closely resembles Hanuman's. Not much is known about him.
- The meeting of Sulabha and Janaka is narrated in the Bhisma Parva of the *Mahabharata*. It describes how she enters his mind using yogic powers and how he resists. The name of the Janaka Sulabha meets is Dharmadhvaja, sometimes identified as Sita's father.
- The idea of female monks and intellectuals was not unknown in Vedic times, but it was not actively encouraged. It is said that initially even the Buddha hesitated to include women in his monastic order, until he saw the pain of his stepmother at the death of his father and realized that pain is gender-neutral.
- Vedic hymns are used in three ways: in rituals, described in the Brahmanas; in solitary visualizations, described in the Aranyakas; and in intimate conversations, described in the Upanishads. All three thrived in the pre-Buddhist period. When Buddhism started waning in India after the fifth century CE, these works once again gained prominence because of the works of acharyas such as Shankara, Yamuna, Ramanuja and Madhava.
- Janaka is a common participant of the intimate conversations that make up the Upanishad. In the Brahmanas, the raja or king is the patron while the rishi or sage is the conductor. The Aranyakas are the works of rishis alone while in the Upanishads we find kings equally engaged.
- In the eighteenth and nineteenth centuries, European scholars, with the memory of the Renaissance (scientific revolution) and Reformation (religious revolution) still fresh in their minds, tried to explain Indian intellectual development along similar lines, with ritualistic priests being overthrown by intellectual kings like Janaka and the Buddha. Such classification and progression is more imposed than accurate. While the tension between the monk, the household priest and the king is not in doubt, we find the ideas in the Brahmanas, Aranyakas and Upanishads often mingling and merging. Revolutions are subtle in India, and the winner does not wipe out the loser; he simply takes the more

dominant position. Thus Shiva, the monastic form of God, and Vishnu, the royal form of God, are two sides of the same coin.

- The Brahmanas, Aranyakas and Upanishads (pre-500 BCE) focus on taking the participant from the form (ritual and hymn) to formlessness (thought), a technique consistent in later-day Agama, Purana and Tantra literature (post-500 CE).

The Upanishad

Sita attended the conference with her father, at first clinging on to his shoulders, then seated on his lap, and finally following him around, observing him engage with hundreds of sages, amongst them Ashtavakra, Gargi and Yagnavalkya.

When Ashtavakra was still in his mother's womb, he had corrected his father's understanding of the Vedas. Infuriated, his father had cursed him to be born with eight bends in his body, hence his name, one who has eight deformities. 'Without realizing it, I threatened my father,' Ashtavakra said to Janaka. 'Animals fight to defend their bodies. Humans curse to defend their imagination of themselves. This imagined notion of who we are, and how others are supposed to see us, is called aham. Aham constantly seeks validation from the external world. When that is not forthcoming it becomes insecure. Aham makes humans accumulate things; through things we hope people will look upon us as we imagine ourselves. That is why, Janaka, people display their wealth and their knowledge and their power. Aham yearns to be seen.'

Gargi was a lady who questioned everything: 'Why does the world exist? What binds the sky to the earth? Why do we imagine? Why do we flatter ourselves with imagination? Why does Dashratha yearn for sons? Why is Janaka satisfied with daughters? What makes one king so different from another?' This angered many sages, who told her, 'If you ask so many questions your head will fall off.' But Gargi persisted, undeterred. She was hungry for answers. She did not care if her head fell off; she would grow a new head then, a wiser one.

Yagnavalkya revolted against his own teacher who refused to answer questions. He refused to accept that the purpose of tapasya and yagna was to compel nature to do humanity's bidding. He approached the sun-god, Surya, who sees everything, for answers. Surya explained to him how fear of death makes plants seek nourishment and grow towards sunlight and water. Fear of death is what makes animals run towards pastures and prey. At the same time, yearning for life makes animals hide and run from predators. But human fear is unique: fuelled by imagination, it seeks value and meaning. 'Do I matter? What makes me matter?'

Thus informed, Yagnavalkya shared his understanding of manas in the court of Janaka. 'Every human creates his own imagined version of the world, and of himself. Every human is therefore Brahma, creator of his own aham. *Aham Brahmasmi*, I am Brahma. *Tat tvam asi*, so are you. We knot our imagination with fear to create aham. Tapasya and yagna are two tools that can help us unknot the mind, outgrow fear and discover atma, our true self.'

'Tell me more about atma,' said Janaka.

Yagnavalkya said, 'Atma is the brahman, a fully expanded mind. Atma is the mind that does not fear death or yearn for life. It does not seek validation. It witnesses the world as it is. Atma is ishwar, also known as Shiva, who performs tapasya, is self-contained and self-sufficient. Atma is bhagavan, also known as Vishnu, who conducts a yagna to nourish everyone even though he needs no nourishment.'

'May Brahma's head keep falling off till he finds the brahman,' said Ashtavakra.

'Who will facilitate this?' asked Gargi.

'The brahmin, transmitter of the Vedas,' said Yagnavalkya.

- Vedic knowledge is contained in hymns composed in the Sanskrit language. The fine intonations of Sanskrit, and the nuances of the ritual to which the hymns were attached, cannot be captured in totality in writing. So Vedic knowledge could only be transmitted orally through people. The community of people who were entrusted with this responsibility was that of the brahmins. They spent all day memorizing and transmitting their knowledge. Since they were the carriers of this lore, they became highly valuable. Killing a brahmin was the greatest of crimes as it meant loss of Vedic knowledge. Brahmins were essentially transmitters and stewards of Vedic hymns and rituals, not its interpreters or owners. Over time, however, they used their exalted position to dominate society and claim entitlements. It was an irony of history that those who carried knowledge of how to expand the mind failed to expand their own minds, and chose the common path of domination instead.

- The Upanishadic times, dated between 1000 BCE and 500 BCE, was a period of great intellectual fervour in India. It marked the rise of the shramanas or the monastic orders, which preferred tapasya to yagna. The shramana orders that were most successful were the Buddhists and the Jains. These orders compelled Hinduism to redefine itself and narrow the gap that had emerged between its intellectual side and its social side.
- The Upanishadic gathering at Mithila is believed to be the forerunner of the Kumbha melas held at Prayag, Ujjain, Nashik and Hardwar, where hermits and householders gather to discuss worldly and other-worldly matters.
- The story of Ashtavakra comes from the *Mahabharata*. He is the author of the *Ashtavakra Gita*.
- The story of Gargi and Yagnavalkya is found in the Brihadaranyaka Upanishad. Yoga Yagnavalkya is a conversation between the two. In some retellings, Gargi is Yagnavalkya's challenger; in others, she is his wife.
- 'Cutting off the head' is a recurring metaphor in Hindu mythology, which refers to the mind being forced into realization through trauma.
- The Upanishad documents stretch over centuries and there are references to many Janakas, indicating patronage by a line of kings. That the *Ramayana* identifies Sita's father as Janaka and his kingdom as Videha is significant. A man of great wisdom, who looks beyond all things material, raises the goddess associated with fertility, vegetation and material abundance. Janaka is no Brahma who simply creates aham; he is a true brahmin, seeking to outgrow aham and discover the brahman. And so is his daughter.

Sunaina's Kitchen

All the sages were convinced that the Upanishad captured the essence of the Vedas. The wisdom squeezed out of the many conversations at Janaka's court was called Vedanta. Janaka gave all the sages many cows. 'May their milk provide you food for the rest of your life. May their dung provide you fuel for the rest of your life. You gave me Saraswati, wisdom; I give you Lakshmi, wealth,' said the very happy king of Videha.

Yagnavalkya took the cows he received to his two wives, Maitreyi and Katyayani. Maitreyi did not want the cows; she wanted only knowledge gathered at the Upanishad. Katyayani, however, took the cows saying, 'Eventually, even the wise need to be fed.'

Overhearing this, Sita wondered: who fed the hundreds of sages who had made Mithila their home, who gave them a place to sleep, who filled their pots with water to moisten their mouths parched by intense conversations?

The enquiry took Sita to her mother's kitchen. There she found Sunaina surrounded by grains and pulses and vegetables and fruits, busy supervising the preparation of the next meal. 'Fetch the bitter-gourds from that corner,' said the queen. Sita did as she was told and watched her mother slice them up neatly.

Before long, Sita found her feet around the kitchen: peeling, cutting, churning, pickling, steaming, roasting, frying, pounding, mixing, kneading, experiencing various textures, aromas, flavours and chemistry. Her senses became familiar with the secrets of spices, and every kind of nourishment provided by the plant and animal kingdom.

Sita's father never knew of the world that was the kitchen. Sita's mother never knew the world that was the court. But Sita realized she knew both. This is how the mind expands, she thought to herself. This is how Brahma becomes the brahman. She was a brahmin, she realized, seeker of wisdom as well as transmitter of wisdom. And that thought made her smile.

- The kitchen is the first yagna-shala, for the kitchen fire turns raw food into edible cooked food that nourishes the body and prepares the mind for intellectual enquiry.
- While tapasya focuses more on the mind, the yagna also pays attention to the body. While the Vedas focus more on the mind, the Tantra also pays attention to the body. Thus, Indian thought, while valuing thought, also values food. Food is nourisher, healer as well as happiness provider. Thought may be God but food is the Goddess. One cannot exist without the other.
- Sita's kitchen is part of folklore. In one story from Himachal, a crow once carried the food she cooked during her exile to Lanka and it was so tasty that Ravana was even more determined to bring Sita to Lanka so that she would cook for him.
- In Ayodhya, even today, we have the Sita-ki-rasoi, or Sita's kitchen, where the objects of worship include the rolling board and rolling pin used to make rotis.

BOOK TWO

Marriage

'Janaka told her to bring happiness into marriage, rather than seek happiness from it.'

The Origin of Rules

Animals compete for mates and fight over territory. Humans do not have to. Rules ensure this. Animals do not eat more than they have to. But humans do. Rules prevent this.

Long ago, there were no rules. A man called Vena plundered the earth for all its resources. Disgusted, the earth took the form of a cow and ran away. So the rishis picked up a blade of grass, chanted mantras to turn the grass into a missile, and directed it to kill Vena. When Vena died, his body was churned. All that was undesirable in him was cast away.

From the purity that remained was created a man called Prithu. Prithu pursued the earth-cow and begged her to feed his people. The earth-cow refused. So Prithu raised his bow.

The earth-cow shouted, 'If you kill me, who will feed your people?'

Prithu shouted back, 'If you keep running away, who will feed my people?'

Finally the earth-cow stopped and allowed Prithu's people to milk her. 'How will you stop them from milking me till my udders are sore?' she asked.

'I will create rules,' said Prithu. 'In nature, there are no rules. But culture shall be based on rules.
The king shall uphold rules.'

Prithu was the first king. The bow was his symbol. The ruler was the shaft and the rules were the string. Too loose, the bow was useless; too tight, and the bow would break. Prithu was Vishnu, upholder of social order, preserver of the balance between nature and culture. He promised the earth-cow that whenever rules of society were disrupted and she was exploited, he would descend on earth to set things right. The earth was so pleased that she called herself Prithvi, daughter of Prithu.

- Prithu's story comes from the Vishnu Purana and the Bhagavat Purana. Like Sita, Prithu is ayonija, not born from a woman's womb, indicating his special status. He is Vishnu's avatar, albeit not a popular one. His story indicates the shift of hunter-gatherer communities to agricultural societies based more on rules, less on force.
- The rest of Vena's body turns into Nishada, founder of the tribal communities who live in the forest, content with subsistence farming and animal husbandry, and who do not have personal property. The narrative draws attention to the difference between tribal and non-tribal societies, and makes us wonder what constitutes civilization. Tribal societies tend to focus on survival and maintenance of the social rhythm of the collective in harmony with nature while non-tribal societies tend to allow disruption of the old order and constantly seek something new either in terms of intellectual or material development often at the cost of nature.
- In the seventh century CE the Chinese scholar Hiuen Tsang recorded that Prithu was known as the first person who obtained the title of raja (king).
- The king is equated with a cowherd (Gopala) who considered earth as the cow who provided him with resources (Gomata). He took care of her and she nourished him.
- The cow is the symbol of sustenance. When a sage has a cow, his basic needs of food (milk) and fuel (dung) are taken care of. He can focus on intellectual pursuits. This is why the cow came to be associated with the earth and worshipped. Without the cow, the rishis would not have been able to hear the Vedas.

Parashurama's Axe

But rules do not take into account human desire.

One day, Renuka saw a gandharva bathing in the river. He was so handsome that she desired him intensely. Until then, Renuka's chastity was her tapasya and it granted her siddha: she could collect water in unbaked pots made of river clay. But with her desire for the gandharva, this power disappeared. She could not carry water now as she had earlier.

Her husband, the sage Jamadagni of the Bhrigu clan, accused Renuka of adultery: 'How can you be trusted if desire makes you disregard the rules of marriage?' He ordered his sons to cut off their mother's head. The older four refused, but the youngest swung his axe and did the needful. His name was Rama. Since he used the axe in so dreadful a manner he became known as Parashurama, Rama of the axe.

Pleased with Parashurama's unconditional obedience, Jamadagni offered his son a boon. 'Bring my mother back to life,' he said. Jamadagni did so using siddha.

Jamadagni had a cow called Nandini, descendant of the celestial Kamadhenu, who could satisfy all desires. King Kartavirya saw this cow and tried to claim it by force.

Kartavirya had been blessed with a thousand hands. Resisting him was impossible. 'These arms you have are meant to help the world,' said Jamadagni, 'instead you use them to plunder and steal. You are no king, you are a thief.' Kartavirya did not care to heed these words. He pushed Jamadagni away and dragged out the cow.

An angry Parashurama once again picked up his axe and hacked off the wicked king's arms until he bled to death.

Kartavirya's sons avenged their father's death by beheading Jamadagni. So Parashurama raised his axe a third time, and took an oath, 'If the rules of society are not respected by kings themselves, how are we any different from animals who live by force? I shall kill every king who disrespects the rules of society; rules of society are greater than any king.'

Parashurama went around the world killing all rulers he found unworthy. Hundreds

were thus slaughtered. A few survived by hiding behind women. From these cowards were born the next generation of kings, who were too timid to govern.

'Will I ever find a perfect king who respects the rules of marriage and the rules of property?' wondered Parashurama.

- Parashurama is a violent avatar of Vishnu who enforces rules; he is very different from Ram who upholds rules and Krishna who bends rules. Parashurama has no wives, Ram has one wife and Krishna has many. The Goddess manifests as Parashurama's mother (Renuka), Ram's wife (Sita) and Krishna's friend (Draupadi). Thus there is a pattern of progression in the three avatars.
- Parashurama's story reveals a period of great unrest between kings and sages. It marks the rise of the notion of property. Both women and cattle are seen as property, an early indicator of patriarchal thought.
- Parashurama's story is a harbinger of things to come, for Ravana will tempt Sita with a golden deer and seek to possess her, even though she is another's wife. Kaikeyi will seek the throne of Ayodhya for her own son as Kartavirya seeks Jamadagni's Nandini.
- Many communities like the Chitpavans of Pune and the Nairs of Kerala trace their ancestry to Parashurama. Though traditionally priests, these communities play a key role in political matters of their respective societies.
- In the Deccan region, especially Karnataka, Andhra Pradesh and Maharashtra, Renuka's head and headless body are worshipped as the goddess Yellamma, Ekavira or Hulligamma. Yellamma shrines have been associated with the infamous, and now illegal, devadasi practice of dedicating young girls to the deity and compelling them into prostitution.

Kaushika Becomes Vishwamitra

Kaushika was a king who performed many yagnas to satisfy the hunger of his subjects. Then one day, he met a rishi called Vasishtha who had with him a cow just like Indra's Kamadhenu who could fulfil any wish. Kaushika felt that such a cow should belong to a king so that he could feed his entire kingdom effortlessly.

Vasishtha, however, refused to part with the cow, stating, 'The wish-fulfilling cow only comes to one who has no desires.' Kaushika tried to take the cow by force but the cow resisted. From her udders emerged a band of fierce warriors who repelled every attack of Kaushika's.

Kaushika realized that the only way to possess a Kamadhenu was to become a rishi like Vasishtha and compel Indra to give him one of the magical cows that grazed in the paradise known as Swarga. For that he had to acquire siddha. For that he had to do tapasya. For that he had to live in the forest like a hermit. For that he had to renounce his kingdom and his crown.

A determined Kaushika did it all. In time, he had enough siddha to make nature do his bidding.

But while Kaushika was busy restraining his senses and gathering siddha, his family was left neglected. No longer in the palace, they had to fend for themselves. They found it difficult to find food. They would have starved had it not been for the generosity of a man called Trishanku.

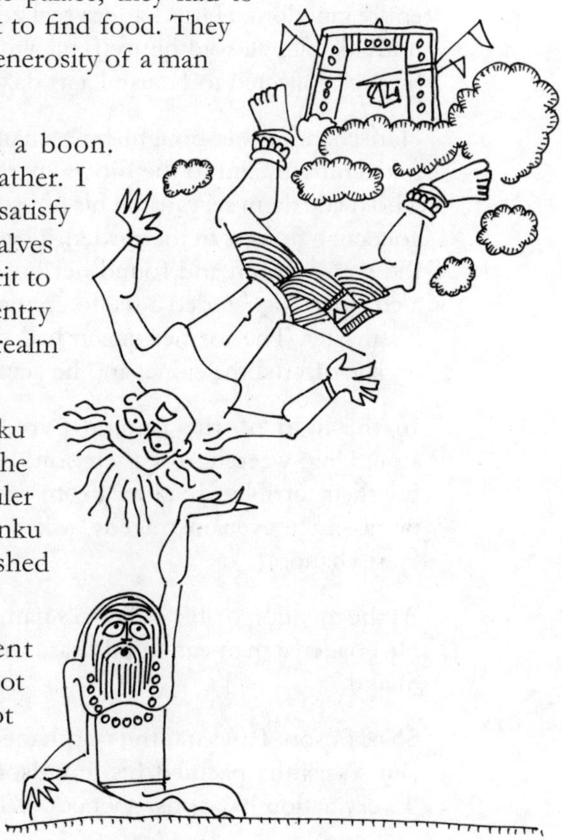

A grateful Kaushika offered Trishanku a boon. Trishanku said, 'I have disrespected my father. I have forced myself on a married woman. To satisfy my hunger, I have killed cows and made calves weep. As a result, I do not have enough merit to enter Swarga. Use your siddha to force my entry into that garden of delights located in the realm of the stars.'

Using his siddha, Kaushika caused Trishanku to rise from the land of humans through the sky towards the land of the devas. Indra, ruler of Swarga, did not take this kindly. Trishanku was an unworthy, uninvited guest. He pushed Trishanku back towards the earth.

Kaushika had enough siddha to prevent Trishanku from crashing to the ground, but not enough to overpower Indra. So Trishanku got stuck midway, suspended between the earth and sky, between the land of humans and the land of the devas.

Kaushika continued his austerities, determined to gain more siddha and defeat Indra. Fearing the worst, Indra sent the apsara Menaka to seduce the former king. Menaka danced before the meditating sage and it was only a question of time before he succumbed to her charms.

Frustrated at not being able to turn into a rishi as powerful as Vasishtha, Kaushika resumed his austerities. Just when he was about to regain his siddha, a king called Harischandra who was out hunting disturbed his concentration. Enraged, Kaushika was about to curse the king and his clan when the king offered his entire kingdom as compensation. Kaushika accepted this compensation as it allowed him to feed his starving family.

To ensure that Harischandra's compensation was not mistaken as alms or bhiksha, or as charity or daana, Kaushika asked the king for dakshina, a service fee for liberating him from the karmic obligation of his crime. Having given away his entire kingdom, Harischandra realized he had nothing more to give. So he did the unthinkable: he sold himself, his wife and his son as slaves and gave the money he thus collected to Kaushika as dakshina.

Harischandra was bought by a chandala, the caretaker of a crematorium, who asked him to tend to the funeral pyres. His wife and son were bought by a priest, who made them servants in his household. The son died of snakebite while he was collecting flowers in the garden. The distraught mother brought her son's body to the crematorium and found her husband there. Harischandra, once a king, now a chandala, demanded a fee to cremate his own child, for those were the rules of his master. The former queen had nothing to give but the clothes on her body. So she offered the same, and he accepted it as fair payment.

In the light of the funeral pyre, Kaushika saw the naked queen and the stoic king, weeping for their son, but neither blaming nor reproaching anyone for their terrible situation. From where comes this wisdom that enables you to be at peace even in tragedy, asked Kaushika. 'From my guru, Vasishtha,' said Harischandra.

At the mention of his old rival's name, Kaushika's envy reared its ugly head again. He goaded a man-eating rakshasa called Kamlashpada to devour Vasishtha's son, Shakti.

Shakti's son, Parasara, thus orphaned, decided to destroy all rakshasas on earth. But Vasishtha pacified his grandson by explaining to him the laws of karma: 'Every action has consequences. Why blame the instrument of karma for what

is determined by our own past actions? By denying Kaushika the Kamadhenu, because he did not deserve it, I ignited rage in his heart, which led him to goad Kamlashpada to kill your father. I am as much responsible for Shakti's death as Kamlashpada and Kaushika are. I wish I had more sons that Kaushika could kill until he has his fill of anger.'

Hearing this, Kaushika realized that it is not siddha that makes a man a rishi, it is the ability to care for others. To care for others, we have to first see them, understand them truly. Vasishtha had seen Kaushika in a way that Kaushika had not seen himself. And Kaushika had failed to see Vasishtha as he truly was. His gaze was coloured by rage. He realized Vasishtha was a wise seer, and he a powerful sorcerer at best.

'The purpose of yagna and tapasya is not to increase my wealth and my power. It is to make me unknot my mind, move from aham to atma, see the world from another's point of view. Only then can I be a rishi,' Kaushika thought.

With this realization, Kaushika was transformed. He stopped being Vishwashatru, enemy of the world, and became Vishwamitra, friend of the world. He no longer wanted to change the world; he wanted to help the world. He decided to use his learning and his experience to create noble kings that even Parashurama would admire.

- In narratives, kings perform a yagna to harness material wealth from nature, and sages perform tapasya to get magical powers that enable them to control nature. Shiva encourages one to outgrow the hunger for material wealth and magical powers. Vishnu encourages one to pay attention to this hunger in others.
- Kaushika, the raja or king, becomes Vishwamitra, the rishi or sage. His rivalry with Vasishtha is a recurring theme in the scriptures. In tales, Vasishtha comes across as wise but idealistic while Vishwamitra comes across as impatient but pragmatic.
- Kaushika and Parashurama embody attempts to bridge the gap between warriors who value things and sages who value ideas. Kaushika the warrior wants to be a sage. Parashurama the sage wants to be a king.
- Trishanku is a metaphor for a person who belongs nowhere: the outlier trapped between worlds.
- Menaka is a metaphor for temptations that prevent us from achieving our goal.
- Harischandra is a metaphor for honesty; he suffers personal tragedy but remains true to his word.
- In Varanasi, on the banks of the Ganga, stands the Harischandra Ghat where bodies are cremated. The keepers of this ghat trace their ancestry to the chandala who bought Harischandra as a slave.

The Yagna of Vishwamitra

Wild, the forest is of no value to humans, for in the wilderness humans are no different from animals. Domesticated, the forest grants humans value by turning into fields and orchards of which man is master.

But when the human mind is domesticated by rules, the mind is restrained. What should a king be, an enforcer of rules or an expander of minds? Should he turn his subjects into domesticated, obedient beasts or into brahmins?

These questions plagued Vishwamitra. So he established the Siddha-ashrama, a hermitage in the middle of the forest. He decided to conduct a yagna there, risking attack by rakshasas. This was the best way to help new kings appreciate the principles of domestication.

He sent invitations to the kings whose kingdoms were located up and down the river Ganga, asking them to send their sons to protect his fire-hall, the yagna-shala, from rakshasa attacks. 'In exchange, I will grant them practical knowledge about war and weapons. I will even teach them spells with which they can turn ordinary arrows into potent missiles with the power of fire, water, the sun, the moon, wind and rain.'

But no kings sent their sons; they were terrified of the forests and the rakshasas.

When no student comes to a teacher, a teacher goes in search of a student. Vishwamitra decided to find a student and turn him into a perfect king. And who better than a student of his arch-rival Vasishtha whose wisdom he had begun to grudgingly admire?

- Rishis or seers came from all communities. Vyasa was born to a fisherwoman; Vasishtha and Agastya were born to apsaras, celestial damsels who were bound to no man; Vishwamitra emerged from a line of kings. Most of them renounced all connections to their earlier life and were hence considered the mind-born sons of Brahma, reborn in thought.
- In Vedic society, children were often sent away from home to learn from sages. These sages were often family elders who were expected to renounce their social role, and eventually society itself, to make way for the next generation. They lived in the forest, or vana, away from society. This was vanaprastha ashrama, the stage of forest dwelling, a twilight space of transformation that prepared the old to leave society as hermits, even as they taught the young to enter society as householders. Vishwamitra probably fits into this ashrama, having completed his worldly duty as king.

Students of Vasishtha

When Dashratha had asked the rishi Vasishtha to teach his four sons the ways of kings, Vasishtha had said, 'I will try my best to make them brahmin.'

'But I am a king, my sons are princes, they must be trained to be rulers, not priests,' Dashratha responded in alarm.

'You confuse brahmin-jati with brahmin-varna,' Vasishtha had clarified. 'He of brahmin-jati is a priest, transmitter of hymns and rituals of the Veda. He of brahmin-varna is one who inspires the Brahma of limited mind to move towards being brahman of limitless mind. Whether priest or warrior, farmer, herder or trader, man or woman, everyone must expand their minds, rise from shudra-varna, the mindset of a follower, to vaishya-varna, the mindset of a trader, to kshatriya-varna, the mindset of a master, to brahmin-varna, the mindset of a seer.'

'How can a king be a servant or a trader or a master or a seer?' wondered Dashratha.

Vasishtha said, 'A king is a servant when he mimics other kings without understanding. A king is a trader when he uses rules to get all the things that he desires. A king is a master when he uses rules to impose his thoughts on those around him. A king is a seer when he understands the thought behind the rules and so appreciates the many reasons why a rule is followed and why another rule is not. For a king with a mind of brahmin, rules are merely functional, they are never right or wrong, and like all actions they have consequences. For him rules are not tools of power to dominate and control. For him rules are merely instruments of society that enable even the weakest to have what is otherwise cornered by the strongest.'

'May you make my sons brahmin,' said Dashratha on being enlightened so.

When their education was complete, the four sons of Dashratha were sent on a pilgrimage to the hills. When they returned, the eldest prince, Ram, felt there was

more merit in being a hermit than a householder. Vasishtha then explained to him how he could be a hermit while leading the life of a householder.

'Conduct your yagna as only a tapasvi can. Ignite the fire, tapa, which needs no fuel, within your mind. Light the outer physical fire, agni, which demands fuel. Tapa will transform you while agni will transform the world around you. Tapasya will burn your hunger. Yagna will feed the hungry. Tapasya will reveal fear that generates aham. Yagna will help you discover love that reveals atma. Tapasya works on the self so that we can focus on the other. Yagna focuses on the other so that we can work on the self. Tapasya helps you understand rules. Yagna helps you impose rules. He who understands this walks the path of Vishnu.'

- The confusion between varna (mindset) referred to in the Vedas and jati (community) that shapes Indian society has created much negativity. Both brahmins like Manu and later academicians have tried to force-fit various jatis into varnas, the assumption being that certain mindsets thrive in certain communities. But the Vedas are more psychological than social, referring to how a person of any profession or gender can have the mindset of a follower, a trader, a master or a seer.
- What the word 'brahmin' actually means is the subject of many conversations in the Upanishads and the *Mahabharata*. In all these conversations, the focus is always on worldview, never profession. But it is the focus on the latter that was always preferred in society, by both academicians and politicians.
- Vasishtha is driven more by the mind while Vishwamitra is driven more by society. For Vasishtha, if the mind is clear, everything else becomes clear. But Vishwamitra thinks more in terms of action. In many ways, Vishwamitra represents what we call the modern Western 'just do it' action-oriented mindset. Vasishtha observes without resistance.

Dashratha Lets Go of His Sons

'What your sons have learned till now under Vasishtha is rather theoretical. Time for some practical experience from one who was once a king,' said Vishwamitra to Dashratha.

Dashratha, however, was not willing to part with his sons. 'They are too young. Take my army instead. I myself shall come with you if you want.'

'Nonsense,' said Vishwamitra. 'You are too old. And your boys are on the threshold of kingship. Let them come with me.'

Seeing Vishwamitra's nostrils flare in rage, a terrified Dashratha said, 'I will give you two. But two will stay back, just in case.'

Vishwamitra smiled at the insecure father who did not trust the capability of his sons. Two sons of Dashratha set out with Vishwamitra towards the hermitage. They came to a fork on the road. 'Which one shall we take? The short route that is safe or the long one that is swarming with rakshasas?' asked Vishwamitra.

'Taking the short, safer route makes sense,' said one of the princes. The other prince, his younger brother, nodded in agreement.

Vishwamitra immediately turned back and returned to Ayodhya and told Dashratha, 'These two sons of yours are not yet ready. Let me take the other two.'

'No, no, not Ram,' said Dashratha, clearly identifying his favourite. But Dashratha knew he had to yield; he did not want to risk the rishi's curse. So Bharata and Shatrughna stayed back, while Ram and Lakshman went forth.

When Vishwamitra reached the fork on the road, he once again asked, 'Which one shall we take? The short route that is safe or the long one that is swarming with rakshasas?'

Ram replied, 'Let us take the long, fearsome route. That is the path of knowledge.' Lakshman agreed. Vishwamitra was pleased with the answer.

This boy with long, lithe limbs, broad shoulders, thick, curly hair and eyes the shape of lotus buds renewed his hope. Was he the perfect king?

- The Bala-kanda, the first chapter of the *Ramayana*, often seen as a later addition, speaks not just of Ram's birth but also his education under Vasishtha and Vishwamitra. Vasishtha focuses on his mental development while Vishwamitra focuses on his martial and social duties.

- The story of Dashratha sending Bharata and Shatrughna first to Vishwamitra's yagna, and not Ram and Lakshman, comes from the Bengali *Ramayana* of Krittivasa Ojha known as 'Ram Panchali' or 'diary of Ram'. From the twelfth century onwards, much of Bengal was under Muslim rule and Krittivasa refers to being garlanded by Gaudeshwara, lord of Gaud (Bengal), his patron, who in all probability was Sultan Jalal al-Din Muhammad Shah who ruled in the fifteenth century.
- Dashratha's refusal to let his sons go into the forest reveals his fears, and his attachment to his sons, especially Ram, his son by Kaushalya. Such preferential treatment for one child is assumed to be normal, even natural, but is it the best use of human potential?

The Killing of Tadaka

On the way to the hermitage, Vishwamitra taught Ram and Lakshman the many spells he knew to turn arrows into missiles by telescoping into them the power of animals, planets and elements. Ram learned how to set a tree aflame by shooting an arrow, how to bore a hole in the ground and cause water to spring forth and how to summon the wind. He learned how to make arrows fly like a hawk, pounce like a tiger and pound like an elephant.

When they eventually reached Siddha-ashrama, Vishwamitra was pleasantly surprised to find Kushadhvaja there along with the four princesses of Videha. 'We do not have sons but Janaka felt his daughters needed to witness a yagna performed in the forest.'

Lakshman looked at the four princesses of Videha, but the girls were more interested in the yagna, as was Ram. He realized he had never had a sister. Only brothers surrounded him. He wondered what it would be like to have a sister to play with.

Vishwamitra's sons, once princes, were dressed in clothes of bark. They had strings of beads made of seeds around their neck and arms. Their wives, anointed with sandal paste, wore garlands of flowers and assisted them to prepare for the ceremony. The whole precinct was full of clay bricks and pots, wooden spoons and wicker baskets and mats of bamboo and the skin of deer. Seven types of fruits, seven types of leaves and seven types of flowers had been collected. 'We must bow to Shakti, ask her permission, before we light the fire that will eventually turn the forest into a field,' said Vishwamitra.

'Why do you address the forest as a goddess?' asked Sita.

Knowing that the daughters of Janaka were well versed in the Upanishads, Vishwamitra saw that he would have to give a considered answer. So he framed his answer carefully. 'Because I see the mind as a man,' he said. 'This mind of ours seeks to control nature as man tries to control woman. The mind assumes ownership of nature as a man assumes ownership over his wife.'

'So my mind is male and the nature around me is female?' said Sita.

'Did you hear what she said?' Vishwamitra overheard the younger prince of Ayodhya ask his elder brother. Vishwamitra waited with bated breath to hear Ram's reply.

'That is a figure of speech,' said Ram to Lakshman. 'The rishis have found it easy to explain the mind using the male body and nature using the female body. Do not take it literally.'

Vishwamitra was pleased with Ram's response. Sita was impressed too, he could see. There was reason to be: a prince with the mind of a sage is not common to find, especially one so young and handsome and brave.

Vishwamitra, with his wife by his side, drilled the fire-stick and lit the fire in the altar. The princes and princesses watched the ceremony with fascination. Vishwamitra declared himself the yajaman, and sang hymns invoking the gods. His sons sang hymns in praise of Indra, the sky-god; Surya, the sun-god; Chandra, the moon-god; Vayu, the wind-god; Varuna, the water-god; and Agni, the fire-god. These powers that exist above the earth had to be invoked so that collectively they would help domesticate the forest and unknot the mind.

As the chants filled the air and the fire blazed brilliantly, Sita looked up and saw Ram. A glance was exchanged, both hearts missed a beat, and she looked away.

Then came the angry sounds that drowned the songs of Vishwamitra and his sons, first from a distance, then louder and louder, until it seemed they encircled the entire hermitage.

Sita, well versed in many languages due to her interaction with many rishis, fathomed the words of the rakshasas: 'We will behead Vishwamitra as Shiva beheaded Brahma. We will destroy Vishwamitra's yagna as Shiva destroyed Daksha's yagna. We will not let sanskriti destroy prakriti.'

'You understand what they say, don't you, Janaka's daughter,' said Vishwamitra. 'Sanskriti is culture, where everyone acts with affection. Prakriti is nature, a place where all actions are propelled by fear of starvation and fear of attack. Though Brahma and Daksha conducted yagnas, they were not creating sanskriti. Brahma feared the untamed and used the yagna to control nature. Daksha used the yagna to make everyone do his own bidding. That is why Shiva attacked them. The point of the yagna is to outgrow fear, not indulge it. I conduct this yagna to transform kings into Vishnu, who uplifts with affection rather than subjugates with rules.'

'The rakshasas don't know that,' said Sita as the chanting of the rakshasas was replaced by the clamour of weapons.

'They will not until we connect with them. For now, we are strangers. We are threats. There is no room for conversation. We must not resent their hostility.'

As they spoke, sticks were hurled into the precincts, followed by stones and bones. But before they touched the ground, arrows shot by Ram and Lakshman diverted or shattered them. Vishwamitra said, 'Now is the time to use the mantras I taught you.' So Ram and Lakshman shot a series of arrows creating a fence around the hermitage and a roof over the yagna-shala. The sticks, stones and bones hurled against them simply bounced back. Everyone felt safe.

Then a blood-curdling yell was heard from beyond the trees. A woman's voice. 'That's Tadaka, matriarch of this herd of rakshasas, stronger than all the others put together,' Vishwamitra said. 'Use the mantras that will turn your arrows into missiles imbued with the power of the sun, the moon, wind, water and fire. Shoot her dead, for she alone can force her way into the hermitage and destroy the yagna-shala.'

'But that is a woman. The scriptures tell us not to hurt women,' argued Lakshman.

'Villains have no gender. Shoot!' shouted Vishwamitra.

Sita watched Ram chant a hymn softly, mount the arrow to his bow, pull the bowstring and with a calm expression shoot the arrow in the direction of Tadaka's voice. The arrow struck Tadaka just as she was emerging from the trees. She was tall and strong and fierce-looking. But she fell silent as the arrow ripped its way through her heart. And then like a giant tree she fell down with a tremendous thud.

Behind Tadaka were two men: Subahu and Marichi, both tall and fierce with hair like flames. Subahu ran to strike Ram, but another arrow brought him to the ground. Marichi turned around and fled.

No more sticks, stones or bones were hurled thereafter. The yelling and screaming stopped, and was replaced by an eerie silence. The rakshasas had withdrawn.

Vishwamitra spoke, 'They see us as the new dominant beast who has marked this territory. They will return to reclaim the territory when we grow weaker or they grow stronger.'

'If you wish, we will guard this compound forever,' said Lakshman.

'Then this space will never have sanskriti,' said Ram, frowning as his mind was flooded with thoughts. Vishwamitra was pleased to see this. He asked his sons and Dashratha's sons to gather wood to cremate Tadaka. 'Let us facilitate her journey across the Vaitarni. Who knows how she will be reborn? Hopefully as a friend, not a foe.'

'But why should we disturb the jungle way? Why don't we just leave them alone?' asked Shrutakirti, the younger of Kushadhvaja's daughters, as she watched the funeral rites of Tadaka being conducted.

'The forest belongs to no one. Without human intervention, it will stay a jungle, a place of fear, of hostility not hospitality, where might is right and only the fit survive. Without tapasya and yagna there will be no civilization,' said Vishwamitra.

'But we just killed Tadaka,' said Urmila.

'To light a fire, wood must burn. To feed the cow, the grass must be cut. Until the rakshasas learn to trust us, we will be seen as threats and rivals. Until then there will be violence. They will be hurt. We will also be hurt. What matters is our intention. Eventually relationships will be introduced and affection will prevail.'

'They fear we will destroy their way of life. Will we? Can we?' said Mandavi.

'Indeed we can, if we stay animals and find pleasure in domination, and believe there is nothing to learn from them. That is adharma. Dharma is about exchange, about giving and receiving. It is about outgrowing animal instincts, outgrowing fear, discovering the ability to feed others, comfort others, enable others to find meaning.'

It did not escape Vishwamitra's notice that Janaka's daughters asked questions like Gargi of the Upanishad; Dashratha's sons preferred obeying commands. Different seeds nurtured in different fields by different farmers produce very different crops indeed.

- In Bhavabhuti's Sanskrit play *Mahavira-charita*, or the tale of the great hero, dated to the eighth century CE, Sita is present during Vishwamitra's yagna. She comes along with her sister Urmila and her uncle, Kushadhvaja.
- The suggestion of romance between Ram and Sita before their marriage is suggested in the *Ramayana*s of Bhavabhuti, Kamban and even Tulsidas. This is in keeping with the shringara rasa or romantic mood found in Sanskrit kavyas.
- In Kalamkari fabric paintings of the *Ramayana,* Ram is shown facing the other way when he shoots Tadaka because, the artists say, the only woman Ram will see, other than his mothers, is Sita.
- In the *Ramayana* many women are killed or mutilated on the grounds of them being demons: Tadaka is the first amongst them and Surpanakha is the most well known. But there are others such as Ayomukhi, Simhika, Surasa, Lankini and even Mandodari, the wife of Ravana, and Chandrasena, the wife of Mahiravana. It is difficult to digest that these are simply metaphors for wild, untamed nature. There is clearly an acceptance of male violence against women.
- Tadaka and her rakshasa hordes are often visualized as troublemakers, with the rishis assuming the right to conduct a yagna in their forests. Vishwamitra's yagna can be equated with the burning of the Khandava forest by the Pandavas to build their city of Indraprastha. A yagna may be a metaphor for clearing forests, creating fields for human settlements. It is easy to read this as the incursion of Vedic Aryan tribes from the Gangetic plains into the dense southern forests. The action of the rishis can easily be equated with proselytizing efforts of missionaries and evangelists. European colonizers popularized such interpretations to justify the colonization of India, putting the rulers, landowners and priestly communities of India on the defensive.

The Liberation of Ahilya

When the yagna drew to a close, Vishwamitra said, 'Let us go downstream to the hermitage of Gautama. We are needed there.'

Everyone followed Vishwamitra along a narrow, rocky path lined with flower-bearing trees until they came to a rock in the middle of a dilapidated, neglected hermitage. Vishwamitra then proceeded to tell its tale.

Ahilya, a beautiful princess with many suitors, was given in marriage to the sage Gautama, much older than her. Gautama spent all day conducting yagnas or performing tapasya while Ahilya took care of his needs. She longed for his friendship and companionship but he was too distracted to pay her any attention.

Then one morning, Gautama behaved very differently. Instead of going to the mountains to meditate after bathing in the river, he returned home and spent the afternoon with Ahilya, being extremely attentive, caring and gentle, giving in to all her demands.

But as evening drew close, Ahilya saw another sage who looked just like her husband approaching the house; the only difference was that the one outside looked stern and the one in her arms was extremely generous. It dawned on her that the loving man in her arms was not Gautama: he was an impostor. He turned out to be Indra, who had taken the form of her husband to exploit her loneliness. Her real husband stood outside.

Gautama was unforgiving. He cursed Indra that he would lose his manhood and that his body would be covered with sores. Then he cursed his wife that she would turn into stone, unable to move or eat. Animals would urinate on her. Travellers would walk over her.

'If you, heir of the Raghu clan, prince of Ayodhya, touch her without judgement, she will be liberated from her curse,' said Vishwamitra.

'But isn't adultery the worst of crimes, for it marks the end of trust? Renuka was beheaded for just thinking about another man; this is far worse,' said Lakshman.

'How much punishment is fair punishment? Who decides what is enough? A king needs to intervene, balance his ruthlessness with compassion.'

Ram immediately touched the rock that was Ahilya. It moved. He stepped away and she materialized, letting out a sigh, and then a wail, for she had been relieved of the burden of shame.

Gautama appeared from the shadows, looking confused, happy to have his wife back, yet unable to forget his humiliation.

'Let go of your self-pity and your rage, noble sage. Let the knots of your mind unbind until aham gives way to atma. Only then will you be able to restore your hermitage and bring back joy to your world,' said Ram with the demeanour of a king.

Gautama stretched out his hand. Ahilya, once beautiful, now gaunt, paused for a moment, and then accepted it. Vishwamitra poured water over their joined hands so that the two could start life afresh.

A curious Mandavi wondered why fidelity is so important in marriage. The rakshasa women, she had heard, did not restrict themselves to their husbands and the rakshasa men did not restrict themselves to their wives. In nature, all kinds of unions existed: swans were faithful to each other, the male monkey had a harem of females that he jealously guarded, the queen bee had many lovers. Why then was fidelity so important to the rishis?

'It is a measure of how satisfied we are with the offerings of the spouse. The dissatisfied seek satisfaction elsewhere,' said Vishwamitra.

'I shall always strive to find all my satisfaction in a single wife,' declared Ram.

'What if your wife does not find satisfaction in you?' asked Vishwamitra, eager to hear the response of the prince. But it was a princess who responded.

'If she is wise, she will accommodate the inadequacy. If he is wise, he will strive to grow,' said Sita, still looking at Ahilya and the hesitant tenderness of Gautama.

Kushadhvaja noticed the smile that appeared on Ram's face. So he went up to Vishwamitra with a proposal. 'Come with us to Mithila. Bring the princes of Ayodhya with you. I would like Ram to try his luck with the bow of Shiva. Who knows, he may just return home with a wife.'

- Ahilya's relationship with Indra is alluded to in hymns found in the ritual texts known as the Brahmanas, composed at least 500 years before Valmiki's *Ramayana*.
- In some retellings of the *Ramayana* as in the Brahma Purana, Indra tricks Ahilya. In others, like the *Kathasaritsagar*, she recognizes Indra but enjoys his company. In other words, she is an innocent victim in some tales and a consenting partner in others.
- In the Valmiki *Ramayana*, Indra is castrated and Ahilya made invisible, forced to subsist on air. In the Brahmavaivarta Purana, Indra's body is covered with a hundred vulvas, which turn into a thousand eyes when he worships the sun. In the Brahma Purana, Ahilya is cursed to be a dried-up stream. In the Padma Purana, she is stripped of her beauty, and becomes just skin and bones. In the Skanda Purana and Brahmanda Purana, she is turned into stone.
- In the Valmiki *Ramayana*, Ahilya is merely invisible and is liberated when Ram acknowledges her presence and touches her feet. But in regional *Ramayana*s, written a thousand years later, she is a stone that is liberated after Ram steps on her.
- Ahilya is also known as Ahalya. Hala means plough and so Ahalya means 'one who is not ploughed', meaning she is either a version or an allegory of a field that is yet to be ploughed.
- The amount of discussion on female infidelity is not matched by discussion on male infidelity indicating that women are seen as properties whose boundaries must not be violated; men are not seen so. Traditionally, a holy woman is one who is chaste and attached to one husband while a holy man is one who is celibate and attached to no woman. She is called sati and he is called sant.
- European scholars often equated Indra of Hindu mythology with Zeus of Greek mythology. Both are leaders of the gods, both rule the sky, wield the thunderbolt and are known for their love of women. This cosmetic similarity falls apart, however, when we delve deeper. Zeus rapes many nymphs and princesses, often by taking various deceptive forms such as a goose or a ray of sunlight or even the likeness of husbands, and the women end up giving birth to great heroes such as Perseus and Hercules. Scholars see this as the spread of the male sky-cult and the subjugation of female earth-cults. Indra's roving eye, however, has a different purpose. He is associated with fertility and is an enemy of the monastic order of hermits. A balance between hermits and householders is achieved through Shiva, the hermit who becomes a householder, and Vishnu, the householder who thinks like a hermit.
- In later regional retellings, especially South Indian ones and those from South-East Asia, Ahilya has three children. Doubting their paternity, Gautama turns them into monkeys. The girl is Anjana, mother of Hanuman, and the boys are Vali and Sugriva. Anjana is Gautama's daughter. Vali and Sugriva are sons of Indra and Surya. In some versions, Ahilya curses her daughter for revealing her secret, while Gautama curses the boys for keeping quiet.

The Bow of Shiva

Shiva, the supreme tapasvi, had destroyed hunger. So he sat atop a mountain of stone covered with snow, where no vegetation grew. This was Mount Kailas, located under the Pole Star.

Nature, taking the form of Shakti, said to him, 'Hunger distinguishes creatures alive from creatures that are not alive. If you have no hunger, you should be called shava, corpse.'

'A plant grows towards the source of food. An animal runs towards food. A human can outgrow the need for food through tapasya. That is the distinguishing feature of humanity,' said Shiva.

'A human can also sense another's hunger and produce food through yagna to satisfy another's hunger. That is also the distinguishing feature of humanity,' said Shakti. 'When tapasya is done without yagna, solitude thrives, no relationships are established and society collapses. You become the destroyer.'

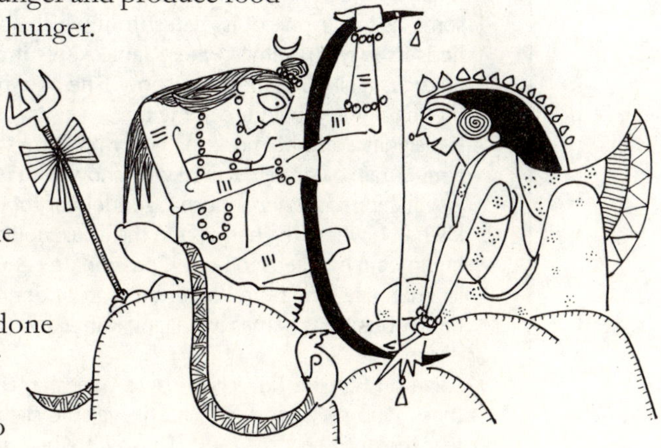

Shiva then said, 'When yagna is done without tapasya, we exploit other people's hunger to satisfy our own. Thus a corrupt society comes into being.'

'Indeed. Tapasya is like the shaft of the bow. Yagna is like the string of the bow. Individually, they do not create the bow. To create the bow, the shaft has to bend and the string has to become taut.'

'Too loose, the bow is useless. Too tight, the bow will break,' said Shiva repeating Vishnu's words when Prithu became king.

'Come, let us create the bow that joins yagna and tapasya. Let this be the symbol of all relationships, of man and woman in marriage, of king and kingdom in kingship.' So saying the Goddess took the form of Parvati, daughter of the mountains, and led Shiva down the slopes to the bustling city of Kashi on the riverbank. Here she became Annapoorna, goddess of food, and he transformed from Shiva, the hermit who has no hunger, to Shankara, the householder who cares for the hunger of others.

From their conversations came a bow. He who could string this bow would be the perfect king. Shiva gave the bow to Janaka, patron of the Upanishad. Vishwamitra was keen that his students should see this bow, though he was not sure they would be able to string it. But there was no harm in trying.

- In 1609, a Portuguese Jesuit missionary named Jacobo Fenicio, who lived in the court of the Zamorin of Calicut and travelled the Malabar Coast, put together the first well-researched document on Hindu mythology for Western audiences (though the work of a plagiarist called Baldeus dated 1672 became more popular). In it, he records an oral retelling of Sita's birth. Shiva serves Lanka for a while as its guardian and one day drops some ash near one of its gates from which springs a great tree. A branch of that tree finds its way to Mithila where Janaka sets it aflame as part of a yagna. From the fire emerges a girl, Sita, bearing a bow. The bow bears an inscription that she would marry the man who would break the bow.
- It is significant that Shiva, the god who knows no hunger, who lives atop Mount Kailas, a mountain of stone covered with snow with no vegetation, has as his wife Shakti, who is worshipped as Annapoorna, goddess of food, in Kashi, the city on the riverbank. Her kitchen is where the hermit and the householder make peace, for the hermit may not be hungry but he needs to be compassionate enough to care for those who are not hermits like him. He may burn Kama, the god of desire, and become Kamantaka, destroyer of desire, but she is Kameshwari, and Kamakhya, the goddess who appreciates and satisfies desire.
- Shiva and Shakti have two sons: Ganesha, the elephant-headed scribe, who satisfies those who seek food, and Kartikeya, the six-headed warrior, who defends those who fear they will become food. Thus with Shiva by her side, Shakti creates a forest where both predator and prey are happy.

Sita Picks Up the Bow

The bow of Shiva was so heavy that even a dozen men could not pick it up. So it was hauled on to a cart and taken to the armoury of Mithila where it was kept, admired from a distance by all the warriors who passed through the land. Every day Janaka would smear it with ash and light lamps around it in reverence.

One day, Sita entered the armoury with her three sisters and a dozen maids. She had been given the responsibility of cleaning the entire palace. 'Make sure no corner, no courtyard, no pillar, no wall, no roof or floor goes unattended. And don't forget the weapons. They need to be wiped, so that the wood does not gather mould, and the metal does not rust,' her mother had said. While the other girls busied themselves wiping the swords, the spears, the knives, the shields, the arrows, the bows and the maces, Sita headed straight for Shiva's bow.

'That's too heavy,' said one of the maids, 'no man can pick it up.'

'Still it needs to be cleaned,' said Sita, effortlessly picking up the bow with one hand and vigorously wiping its undersurface with the other.

News of this amazing feat reached the king and the queen. They rushed to the armoury and asked Sita to pick up the bow again. She did it with great ease, wondering what the fuss was all about.

'She is too strong. Who will marry her now?' wondered her mother with a smile on her face but concern in her heart.

'Someone who is equally strong, or maybe stronger,' said her father.

'And wise,' said Sunaina, knowing how much Janaka valued wisdom over strength. 'The perfect king.'

Janaka sent word across Aryavarta to kings and princes, inviting them to Mithila to string the bow of Shiva and claim both the bow and his daughter. Unlike in the Upanishad, when the city was full of sages seeking wisdom, the city was now full of princes who were motivated by power, property and pleasure.

Many came, many tried, all failed.

Amongst the many men who came to the city to pick up the bow was a man who came from faraway Lanka. He was taller than any man in the city, and his hair was thick and curly, his chest wide and his stomach firm. He smeared his body with ash, an indicator that he admired Shiva. No one looked at his face; his stare was so intense that everyone around him lowered their eyes. The man bent down to pick up the bow of Shiva and almost succeeded, but then he sneered, and lost balance; the bow pinned him to the ground like an angry python.

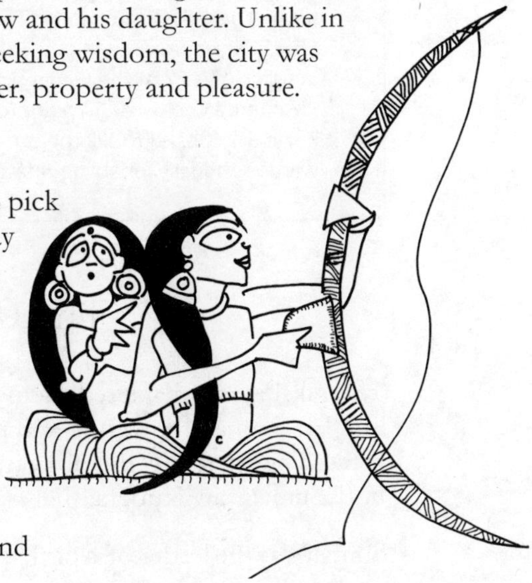

Janaka and his warriors rushed to his aid, but failed to pull him out from underneath. As the ash-smeared, fiery-eyed stranger gasped for breath, Sita was sent for. She picked up the bow with one hand, and kept it aside. The man was not grateful. He roared, 'If I could not pick up this bow, then no man can. Your daughter will die a lonely spinster, Janaka.'

Unflustered by these words, Janaka said, 'Alone maybe, but never lonely. She is not you.'

The man disappeared and was never seen again. But there were whispers on the streets of the city that he was none other than Ravana, son of the rishi Vishrava, king of the dreaded rakshasas.

- The Valmiki *Ramayana* does not depict Sita as having the strength to lift the bow, but it is part of folklore. Films like *Sita Swayamvar* (1976) show this episode. Parashurama advises Janaka to make sure that the man who marries Sita has the ability to string the bow that Sita is able to pick up.
- The story of Ravana trying to pick up Shiva's bow is also not found in the Valmiki *Ramayana* but is again part of folklore. It is one of the themes performed by Chhau dancers of Odisha, Jharkhand and Bihar. The reason given for Ravana's failure is his pride and overconfidence.
- The idea of Sita's strength has its origin in Sita being seen as the Goddess. She is Kali, the sovereign goddess of nature, who chooses to be Gauri, demure and domesticated, for the benefit of humanity. This idea is made explicit in the *Adbhut Ramayana* and in Shakta literature.
- In folk songs from the Gangetic plains, Sita prays to Shakti, the Goddess, to get a good husband. When a demon approaches her, she gives him a letter to deliver to Shakti. In it she asks Shakti to kill the presumptuous demon. Shakti kills the demon as Durga, the warrior-goddess, enabling Sita to marry Ram.

The Origin of Ravana

The rakshasas considered themselves rakshak or guardians of the forest way of life that favours the strong and the cunning, where there are no rules, only brute force. They naturally did not care too much for the tapasya or yagna of the rishis, until Sumali saw Kubera, that is.

Sumali was the leader of a pack of rakshasas who prowled the jungles of the south.

One day, he encountered Kubera, leader of the yakshas, who had built a city of gold called Lanka on the island of Trikuta in the middle of the southern sea; he travelled around the world on a flying chariot, the Pushpak Vimana.

Sumali learned that Kubera's mother was a yaksha called Idavida but his father was a rishi called Vishrava. Knowledge of tapasya, yagna and the Vedas obtained from his father had enabled Kubera to become rich and powerful. Sumali desired a child as powerful and capable as Kubera. So he asked his daughter, Kaikesi, to go to Vishrava and have a child by him. That is how Ravana was born.

Vishrava taught Ravana all about tapasya, yagna and the Vedas. Ravana expanded his mind so much that he needed ten heads to accommodate all his knowledge and twenty arms to accommodate his strength.

His grandfather Sumali constantly compared him with Kubera, so Ravana grew up with the desire to be stronger, faster and better than Kubera. He was determined to be the dominant one, feared and followed by all. It was not easy, for Kartavirya of the Haiheya clan had a thousand arms while he had only twenty. And Vali, the monkey-king of Kishkindha, had just one tail but it was stronger than all of Ravana's arms put together.

So Ravana invoked Brahma and obtained from him a pot of nectar that he hid in his navel. As long as he had this pot of nectar with him, he could not be killed.

Ravana then invoked Shiva. He cut off his head and created out of it a lute called Rudra-veena. Pleased with this, Shiva gave him a crescent-shaped sword, the Chandrahas, that would always secure him victory in battle.

Raising Chandrahas high above his head, Ravana overran the island of Trikuta with his rakshasa hordes, kicked Kubera out and declared himself king of Lanka and master of the Pushpak Vimana, much to Sumali's delight and Vishrava's disappointment.

Kubera ran north, to the mountains, and sought refuge in Shiva's shadow.

There he built another city, Alanka, the opposite of Lanka, more popularly known as Alaka.

'Both are your devotees, but whom do you prefer: Ravana or Kubera?' Shakti asked Shiva.

'Neither is really different from the other. Ravana grabs, while Kubera hoards. Both believe their identity stems from their property. That is why they value things rather than thoughts. That is why they refuse to expand their minds, even though both are sons of a brahmin,' Shiva said.

- The earliest versions of Ravana's life come from the Uttara-kanda, the last chapter of the *Ramayana*.
- In the fifteenth century, Madhav Kandali wrote the *Saptakanda Ramayana* in Assamese where he describes Ravana as the one who stole the staff of the god of death, the throne of the king of the gods, the noose of the god of the sea, the rays of the god of the moon, and who changed the planetary alignments at will. But unlike in Tulsidas's sixteenth-century Avadhi *Ramayana*, in the Assamese version Kandali treats Ravana more sympathetically and is in awe of the rakshasa-king's wealth and splendour.
- The words asura and rakshasa are often used interchangeably but they refer to two different groups of beings. Asuras are children of Kashyapa; they live under the ground and fight the devas. Rakshasas are children of Pulastya; they live in forests and fight humans. Kashyapa and Pulastya are Brahma's mind-born sons.
- While Ravana is reviled as a demon, Kubera gets the status of a god. Ravana is associated with the south, the direction indicative of death, while Kubera is associated with the north, the direction indicative of permanence and stability. The rakshasas are associated with stealing and grabbing, while the yakshas are associated with hoarding.
- In his Jain *Ramayana*, Vimalasuri says that Ravana did not have ten heads. When he was born, his mother put a necklace with nine mirrors around his neck, each of which reflected his head. So his mother called him Dasanan, one with ten heads, and the name stuck.
- Kubera is a highly revered character in Hindu, Buddhist and Jain mythology. He is the potbellied treasurer of the devas, the only one whose vahana or mount is a human.

- While temple images show the Rudra-veena with only one head of Ravana, the Rudra-veena used by musicians always have two gourds (heads).

The Descent of Ganga

Vishwamitra, Kushadhvaja, the two princes of Ayodhya and the four princesses of Mithila made their way south to Videha along the Ganga. On the way, Vishwamitra told everyone the story of Ganga.

King Sagara was performing the Ashwamedha yagna where the royal horse is let loose; all the lands that the horse traversed unchallenged would come under his rule. Fearing the horse would reach Amravati and that Sagara would become his master, Indra stole the horse and hid it in the hermitage of a tapasvi called Kapila.

When the sons of Sagara finally traced the horse, they accused Kapila of theft. Kapila, until then lost in tapasya, was so annoyed that when he opened his eyes flames of tapa emerged from them and burned Sagara's sons alive, reducing them to a pile of ash.

'Will my sons never live again?' cried Sagara.

'They will,' said Kapila, 'provided you immerse these ashes in the Ganga, the river that flows in Amravati, the city of the devas, the river that you see in the sky as Akash Ganga, the Milky Way.'

Sagara was too old to perform tapasya and use the power of siddha to compel Indra to let the celestial Ganga flow on earth. And he had no sons left who could do it for him. His widowed daughters-in-law were as yet childless. He saw no hope for his sons.

But one of Sagara's sons had two wives; they were determined to bear a child. So they called a sage and asked him to conduct a yagna that would yield a potion that could make barren women pregnant. When the potion was created, one queen drank the potion in her capacity as wife while the other queen made love to her pretending to be their late husband. From this union a child was born. But as no male had been involved in the conception, the child had no bones or nerves, only flesh and blood. The queens took this mass of flesh and blood to Kapila who used his siddha to create bones and nerves for the child. The child thus became complete and came to be known as Bhagiratha.

Bhagiratha performed tapasya and got Indra to let Ganga leave the sky and flow on earth. Ganga laughed, 'When I fall on earth, I will break all the mountains and sweep away all the forests, such is my force.'

Fearing the worst, Bhagiratha invoked Shiva and begged him to break Ganga's fall by catching the celestial river in the matted locks of his hair. Shiva agreed. Ganga jumped from the sky and fell straight on to Shiva's head. Before she realized it, she had become completely entangled and trapped in his hair. 'Let me go,' she yelled.

'Only if you treat the earth with respect,' said Shiva.

When Ganga agreed, Shiva let her flow out gently. She meandered her way to the sea, creating fertile riverbanks on either side. In her waters, Bhagiratha cast the ashes of his fathers, and he heard them cry out in gratitude.

Vishwamitra told everyone, 'Just as Ganga enables the rebirth of humanity and of vegetation, a woman enables the rebirth of a family, for she holds in her body the promise of the next generation.'

'To be a wife, must a woman be tamed as Shiva tamed Ganga?' asked Urmila.

'Ah, look at the idea beyond the gender,' Vishwamitra urged her. 'To be a good spouse, wife or husband, the wilfulness of Ganga needs to be balanced with the serenity of Shiva. Only then will the river of marriage create fertile riverbanks.'

Vishwamitra observed how much thought was provoked and wisdom realized each time Janaka's daughters asked a question. The men who married them would indeed be fortunate.

- The early Vedic scriptures refer to the rivers of Punjab, Rajasthan and Jammu. The later Vedic scriptures refer to the Gangetic plains, indicating a spread of this culture eastwards. Some attribute this shift to the drying up of the mighty river Saraswati in the west (now the tiny river Ghaggar), which led to an eastward shift in culture. As the population increased, the culture spread southwards.

- Ganga's story underlines the belief in rebirth which forms the cornerstone of philosophies that originated in India. In the earliest of Vedic scriptures, rebirth is implied and alluded to. The theme becomes dominant in the Upanishadic period. Belief in rebirth stems from a belief in impermanence. Nothing is forever: neither life nor death. This makes existence a merry-go-round that goes on forever. The tapasvis and shramanas proposed the idea of liberation (mukti, moksha, kaivalya) from the wheel of rebirths. These twin destinations of life and death are indicated by the fire in Kapila's eyes and the water that comes with Ganga's descent. Flames rise up, burning bonds to the wheel of rebirth; water flows down, ensuring the dead are reborn.
- That Vishwamitra tells this story of the sea and the river to Ram is an important part of his education. Ram needs to learn that life is a cycle. He is being told that one of his duties as a man is to marry and produce the next generation of kings, for nothing will last forever, not even his reign.
- The story of the two queens giving birth to Bhagiratha is found in Krittivasa's Bengali *Ramayana* and the Bengali version of the Padma Purana, and suggests same-sex relationships were not unheard of in those days. It is based on a Tantric belief that soft tissues like flesh and blood come from the red seed of woman and hard tissues like bones and nerves come from the white seed of man. In the Krittivasa *Ramayana*, the boneless Bhagiratha waves out to Ashtavakra from a distance. Unable to figure out if the boy is taunting him or greeting him, Ashtavakra, sensitive about his deformed body, invokes the gods to reduce the boy to ash if he is making fun of his deformity or cure him if he is genuinely deformed. Bhagiratha is thus cured.

The Breaking of the Bow

When Vishwamitra and the youngsters reached Mithila, Sunaina rushed out to see her daughters, who excitedly told her everything they had seen and heard during their trip to and from the hermitage.

Janaka welcomed Vishwamitra and his two young students. 'You are indeed blessed to be students of both Vasishtha and Vishwamitra,' he told Ram and Lakshman. 'Tell me what matters more: the theoretical knowledge of Vasishtha or the practical training of Vishwamitra?'

'Neither is better or worse,' replied Ram. 'The pursuit of theoretical knowledge develops the mind, while practical knowledge develops the body. Both have value and both come at a cost. It is aham that creates notions of better or worse. Atma observes it all, and smiles.'

These words were like music to Janaka's ears. The boy was not just strong and obedient; he was also wise. He hoped the boy would succeed in stringing the bow.

When they entered the armoury, Janaka requested Vishwamitra to formally introduce Ram. 'Let the bow of Shiva know who comes to string it.'

So Vishwamitra introduced the lineage of Ram. 'In the beginning, Narayana slept a dreamless slumber and the world did not exist. When he awoke, a lotus rose from his navel and within it sat Brahma, who was so terrified of being alone in the world that from his mind he created sons. One of these sons was Daksha. Another was Manu. Shiva beheaded Daksha. Manu had a son called Ikshavaku and another called Ila. From Ikshavaku came the Suryavansis, the solar line of kings, and from Ila came the Chandravansis, the lunar line of kings. In the Ikshavaku line of kings was one Raghu, who performed many yagnas. From him comes the clan of Raghavas or the Raghu-kula. In this clan was one Sagara, whose sons dug a hole so deep, in search of their missing horse, that rainwater collected in it to create the ocean. In this clan was one Bhagiratha, who brought Ganga from the skies to flow on earth. In this clan was one Dilip, who to save a cow from a hungry lion offered his own flesh. In this clan there was one Harischandra who kept his word even if it meant losing all his fortune, his dignity, even his son. In this clan was one Aja, who loved his wife Indumati so much that he died the instant she passed away. From Aja came Dashratha and from Dashratha comes Ram.'

'May I?' Ram asked Janaka for his permission.

Janaka nodded. He watched Ram invoke his ancestors, his parents, his teachers and seek their support. Only then did the eldest son of Dashratha reach out to hold the shaft of the bow. Slowly, he picked it up, looking surprised that it was not as heavy as everyone claimed it was. Janaka held his breath as Ram fixed the lower end of the shaft with his right toe and stretched the string with his right hand while bending the shaft with his left hand, determined to tie the loose end of the string to the free end of the shaft.

Anticipation and anxiety filled the room. Sita was filled with dread. The rules were clear: she could only marry a man who could string Shiva's bow. But her heart did not care for rules: it had given itself to him. In him she would find all satisfaction. But what if he did not succeed?

Then something happened. Ram looked into Sita's eyes; his concentration wavered, but for a moment. And in that moment, he put too much force on the shaft and it broke into two.

The sound of the crack was like the clap of a thousand thunders. Everyone heard it: the devas in the sky and the nagas under the earth. Everyone was stunned. Had Ram succeeded or failed? All eyes turned to Janaka.

And he said, 'From today, Ram, you shall be known as Janaki-vallabha, the beloved of Janaka's daughter Sita.' The court erupted in cheer.

- In the ninth century (though some argue the twelfth century) Kamban, a temple musician and follower of the poet-saint Namalvar, wrote the Tamil *Iramavataram*. This was the first regional retelling of the *Ramayana*, ten thousand verses long, full of songs. It was first presented in the Srirangam temple and the tale goes that so pleased was the deity that Narasimha emerged from the pillar to growl in satisfaction. The king had commissioned two poets to write it, but by the time inspiration struck Kamban his deadline was only two weeks away. He wrote furiously, day and night, with the Goddess herself holding the light so he would put down the thoughts through the night, enabling him to present his work first. In his work, Kamban visualizes Ram and Sita meeting in a bower and falling in love long before the bow is broken. This idea of falling in love was a key motif in Sanskrit drama. Sita is not just the prize of a contest; she is in love before she is given in marriage.
- Shiva uses his bow Pinaka to shoot arrows that pin Brahma to the sky when he is about to chase his own daughter. It is also used to destroy three worlds, the Tripura, which is why Shiva is called Pinaki (bearer of the Pinaka) and Tripurantaka (destroyer of three worlds). The bow is a metaphor for a sharp mind that is able to shoot the arrow of yoga to align nature (prakriti), culture (sanskriti) and imagination (brahmanda).
- The lineage of Ram reveals his ancestors were known for their uprightness and integrity. Of significance is Aja, Dashratha's father who died the moment his wife, Indumati, died. Such love of a husband for a wife is not common in the scriptures. Indumati dies when a sage's garland falls around her neck from the sky. The flowers remind her that she was once an apsara, and is living on earth as a result of a curse. With that memory comes death. And her death breaks Aja's heart. This story is described in Kalidasa's *Raghuvamsa*.

- Ram is renowned as maryada purushottam, one who always follows the rules. That he breaks the bow he is meant to bend and string is not insignificant. It indicates a wavering of the mind, or perhaps a momentary loss of balance. That he breaks the bow of Shiva, who is associated with detachment, perhaps indicates a moment of attachment to Sita. This makes exile a necessity, for in the forest the prince shall learn about detachment before he is ready to be king.

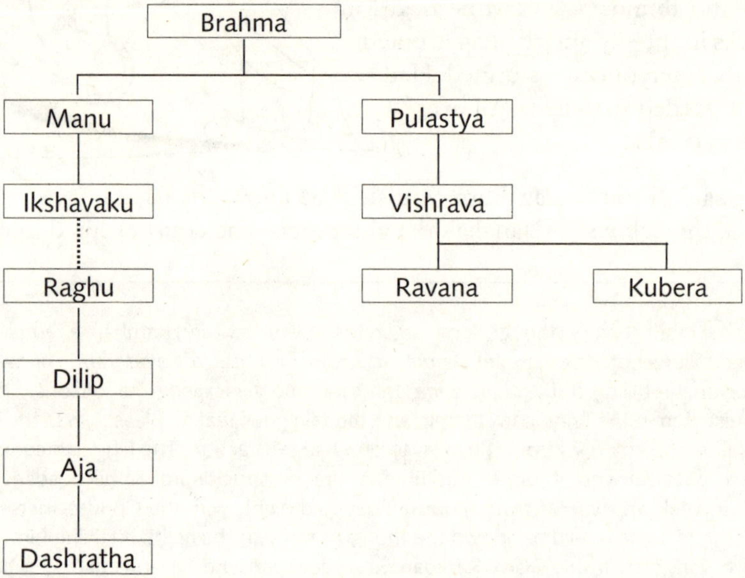

* *Abbreviated family tree*

Parashurama's Rage

Hearing the sound of the bow breaking, Parashurama raised his axe and rushed into Mithila. His presence frightened everyone. 'Who is this man who dares break the bow of Shiva when asked to bend it?' Parashurama thundered.

Janaka was about to get up and cajole the agitated warrior-priest but Vishwamitra grabbed his arm and stopped him. 'Let the boy handle this,' he whispered to the king.

With not a trace of fear on his face, Ram said, 'I did.'

'And you are?'

'Ram, son of Kaushalya, scion of the Raghu clan, prince of Ayodhya.'

'He who liberated Ahilya, who was adulterous in deed. Do you know who I am?'

'My namesake, Rama of the Bhrigu clan, also known as Rama of the axe, Parashurama, who beheaded his mother, Renuka, on his father's instructions, for being adulterous in thought.'

'When a warrior breaks a bow when asked to bend it, it indicates a mind that does not know when to stop, like my mother's who could not control desire and like Kartavirya's who could not control his greed,' declared Parashurama.

'What kind of a mind cannot overcome rage and keeps killing king after king, in clan after clan, generation after generation, in the hope that repeated punishment will create a perfect world?' asked Ram.

Parashurama had no answer. He had not expected such a sharp retort from this young man. The air was filled with tension. Those around dared not breathe. 'Are you saying control is bad?' asked Parashurama.

'Control creates domesticated animals. The purpose of society is to inspire humanity, not tame them,' said Ram.

'What then will create culture? Why not live like rakshasas? Without rules, the strong will dominate the weak and no one will help the helpless,' Parashurama shouted.

'Rules cannot be used to compel people to care. It will only amplify fear. The whole purpose of sanskriti is to outgrow fear so that we do not feel the need to grab, control or dominate. Your mother was beheaded not because she desired another, but because your father felt inadequate. Your killing of Kartavirya only sowed the seeds of vengeance in his sons, just as their killing of Jamadagni sowed the seeds of vengeance in you. You call it justice, but how much punishment is adequate – when is it fine to forgive and move on? A society that does not make room for imperfection can never be a happy society.'

These words uttered by Ram pleased Parashurama. Not every king on earth was like Kartavirya. There was still hope. He smiled. Everyone heaved a sigh of relief.

Parashurama offered Ram his bow. 'You broke Pinaka, which is Shiva's bow. Let me see how well you handle Saranga, which is Vishnu's bow.'

Ram took the bow, bent the shaft, strung it, mounted an arrow on it and pulled the string back effortlessly. Parashurama was impressed. This bow had been with the Bhrigu clan for generations and none but he had been able to hold it, let alone wield it.

'I have mounted an arrow on this bow. What should I strike? This arrow cannot go in vain,' said Ram.

'Strike my mind with it, for I had assumed I alone would solve the world's problems by enforcing rules. Shatter the boundaries of my mind, help me appreciate that the rules have to be followed voluntarily to create a happy society.'

Ram released the arrow and it struck Parashurama's mind, shattering all limitations. Everyone had seen arrows strike physical targets. For the first time they saw an arrow strike a mental target.

Parashurama was so pleased that he declared he would withdraw from the world. 'The Krita yuga ended when Kartavirya tried to steal my father's cow and broke our faith in kings. Now I see the Treta yuga has dawned with Ram who will reinforce humanity's faith in kings. No more will I kill warriors, or frighten them into being good, because now there is one amongst them who will show how to be good. My task is done.'

Parashurama hurled his axe into the sea and retired to Mount Mahendra, renouncing violence forever.

- The confrontation of Ram and Parashurama is handled differently in different retellings. It is a verbose argument in Bhavabhuti's *Mahavira-charita*. In Ram-leela performances popular in the Gangetic plains, Sita gets from Parashurama the boon of being 'akhanda soubhagyavati', one who is always fortunate, a phrase meaning her husband will outlive her. That is why Parashurama cannot hurt Ram.
- In some traditions, there is a hierarchy between Vishnu's avatars: Ram is greater than Parashurama and Krishna is greater than Ram. Krishna alone is called purnavatar, the complete form of Vishnu on earth.

- Every society goes through four phases, or yugas, according to Vedic thought. These are numbered in the reverse: Krita (4), Treta (3), Dvapara (2) and Kali (1) followed by pralaya (0) and then back to 4, 3, 2, 1. Every society begins idealistically and eventually collapses. Each yuga comes to an end with a different avatar: Parashurama in Krita, Ram in Treta, Krishna in Dvapara and Kalki in Kali.
- Parashurama is closely associated with the western coast of India, stretching from Gujarat to Kerala. It is said that when Parashurama threw his blood-soaked axe into the sea, the sea recoiled in horror and the western coast came into being.
- The colloquial term 'Ram-bana' stands for an arrow that never misses its target and refers to a sure cure for ailments or a guaranteed solution to a problem.

Four Brides for Four Brothers

Ram had impressed everyone: everyone hailed him as a worthy groom for Sita. And so, in the presence of Vishwamitra and Parashurama, Sita garlanded the eldest son of Dashratha. She would be his wife, and he would be her husband.

Messengers were sent to Ayodhya and Dashratha came to Mithila with his guru, Vasishtha, and his other two sons. Janaka had a proposal: 'You have three more sons and my family has three more daughters. Let the four brothers marry the four sisters and let your house be united with mine.'

Dashratha accepted this proposal and a grand wedding was organized to mark the union of four couples. Lakshman married Urmila, Bharata married Mandavi, and Shatrughna married Shrutakirti.

The brides and grooms were bathed in turmeric water. The boys were dressed in white, a reminder of the white seed contained in their body. The girls were dressed in red, a reminder of the red seed contained in their body.

Together they would produce the next generation, enabling the dead ancestors to be reborn.

Janaka gave his daughters to the sons of Dashratha, saying, 'I give you Lakshmi, wealth, who will bring you pleasure and prosperity. Grant me Saraswati, wisdom. Let me learn the joy of letting go.' This ritual came to be known as kanya-daan, the granting of the virgin bride. Unlike dakshina, where wealth is asked in exchange, and bhiksha, where power is asked in exchange, in daan only wisdom is sought in exchange.

The four couples took seven steps together in front of their elders. This made them lifelong companions who would share seven things: a house, fire, water, income, children, pleasure and conversation. Placing their palms one below the other they made offerings of ghee and grain to the fire so that the smoke carried them up to the realm above the sky where the devas could feast to their satisfaction. Offerings were also made to the cow, the dog, the crow and the serpent, to the banana plant and the banyan tree, to the rocks and to water, a reminder that humanity does not live in isolation.

The sons of Dashratha did as they were told without question. The daughters of Janaka smiled, for every ritual spoke to them: questions they had asked long ago had revealed to them the language of symbols.

When it was time for them to leave, Janaka blessed his daughters, 'May you take happiness wherever you go.'

Sunaina said nothing. She just gave all the girls two dolls each, one male and one female, made of red sandalwood. These were symbols of domestic bliss to be kept in the most sacred corner of their courtyards.

Finally, a fistful of rice was given to the four princesses of Videha. They threw it back over their heads. Sunaina burst out crying. No amount of wise words could stop the flow of her tears. That rice symbolized repayment of a daughter's debt to her parents. Now she was free to start her life elsewhere. The umbilical cord had been cut.

Sita, Urmila, Mandavi and Shrutakirti wanted to turn back, but they did not. They were Janaka's daughters. They knew that there is wisdom in letting go and moving on.

A huge caravan of horses, elephants, donkeys and bullocks left the city of Mithila, carrying the gifts from the home of the brides to the home of the grooms. There

were fabrics, jewels and weapons. Craftsmen and their families also travelled alongside to carry skills from the land of Videha to the land of Kosala. Sita especially paid attention to the seeds of pulses and grains, vegetables and fruits, herbs and spices. These would be grown in her husband's garden to remind her of home. For when a bride enters the husband's house she brings with her not just the promise of a new generation but also new food, a new culture and with that new thoughts that enrich her husband's household.

- Usually a king would give all his daughters to the crown prince. That the daughters are given to all the sons of Dashratha is a reminder of what the epic considers ideal: monogamy, something that is not prevalent in most stories.
- Marriage, since Vedic times, is not just the union of a man and a woman but an opportunity for two cultures to intermingle so that new customs and beliefs can enter an old household and revitalize it.
- Wedding rites in India have symbols that are rooted in agricultural practices that the modern mind may consider distasteful, ideas that describe the man as the farmer who plants the seed and the woman as the field who germinates the seed.
- In Tamil Nadu, Andhra Pradesh and Karnataka man–woman dolls of red sandalwood are given to girls either during their first menstrual periods or during their marriage. These 'king–queen' dolls are displayed along with other dolls during Navaratri festivals and are indicators of domestic bliss.
- By making Janaka a character in the epic, Valmiki is clear he wants to question the mindless materialism of kings, herdsmen and farmers. The daughters of Janaka are

expected to find happiness not through things but through thoughts.

- Mithila (the home of Sita) is south of Ayodhya (the home of Ram) and Ayodhya is south of Mathura (the home of Krishna). All three are in the Gangetic plains. Culturally, even today, these three areas have very distinct cultures. Mithila is associated with village arts and crafts; Avadh or Ayodhya was the centre of urban sophistication; Vraja or Braj was the centre of earthy devotion. Each has a different dialect: Maithili, Avadhi and Brajbhasha.
- Many scholars distinguish Ram the mortal hero from Ram who is God incarnate. They separate the sections written later, the Bala-kanda and the Uttara-kanda, chapters 1 and 7 respectively, from the original core of the narrative. However, the magic of the *Ramayana* comes from the efforts of a human struggling to realize his divine potential. Can we rise above aham and realize atma? Is aham essentially selfish and is atma essentially fair? Who is more affectionate, caring and fair – the mortal Ram or the divine Ram? It delves into the human question of trying to live a perfect life in an imperfect world where everyone's notion varies.
- The Janaki mandir is located at Janakpur in Nepal where the seventeenth-century saint Surkishoredas found a gold image of the Goddess and preached Sita-upasana or worship of Sita. Here the wedding of Sita is enacted every year around November–December.

BOOK THREE

Exile

'She followed her husband to ensure he never felt incomplete.'

Crossing Over into Ayodhya

Three queens stood at the gates of Ayodhya to greet the four women who would transform their sons into men. Conch shells were blown and tongues oscillated in ululation to attract positive energies and push away negative ones. Music filled the air: drums, pipes and cymbals. The city was decorated with leaves and flowers and lamps. Bright white patterns had been painted in front of every house to welcome the brides, who were seen by all as diminutive doubles of Lakshmi, the goddess of wealth.

Like the goddess the brides were garlanded with lotus flowers. There were beaded strings around their necks, rings around their toes and bangles on their arms. In the parting of their hair was vermilion informing Indra that they were married women, unavailable to anyone but their husbands.

Pots filled with rice were placed at the gates and the brides were asked to kick them in. They were made to walk on red dye and their footprints were collected on fine cotton muslin. They were made to dip their hands in red dye and their palm prints were emblazoned on the bodies of white cows. They were taken around the palace, the verandas outside where men resided and the courtyards where the women lived. They were taken to the cowshed, the horse stables, the elephant stables, the kitchen gardens and finally the kitchens. They were made to use the ladles and stir green vegetables that were being cooked over the fire. They were made to watch boiling milk overflow. They were shown lovebirds in a cage and asked to set them free, and watch them fly together as a pair towards the sky.

The four princes were asked to display their valour. Arrows were shot towards the sky; they transformed into flowers and fell on the cheering crowds that lined the city streets. Swords were held aloft and spears swung with agility and grace. This display of skill impressed one and all.

And finally, rings of pearls and diamonds were pierced into their nostrils: on the left side of the brides and the right side of the grooms.

Everyone in Ayodhya felt assured that the future was safe, and fertile.

Vasishtha told the boys, 'Before your wife came into your life, you were a student with no claim over property. After your wife leaves your life, you must become a hermit, with no claim over property. Only as long as she is by your side do you have claims over wealth. Without her, you cannot perform yagna; you must only perform tapasya.'

Arundhati, Vasishtha's wife, came to meet the brides and told them her tale. 'We were seven couples in the forest. Our husbands were rishis well versed in the understanding of yagnas and tapasya and we were their faithful wives. One day, after our bath, we went to worship the fire in the yagna-shala. The other wives, in their hurry to finish their chores, forgot to wear their symbols of marriage – no beads around the neck, no bangles on their arms, no vermilion in the parting of the hair, no toe-rings. Agni, the fire-god, mistook the women to be without husbands and made love to them. I, however, remained untouched. The rishis abandoned their six wives; they are now known as the Matrikas, forest virgins who are bound to no man. I alone, faithful wife of Vasishtha, serve my husband in the yagna-shala while the other six have become tapasvins, refusing to see women. I have a star by my name in the sky beside the constellation of Saptarishi, named after the seven rishis. And the six women, once

my sisters, form another constellation, the Krittika cluster of stars. The Krittikas were rejected by all except Shiva and Shakti, who made them the wet nurse of their son, the warlord Skanda, named Kartikeya after them.'

Sumitra told the daughters-in-law that at night they should ask their husbands to show them the star called Arundhati. That would be the first time they would touch their bodies, holding their hands until the fingers pointed to the star that has come to be the symbol of marital fidelity in Aryavarta, the land of Vedic wisdom.

'But that is some time away,' said Kaikeyi. For the girls were still young. They would not be given courtyards of their own. They would sleep in the beds of their mothers-in-law while the boys, now men, would leave their mother's courtyard and sleep in the courtyard of their father, the king.

In time, when the lotus bloomed, the love-god Kama would be invoked to strike the young hearts and the grooms would be invited as bees to the flower-bedecked bedchambers of the brides.

- The threshold plays a key role in the Indian household. It separates the domesticated inside from the wild outside. And so there is great fear when the daughter leaves the household and the daughter-in-law enters the household. Both events are marked by ceremonies aimed at drawing positive energies and keeping out negative energies.
- Even today, grooms of many communities are expected to hold a sword during the wedding ceremony, as a reminder of times when brides, along with their dowries, were at risk of being abducted by bandits.
- In Jagannath Puri, the image of Krishna sports a nose-ring on the right side. In ancient times, in many communities, men too wore nose-rings. The practice disappeared with time.
- The Saptarishi constellation is known as the Great Bear in English; Arundhati is known as Alkor; Krittika is known as the Pleiades or the Six Sisters. The twin stars of Alkor and Mizar in Ursa Major are known as the Arundhati and Vasishtha stars, Arundhati being fainter than Vasishtha.
- The Krittikas or the six virgin goddesses (sometimes seven) are fierce forest maidens who are revered and feared by women unable to bear children or whose children suffer from fevers and rashes. Their open-air shrines are found in rural communities throughout India. In the *Mahabharata*, they collectively bear the seed of Shiva and give birth to the six-headed son of Shiva, Kartikeya, who leads the armies of devas into battles. In later narratives, they become gentle wet nurses. They embody nature's raw power undomesticated by social rules, marriage in this case.
- In the Valmiki *Ramayana* Ram and Sita are rather young but they are much older in later versions, perhaps indicating what different communities considered a suitable age for marriage.

- Child marriage does not imply immediate consummation. Marriage in many parts of India takes place in two stages. In the first stage, the relationship is formal as the bride and groom are very young. In the second stage, the relationship is consummated after the girl attains physical and mental maturity. Until then the girl lives with her mother or mother-in-law. The point is to help her fit into the husband's household from an early age. Ceremonies mark her entry into womanhood and the groom is invited to come and claim his wife. This ritual is called 'gauna' in Bihar. There are many folk ballads that speak of women married in childhood waiting in their parental house for their husbands to come and claim them. Failure to understand the difference between the formal ritual and the actual marriage has led to many social problems.

Kaikeyi, the King's Charioteer

Sita stayed with Kaushalya while Mandavi stayed with Kaikeyi. Urmila and Shrutakirti stayed with Sumitra. They spent all day and all night listening to tales of the sons told by their adoring mothers.

Kaushalya said, 'Once Ram refused to sleep, for he wanted the moon to sleep beside him. Finally, to appease him, we put a pot of water on his bed. Reflected in the water was the moon. Thus he slept with the moon and, from that day, we decided to call him Ramachandra, Ram of the moon, even though this family worships the sun.'

Sumitra warned her daughters-in-law about the affection of their husbands for their brothers. 'You have to work hard so that they prefer you to them.'

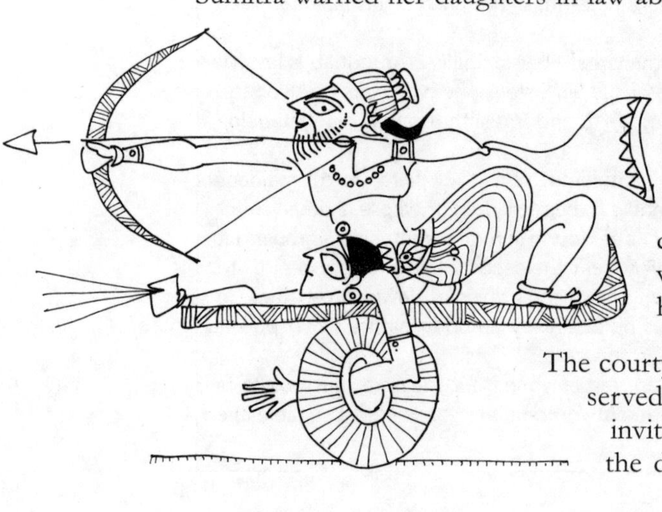

'At night at least,' chuckled Kaikeyi, making the women blush.

In the common courtyard of the three queens, Kaikeyi was most in demand. She was the most beautiful queen, dazzling in her daring.

The courtyard walls had murals showing how she served as the king's charioteer when he was invited to fight the asuras by Indra, king of the devas. She had shielded the king from arrows and motivated him with her words while she steered the horses through the battlefield. At one point the axle of the chariot broke. Without a moment's hesitation, she bent down and shoved her hand into the wheel, using her forearm to replace the broken axle.

Kaikeyi's stories were delightful, especially those about horses, for she came from the land of horses in the north-west. Her maid Manthara, who had nursed her as a child, and had also nursed her son, Bharata, was a great cook. So the girls spent hours with her in the kitchen understanding the different ways in which food was cooked in Kekaya, Kosala and Videha.

Kaushalya made dolls for the girls. Sumitra fashioned their hair, decorating it with jewels, but it was Kaikeyi's stories and Manthara's food that got the most attention.

'She knows how to become everyone's favourite,' said Sumitra.

'She may be the king's favourite queen,' said Kaushalya, 'but Ram is his favourite son.'

Manthara overheard this conversation and accidentally squeezed lime into boiling milk, curdling it.

- The story of Ram's love for the moon is commonly told to children across India. Ram is also called Ramachandra because his later decisions regarding Surpanakha and Sita brought a blemish to his solar glory.
- The story of Kaikeyi saving Dashratha's life in battle comes from later narratives.
- The Valmiki *Ramayana* acknowledges Kaikeyi as Dashratha's favourite queen, perhaps because it was foretold that she would bear an illustrious son and he was eager for one.
- Kekaya is located to the north-west of India, near Pakistan and Afghanistan. Many epic princesses, like Gandhari and Madri of the *Mahabharata*, belong to this land. It is associated with horses, which is why Kaikeyi's father is called Ashwapati, master of horses.

The Three Queens

Sita knew that people called her Janaki, Maithili and Vaidehi referring to her as the daughter of Janaka, resident of Mithila, from the land of Videha. But she had a name, Sita. She wondered what the real name of Kaushalya was, for her name simply meant princess of Kosala.

Dashratha was king of North Kosala with his capital at Saket. Kaushalya's brother was king of South Kosala with his capital at Kashi. Great wars were fought between the two. Peace followed after the princess of South Kosala insisted on marrying the king of North Kosala. When Kaushalya became Dashratha's queen, the two kingdoms merged into one, and Saket came to be known as Ayodhya, where wars are not fought.

Sita also wondered what the real name of Kaikeyi was, other than 'princess of Kekaya'. Her father, Ashwapati, was famous for the horses he owned. Her brother, Yudhajit, was a great warrior. Kaikeyi spoke often about her brother's exploits; they were very close as they had lost their mother when Kaikeyi was very young.

Sumitra once told Urmila and Shrutakirti what she had heard of Kaikeyi's mother. King Ashwapati had been gifted the power to understand the language of birds but he had been warned that if he ever shared what he heard from the birds with anyone he would die instantly. One day, Ashwapati was sitting with Kaikeyi's mother next to a lake when he heard the swans speak. Their conversation amused him and he laughed. The queen wanted to know what he had overheard. The king said he could not share what he had heard for that would lead to his death. The queen said, 'If you love me truly, you will tell me what you heard.' The king felt his wife was either too uncaring about his well-being or too stupid. Either way, he did not want her around him. He had her sent back to her parents' house. Rendered motherless, Kaikeyi and Yudhajit were handed over to the wet nurse Manthara, who raised them both.

And Sumitra? It was clear she was no princess. Manthara one day told Mandavi in hushed tones, while she was grinding wheat, 'Not of royal blood. Not a brahmin's daughter. Perhaps a trader's or a cowherd's or a charioteer's. Perhaps a servant's. It is said marrying a woman of a lower social order increases the chances of fathering a son. But even this did not work and so a yagna was needed. That is why her sons are so servile.'

One day as the four princes sat with their brides in the common courtyard of the queens, Sita hesitatingly asked Ram, 'Your father has three queens, one whom he respects, one whom he loves and one who serves him. Which queen will I be?'

Ram replied without a moment's hesitation, 'He may have three but I will have only one. I shall be satisfied with whatever this wife of mine offers me and hope that she is satisfied with whatever I offer her.'

Sita noticed the formal tone of his voice. 'I asked you about queens, not wives,' she said softly, with a smile.

'I am a husband now who has a wife. Should I be king, then my wife will also become queen. The two are not the same, Sita. My wife sits in my heart; I exist for her satisfaction. The queen sits on the king's throne and she exists for the kingdom's satisfaction,' he said, still formal.

'Does this husband know his wife?' asked Sita.

'Why does the wife need to ask? Does she doubt it?'

'The wife has not really spoken to the husband,' said Sita.

'Indeed,' said Ram, suddenly thoughtful. Rites, rituals and rules had bound their relationship until then, not conversation. They held each other's hand because they had to in ceremony. They sat next to each other because they had to in ritual. They fed each other as was tradition. She walked beside him as was the norm. But did he really know her? Did she know him? Did they see each other? What did they see of each other: the body or the mind? They were still prince and princess, not husband and wife.

Ram looked at Sita, curious and intent. Then his eyes lit up in wonderment. Sita immediately looked away, suddenly shy, becoming formal herself, trembling at the intensity of his gentle gaze.

- Jain and Buddhist documents refer to Dashratha ruling Kashi and later moving to Ayodhya.
- Saket is an ancient name for Ayodhya but is also identified as a separate city.
- In the southern text of the Valmiki *Ramayana*, Sumantra, Dashratha's charioteer and counsellor, speaks of Kaikeyi's father abandoning her mother. Details of the story are part of folklore in Odisha and Andhra Pradesh. Backstories such as these are common to explain people's behaviour, for in India all actions are seen as consequences of prior events. Nothing happens without a reason.
- In the Jain *Paumachariya*, Sumitra is the daughter of Subandhu-tilaka, king of Kamalasankulapura. Regional retellings identify Sumitra as a princess too. But not much is mentioned about her royal past. Unlike Kaushalya and Kaikeyi who are named after

the kingdoms they come from, Kosala and Kekaya, Sumitra is not named so, alluding to her non-royal station.

- Sumitra's name is very similar to Sumantra, leading to speculations that she could be his daughter. In folk songs from the Gangetic plains, Sita is visualized as a lucky and much-loved daughter-in-law for whom a well is made in the house by her father-in-law, husband and brothers-in-law. She does not have to go to the village well or the river to fetch water.
- In ancient India it was considered normal for a man, especially a king, to have many wives. Though Draupadi has five husbands, it is more the exception than the rule. There are tribes in India in the Himalayas and down south where a woman marries many brothers, but this was never the norm.

The Hunting of Shravana

Dashratha was happy. Three wives, four brave sons, four wise daughters-in-law. The future of Kosala was safe. What more could a man want?

Joyfully, he went out hunting. He shot birds flying overhead and rabbits on the ground. He stalked a tiger and successfully ambushed it. He chased deer. Then, to test his skills, he decided to blindfold himself and shoot game using merely sound to spot the target. He heard what he thought was a deer drinking water from a pond and shot an arrow in its direction. Immediately a human scream was heard.

Ripping away his blindfold, Dashratha ran towards the terrible sound. He had, as he feared, shot a human being, a boy. The arrow had gone right through his chest. He had but a few moments to live. 'My parents,' he gasped, 'please, kind stranger, find my parents, take them to safety. This hunter who shot me may hunt them down too.' Then he died.

Dashratha noticed a pot of water floating in the pond. The sound he had heard was the sound of that pot being immersed in water. It hadn't been a deer.

A guilt-ridden Dashratha carried the body in his arms and looked for the boy's parents. 'Is that you, Shravana?' he heard a feeble man's voice. 'Your footsteps sound so heavy. What are you carrying?'

Dashratha saw the boy's parents: they were old and almost blind. They sat in two baskets, which were tied to the ends of a long stick. The boy, he deduced, had slung the stick over his shoulders to carry his parents around. 'I am Dashratha, king of Kosala. What are you doing in the forest?' he said.

'Our son,' said the mother, 'is taking us on a pilgrimage. He moved away from the pilgrim path to fetch some water. We were very thirsty. Shravana saw a tiger and a deer walking together. He realized they were both going to some waterbody. So he followed them with a pot. He should be returning soon.'

'Forgive me,' said Dashratha, throwing himself at the feet of the old couple. He then told them what had happened.

The parents pulled their son's body from Dashratha's arms. They checked his pulse and his breath. He was indeed dead. The mother then let out a wail. And the father spat out a curse, 'As my wife wails so shall you, when you will be forced to separate from your son. As my heart is ripped in pain, so shall yours, when the joy of the future is stripped away from you.'

'Please, let me help you. Please understand.'

'No, stay away from us. Let us die here holding our son's body. Let the tiger feed on us while we are still alive. Let the vultures eat us when we are dead. That pain will be more bearable than the pain you have caused us.'

Dashratha fled from the old couple, and returned to the palace, guilt-ridden and terror-struck. 'My sons . . . I want my sons before me,' he ordered. Ram and Lakshman, who were in the elephant stables, rushed out to be by their father's side. 'Where are Bharata and Shatrughna? Has something happened to them?' asked Dashratha.

'Don't you remember, Father?' said Ram. 'Before you left for the hunt you bid them farewell. Uncle Yudhajit had sent a chariot from Kekaya to fetch them. Old King Ashwapati is ill, and wanted to see his granddaughters-in-law before he died.'

'And what if I die today?' said Dashratha, as the servants wiped the sweat from his brow and fetched him water and pressed his feet. Everyone looked at each other.

What was the matter with the king? Why was he so frightened? 'No, it is time to appoint the next king. Ayodhya needs a young king; let the old king retire. Yes, let me withdraw from my throne, before anyone withdraws my sons from me.'

Nobody understood what the king was rambling on about. But when Vasishtha came, Dashratha made it very clear: 'Tomorrow morning, I wish to place the crown on the head of my eldest son, Ram. He has a wife now. He has killed and forgiven already. He is ready to lead the Raghu clan. And I am ready to retire, sit in the shadows, watch him rule and train his sons as Kaushika trained my sons.'

This was a good idea, thought Vasishtha. The king was respecting the ashrama system of Vedic society, according to which every man has to spend the first quarter of his life as a celibate student, the next quarter as a productive householder, the third quarter in retirement, supporting his son and teaching his grandson, and the final quarter as a sanyasi, renouncing home and wife. The system ensured no generation dominated society; every generation made room for the next. But he was suspicious of the king's impatience.

- The story of Dashratha killing Shravana is found in the Valmiki *Ramayana*, but the name given to the boy is Yagnadatta. His mother's jati is shudra and his father's vaishya. This reference to caste is significant, for if the boy was a brahmin his killing would have been the greatest of crimes.
- Boons and curses are narrative tools to explain karma: all actions have consequences.
- According to the Valmiki *Ramayana*, twelve years pass between Ram's marriage and the decision to coronate Ram. In later retellings, the decision is almost immediate.
- Dashratha struggles to change his fate. First he wants to father a child, even if it means marrying three times and getting a priest to intervene. Then he wants a quick coronation before anything happens to his sons. But in doing so, he sparks off events that hasten the inevitable.
- The image of a son carrying his old parents to a pilgrimage is at once a reflection of nobility as well as burden. Children who care for their old parents are often called Shravana.
- The kavadi or the bamboo staff slung over the shoulder, weighted on either side by feathers and auspicious symbols like pots, is a symbol of household responsibilities that young men carry as part of many temple rituals associated with Shiva. In the south, devotees of Shiva's son Murugan carry this. In the north, devotees of Shiva carry water from the Ganga on kavadis to their local temples, making sure the kavadi never touches the ground along the way.
- In the Unnao district of Uttar Pradesh there is a place called Sarvan associated with the death of Shravana. There is a stone image there whose navel can never be filled with water, indicating the eternally unquenched thirst of the dutiful son killed by Dashratha.

The Venom of Manthara

Word spread rapidly from the king's courtyard to the city and then across the land. At dawn the following day, a new king would be crowned while the old king would retire; thus continuity and stability would be assured for the city of Ayodhya and the land of Kosala.

This led to utsav, a spontaneous celebration. The farmers returned home early from the fields, herdsmen from the pastures and fisherfolk from the waters to join in the celebrations. The houses were cleaned and decorated with flowers. The streets were swept clean and watered to prevent the dust from rising. Lamps were lit. Flags were prepared, to be raised at dawn the next day. Special food was cooked – nothing sour, only sweet, all rich in butter and ghee. The men and women took out their finery to greet the king when he would ride out on the royal chariot under the ivory parasol after the coronation ceremony. A feast was organized in the city square. Wrestlers, entertainers and musicians rushed to the city to take part in the festivites.

The news thrilled everyone in the queen's courtyard. Kaushalya said, 'But surely this can wait till Bharata and Shatrughna return?'

'Indeed,' said Manthara, 'I wonder why this impatience. Or was this all planned?' Her mind wandered. As it wandered further and further, her thoughts transformed from a gentle breeze to a storm. Suddenly she saw patterns that no one else saw. And these patterns frightened her. She ran to Kaikeyi and found her busy selecting her favourite jewels.

Manthara shut the doors and windows, sat in front of Kaikeyi and began to beat her chest, staring at the floor. Again and again, repeatedly, with increasing frequency, till Kaikeyi took notice. 'What is it, Mother?'

'You are beautiful, brave and intelligent and destined to be the mother of a king. You should have been the first wife of a great king. But no, your father gave you to this wretch who already had a wife. He promised your father that your son would be his heir. Then he blamed you for not giving him a son. Calls himself king but does not take responsibility for his own sterility. Even that servant's daughter's womb could not germinate his weak seed. So he calls a priest and conducts a yagna and invokes the gods and gets a potion to become a father. And what a horrible father, preferring his first wife's son to the others! Holding him back in the palace and letting your son go to the forest with that wretched Vishwamitra. And then giving your son an inferior wife, sister of the eldest bride, not a queen in her own right. And now, when your son is away, prepares to crown his dear Ram king.

That will make Kaushalya the queen mother and where will that leave you? Your son will be servant of the king and you, my beautiful, brave, intelligent, fertile Kaikeyi, will be Kaushalya's maid. And I will be maid to a maid. With a heavy heart I accepted being maid to the second queen in the hope that one day you would be queen mother. But now, that hope is dashed. All because your charms did not work with the king. Kaushalya's did.'

Kaikeyi, who had been happy until that moment, and had never seen things the way Manthara did, suddenly felt fear creeping into her heart. Did she matter to the king? Did her son matter? No more would she be the favoured queen; she would be servant to the queen mother. And Bharata? Would he be Ram's servant? Then she thought: but Ram is the eldest son and a good son, a brave, strong and wise man. Surely Ayodhya deserves him. What is wrong in serving a worthy king and his noble mother?

'Sacrifice is good,' continued Manthara tauntingly. 'The poor always sacrifice for the rich, the weak for the strong, the servant for the master. Let us accept our place, at the feet of Kaushalya. Since I raised you, not your royal mother, I guess you are bound to display servant qualities just like me.'

Like a snake whose tail had been struck, Kaikeyi raised her hood. 'Never. I am no one's servant. I will always be queen. I will go to my husband and tell him to stop. He will listen to me. He always does.'

'Yes, he does. But not now, not when Vasishtha and Kaushalya sit beside him. Get him here, alone. And don't ask him. Demand that he keep his word.'

'Word?'

Manthara reminded Kaikeyi of the two boons Dashratha had granted her long ago, in the battlefield when she saved his life, boons that she had yet to claim. 'Oh yes,' said Kaikeyi, with a wily smile.

- From desire come all problems. And all desires come from fear. Manthara fears for her own well-being, and so does Kaikeyi. Neither trusts Dashratha. Each one imagines the consequences of Ram's coronation and is not happy with the picture that emerges.
- In ancient times, there were special chambers known as kop-bhavan or anger rooms where queens went to declare their rage. Kings were expected to then appease them and draw them out of their kop-bhavan. This is where Kaikeyi goes; she removes her finery and hurls herself on the floor to dramatically display her sorrow.
- Manthara is a common literary device whereby an aspect of the protagonist's personality is turned into a character in a story. Manthara embodies and voices Kaikeyi's deepest fears.
- In many retellings, both Manthara and Kaikeyi are compelled to do what they did in order to ensure that Ram goes into the forest and kills the demons there. In the *Adhyatma Ramayana*, for example, the goddess of knowledge Saraswati influences the two women. Such narratives attempt to humanize the villains, make them critical pawns in a larger narrative.
- The narrative reveals the anxieties of the palace. In every organization there are hierarchies which determine power. To rise, some use talent, others use loyalty and still others use connections. That the eldest should inherit the throne is a human construction. In nature, the strongest leads the pack. Stories that show Ram as not just elder but also wiser and stronger establish his claim to the throne.
- Bhavabhuti's *Mahavira-charita* describes how Ravana's uncle and minister Malyavan plots against Ram. First he provokes Parashurama to fight Ram. Then he gets Surpanakha to possess Manthara's body and influence Kaikeyi, thus forcing Ram to enter the forest where he would be overpowered by Ravana's ally, the monkey-king Vali, and be forced to marry Surpanakha while Ravana would claim Sita. Murari's Sanskrit play *Anargha-Raghava* has a similar take.

Two Boons for Kaikeyi

When a king has several wives, he is supposed to divide his time equally between them. Dashratha, however, preferred spending most nights with Kaikeyi, something that always created tension in the inner courtyards. But Kaushalya was too gracious to protest and Sumitra too mild.

That night, like most nights, the king came to Kaikeyi's courtyard. He expected to be greeted with the fragrance of perfumes and the aroma of Manthara's cooking, especially tonight, when the whole city was fragrant and everyone was busy preparing for the next day's event. But what greeted him was darkness and silence.

Manthara was crouched in a corner, beating her chest with her hands and striking her head on the wall. And Kaikeyi lay on the floor, her hair unbound, her clothes unravelled, her jewels cast on the floor, whimpering and sobbing. What was going on?

'I mourn the shame you will bring to the Raghu clan when you fail to keep your word,' said Kaikeyi.

'That will never happen! That can never happen. How can you say that?'

'I want something, something that you promised me long ago, that you may not want to give me any more,' said Kaikeyi, slowly ensnaring the king into her trap.

'As scion of the Raghu clan, I will always keep my word lest people doubt my family's integrity, you know that,' said Dashratha indulgently, looking forward to the prospect of spending all his time with Kaikeyi after handing over the royal responsibilities to Ram.

'Then give me the two boons that you promised me when I saved your life in the battle between the devas and the asuras. Let Ram be sent to the forest where he has to live as a hermit for fourteen years. Let Bharata be made king of Ayodhya.'

Dashratha flinched as if stung by a scorpion. He looked at Kaikeyi. No, she was not joking. This was real. As scion of the Raghu clan, he had to keep his word. The curse of Shravana's father was coming true. His legs felt weak. He sat down. 'I will have to ask Ram,' he mumbled.

'Manthara can go and fetch Ram. Let us see if he is truly a scion of the Raghu clan,' said Kaikeyi, enjoying the king's discomfort. 'Should she?' The king nodded reluctantly.

Manthara ran to Kaushalya's courtyard and found Ram, looking radiant, being fed by his mother. Bowing low, Manthara said, 'The king wants to see you. It's a bit urgent.'

'Let him finish his food,' said Sumitra, who was feeding Sita, the queen-to-be. But Ram had already stood up. Kaushalya did not mind; she knew her son and the rules of the royal family.

- Why did Kaikeyi send Ram into exile for fourteen years and not forever? This is a mystery that is not easy to solve. It suggests that Kaikeyi wanted Ram to return. Different retellings offer different explanations. In one version, a fortnight of the devas is fourteen years for humans, and that is what Kaikeyi sought because that is the time Ram would need to kill Ravana. In another version found in Assam, it had been foretold that whosoever sat on Ayodhya's throne for those fourteen years would die, and so Kaikeyi wanted to protect Ram even if it meant the death of her own son, Bharata. Somehow, there is an eagerness in storytellers to understand and forgive Kaikeyi rather than condemn her, a trait typical of Indian storytelling.
- In Bhasa's *Pratima-nataka*, Kaikeyi tells Bharata that she wanted Ram to go into exile for fourteen days but said fourteen years by mistake. The play tries to clear Kaikeyi's name.
- In the Buddhist *Ramayana*, Ram is sent into exile by his father to protect him from his ambitious stepmother. Dashratha tells him to return after his death and claim the throne by force.
- In the Jain *Paumachariya*, fearing that Bharata will become a monk in his footsteps, Dashratha asks Ram to go into exile.
- When Ram is summoned, the Valmiki *Ramayana* describes him as seated amongst the elders of the city looking like the bright moon and Sita appearing as a constellation of stars.

Upholding the Reputation of the Raghu Clan

Ram found his father in a state of distress, mouthing incoherent words, when he entered Kaikeyi's courtyard. Kaikeyi spoke in his stead: 'Your father, king of Ayodhya, scion of the Raghu clan, had promised me that he would grant me not one but two wishes. Tonight, I told him what I desire. I want you to live as a

hermit in the forest for fourteen years while Bharata is crowned king instead. What do you have to say to that? Your father clearly struggles with the idea.'

Ram said, his face as calm as before, 'A word given must be kept. I shall set out for the forest immediately and gladly make way for my brother to sit on the throne. Let it not be said that any member of the Raghu clan does not keep his word. Let people never doubt the integrity of the kings of Ayodhya.'

Dashratha broke down. It would have been so much easier if the boy had resisted, if he had asked for an explanation, shown a hint of rage.

Kaikeyi chuckled, 'No wonder he is your favourite. He obeys you unquestioningly.'

'You are blind, wicked woman. This is not a son obeying his father. This is a prince of the Raghu clan upholding royal reputation.'

Kaikeyi did not care to hear this. And Manthara cackled in glee as she ran to Kaushalya's courtyard to tell everyone the news.

- In society, a man is valued on the basis of what he has. But Ram does not value himself so. He does not see Ayodhya as his property or entitlement. So he can let it go easily. It indicates wisdom. Tapasya enables a human being to determine how he values himself; this dictates the way he conducts yagna in society. But what seems noble at the start of the epic when Ram detaches himself from Ayodhya seems horrifying at the end of the epic, when Ram detaches himself from his wife. The epic draws attention to the dark side of detachment. It is not always as noble as it is made out to be.
- Ram is celebrated as maryada purushottam, one who follows the rules. So his decision is not based on emotions, but on the model social behaviour expected of a prince. This distinction is critical. That Ram gives more value to rules than to his feelings is revealed starkly in the way he treats his wife later in the epic. The rule-follower keeps the royal word and upholds royal reputation. It does not matter that one decision breaks his father's heart and the other breaks his wife's. The rule-follower is neither an obedient son nor a loving husband; he is just a rule-follower. In a way, this seems like an ancient

indictment of the institution model of society, where rules and systems are given more value than people.

- The Valmiki *Ramayana* clearly states that Dashratha secured Kaikeyi as his wife on the condition that her son would be his heir. Ram is aware of this and so never blames Kaikeyi.
- Until the fifth century CE, Ram was hailed as a great human hero, even though the Valmiki *Ramayana* alludes to Ram sensing his divinity, though never revealing it. From the fifth century onwards, Ram was increasingly seen as a form of Vishnu on earth, a model king, who valued his word over all things. By the tenth century, there was no doubt of Ram's divinity. In Kamban's Tamil retelling, *Iramavataram* ('This avatar called Ram'), Ram struggles with his divinity and gradually slips into silence, as his actions often seem contrary to what is conventionally expected of the divine. By the twelfth century, following the work of the Vedanta scholar Ramanuja, Ram became equated with God himself and this marked the beginning of Ram-bhakti, where Ram is assumed to be God and does not have to prove he is God. Everyone in the epic knows he is God and approaches him accordingly.

Ram's Companions

Kaushalya and Sumitra rushed into Kaikeyi's courtyard, followed by Lakshman, Sita and Urmila. Lamps had been lit in the courtyard that was still dark. In the flickering light, they saw the king on Kaikeyi's bed and Ram at her feet. The king looked shattered, Kaikeyi looked triumphant, while Ram looked calm, unclasping his jewels, letting them drop to the floor.

Kaushalya felt faint, but was held upright by Sumitra. It was all true.

Lakshman declared, 'I will come with you. I have been your shadow in the palace. I will be your shadow in the forest.' Ram did not say a word.

'So will I,' said Sita.

'No,' shouted Ram, taken by surprise. Then, toning down the sharpness of his voice, he explained, 'The forest is no place for a princess. Wait for me here in the palace.'

'I do not need your permission. I am your wife and I am supposed to accompany you, to the throne, into war and to the forest. What you eat, I shall taste. Where you sleep, I shall rest. You are the shaft of the bow that is our marriage; you need the string to complete it. My place is beside you, nowhere else. Fear not, I will be no burden; I can take care of myself. As long as I am beside you and behind you, you will want for nothing.'

The words of the young girl stunned everyone in the palace. She was indeed Janaka's daughter, born of the earth, raised amongst sages, the one who could hold aloft the bow of Shiva that crushed everyone else.

'And I will follow my husband,' said Urmila.

Lakshman took his wife aside and said, 'Support me by staying back. I am going to the forest to serve my brother and his wife. If you come along, I will be distracted.'

'Who will serve you?' asked Urmila.

'Serve me by staying here. Let me carry you in my heart.'

Sumitra said what everyone wanted to say, 'Fourteen years in the forest! Do you know what that means? Fourteen years of summer without a fly whisk, fourteen years of winter without a quilt and fourteen years of rains without parasols.'

Sita said, 'Mother, do not worry for your sons. In summer, I shall find shady trees under which they can rest. In winter, I shall light fires to keep them warm. During the rains, I shall find caves where we can stay dry. They are safe with me.'

Kaushalya's heart melted in affection: the child does not know what is in store for her, she thought. She felt as if someone jealous of her happiness was ripping her heart out gleefully. Tears streaming down her face, she took off talismans from her arm and tied them on Sita's.

Urmila hugged Sita and wept uncontrollably. Suddenly, she felt alone.

- The exile of Ram is described very elaborately and theatrically in the Valmiki *Ramayana*. First Dashratha asks Ram to come to Kaikeyi's palace. Then Ram goes to Kaushalya's palace and then to Sita's palace to convey the news. Finally Ram returns to Dashratha's palace, ready to leave.

- Is Sita following Ram because it is her duty or because she loves Ram and cares for him? Is the decision based on social norms or emotion? This is not clarified in the epic. But while Ram tilts more towards rules, Sita balances him by tilting more towards emotions. He aligns; she understands.
- Unlike conventional narratives that portray Sita as a demure, obedient wife, the Sita of the Valmiki *Ramayana* has a mind of her own. In fact, she rebukes Ram for not being man enough and for being afraid of taking his wife along.
- In the *Adhyatma Ramayana* what finally makes Ram agree to Sita accompanying him to the forest is her argument that she has always accompanied him to the forest in all the earlier *Ramayanas*. This alludes to the many retellings of the epic, or to a prior life, when he was Ram before. Thus the narrative implies knowledge of the belief that the *Ramayana* is an eternal cyclic story, taking place again and again, both simultaneously and sequentially, in different ages and told through different poets, and we have access to just one of its many repetitions.
- In Vaishnava literature, when Vishnu descends on earth, he is accompanied by Adi Sesha, the many-hooded serpent on which Vishnu reclines, as well as his weapons which take human form. When he descends as Ram, Adi Sesha takes the form of Lakshman and his weapons, the disc and the mace, descend as his brothers, Bharata and Shatrughna.

Clothes of Bark

Everything was happening fast. At dusk, the palace was a place of celebration. By midnight, it had become a place of gloom. The servants went around the palace to tell musicians to stop playing music, the cooks to stop preparing food, the maids to stop stringing garlands, the attendants to stop lighting the lamps and the priests to stop chanting hymns. The chatter of excited entertainers preparing for the next day was replaced by worried whispers.

Soon the word spread from the palace to the city like the tentacles of an octopus. The unimaginable had happened: Ram who was to be crowned king at dawn had been banished from the palace and asked to live as a hermit in the forest for fourteen years. The people of Ayodhya, who had stayed awake preparing for the next day, left all their chores and walked towards the palace wondering if what they had heard was true or if it was a cruel prank played by a mischief-maker.

Meanwhile, Manthara organized clothes of bark for Ram, Lakshman and Sita. Ram replaced his rich royal robes very comfortably, for he had worn such clothes when he was a student at Vasishtha's hermitage. Sita had seen these on the many ascetics who attended the Upanishad, but had never worn them herself. She looked unsure.

'Let me help you,' said Ram.

'Stop,' said Kaushalya looking at Sita. 'Ram has been told to live like a hermit. Not you, my daughter-in-law. You embody the prosperity of the Raghu clan. Never ever should you be seen distressed or poor, stripped of jewels or colour. It will annoy the devas and bring misfortune to the household of your husband. Tell her, Kaikeyi. Or do you want your son's kingdom to face the wrath of the Goddess?'

Kaikeyi, heady with the unexpected and wonderful turn of events, decided to be gracious. 'Yes. Ram needs to be a hermit. Sita, you need to continue to be the bride. You will embody the reputation of the Raghu clan even in the forest. Guard her well, Ram. Do not forget to carry your weapons. Never let Bharata doubt your loyalty.'

Manthara chuckled, 'Oh my, the girl will become a woman in the forest. Will the hermit stay a hermit then?'

'I will cut your tongue out, vulgar witch,' said Lakshman.

'I am leaving now,' said Ram curtly to Lakshman. 'If you wish to follow, then follow me now. If you wish to stay and cut out tongues, then stay.'

Ram walked out of Kaikeyi's courtyard, dressed in bark, carrying nothing but his weapons: a sword, a spear, an axe, a bow and a quiver full of arrows. Sita followed him, dressed in red, laden with jewels meant for a queen who sits on the throne beside her husband, the king. Lakshman followed her, barely hiding his rage. The attendants who carried parasols and fly whisks meant for the crown prince stood aside, numb, not knowing what to do.

Had they been going to war, no one would have cried. But this was unbearable, unacceptable even: children being sent to live in the forests while their parents continued to live in the palace. As they crossed the threshold, Dashratha could not contain himself. Royal composure gave way to a father's wail. Kaushalya and Sumitra who tried to comfort him also began to cry. Watching them cry, the maids and servants began to cry as well, the warriors began to cry, the priests began to cry, the elders began to cry. It was like someone had died.

- Sodden strips of the fibrous inner bark of trees and plants such as the banyan and the banana are beaten into sheets to make cloth of bark.
- Ram mats his hair using the juice of the banyan tree.
- In miniature art, Ram is often shown wearing clothes made of leaves and he also wraps animal hide around his body. These were the clothes of mendicants.
- Not all versions agree on whether Sita followed Ram in royal robes or in clothes of bark. In Kamban's *Ramayana* she wears bark.

Departure

When the people of Ayodhya heard the wailing from the inner chambers of the palace, they blocked the palace gates. They would not let Ram go. Whatever the palace politics, this was about their future too. They would not be silent witnesses.

To avoid the commotion at the gates, it was decided that Ram, Lakshman and Sita would be taken out on the royal chariot, which would make it easier for them to cut through the crowd. Sumantra, the king's charioteer, ordered the warriors to use whips and sticks to push the people away and make a path.

But as the chariot rolled out, the crowds rushed forward, refusing to be intimidated. They threatened to throw themselves under the wheels and kill themselves. 'We will kill Kaikeyi. We will kill Bharata. Revolt, Ram, we are with you. Do not submit to this injustice,' they said.

Ram finally stood up and said in a voice that was clear and soothing, 'Know this, Ayodhya is not mine to give or Bharata's to take; Ayodhya is the responsibility of the Raghu clan, not our property. It will be injustice if the kings of the Raghu clan do not keep their word, it will be injustice if the wishes of Kaikeyi are not fulfilled. My father promised to fulfil her wishes and he is obliged to fulfil them, as am I. Do not blame her for asking what is due to her. Yes, the event is unfortunate but it is but one event in our lives; we can call it a tragedy if we wish. Blaming helps no one; let us take responsibility for it. For nothing in life happens spontaneously: it is the result of past actions. This moment is as it is supposed to be. I am repaying the debt of the past and so are you. We cannot choose the circumstances of our life, but we can make our choices. I have chosen to be true to my clan. My wife has chosen to be true to her role as my wife. My brother has chosen to be true to his feelings. Allow us our choices. Come to terms with our decisions. You are angry not with the queen or her son, or the king, you are angry that life has not turned out the way you thought it would. In a moment, the world you so took for granted has collapsed. Expand your mind and understand that the pain comes from your assumptions and expectations. Choose love over hate, by accepting the fears and fragilities of humanity that lead to situations such as these. This moment is the outcome of some curse, or maybe it is a boon in waiting. Who knows? Varuna has a thousand eyes, Indra a hundred, you and I, only two.'

After this there was no more agitation. The chariot rolled without resistance and the people stood quietly by.

When the chariot crossed the city gates, the people felt emptiness in their hearts, and spontaneously began following the chariot. They would not stop the chariot but they could not stop their feet either. Before long the city was deserted, and a long stream of people made their way behind the chariot, with its fluttering royal flags, which made its way towards the frontiers of Kosala.

Dashratha dragged himself out of Kaikeyi's courtyard assisted by his wives. From the palace gate he watched the chariot carrying his sons roll out. He stood on

his toes and strained his neck, watching the chariot until it disappeared over the horizon. 'Ram is gone. Bharata is not here. Neither is Lakshman or Shatrughna. What will happen to Ayodhya if I die now?' he said.

'Nothing,' said Kaushalya wistfully. 'The sun will rise. The birds will chirp and the city will go about its business. The world does not need us, my husband. We need the world. Come, let us go inside and prepare for Bharata's coronation. Fortunes and misfortunes come and go but life continues.'

- The motif of the beloved leaving on a chariot is a recurring one in the *Ramayana* and the *Mahabharata*. Ram leaves Ayodhya on his chariot and the people of Ayodhya try to stop him. Krishna leaves Vrindavan on his chariot and the milkmaids of Vrindavan try to stop him by hurling themselves before the chariot. Krishna does not keep his promise to return but Ram does.
- Unlike the departure of the Buddha that takes place in secret, Ram's departure is public, with everyone weeping as the beloved is bound by duty to leave.
- Ram's stoic calm while leaving the city is what makes him divine in the eyes of most people. He does what no ordinary human can do; he represents the acme of human potential.
- According to the Kashmiri *Ramayana*, Dashratha weeps so much that he becomes blind.

Guha, the Boatman

The chariot stopped when it reached the banks of the river Ganga. 'Let us rest,' said Ram. So everyone sat on the ground around the chariot.

Slowly, the night's events began to take their toll. People began to yawn and stretch. No sooner did their heads touch the ground than they fell asleep. Sita saw Ram watching over the people with a mother's loving gaze. 'Why don't you sleep for some time?' asked Sita.

'No, the forest awaits.' As the soft sounds of sleep filled the air, Ram alighted from the chariot and told Sumantra, 'We will take our leave as they sleep. When they awaken tell the men and women of Ayodhya that if they truly love me, they must return home. I will see you, and them, again in fourteen years. No eclipse lasts forever.'

Ram walked upriver. Sita and Lakshman followed him. Sumantra watched them disappear into the bushes. The sky was red by the time they reached a village of fisherfolk; the sun would soon be up. 'Guha,' Ram called out in hushed tones.

'Who is it?' The voice was gruff. From under an overturned boat emerged Guha, the king of fisherfolk. He recognized Ram immediately and beamed. 'What are you doing here so early?' He then noticed Sita and Lakshman behind him, and the clothes Ram and Lakshman were wearing. 'Is this some royal game, or ritual? Are you going on an excursion to the forest?'

'Yes,' replied Ram, 'for fourteen years.' Ram told Guha what had transpired at the palace. He then asked Guha for a favour: 'Take us across. And do not ferry anyone else across these waters for the rest of the day. I do not want anyone to follow us.'

'Why don't you stay here, with us? My hut is not a palace, and it is as bad as any forest, but I will make your stay comfortable.'

'I cannot,' said Ram. 'A forest is defined as a place from where we cannot even see the light of the lamps of human settlement.'

'Humans are not meant to live like that. Certainly not princes, or princesses,' Guha said looking at Sita. She was so young and dainty. How would she survive in the forest? This was madness.

'Guha, the boat,' said Ram, his firm voice a command.

'Eat some rice before you go,' pleaded Guha. 'I will cook it myself and flavour it with pepper.'

'No cooked food for a hermit. Just what we pluck from trees or pull out from the ground.'

'Let me come with you, serve you.'

'No servants for hermits.'

As the harshness of the exile kept unfolding before Sita, she was confident that she would find the strength to bear and ease the suffering of her husband and his brother. Never ever would she make Ram regret her companionship. She would help realize Janaka's blessings before she left, 'May you bring happiness wherever you go.'

As Guha dragged the boat into the waters, he tried to make light of the situation. 'The touch of your feet turned a stone into a woman, I heard. Hope you don't turn this boat of mine into something else; it is my only source of livelihood.'

Ram smiled and hugged Guha, the kind boatman, who then ferried the three to the other side from where began the Dandaka forest, realm of the rakshasas.

The sun rose and in the first light Ram turned to have a last glimpse of Kosala. On the other side, he saw the people of Ayodhya. They had noticed his absence and followed him silently to the village of the fisherfolk, but had let him go without a word of protest. Ram bowed to them, in appreciation of their wisdom, and they bowed back, in appreciation of his nobility.

- In the Valmiki *Ramayana*, Ram leaves while the people are sleeping and the chariot turns around and returns to Ayodhya; everyone presumes that Ram has probably changed his mind and returned home. Instead, Ram crosses the river and goes into the forest.
- To go into exile, Ram crosses two rivers, the Ganga and the Yamuna, which water the plains commonly associated with Aryavarta. The river divides culture from nature, the realm of humans from the realm of animals.
- Guha is an important character in devotional songs and literature. Ram treats him as a friend, not a servant, and Guha reveals his naivety when he fears Ram's foot will turn his boat into a woman.

The Sleep Goddess

They walked all day, moving away from Kosala, not looking back. Ram kept turning only to see if Sita was comfortable, while Sita was busy collecting berries and fruits she found on the way. No word was exchanged, but each one had taken up a responsibility: Ram would find the path they would all follow, Sita would collect food and water, and Lakshman would keep an eye out for predators.

They found a huge rock next to a lake. 'We will spend the night here,' Ram said. They were all very tired after the events of the previous night and having walked all day. Ram and Sita could hardly keep their eyes open.

But Lakshman refused to sleep. 'You must,' said Nidra, the goddess of sleep, appearing before him, 'it is the law of nature.'

'If I sleep, who will protect my brother and his wife? No, I wish to stay awake.' He begged Nidra to go to his wife Urmila in the city of Ayodhya and tell her to sleep on his behalf. 'Let her sleep all night for herself and all day for me.'

When Nidra appeared before Urmila and told her of Lakshman's wish, she was more than happy to help. 'Let his exhaustion come to me so that he stays always fresh and alert as he serves his brother and his wife.'

And so it came to pass that for the next fourteen years Urmila slept all day and all night, while Lakshman remained without sleep in the service of Ram.

- The episode of Urmila sleeping and Lakshman staying awake for fourteen years comes from Buddha Reddy's *Ranganatha Ramayana*.
- Many poets have wondered about Urmila, the wife abandoned by the husband who considers duty to his elder brother more important. Through her, they have expressed the status of the Indian woman, as being servile to the larger institution, the husband's family. Even the husband is servile to his family. In the Indian social order, the individual is inferior to the family. Individualism is expressed only as a hermit; else one has to submit to the ways of the householder. The household is thus bondage, from which one yearns for liberation. In the *Ramayana*, this bondage is visualized as yagna, conducted out of sensitivity for the other. The hermit, on the other hand, is seen as one who is indifferent to the hunger of the other.
- Rabindranath Tagore in his writings criticized Valmiki for overlooking the contribution of Urmila, inspiring the poet Maithili Sharan Gupt to give prominence to Urmila in his *Ramayana* titled *Saket*.

Meeting Bharata

The forest was no sylvan retreat, the princes realized. It was different travelling through forests in the company of Vasishtha and Vishwamitra, or hunting there with Dashratha, or exploring it with servants in tow. Now it meant walking on uneven ground strewn with sharp stones and thick, prickly bushes, avoiding snakes and scorpions, finding their own food and water, sleeping on the ground, under trees or the open sky, and being constantly wary of predators, for the animals of the forest did not care that they were Dashratha's children.

Occasionally they met tapasvis, like the rishi Bharadwaja, at Prayag, the confluence of the Ganga and the Yamuna, who sympathized with their situation and gave them advice on how to spend their time in the forest fruitfully.

Two moons into the exile, Ram and Sita were resting under a banyan tree while Lakshman kept a lookout from atop one of the branches. He heard the sound of conch shells and drums. Then he saw fluttering flags coming towards them, following the path they had taken from Ayodhya. He recognized the flags: they were his father's.

'I think it is Father, coming to fetch us back,' said Lakshman.

'No, we have to keep his word. Stay for fourteen years as is desired by the queen.'

When the flags came nearer, Lakshman saw no sign of their father. Instead, on the chariot he saw Bharata and Shatrughna. 'They have come to kill us,' shouted Lakshman.

'No,' said Ram, who had also climbed the tree. 'Look carefully. They bear no weapons. And look, their heads have been shaved.'

Lakshman turned to look at Ram, his face ashen. 'Do you think . . . ?'

Ram alighted from the tree, his shoulders drooping. 'I think my father is dead.' Sita rushed to comfort him. Could things get worse? They could, considering Bharata was coming with an entourage of warriors. So Lakshman picked up his bow, just in case. 'No, Lakshman. Have faith in Bharata. He too is Dashratha's son,' said Ram.

'And Kaikeyi's,' said Lakshman, his grip tightening over his sword.

The chariot stopped at the sight of Ram. Bharata alighted from the chariot and ran towards his elder brother, no weapons in his hands, tears streaming down his cheeks. 'Brother,' he cried, as he hugged Ram.

- The place where Bharata and Ram meet, Ram's first major camp after his exile, is called Chitrakut.
- Across India, there are cities that are divided based on the events that occur in the *Ramayana*. In Varanasi, for example, there are portions of the city identified with Ayodhya (Ram Nagar) and with Lanka. They are located on either side of the river Ganga. Then there are specific locations identified as Chitrakut where Ram meets Bharata and as Panchvati from where Sita gets abducted. Thus the grand epic becomes particular and intimate. Similar mapping is seen in Wayanad in Kerala.
- *Bharat Milap* (1942) is a popular Hindi film based on the meeting of Bharata with Ram.
- In the Buddhist *Dashratha Jataka*, Dashratha who is king of Varanasi exiles Ram into the forest to protect him from his ambitious second queen. Astrologers tell Dashratha he will live for twelve years and so he tells Ram to return after twelve years. But when Dashratha dies only nine years later and Bharata goes to fetch Ram, Ram insists on keeping his word and staying in the forest for twelve years. He speaks of the impermanence of all things, thus revealing himself to be the Bodhisattva. This display of integrity makes him noble and worthy of reverence.
- In the *Dashratha Jataka*, Ram and Sita are described as siblings. The assumption that this indicates a prevalence of incest has riled the Hindu orthodoxy. Beyond such titillating interpretations that get media coverage, the story probably resonates the ancient belief in Indic faiths that there was once a golden age (the sushama-sushama period or the yugalia era of Jain cosmology, for example) where couples were not husbands and wives but brothers and sisters, twins actually, as there was no need for sexual activity since the mind was so highly evolved that the body did not crave sensual pleasure and children were born out of thought. With time, pollution crept in, and sexual activity emerged, giving rise to marriage laws and incest taboos. Thus Jain Agama speaks of Rishabha having two wives, Sumangala who is his twin and Sunanda whose twin dies in an accident. Further, in India, where child marriages were prevalent, husbands and wives addressed each other as brother and sister, until they were deemed old enough to consummate the marriage.

The Last Rites of Dashratha

When the tears stopped flowing, Bharata told Ram the terrible events that followed after Ram had left the city.

Bharata had left Kekaya and returned home after receiving urgent word from his mother. He found the city shorn of all joy. No music, no smiles, no fragrances, no colour. Glum faces everywhere. At the palace gate, Manthara greeted him, but no one else. In his mother's courtyard, he found his mother with a shaven head, wearing the ochre robes of a widow. Rather than telling him how the king died, she told him excitedly how he would now be king. When he insisted on knowing about his father, she revealed how he had collapsed on the threshold of the palace shortly after Ram's departure to the forest. He died without his sons by his side, or his subjects around him. His body had been kept in a vat of oil, to prevent decomposition, waiting for one of his sons to perform the last rites.

'But I did not perform the last rites,' said Bharata. 'Sumantra told me the king's last wish very clearly. He did not want Kaikeyi's son to light his funeral pyre. Shatrughna, the youngest, had to do what is supposed to be done by the eldest.'

Shatrughna then said, 'Yes, the rituals are complete but our father's spirit refuses to cross the Vaitarni. Yama's crows refuse to eat the funeral offerings. I have been tormented by dreams. Father wants the meat of the one-horned rhino, hunted by his four sons together. That is why we have come to see you.'

Ram realized how desperately his father wanted to see his children united. 'Then let us go hunting. Let us work as one and give our father the food he is hungry for.'

While the royal entourage waited, the four brothers went deeper into the forest in search of the one-horned rhino. They returned shortly with its carcass, and performed the necessary ceremonies. The crows accepted this offering, indicating that Dashratha was finally ready to leave the land of the living.

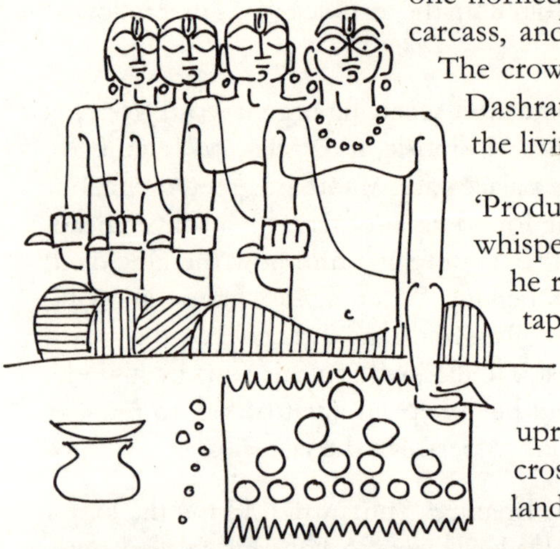

'Produce sons soon,' the spirit of Dashratha whispered in his sons' ears before he left. But he realized that all four sons would live like tapasvis until Ram's return fourteen years later. He would have to be patient until then. Enraged, he caused the wind to uproot a few trees in the forest, before he crossed the Vaitarni to await rebirth from the land of the dead.

- Traditionally, the eldest son performs the last rites of his father. In the Valmiki *Ramayana*, the tragedy of Ram not being able to perform the last rites of his father, even though he is the eldest son, is highlighted.
- The detail of Bharata being denied the right to perform the funeral comes from Kamban's *Ramayana*.
- The hunting of the rhino episode is based on the *Ramayana* play performed in rural Odisha.
- Hindus believe that the river Vaitarni separates the land of the living from the land of the dead. In the land of the living live the sons or Putra. In the land of the dead live the forefathers or Pitr. Pitr are reborn through Putra. Those who fail to produce Putra are doomed to be trapped in the hell known as Put. Scholars are divided if Putra and Pitr are gender-neutral terms or refer specifically to sons and forefathers.
- In Bhasa's play *Pratima-nataka*, Ravana takes advantage of Ram's desperation to perform the last rites of his father. Pretending to be a brahmin well versed in funeral rituals, he advises Ram to offer a golden deer found in the Himalayas to please the departed soul of his father. Thus Ram is encouraged to leave the hermitage, enabling Ravana to abduct Sita.
- Gaya in Bihar is favoured by Hindus for making funeral offerings to ancestors. The river Falgu has no water here, even though there is water upstream and downstream, because it runs underground. Digging the riverbed reveals the waters. It is said that Ram came to this spot with his brothers to perform Dashratha's shradh rituals and while he was away bathing, the spirit of Dashratha appeared before Sita and asked her to feed him immediately. She did not have any rice or black sesame seeds, so she gave him pinda

balls made of riverbed sand. This pleased Dashratha. When Ram returned, she told him what had happened. He did not believe her. Sita pointed to her witnesses – the banyan tree, the river, the cow, the tulsi plant and the priests. Unfortunately, none but the banyan tree spoke up. Enraged, Sita cursed the river that henceforth it would lose its water in Gaya, the cow that it would henceforth be worshipped from the back not the front, the tulsi plant that it would not be worshipped in Gaya and the priests that they would always be hungry. She blessed the banyan tree that it would have the power to accept funeral offerings made not just to deceased parents but also deceased friends, enemies, strangers and even oneself if one is childless.

The Sandals of Ram

All ceremonies of death were performed facing south. When the mourning period was over, Dashratha's sons were asked to face east, and resume the ceremonies of life. Bharata said, 'It is now time to return home. End this nonsense. You shall be king as you are meant to. And I shall serve you.'

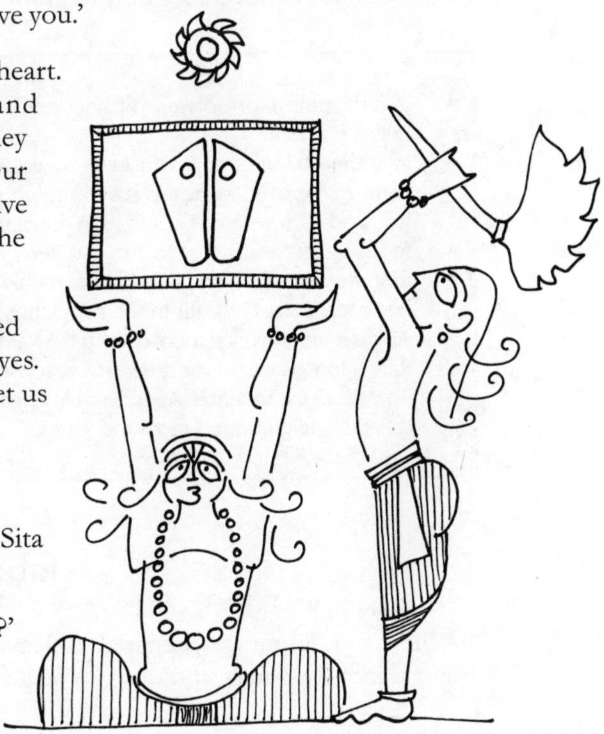

Memories of his father rose in Ram's heart. He enfolded Bharata, Lakshman and Shatrughna in his arms and wept. They were orphans now. Then he said, 'Our father died keeping his word. Let us live keeping his word. I will have to stay in the forest for fourteen years.'

'Look at all the people who have followed me. Look at the expectation in their eyes. They all want this bad dream to end. Let us go back to things as they were.'

'No, Bharata,' said Ram calmly.

'I will follow you then,' said Bharata, 'as Sita and Lakshman do.'

'Who then will take care of Ayodhya?' asked Ram. 'We are kings, Bharata. Let us not sacrifice responsibility at the altar of sentimentality. Father was not obliged to give our mother a boon; but he did, not one but two. While expressing gratitude to his wife who had saved his life, he forgot he was also a king and his boons could have far-reaching implications. We now have to face the consequences of that lapse. The Raghu clan must not be seen bending their rules for the sake of convenience. We need to be dependable kings.'

'But I do not have to be king to take care of the subjects. I renounce what has been given to me by my mother's deceit. I shall rule Ayodhya as your regent, awaiting your return.'

Ram realized that Bharata was determined. He could not be stopped. He could not be forced to be king. Never before and nowhere had anyone seen princes of a royal clan each willing to give up the throne for the other. They realized why the Raghu clan was truly illustrious, a worthy branch of the solar dynasty.

Bharata then asked Ram to step into the royal golden sandals worn by the kings of Ayodhya. 'Claim these by stepping into them. I shall place them on the throne till you come back. They shall symbolize you. I too shall live like a hermit till then, for it does not behove a servant to enjoy the pleasures denied to his master.'

- Worshipping the footwear of an elder, a holy man, a king or a teacher is common practice in India.
- In Vishnu temples of South India, devotees are not allowed to touch the feet of the deity. In blessing, a priest places a crown, with the footwear of the deity on its top, on the head of devotees. Thus though the devotee cannot touch the deity's feet, the deity's footwear makes its way to the devotee's head.
- In some versions, Ram gives to Bharata his forest sandals made of kusha grass. In others, he simply places his feet in the royal shoes that Bharata carries with him.
- Across India, in sites associated with the *Ramayana*, pilgrims are shown Ramcharanchinnha, Ram's footprints, which are much revered.
- Bharata does not enter Ayodhya. He rules from the outskirts of the city, from a village called Nandigram that faces the forest.

Jabali

As the royal entourage prepared to leave, Jabali, a rishi who had accompanied Bharata into the forest, spoke up: 'You give too much value to your father's words

and your family reputation. It burdens you, prevents you from enjoying life. Values are artificial – created by man, for man. Hold on to them if they create a happy society; abandon them if they create an unhappy one. In nature, the only purpose of plants and animals is to grab nourishment and survive, often at the cost of others. So there is nothing wrong in grabbing pleasure and enjoying life. Don't let these silly human notions of appropriate conduct burden your life. Let go of these troublesome vows, return to the city, enjoy what you are so lucky to receive by the accident of your birth into a royal family.'

Ram bowed before the sage and said, 'You crave for the king's life that you see me being denied. You see me as a victim, stripped of a wonderful life that should be mine. You see me as a fool for submitting to the will of my father, and for not looking at life the way you do. You feel all that I value is false and all that you value is true. But what you value and what I value are both imaginary. The difference is you seek to change the way I see things, you want me to subscribe to the way you see things, while I seek to understand why others do not see things the way I do. I don't see myself as a victim. I don't crave for the king's life. I don't feel living in the forest, bereft of royal comfort and authority, is a tragedy. I see it as an opportunity and wonder why others do not think like me. I want to understand what is so wonderful about a kingdom that Kaikeyi craves for it and what is so terrible about the forest that Kaushalya fears it. Away from society, away from responsibilities, I will finally have the opportunity to do tapasya so that when I return I can be better at conducting yagna.'

Awestruck by these words, Jabali said, 'Most people seek to enjoy life. Most people crave dominion over people and property. Most people see a life without enjoyment and dominion as a lesser life. But not you. You are a sage, who seeks to understand life. You are a worthy son-in-law of Janaka. I bow to you.'

Jabali touched Ram's feet. So did everyone from Ayodhya who had followed Bharata to persuade Ram to return. This was no child. This was no hero. This was God, what humans can become.

- Jabali embodies the philosophy of materialism and hedonism known as Charavaka. It rejects the notion of soul, of God, or that life has any purpose at all. It mocks all ritualism and reflection.
- The notion that the world is more than what we sense and that life has meaning forms the heart of most world philosophies and ideas. But like all ideas, these are countered by philosophies that reject the notion of any grand plan or purpose or meaning in the world. The *Ramayana* became popular across the Indian subcontinent because through the narrative it made people speculate on the nature of existence. Ram became revered because he functioned on the basis of the principle that life was not just about pleasure and hoarding things: it was about finding meaning and purpose.
- The *Ramayana* seeks to construct a family and a society based on certain principles of mutuality and empathy. The epic also reveals the heavy cost of social rules and the dark side of civilization.

The Previous and Next Life of Manthara

When Bharata and all the residents of Ayodhya headed for Kosala, one woman stayed back. It was Manthara. The light of victory had disappeared from her face. She stooped more than before, her visage was that of one crushed in battle. 'I am to blame. I, a servant, destroyed the great Raghu clan. Forgive me,' she cried, banging her head on the ground before Ram's feet.

'No, Manthara, you are not to blame. You ignited Kaikeyi's latent fears and she revealed the irresponsibility of my father. He could have chosen not to give her open-ended boons. She could have chosen not to exercise them. Everyone is responsible for their actions. I do not blame you or hold you responsible. Go back home in peace.'

But Manthara, old, bent and gaunt, kept weeping and beating herself. Sita tried to comfort her and sensed how lonely she was. Ugly, she had clearly been rejected by her parents, never been cherished by a beloved; she had secured all her importance by serving Kaikeyi, protecting her fiercely as a dog protects its territory, fighting for her, seeking her approval, whining when she expressed unhappiness. Should she be discarded because her loyalty made her venomous?

Finally Ram said, 'Hear this, Manthara. You are acting out the will of Brahma. In your past life, you were a gandharvi and you were told by our common father to take birth as Manthara and ensure that the eldest son of Raghu-kula is exiled into the forest where he can put an end to the rakshasa way of life, expanding their minds so that they outgrow their animal instincts. In your next life, you will once again be born as an ugly, bent woman. You will be called Kubija or Trivakra. Then you will meet me again. I will be Krishna. I will embrace you passionately and straighten your back and make you feel beautiful again. This I promise you.'

Sita and Lakshman were astonished to hear this.

Ram continued, 'As Vishnu, in defence of Indra's Swarga, I beheaded the wife of Bhrigu and the mother of Shukra who had been sheltering asuras. For that crime, I was cursed to be born on earth as Ram and live a life of great hardship, live as a hermit in the forest though entitled to live like a prince in a palace. And just as I denied Bhrigu the company of his wife, I was cursed that I would constantly be denied the pleasure of mine. So it is that Sita, though my wife, shall always be at arm's length so that I keep my promise of living as a tapasvi. And I fear even the pleasure of her company will be denied me by the rakshasa hordes and maybe eventually Ayodhya too will be thus deprived. But we cannot blame anyone for our misfortunes, as all calamities are an outcome of our past deeds. We have to take responsibility for all the good that happens to us and all the bad. We are the cause, and we have to face the consequences. This is the law of karma.'

- The story of Manthara's previous life as a gandharvi comes from the Ramopakhyan, the retelling of Ram's story in the *Mahabharata*.
- That the *Ramayana* is part of a larger narrative becomes apparent through stories such as the one where Vishnu kills Bhrigu's wife, found in the Puranas.
- Hindu philosophy is based on the notion of karma. Every event is a reaction to a past event. So Ram's exile is predestined. Manthara and Kaikeyi are but instruments of karma. It is foolish to blame or judge anyone, as we are unaware of the many forces at work that make an event happen.
- The gentle wisdom of Ram as he goes into exile is what transforms him from an ordinary hero into a divine being. He does not see himself as a victim. It is significant, however, that when Sita is later banished into the forest, the authors of the epic do not grant her the same gentle wisdom. They prefer visualizing her as victim, not sage. This gender bias continues even in the most modern writings.
- In Sanskrit plays, Ram appears as an upright hero. In regional literature, Ram appears as a personification of God. But scholars are divided on how Valmiki portrays him. Some believe Ram of the Valmiki *Ramayana* is not divine. Some conclude he does not know his divinity. Some others believe Ram is aware of his divinity. This is in stark contrast to Krishna who is fully aware of his divinity right from his birth. This is why Krishna, not Ram, is the more popular avatar of Vishnu and called the purnavatar or the complete incarnation.
- According to astrological calculations based on lines from the Valmiki *Ramayana*, Ram goes into exile in the year 5089 BCE, which means he was twenty-five years old at the time of exile.

BOOK FOUR

Abduction

'Her body could be imprisoned, but never her mind.'

Into Dandaka

Sita, along with Dashratha's sons, left the woods of Chitrakut, crossed rivers and mountains, and made her way into the forest of Dandaka.

This was once a kingdom called Janasthan, ruled by one Danda. While out hunting one day, Danda came upon a beautiful woman called Aruja and forced himself upon her. She ran crying to her father, a rishi by the name of Shukra. 'A land where boundaries are not respected is no different from a jungle,' said a furious Shukra, cursing that dust storms and thunderstorms would wipe away Danda's kingdom of Janasthan, leaving no trace of it and replacing it with a jungle. And so this land had become the most dreadful of forests that few dared cross.

In the forest there are no boundaries, no rules. As he stepped in, Ram remembered his ancestors and said, 'Ram may leave Ayodhya, but Ayodhya shall never leave Ram.' Then glancing towards Sita, he added, 'As Videha has never left Sita.'

- Dandaka was the great forest south of Aryavarta that thrived on the Gangetic plains.
- That the rape of his daughter makes Shukra turn a kingdom into a wilderness draws attention to the sanctity of boundaries. Humans create boundaries and humans violate them as well. To respect boundaries is the hallmark of humanity, an indicator of dharma. To disrespect them is to be bestial, to follow the path of adharma. Animals, who do not have imagination, do not have the wherewithal to create boundaries or violate them. This is what makes them innocent.
- The epic *Ramayana* is aligned along the Dakshina-patha or the south highway that connects northern India to southern India while the epic *Mahabharata* is aligned along Uttara-patha or the north highway that connects western India to eastern India. Thus the two great epics cover the length and breadth of India.
- Based on the details found in Valmiki's Sanskrit *Ramayana*, many scholars are of the opinion that the events of the *Ramayana* did not take place beyond Central India. But for the faithful, based on the tales of pilgrims, sites of the *Ramayana* are located across the subcontinent and beyond, in Sri Lanka. Here one finds footprints (charan-chinnha) of Ram and temples of Shiva established by Ram.

Meeting Shanta

The trio decided to spend the night at the edge of the dreadful forest. Ram could not sleep. As the wind whistled, he watched the stars and sensed Sita watching him. 'This too shall pass,' she said. He knew that too, but knowledge is no antidote to anxiety. His mind was like the restless comet. 'Let us enjoy what we have, my husband, rather than wonder about what we had or could have. Let us enjoy the stars,' she said. So while Lakshman watched over the fire, Ram and Sita watched the skies until they were overtaken by sleep. Before he shut his eyes, however, Ram placed his bow between him and his wife, just in case.

At dawn, Sita woke up to find Ram and Lakshman at the feet of a beautiful woman. She had large eyes, a generous smile and a sensuous figure. Who was she? The lady noticed Sita, and called out, 'Come here, little one. I am your husband's elder sister, Shanta.'

Shanta made Sita sit on her lap and said, 'Your decision to follow your husband to the forest is indeed a noble one. But it will not be easy for you to travel dressed as a bride, with two handsome men beside you, neither of them looking at you, one because he is a hermit and the other because you are his brother's wife. Everywhere around, you will hear the mating calls of birds, you will see snakes and frogs and deer and tigers in intimate embrace, and you will smell flowers calling out to the bees and butterflies. Your body will cry out; how will you resist the call of your senses, Sita? And the rakshasas: they do not know the meaning of celibacy and fidelity. They will compel you and these two brothers of mine to satisfy their desires, for it is the most natural thing to do. What will you do then, Sita? How will you save yourself from your desires and those of the men around you? There are no boundaries in the forest, Sita. Where there are no boundaries, there is no violation.'

Sita wondered why Shanta was telling her these things. She had heard the feelings Shanta spoke of in the romantic stories and love songs of bards, but had never really felt them. Yes, she liked the way she had felt when Ram looked at her during the wedding ceremony and the few times they had met in the women's courtyard, but now he never looked at her, at least not in that way. Is that what Shanta spoke of, or was it something else?

Sensing her thoughts, Shanta elaborated, 'You are still young but your body is changing, my child. I can sense it. You will sense it too. It is as if your stepping into the forest has caused it to bloom. You are truly the daughter of the earth.'

- Songs depicting conversations between Sita and Shanta are often found in South Indian folklore.
- An implicit assumption is often made that Ram and Sita had conjugal relations before and during the exile. In fact, these are made rather explicit in some Sanskrit plays. But there is no child born of that supposed union, which is highly unlikely, considering that both are in the prime of their youth. So it is most likely that they lived celibate lives, Ram because he had sworn to be a hermit and Sita because she was the chaste wife of a celibate hermit. Lakshman was under no such obligation but he too chose celibacy out of solidarity with Ram and Sita. This celibacy adds to the tension of the narrative.
- In the tales of Ram that are part of Tamil temple lore and Sri Vaishnava tradition, Ram sleeps with his bow between him and Sita, thus indicating his desire to live a celibate life.

Anasuya and Atri

Shanta took Sita to the hermitage of Anasuya and Atri. Anasuya, like Arundhati, was renowned for her chastity. Unlike Renuka, she had never wavered even in thought. And unlike Ahilya, she had never wavered in deed.

Once three handsome tapasvis came to her, while her husband was away, and said, 'We have been fasting for twelve years. To break our fast we have to suckle on the breasts of a rishi's wife. Will you help us?' Anasuya agreed. She saw the three youths as the children she never had. So she uncovered herself and the three youths, of questionable intent, turned into three infants.

The wives of the youths then begged her forgiveness and Anasuya was surprised to learn their true intentions: they were seeking to seduce her, to destroy her reputation as the most chaste woman on earth. Anasuya forgave the tapasvis unconditionally, for in her view, despite performing tapasya, the youths were still children, seeking pleasure in trickery. She restored them to their original youthful forms and offered them food from her kitchen to break their fast.

In gratitude, the three youths blessed Anasuya that she would be mother of a great son, Datta, who would need no teacher; he would learn from all the things he saw: the sky, the earth, fire, water, wind, rocks, rivers, plants, animals, birds, insects, men and women. He would become Adinath, the primal teacher.

Anasuya welcomed Janaka's daughter and took her under a flower-bearing tree, where she revealed to her the secrets of her body that had finally started to unfold. She gave Sita a garment, a garland and a pot of cream. The garment would never become dirty, the garland would never wither and the cream would always soften her skin.

'Had you been in the palace, this would have been a great ceremony. Your father would have sent you gifts, so would your mother. Your mothers-in-law would bathe you in turmeric water and bedeck you with flowers. You would be given a courtyard of your own and when you felt ready, you would send areca nuts wrapped in betel leaves to your husband and invite him to show you the Arundhati star. But alas, for that to happen, you have to wait for fourteen years. What can I give you to compensate?'

'The strength to survive these fourteen years in the forest, being true to both mind and body. My sister-in-law says it will not be easy,' said Sita.

'If you see chastity as an obligation, it will be tough, not otherwise,' said Anasuya. 'If you acknowledge the desires of your body, not suppress them, and reflect on what really matters to you in life, it will not be tough.'

Atri saw his wife bedeck Sita. So he asked Ram and Lakshman, 'It is spring and the flower has bloomed. Can the bee resist the nectar?'

Lakshman spoke first: 'My flower sleeps in Ayodhya. She will bloom fourteen years hence.'

Then Ram said, 'I am not a bee. Neither am I a butterfly. I am a human, scion of the Raghu clan, who has to live as a hermit in the forest for fourteen years. Nothing will make my mind waver.'

Wondering if this was just a grand oration meant to impress or the genuine wisdom of a young prince, Atri said, 'Do not punish yourself if you waver. Humans judge, nature does not.'

- In folklore, the three ascetics who try to seduce Anasuya are Brahma, Vishnu and Shiva.
- Datta or Dattatreya, son of Atri, is worshipped as Adinath, the primal teacher, and is considered a form of Brahma, Vishnu and Shiva. He is called Adinath because he has no guru and has gained wisdom by observing the world around him, according to the Avadhut Gita of the Bhagavat Purana.
- The gift of cloth and cosmetics that Anasuya gives Sita reinforces the great value given to shringara, or beautifying the body, in Vedic times.

Sharabhanga's Heaven

After bidding farewell to Anasuya and Atri, Sita and Dashratha's sons came upon the hermitage of the old sage Sharabhanga, where they saw a wonderful sight. They saw Indra leaving the hermitage on his elephant that had white skin, six tusks and seven trunks.

On enquiry, the sage explained, 'Indra invited me to his garden, Nandana-vana, located in the city of the devas, Amravati, located in the realm of the stars, where stands the Kalpataru tree under which all desires are fulfilled. But I have no desire for it.'

Lakshman asked the sage, 'Is it not the purpose of yagna and tapasya to secure all that Indra possesses?'

'No, son,' said the sage. 'Indra has everything, yet he lives in fear of losing it all. Swarga may be paradise, but it is no heaven.'

'What is heaven then?'

'Heaven is a place where there is no hunger.'

'Does such a place exist?'

'Under the Pole Star sits Shiva on a mountain of stone covered with snow. No grass grows there, but his bull, Nandi, does not complain. Nandi does not fear being eaten by Shakti's tiger either. The snake around Shiva's neck does not fear being eaten by Kartikeya's peacock and it does not seek to eat Ganesha's rat. Clearly, that is a place where there is no hunger. In Swarga there is prosperity, but no peace. I seek peace, I seek Kailas. That must be heaven.'

'May we find the strength to outgrow hunger in these fourteen years,' said Ram.

'Brahma created the yagna to satisfy human hunger. Daksha created rules of society to compel people to satisfy each other's hunger. Both were beheaded by Shiva, hoping they would realize the human potential to outgrow hunger itself.'

Sita said, 'Not everyone can be Shiva. We need people who can feed us, comfort us, grant us meaning. We need people who care for others.'

'You describe Vishnu: who has no hunger like Shiva, but cares for other people's hunger. He is not driven by rules. He functions in affection.'

'But society needs rules, until everyone can be Vishnu. Otherwise everyone will remain Indra,' said Ram.

'Indeed,' said the sage, impressed by the young prince and his wife.

'Brahma, Indra, Vishnu, Shiva. Where can we find them?' asked Lakshman.

'In your mind, Lakshman. We are all Brahma. We are all Indra. We are all Daksha. We can be Shiva. We can be Vishnu too,' chuckled the sage, shutting his eyes and smiling in peace.

- Indra is a deva, which European scholars translated to mean god in the Greek sense of the term. But in Hindu mythology, the word refers to a special class of beings who are adored but not quite enshrined in temples. A deeper reading reveals that Indra is a state of the human mind that craves a life of pleasure and power.
- In Vedic hymns, Indra is much adored as a great warrior, but in Puranic texts, he is seen as an insecure god who fears ascetics who perform tapasya and kings who perform yagna. European scholars concluded, in keeping with the trends they saw in Mesopotamian mythology, that Indra was an old god who was replaced by new gods like Shiva and Vishnu. But Hindus saw it differently. Indra is a god who celebrates material pleasure and is an essential component of the divine hierarchy, albeit at a lower level.
- What distinguishes Jain, Buddhist and Hindu scriptures is the notion of multiple heavens occupied by different beings depending on the karmic balance sheet. Stay in no heaven is permanent. Each offers different degrees of pleasure and pain. In the highest heaven there is neither pain nor pleasure, only wisdom. This needs to be contrasted with the notion of heaven and hell popular in Christianity and Islam, which is based on ethical and moral conduct, and more importantly on faith in the doctrine. The faithful rise up to heaven and the faithless go to hell.

Sutikshna's Request

Sita, Ram and Lakshman then proceeded to the hermitage of Sutikshna, who welcomed them and told them of the plight of many sages who had ventured southwards. He told them the story of the great migration.

Coaxed by Shakti, the serene Shiva had opened his eyes and then his mouth to explain the essence of the Vedas. To hear him, all the rishis on earth moved northwards, causing the earth to tilt. The Vindhya mountain range that separates the north and the south was so eager to hear Shiva that he kept growing in size until he blocked the passage of the sun.

To restore balance, Shiva asked his son Kartikeya, the great warlord, to move southwards. Many sages accompanied him, amongst them Vishrava and Agastya.

Vindhya bowed before Agastya, seeking his blessings, and Agastya asked him to stay bent so that the sun could travel unhindered. Agastya carried the waters of the Ganga in his pot and when he poured it out it turned into the mighty Kaveri river in the south.

Kartikeya's spear split the Vindhyas to create valleys through which he could pass. To ensure that Kartikeya did not miss his mountainous home, Shakti asked the asura Hidimba to carry peaks from the Himalayas to the south. These became the Palni range of hills.

'In the south the rishis found rakshasas and yakshas. Vishrava married a yaksha and a rakshasa and had sons by both wives. He taught both his sons the Vedas. The son of the yaksha, Kubera, built a great city of gold. The son of the rakshasa, Ravana, envious of Kubera, attacked the city and laid claim to it by force. Ravana is a great devotee of Shiva but he believes that might is right. And since he is the mightiest there, his way becomes the right way. Long have the rishis tried to make him see the essence of the Vedas, but he dismisses them with disdain. He considers those who perform yagna or practise tapasya as seekers of siddha, hence his rivals; he has turned all rakshasas against rishis. Remember Tadaka? Who sent her to Vishwamitra's Siddha-ashrama? Ravana! Go south, Ram. Let the tragedy of this exile be beneficial to those who live in the forests. Enable rakshasas to follow dharma, liberate them from Ravana's spell. Enable them to expand their minds,' begged Sutikshna.

'Are rakshasas not demons to be killed?' said Lakshman.

'Remember this, students of Vishwamitra, demons are just humans we refuse to understand or tolerate. To reject them, as they reject us, is adharma,' said the sage.

- Ram-kathas often refer to how Vishnu incarnates as Ram to save the world from the tyranny of Ravana. From a literal point of view, it is easy to see Ram's journey along the path of the rishis into the south as an act of colonialism, the gradual spread of the fire-worshipping Vedic Aryans. From a symbolic point of view, the forest is the undomesticated mind, wild and frightening. The arrival of the sages and then Ram is the gradual awakening of human potential.
- Some people see Ravana as the upholder of rakshasa culture who resists rishi culture. But what is culture that does not welcome and exchange? Why do two cultures clash? Should cultures stay independent of each other or should they influence and transform each other? By making Ravana's father a rishi and his mother a rakshasa, Valmiki ponders this question.
- The description of the rakshasas is ambiguous. They are sometimes violent, bearing weapons, with fangs, claws and large eyes, covered with blood and gore. At other times, they are good-looking and sensuous, even gentle. Some are described as shape-shifters.
- Rakshasas are made frightening and demonic to dehumanize them and justify their killing. It is what civilized nations do in order to justify warfare. It stems from the human mind's discomfort with our essential animal nature that seeks to dominate and fight off rivals to create a safe space. The rakshasa, if not excluded or tamed or included, will end up overwhelming us. Engagement is therefore essential.

Agastya and Lopamudra

As Sita, Ram and Lakshman travelled south, they saw a vast plateau garlanded with hills. A sage told them that once mountains had wings and they travelled in the sky like birds, but their movements created so much noise that the rishis called upon the devas and asked that their wings be cut. So they fell to the ground and never moved again.

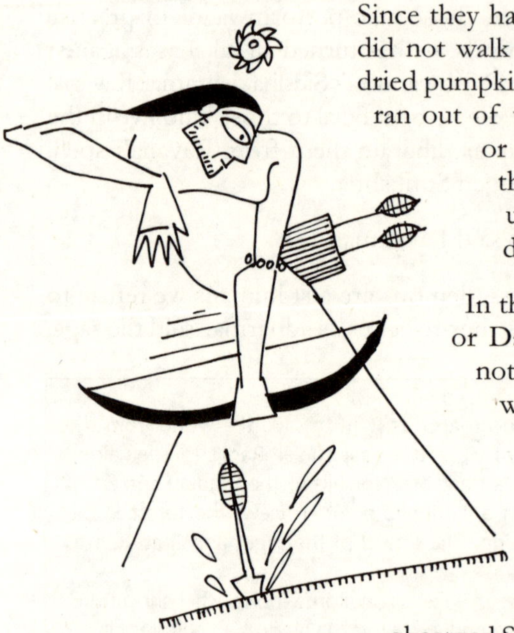

Since they had to avoid human settlements, the trio did not walk along riverbanks. Sita carried water in dried pumpkin gourd shells but sometimes, when she ran out of water before they found a pond, Ram or Lakshman would shoot an arrow into the earth and release water from some underground spring, much to Sita's delight.

In the forest, Sita was not Janaka's daughter or Dashratha's daughter-in-law. Ram could not lay claims to her as a husband, as he was a hermit. She was just a woman, free to do as she pleased. Ram never demanded anything from her and so when she served him he wondered what motivated her. Was it just obligation? Was it simply custom? Was it pity? The more Ram observed Sita, the more he realized it could only be what poets called love.

And Sita noticed a lot about Ram. He always looked away when he spoke to her lest he be ensnared by her glances. And yet, in small gestures he revealed his love, brushing away thorns in her path, moving in the direction of flowers he knew Sita loved, making sure the rocks they climbed were never too big or too slippery for her. And though she waited for him to finish his meal before she ate, she knew he always ate less, making sure she always had more to eat.

Finally, Sita and Dashratha's sons reached Agastya's ashrama. There they saw tigers playing with goats and sheep; it was just like Mount Kailas described by the rishi Sharabhanga, where there is no hunger, hence neither predator nor prey. 'The predator seeks food. The prey seeks protection. Shiva's son, the plump and elephant-headed Ganesh, feeds the hungry predator. Shiva's other son, the mighty Kartikeya, defends the frightened prey. Shiva helps all outgrow hunger and fear,' explained Agastya.

Agastya took them to his house. It was a palace! Unsuitable for a hermit, Sita thought. Agastya then told them his story.

Agastya's tapasya was once disturbed by a vision: he saw his ancestors hanging upside down like bats, weeping, begging him to secure their release from the land of the dead. They begged him to father a child. 'We gave you life, now you give us life. Repay your debt to us by helping us be reborn.'

Agastya went to the king of Vidarbha and asked for one of his daughters as a wife. The king gave him Lopamudra, the most beautiful of his daughters. She said to Agastya, 'To receive something, you must first give. If you want me to bear your children, give me pleasure and satisfaction.'

So Agastya took a bath, untangled his matted hair, smoothened his coarse skin, replaced the ash that smeared his body with sandal paste, put a garland of bright, fragrant flowers around his neck and approached her as a lover should approach a beloved. He ignited fire in the hearth; she turned it into a kitchen. He built her a house; she made it a home. He gave her his seed; she germinated it in her womb and brought forth a child, a poet.

'Alone, I was a tapasvi. But with Lopamudra, I have become a yajaman, and initiated the yagna that is family,' Agastya said. 'But one day, the child will grow up and start a family of his own and not need his parents. I will not need a wife any more and Lopamudra will not need a husband any more. That day, I will become a tapasvi once again, giving away my house with its

courtyard and its kitchen and my cows. What we possess is temporary, but what we become is permanent.'

Ram, Lakshman and Sita stayed with Agastya and Lopamudra. They watched him teach his students Tamil and the secrets of the stars to predict the future and the secret of the herbs to heal and rejuvenate the body. Agastya gave Ram and Lakshman many weapons. Lopamudra and Sita spent hours in the kitchen garden, discussing spices that enable digestion and heal wounds.

- Across India one finds caves associated with Ram, Lakshman and Sita. In many places, Ram's cave is separate from Sita's and Lakshman's, suggesting that they lived as hermits, in isolation, even though they were together.
- Agastya is the great sage of South India, the supreme master of the siddha. He is the fountainhead of language, philosophy, astrology, geomancy and medicine. There are stories about his movement from north to south, clearly suggesting the migration of Vedic ideas and their transformation following contact with the people who lived in the south.
- The hymn of Lopamudra is found in the earliest compilation of Vedic hymns, the Rig Samhita, where she demands that her husband grant her satisfaction as is his duty, and not indulge in his own pursuits.
- Indic thought is a compilation of many thoughts coming from various sources, from nomadic herdsmen to settled agriculturists, from tribes who lived in forests to settlers who established villages and cities. This is why Indic thought keeps transforming from fire rituals to storytelling to temple rituals. What remains consistent is the fundamental Vedic belief in impermanence and the conflict between seeking immortality and accepting change. From this fundamental belief come ideas like karma (action/reaction), kama (desire), maya (perception/delusion) and dharma (appropriate human conduct in a context).

Conversations in the Forest

As the years passed, Sita and the sons of Dashratha criss-crossed the land that they realized was called Jambudvipa because it was shaped like the wood-apple jambul. They took shelter under trees and in caves, often near waterbodies. Sometimes, they would build houses using sticks and leaves, but not for long. As hermits, it was important to keep moving and not stay in one place for long, except during the rainy season when the waters flooded the earth and travel was dangerous.

Sita spent much time observing bees and butterflies and insects. She discovered how to collect honey without upsetting the bees and milk from tigresses who had finished feeding their cubs. She followed herds of elephants to reach secret waterholes atop distant mountains known only to the oldest matriarchs. She understood the migratory patterns of birds and fishes. She learned to communicate with bears and wolves and vultures. They told her where to find the most succulent of fruits and berries, and where the best tubers could be pulled out from the ground. She found leaves that were edible and bark that was nourishing. In the evening, when they set up camp around a fire, she shared with Ram and Lakshman everything she had seen and learned. What was most exciting was to see the deer and tiger drink water next to each other on some evenings because once the tiger had eaten it was no longer a predator and the deer was no longer a prey.

Sita told the sons of Dashratha, 'Flowers make themselves fragrant and offer nectar. Why? To nourish the bees or to get themselves pollinated? Or both? In nature, to get you have to give. There is no charity. There is no exploitation, neither selfishness nor selflessness. One grows by helping others grow. Is that not the perfect society?'

Ram said, 'I see things differently. I see plants feeding on elements, animals feeding on plants, and animals feeding on animals that feed on plants. I see those that eat and those that are eaten. Those who eat are afraid that they may not get enough. Those who can be eaten are afraid they will be consumed. I see fear everywhere. In a perfect society there should be no fear. To achieve that is dharma.'

All day, as they walked, Sita walked behind Ram and in front of Lakshman. She saw neither's face. Over the years she learned to appreciate Ram's broad back, which never once stooped in their days in the forest, darkened by the harsh sun, his hair matted and bleached, so unlike the oiled, perfumed curls of the palace. Lakshman saw only Sita's feet and avoided treading even on her footprints, which he noticed were always to the left of Ram's, closer to his heart. They all waited for the

evening when they could sit around the fire, face each other, let the flames light up their eyes as they shared the experiences of the day.

One day Sita saw a berry tree next to a banana plant. The wind blew hard and the sharp thorns of the berry tree tore the smooth leaves of the banana plant. 'Who is the victim here? Who is the villain?' she asked Ram.

'Neither,' said Ram. 'It is the human eye that gives value to things, turning natural events into epic adventures full of conflict and resolution. That is maya, delusion born of measuring scales.'

'Surely the tigress is the villain when it kills the pregnant doe,' argued Lakshman.

'Would you rather the tigress starve and die? Who will feed her cubs then? You? This is how nature functions: there are eaters and the eaten. The tiger does not resent the deer that gets away. The doe does not resent the tiger that captures her fawn. They are following their instincts. Plants and animals live; humans need to judge, for we need to feel good about ourselves. That is why we create stories, full of heroes and villains, victims and martyrs,' said Ram.

'Our ancestor Dilip was willing to sacrifice himself to save the cow from a lion. Surely he is a hero?' reminded Lakshman.

Ram, with great clarity, replied, 'The cow nourishes humanity with her milk, Lakshman. We need to save it. He is a hero to humans because he saved humanity's food. He is no hero to the starving lion, or to the deer the lion may have to feed on instead.'

Conversations such as these reminded Sita of the conversations of sages she had overheard in her childhood. Often they were the only ones around the fire. Sometimes sages joined them and told them stories, full of heroes, villains, victims and martyrs. Sita enjoyed the tales but realized how each tale contained a measuring scale that converted one into a hero and another into a victim. All measuring scales are human delusions that make humans feel good about themselves. In nature, there is no victim and villain, just predator and prey, those who seek food and those who become food.

Back in the palace at Ayodhya, Kaushalya woke up with a start, 'Is it not time for Ram to return?'

'No, another year,' said Sumitra.

Urmila was still sleeping, watched over by Mandavi and Shrutakirti. There were no men in the house; Bharata had stationed himself in the village outside the city gates. The girls were now grown women. The boys were now grown men. They should have been mothers and fathers. By now the palace should have been filled with the sounds of royal grandchildren. But the only thing that filled the palace was silence. No one spoke, no one sang, no one fought. The silence haunted Kaikeyi the most. She waited for the day Sita and Ram would return. Then, there would be lots to talk about.

- In many retellings, Ram, Lakshman and Sita are teenagers when they leave Ayodhya. They actually grow up in the forest. These are the growing-up years when the mind challenges the certainties of childhood and is able to see the artificial nature of social structures. In the forest an animal or plant does not treat them differently because they are royal. They are seen either as predator or prey. Thus the narrative draws a sharp distinction between the grama or kshetra (settlement) with the vana or aranya (forest).
- Mimansa means enquiry that leads to introspection. This can be done through ritual or through conversation. The former way was called Purva-mimansa and the latter way was called Uttara-mimansa, more popularly known as Vedanta. The forest exile is a time for the royal trio to do mimansa; they transform into sages.

Lakshman's Chastity

During the rains, Sita preferred to stay in caves. They would always select caves with three sections, the central one for Sita, and the ones on either side for the brothers. In summers, they preferred staying next to ponds, the central one for Sita, and the ones adjacent for the brothers. Occasionally they built huts using grass and leaves, straw and sticks, but only for Sita. The brothers had grown used to living outdoors, sleeping under the shade of trees, enjoying the dappled sunlight of the afternoons.

One day, when Ram was out hunting, Sita decided to take a nap while Lakshman kept watch. She spread the hide of a deer and lay down in the shade of a tree. Sleep came quickly as the breeze was gentle and kind. Later, when she was in deep slumber, the wind grew unruly and tossed her clothes all over the place. Sita slept peacefully, unaware that her body had been exposed.

When Ram returned he saw Sita lying uncovered, without a care in the world. Lakshman sat with his back to her, facing the forest. Ram said, 'Oh, who can resist the beauty of one who reclines so carelessly under the tree?'

Lakshman, sensing that Ram was referring to Sita, said, 'He who is the son of Dashratha and Sumitra and brother of Ram and husband of Urmila can surely resist such a beauty who Ram says reclines so carelessly under the tree.'

Ram smiled. His brother's integrity was unquestionable.

But Indra was not so impressed. He decided to test Lakshman and sent an apsara to seduce him. Lakshman shooed her away but the apsara, Indrakamini, decided to play a trick on Lakshman. She dropped some strands of her hair; they clung to Lakshman's clothes of bark.

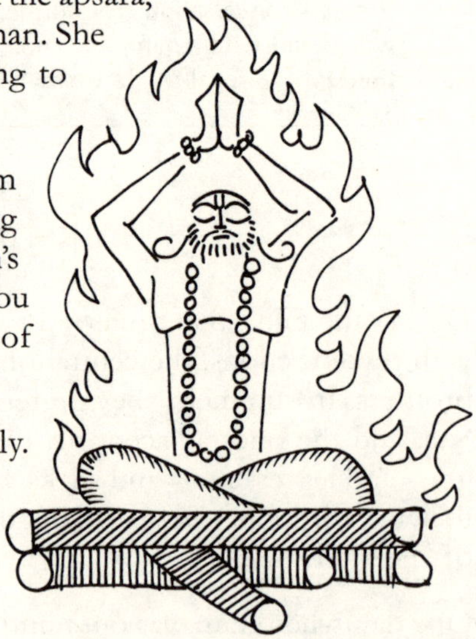

'What is this?' wondered Sita, when she saw them that evening as they rested around the evening fire. 'This is a woman's hair, a refined woman's hair, for it smells of fragrant oils. Looks like you found yourself a wife. Clearly the absence of Urmila is unbearable.'

What was said casually was taken seriously. Lakshman was so angry at the suggestion of being an unfaithful husband that he jumped into the fire around which they sat. Ram was aghast. Sita screamed. 'Look, the fire does not hurt me. Do you need any other proof that I have been true to my wife?' said Lakshman.

That night nobody spoke. Sita realized making light of the integrity of the men of the Raghu clan was not taken lightly.

- In many pilgrim spots such as Nashik in Maharashtra and Rameswaram in Tamil Nadu, and forest reserves such as Hazaribag in Bihar and Simlipal in Odisha, there are separate ponds dedicated to Ram, Lakshman and Sita named Ram-kund, Lakshman-kund and Sita-kund. That they do not bathe in the same pond reinforces their commitment to the hermit's way of life.
- The episode of Sita's clothes being in disarray and the conversation between Ram and Lakshman comes from the Marathi *Ramayana* written by Eknath called *Bhavarth Ramayana*, or the emotional *Ramayana*.
- The episode of Lakshman going through the trial of fire comes from the Baiga *Ramayana*, in which an apsara called Indrakamini is attracted by Lakshman's beauty and tries to malign him when he rejects her. This rare episode draws attention to the value given to male chastity in tribal lore. The Baigas live in Central India.
- There are other stories from tribes of Central India which speak of how Ram, Lakshman and Sita remained indifferent to the charms of the tribal men and women, indicating they were not ordinary mortals. Principles mattered to them more than sensory pleasures.
- Contrary to popular notions of patriarchy that grants all freedom to men, men who claim to be celibate are not respected when they lose control over their senses. Submission to an apsara is seen as failure. But unlike the unchaste woman who threatens the social order, the monk who fails to stay celibate does not threaten the social order, as he is not a member of society. He is a failure in his own eyes and, at best, a failure in the eyes of his monastic order.

Vedavati

One day, the three exiles came upon a woman who identified herself as Vedavati. She wanted to be Vishnu's wife and so rejected all suitors who approached her parents for her hand in marriage. One of the suitors killed her parents and she went to the forest to live as a hermit until she met Vishnu. She was tormented wherever she went by many men who desired her but she was determined to marry only Vishnu. When she saw Ram, Vedavati said, 'You are Vishnu on earth. Marry me. I have been waiting for you for years.'

Ram said, 'I have my Sita. No one shall take her place.'

'Then let me be Sita's servant,' she said.

'No. You will have expectations of me that I will never fulfil. Wait some more time. Vishnu shall return in a different form some day and claim you as a wife.'

Later, Ravana too tried to molest Vedavati. Tired of waiting and being tormented, Vedavati jumped into a fire, hoping to be reborn as one who would be Vishnu's wife.

- The Skanda Purana states that Vedavati becomes Padmavati and marries Vishnu who descends on earth and takes residence on Tirumalai as Venkateshwara Balaji.
- In Jammu, Vedavati is identified as Vaishno Devi who beheaded Bhairava, who sought to make her his wife by force. The head of Bhairava then apologized and revealed that he was practising rituals and for that he needed a woman to help him break free from the cycle of rebirths. 'Then worship me, and I shall grant you liberation,' she said, transforming into the Goddess. While blood sacrifice is common in most Goddess shrines, Vaishno Devi is unique in that she is vegetarian, indicating her close links with Vaishnavism.
- In later versions of the *Ramayana*, Vedavati swears that she will ensure the death of Ravana who tries to molest her. The fire-god does not burn her; he hides her and puts her in Sita's place before Sita's abduction. It is this duplicate Sita that Ravana carries to Lanka. The original Sita returns to Ram after Sita's (Vedavati's) fire trial.
- The story of Vedavati needs to be contrasted with the story of Surpanakha. Both desire to marry Ram. But Vedavati respects Ram's wish to be faithful to a single wife. Surpanakha does not care for his wish; only her desire matters.

The Weapons of Sport and Survival

Ram and Lakshman enjoyed hunting. While one was out chasing game, the other kept watch over Sita while she scoured the forest for food. They mainly hunted tigers and deer, collecting their skin and horns as trophies. Some of the animal hide they used for themselves, as mats to sit on and shawls to cover themselves. Many they gifted to the sages they met. The horns were used to make weapons,

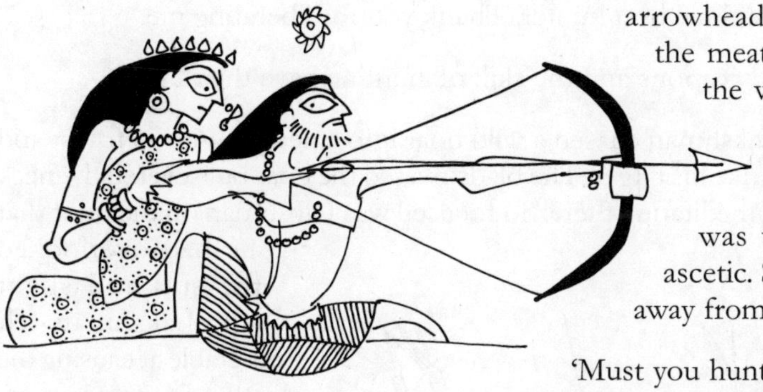

arrowheads mostly. They left the meat on the ground for the vultures to eat. Ram avoided meat, which warriors ate with relish, as he felt it was unbecoming of an ascetic. So Lakshman stayed away from it too.

'Must you hunt these poor beasts?' Sita once asked. 'Can't you just enjoy them as they run through the forests, towards pastures or prey, or away from predators?'

'We are kings, warriors and hunters. That is what we do,' said Ram. 'That is how we ensure our skills remain intact. Sita, do not forget, this is a jungle, not a garden. There is danger lurking in every corner. The fire in the hearth, the fence around our hut and the arrows in our quiver protect us.'

One day, when Sita was collecting flowers to make garlands for Ram, she was grabbed from behind by a rakshasa. Before Lakshman could raise his bow and stop the rakshasa, he fled, carrying Sita on his shoulders. Lakshman pursued the rakshasa and called out to Ram. Ram intercepted the rakshasa and shot arrows at the vile creature. These arrows severed the rakshasa's legs. He fell but refused to let go of Sita. Ram's arrows then severed his arms. Sita could now escape. Blood gushed out of his four limbs, but the rakshasa refused to die.

'I am Viradha,' said the rakshasa. 'Your weapons will not kill me. Bury me deep in the ground, deep enough so that no predator digs me out, so that I can die in peace. Do not leave me here helpless on the ground to be ripped apart by hyenas and vultures.'

So Lakshman dug a hole and Ram pushed the rakshasa who had dared touch Sita into it. They filled the hole with mud, and from the mound arose a handsome being who said, 'I am Tumburu, cursed to remain a rakshasa until

I was hunted like an animal by a hunter. Thank you for liberating me.'

'See, Sita,' said Ram, 'weapons and the skill of hunting have their use.'

Then, another day, Lakshman chased a wild boar into a dense bamboo forest and swung his sword to strike his target. The blade missed the boar but severed the neck of a tapasvi who was meditating there. So focused was Lakshman on the hunt that he had overlooked the still and silent sage. Lakshman felt miserable at causing the death of an innocent. He wished he had listened to Sita and not indulged in this passion for hunting.

But Indra appeared before them and congratulated Lakshman: 'That tapasvi was a rakshasa, nephew of Ravana. Had he succeeded he would have had the power to overthrow me. I sent the boar along so that you would shoot your arrows at him. You think what you did is bad, but I say what you did is good.'

That evening Sita and the sons of Dashratha discussed karma. Lakshman said, 'All events in our lives are reactions to past actions. Today I accidentally killed a man. I think it was bad. Indra says it was good. What impact will it have on the future? Will it generate fortune or misfortune?'

Ram said, 'Events are events. Humans qualify them as good or bad.'

Sita could not help herself and said, 'These days in the forest, I am sure you think they are bad. But I think they are good. There is so much freedom here in the forest, no rules and rituals and rites that bind us back home.'

Ram said, 'All things are good and bad only in hindsight.'

- Did Ram, Sita and Lakshman eat meat during their sojourn in the forest? This question remains best unanswered as there are many who react violently even at the suggestion that consuming meat was not frowned upon in ancient times. Miniature paintings often show Ram and Lakshman hunting and wearing animal hide; a few even show them roasting meat. This is rationalized as consuming meat was permitted to members of the warrior community, the kshatriyas. References to the eating of 'flesh' in Sanskrit works are often translated to mean 'flesh of fruit'. Vegetarian practices became widespread first because of Buddhism and Jainism, and later because of Vaishnavism. Rational arguments aside, to eat vegetarian food continues to be in India a sign of ritual purity that places one higher in the caste hierarchy.
- The episode of Sita's unhappiness over the sport of hunting comes from the Valmiki *Ramayana*.
- Viradha's desire to be buried after death is significant as this goes against the common Vedic practice of cremation. In traditional Hindu society, burial is reserved for sages who have broken free from the cycle of birth and death in their lifetime.
- That Viradha was a gandharva before he became a rakshasa and turns into a gandharva once again draws attention to the role of curses as an instrument of karma.
- The story of the demon accidentally killed by Lakshman comes from Odia, Telugu, Tamil and Malayalam folklore based on the *Ramayana*.

Surpanakha's Husband and Son

The rakshasa that Lakshman killed was Sunkumar, son of Surpanakha, sister of Ravana, king of Lanka.

Ravana's wife, Mandodari, once refused to serve Surpanakha meat and this led to a great household altercation. Their respective husbands tried to pacify the women until, goaded by Surpanakha, her husband, Vidyutjiva, stretched out his enormous tongue and swallowed Ravana. This happened in the heat of the moment and everyone immediately realized the terrible consequences of the household quarrel: Ravana had been consumed and the only way to save him was to cut open the stomach of the man who had swallowed him. This would grant life to Ravana but cause death to Vidyutjiva.

'Do it,' said Ravana to his sister, 'and I will make your son my heir and give you any man you choose as your husband.' Surpanakha then used her claw-like nails to tear open her husband's stomach and liberate her brother. She became a widow but was given the freedom to take any husband of her choice from the forests. And she waited for Ravana to keep his promise to declare her son his heir. But he did

not. When her son grew up, he grew impatient and decided to perform tapasya and obtain a weapon that would enable him to kill Ravana. It was while he was performing tapasya that Lakshman killed him, thus inadvertently saving Ravana.

Having lost her husband and now her son, Surpanakha was furious. She could not punish the man responsible for her husband's death, as he was her brother, but she was determined to punish this hunter, her son's killer.

So she tracked the footsteps of Lakshman and reached the banks of the Godavari, near Panchavati, and found Ram and Lakshman seated there. They were beautiful. All thoughts of vengeance vanished and were replaced by lust.

- The Valmiki *Ramayana* refers to a rakshasa sorcerer called Vidyutjiva, which means 'lightning tongue'. Valmiki refers neither to Surpanakha's husband nor to her son.
- Surpanakha means one whose nails are as long as the winnow.
- The story of Surpanakha's husband and son comes from Tamil folklore. In most stories, Ravana kills Vidyutjiva accidentally as he goes about conquering the world. In the Thai version, Ravana mistakes the long tongue of Surpanakha's husband to be the tower of a fortress or the wall of a castle, and shoots it down. This story adds more passion and domestic energy to the narrative.
- The son of Surpanakha is variously identified as Shambukumar, Darasinha, Japasura, Jambukumar and Sunkumar, in various southern oral *Ramayana*s, often narrated during shadow theatre performances.
- In some versions, Lakshman finds a sword floating in the air. It has materialized for him to kill Surpanakha's son who is behind a clump of bamboo grass, meditating. Not realizing this, Lakshman takes the sword, swings it, and ends up accidentally killing the demon-ascetic, much to Indra's delight.

- The Tamil *Ramayana* of Kamban humanizes the rakshasas and shows them as creatures of passion. This folklore amplifies this trend. Unlike the lustful woman of Valmiki's poem, we have here a lonely woman who has lost her husband and her son and seeks pleasure in a handsome man, only to be brutally disappointed.
- The tale also highlights how lives get entangled accidentally. Had Lakshman not accidentally killed the demon-ascetic, would he have attracted Surpanakha's attention, and hence Ravana's?
- In Kamban's *Ramayana*, it is suggested that Surpanakha draws Ram into a quarrel with Ravana to avenge her husband's death at Ravana's hands.

Disfiguring Surpanakha

Yes, they looked like sages. They had matted hair and beards. Their bodies were covered with ash. And they wore clothes of bark and animal hide. And they carried weapons, like men from the north. But they were beautiful. Tall and lithe, their bodies gleamed like bronze in the sunlight. The smell of their sweat was intoxicating. Surpanakha felt giddy with desire.

She first went to Ram, who she felt was taller and had wider shoulders, and said, 'Come, be my beloved, satisfy my desire.'

Ram, amused by this unabashed display of desire, said, 'I am married.'

'What does that mean?'

'It means I have a woman already with me, and will look upon no other. Perhaps you can ask my brother here who is all alone in the forest.'

When she approached Lakshman, he said, 'No, go away. I am not interested. I serve my brother and no other.'

Surpanakha did not understand. Why would they turn her away? Was she not attractive? Were they not lonely? She then saw Sita seated beside Ram and surmised that perhaps with her around they desired no satisfaction elsewhere. She was the rival. She had to be exterminated. So like a beast in heat, she rushed towards Sita, determined to strike her with a rock and smash her skull. 'Stop her,' shouted Ram, pulling Sita behind him.

Lakshman caught Surpanakha by the hair and pulled her back. Surpanakha resisted

and shoved him away. She was strong, and determined to have her way.

'Don't kill her,' shouted Sita, for she had watched how Ram and Lakshman had mercilessly killed Viradha.

'Then I will punish her,' said Lakshman. 'I will teach her a lesson that she will never forget.' He grabbed a knife and in one swift stroke chopped off her nose.

Surpanakha yelled out loud in shock. What was this? Could so beautiful a man be so cruel? She ran away crying, her mournful wails filling the air. She ran in search of her brothers Khara and Dushana, who would teach these deceptive monsters a lesson.

Sita trembled. 'Don't be afraid, Sita. We will protect you,' said Ram.

And Sita said, 'I fear for all of us. That was no animal, my husband. That was a human. And in her eyes, you are the villain and I am no victim. This action will have a reaction that will not be pleasant.'

- In the Valmiki *Ramayana*, Surpanakha is foul and ugly and demonic. In the Kamban *Ramayana*, she is lovelorn and beautiful. Versions vary about how she looks. In Ram-leela plays of the Gangetic plains, she is comical in her vulgar display of erotic desire. The story makes explicit the conflict between natural desire and social values. It makes one wonder how one should see an erotically aroused woman, with disgust, with sympathy or with amusement. How would women see her – sympathetically or with suspicion? How would men see her – with outrage or embarrassment? The *Ramayana* repeatedly provokes such intense emotions and thoughts and thus draws out the humanity of those who hear the tale.
- In some retellings, Ram orders the mutilation of Surpanakha but in others it is Lakshman's decision. The narrator knows the ambiguous ethics of the action and is uncomfortable attributing it to Ram.
- The most common version of the tale refers to Surpanakha's nose being cut off. But often the cutting of the nose is accompanied by the chopping of her ears. And in the most brutal version, found in Kamban's Tamil *Ramayana*, there is even a reference to her breasts being cut off. In South Indian folklore, the breasts are where a woman's power resides.

- In Tamil oral *Ramayanas*, when Surpanakha's body parts are thus mutilated, Ravana's heads keep falling off. He feels her pain and wonders what is going on. Thus the relationship of the brother and sister is amplified.
- Modern templates, rooted in Western mindsets, thrive on rigid categorizations, fixed power equations, judgement and most importantly separating the narration from the audience. Thus using Western academic templates, scholars tend to see the *Ramayana* only in terms of the suppression of certain emotions, races, communities and gender. It equates dharma with the biblical commandment. It becomes a tale about 'them' and 'us'. This clear demarcation is not part of traditional storytelling, which allows for 'them' to become 'us'. The audience appreciates and rejects both Ram and Surpanakha simultaneously. One is constantly asked to negotiate the cruelty of Ram's actions with Ram's divinity. Is God fair? Must he be fair? Can humans be fair? Who decides what is fair, Sita or Surpanakha, Ram or Lakshman? Thus are thoughts provoked and ideas churned.
- Before her nose is cut, Surpanakha comes across as a villain. After the act, she becomes a victim. One wonders if the brutality of the punishment matches the intensity of the crime. Is it criminal to express desire or is it criminal to disregard the rules of marriage?
- Viradha is killed for touching Sita. Surpanakha is mutilated for attacking Sita. Most people who hear the *Ramayana* forget the killing of Viradha but everyone remembers the mutilation of Surpanakha.

The Force of Khara and Dushana

The next day, as the first light touched the sky, the air was filled with the sounds of roaring rakshasas led by Khara and Dushana screaming for revenge. Ram and Lakshman circled their hut, armed with bows and arrows.

A terrific fight followed that lasted all morning. The rakshasas came screaming, bearing axes and spears and maces, one after the other, in swarms, like mad bees.

Ram and Lakshman directed a shower of arrows at them. They chanted hymns to invoke the power of the wind and water to make the rakshasas slip and fall, and break their necks against rocks and trees. They shot arrows that had the strength of elephants and the speed of leopards. With their arrows they cut the rakshasa horde to pieces. By the time the sun was overhead in the sky, Khara and Dushana and their hordes were all dead. Several dozen corpses littered the forest around Sita's hut.

Vultures came from the skies and cats from the forests to feed on the field of carcasses. Ram ordered Lakshman to shoo them away and then prepared to

cremate the fallen rakshasas. 'You give them too much dignity,' said Lakshman as he lit the pyre.

'It is the only way to remind ourselves that we are still humans,' said Ram. 'Let the forest and its fears not claim you. Stay true to the idea of dharma. Be the best you can be, in the worst of circumstances, even when no one is watching.'

As the fire rose, Lakshman heaved a sigh of relief. 'There, it is over.' His body was covered with blood and sweat and his eyes were gleaming with the excitement of victory.

'No, it is not,' said Ram, who had seen Surpanakha watching the flames from atop a distant hill. 'Strength has failed. They will now use cunning. Like hungry animals on a hunt they will not stop till they get their prey. We should move.'

- Tadaka is associated with two men, Marichi and Subahu; so is Surpanakha associated with Khara and Dushana. They are sometimes called her brothers, sometimes her sons, and one wonders if this mirror relationship is merely coincidental or significant. Temples dedicated to the Goddess often show her flanked by two male warriors, identified as her guards or brothers or sons. Are these rakshasa matriarchs of the *Ramayana* embodiments of forest goddesses, wild and ferocious, who demand hook-swinging and fire-walking for their pleasure, who love meat, alcohol and lemons as offerings? Did Vedic sages encounter such forest goddesses when they entered the jungles of the south? The answers are purely speculative.
- Khara and Dushana are not mere troublemaking rakshasas. They are victims seeking revenge and justice. God, the dispenser of justice, is now victimizer as well as victim. Thus further enquiry is provoked into the idea of God.
- In the Jain *Ramchandra-charitra Purana* written in Kannada by Nagachandra, Ravana asks Avalokinividya to roar like a lion. Lakshman, busy fighting Khara and Dushana, does not hear this. Ram hears it and, fearing for Lakshman's life, leaves Sita alone. Taking advantage of this breach in her security, Ravana arrives in his flying chariot and whisks her away.

The Cunning of the Golden Deer

They moved camp down the river Godavari to a place enclosed by rocks, which gave Ram and Lakshman a chance of spotting intruders from a distance. The forest was some way off. A hut was built here for Sita. The brothers sat on the rocks all day and night, keeping watch.

Days turned into weeks, weeks into months. Viradha and Surpanakha were a distant memory. Once again the forest looked beautiful with its flowers and fruits. The rivers and the mountains had stories to tell. Once again boredom descended and the trio wondered how to spend the day. There was enough food and so there was no point foraging. And hunting made Sita unhappy. There were no hermits around this place to chat with, and all the stars in the night sky were familiar.

'Do animals get bored?' asked Lakshman.

'Do trees get bored?' wondered Ram.

'Let us create board games to fill the time so that we do not think of boredom,' said Sita. And just when she said this she saw a deer, shining like gold. It had two heads and long antlers. As it jumped about, its hooves destroyed the patch of grass that Sita loved and with its antlers it ripped out the flower-laden vine that Sita particularly liked.

'Let me catch him for you, Sita. Alive, it will make a great pet. Dead, its skin will make a lovely mat for you,' said Ram. Sita did not stop Ram. She was spellbound by the creature. She wanted to possess it. And Ram saw this in her eyes. For the first time in all these years, she wanted something. 'I will fetch it for you,' he promised, eager to please the princess who never ever showed signs of discontent.

'Maybe this buck leads a herd,' said Sita, her eyes twinkling with the possibility of seeing hundreds of golden deer.

Lakshman warned, 'Golden deer do not exist. This is unnatural.'

'Or just unique, undiscovered,' said Sita, eager to believe this creature was real enough to be caught, tamed, possessed.

Delighted by the prospect of making the otherwise lofty Sita smile by having a very petty desire fulfilled, Ram set out for the woods. 'Stay by her side, Lakshman, while I hunt this deer down,' he said before running after the golden deer.

The sun had barely risen when Ram left the camp. By the time it was noon, Sita got restless. 'He never takes this long. What is happening?'

'The deer is no ordinary deer if it runs so fast and eludes Ram,' said Lakshman.

Then, mid-afternoon, they heard a cry: 'Save me, Lakshman. Save me, Sita. I am dying.' Sita, who had not eaten food nor sipped water since Ram's departure, became agitated. Once again they heard the voice.

'Go to him, Lakshman. There is trouble,' said Sita.

'No,' said Lakshman, 'I will not leave your side.'

'But Ram needs help.'

'I will obey him and not leave your side.'

'What is wrong with you? Do you want him to die?'

Lakshman flinched at these words. 'Something is amiss. This is a trick. This forest is full of rakshasas who can mimic anyone's voice. I don't think Ram is in trouble. It must be the wind. Hunger and thirst are clouding our minds, making us hear things.'

Sita was furious. 'You seem overly eager not to go to Ram. Do you want him to die? Do you? In the jungle, when the dominant male dies, the next one claims his mate. Is that what you want?'

Lakshman could not believe what he was hearing. His noble sister-in-law, in her panic, was willing to descend to the vulgar to make him obey her. Was she so frightened? Did she not trust Ram? Not wanting the situation to get worse, Lakshman decided to go in search of Ram.

But before he left, he traced a line around Sita's hut. 'This is the line of Lakshman, the Lakshman-rekha. I imbue it with the power of hymns I have learned from Vasishtha and Vishwamitra. Any man who tries to cross this line will burst into flames instantly. Stay within this line. Inside is Ayodhya and you are Ram's wife. Outside is the jungle, you are a woman for the taking.'

- The golden deer marks the end of happiness. The next time Ram and Sita meet is after the war, when issues of fidelity and social propriety strain their relationship.
- The motif of the two-headed deer is commonly seen in miniature cloth paintings from Odisha. It is also found in the *Ramayana* of the Bhils who live in Gujarat.
- The idea of Sita wanting Ram to capture or hunt a deer is not acceptable to many storytellers and so in the Bhil *Ramayana* (*Ram-Sita-ni-varta*) we are told that the two-headed golden deer destroys Sita's garden, upsetting Sita, and Ram is so angry that he decides to pursue and hunt the deer.
- The deer is Maricha, a shape-shifting rakshasa, an innocent victim of the war between Ram and Ravana. He represents the common servant who is sacrificed in the fight of the masters.
- Sita uses all her wits to force the obedient Lakshman to disobey. Frightened, she accuses him of an emotion that is most foul. Since Sita has been positioned as the epitome of female virtue that she would even articulate such a thought is unacceptable to many.
- The custom of a widowed sister-in-law becoming the wife of the younger brother-in-law is common in many communities across India, especially in the north-west and the Gangetic plains. It remains an ambiguous relationship, one of caretaker and child when the husband is alive and one of dependant and support when the husband is dead. The sexual tension between the two is alluded to in many folk songs. This idea becomes explicit later in the narrative when Sugriva takes Tara as his wife after Vali is killed, and Vibhishana takes Mandodari after Ravana is killed.
- In the Valmiki *Ramayana*, there is no mention of the Lakshman-rekha. It is first mentioned in the Telugu and Bengali *Ramayana*s written over a thousand years after the Valmiki *Ramayana* was composed. Many early Sanskrit plays that describe Sita's abduction do not mention this line.
- In Buddha Reddy's Telugu *Ranganatha Ramayana*, Lakshman draws seven lines across the ground in front of Sita's hut, not one, and these lines spit fire each time Ravana tries to cross them.

Feeding the Hermit

Shortly after Lakshman left, a rishi with his body smeared with ash came to Sita's hut with a bowl in his hand. 'Are you the bride of that unfortunate scion of the famous Raghu clan, Ram?'

'Yes, I am,' said Sita.

'The noble Raghu clan, famous for its hospitality?' he reconfirmed.

'Yes.'

'Then you will surely take care of me. I have not eaten for several days and have found neither an edible berry nor a root or a shoot in this wretched forest. I beg you to feed me any morsel that you may have left in the house.'

'Come in,' said Sita.

'I cannot,' said the rishi. 'I see no man beside you. They must have gone to the forest or the river. You are alone in the house. It would be inappropriate to come in. Someone may accuse you of being a Renuka or an Ahilya. No, it is better that you come and feed me.' The rishi spread the hide of a blackbuck on the ground and sat at a distance from the hut, ready to receive his meal.

Sita collected the fruits and berries from within and was about to step out when she remembered the line drawn around the hut. She was suddenly confronted with a dilemma. As long as she stayed inside the line, she was safe. Outside she was vulnerable.

But if the rishi was not fed he would go around the forest maligning the reputation of the Raghu clan because of her, the eldest daughter-in-law. 'They call themselves noble but refuse to leave their house to feed hungry sages. When you meet a member of the Raghu clan, remember Sita, and do not expect any hospitality,' he would say. What was more important, herself or the reputation of the Raghu clan, she wondered. She had to risk vulnerability.

So Sita crossed the line drawn by Lakshman, to feed the rishi.

Ravana looked at her and smiled, 'Inside the line you were someone's wife. Outside you are just a woman for the taking.'

Sita screamed. He grabbed her arm, tossed her over his shoulder and summoned his chariot. It had the power of flight!

- Though the Valmiki *Ramayana* leaves no doubt that Ravana grabbed Sita physically, in many regional versions, written over a thousand years later, Ravana does not touch Sita. In Kamban's *Ramayana*, he picks up the ground under Sita and carries her along with the hut to Lanka. These versions suggest that in medieval times, the concept of contamination and pollution through touch had gained more prominence in Indian society.
- That Ravana is in love with Sita is a common theme, especially in South Indian retellings. Ram is the restrained, civilized, faithful beloved who follows the rules, while Ravana is the unrestrained, passionate lover who cannot handle rejection.
- In Shaktibhadra's ninth-century Sanskrit play *Ascharya-chudamani*, Ram and Sita are given gifts by sages: Ram a ring and Sita a hairpin. These ornaments are special. As long as the two wear them, no demon can touch them and they can reveal demons who use magic disguises. In the play, Ravana approaches Sita not in the form of a hermit but in the form of Ram on a chariot with Lakshman as his charioteer, and tells Sita that they have to rush to Ayodhya which has been invaded by enemy forces. Sita believes him and steps on to his chariot. Ravana does not touch Sita fearing the hairpin, but when Sita touches Ravana, Ravana is forced to reveal his true form. Likewise, Surpanakha meets Ram in the form of Sita. She cannot touch him as he wears the special ring, but when he touches her, she sheds her disguise and reveals her demonic form.
- The story goes that the playwright Shaktibhadra presented his play based on the life of Ram to the great Vedanta scholar Shankara. Shankara had taken the vow of silence and so did not say anything on reading the work. Assuming this to mean displeasure, Shaktibhadra burnt his text in disappointment. When Shankara finally broke his vow of silence and praised the work, Shaktibhadra revealed what he had done. Miraculously, by the grace of Shankara, Shaktibhadra was able to recite the entire play from memory.
- Ravana's chariot, or rather Kubera's chariot, is called Pushpak Vimana. It is a vimana, or chariot that has the power of flight, leading one to believe that ancient Indians knew aeronautics. In fact, long essays have been written of how this ancient airplane would have been fuelled. It is seen as proof of India's great technological achievement in ancient times.
- In Sinhalese, Ravana's chariot is called Dandu Monara, which means flying peacock. In Sri Lanka, Weragantota, about 10 km from Mahiyangana, is identified as Ravana's airport.

The Wings of Jatayu

Sita did not know who this strange rishi was. Was he a rishi at all?

'Know this, pretty one, I am Ravana, king of Lanka, brother of the woman your husband mutilated, leader of the men your husband killed. You are the penalty of his crimes. When he returns to the hut, you will not be there and there will be no footprints for him to follow. He will search around the forest for years in futility like a lovesick fool and then, realizing that you have been taken by some beast or bird, he will come to terms with your loss and find comfort in another woman, probably my sister, who seems so infatuated by him despite the way he has treated her.'

Sita refused to look at her abductor. She would not give him the satisfaction of seeing her wail and whimper in fear. She looked below – a carpet of trees, they were indeed flying. Sita wondered if he was taking her to Amravati, the city of the gods.

Reading her mind, Ravana said, 'I am taking you to the most wonderful place on earth, to Lanka, the city of gold, located in the middle of the sea, far from all human habitation.'

Sita felt a mixture of fear and sorrow. Not for herself but for Ram and Lakshman. Her absence would make them anxious, fill them with guilt and shame. They were

warriors, after all, proud men who would feel they had failed in their duty. And she wondered who would feed them when they returned from the hunt, who would provide them water to quench their thirst and make ready a bed of grass for them to rest on. Sita felt miserable about the situation Dashratha's sons would find themselves in, rather than her own. She would manage; would they?

She wondered how Ram would know where she was being taken. She was clearly being taken south. She pulled off her armlets and anklets, the chains around her neck and her earrings, and began dropping them below, hoping they would create a trail for Ram to follow. She removed everything except her hairpin. She remembered her mother's words, 'As long as you are a married woman and matriarch of a household, your hair must be tied up. Untie it only for your husband in the privacy of your bed, never when you step out of it.'

Suddenly a bird appeared before the chariot. It was the old vulture called Jatayu who often kept watch over their hut. He spread his wings and blocked the path of the flying chariot and challenged Ravana to a duel. Ravana pulled out his crescent-shaped sword and prepared for battle. Jatayu struck Ravana with his wings, biting into his arms with his sharp beak, tearing his flesh with his sharp talons. But Ravana was agile and Jatayu old. Ravana swung the sword in an arc and slashed off one of the bird's wings, causing Jatayu to tumble down to earth from the sky.

- Sita is abducted in the final year of exile.
- The place from where Sita is abducted has been identified as Panchavati, near Nashik in Maharashtra on the banks of the river Godavari. The name of the city of Nashik near Panchavati is derived from 'nasika' which means nose in Sanskrit and Prakrit, alluding to the cut nose of Surpanakha.
- Sita is shown here not as helpless but as alert and resourceful. Realizing she cannot escape, she thinks of a way to let her husband know her whereabouts.
- The hairpin or chudamani is a jewel worn by women to adorn their hair and keep it up. Symbolically, untied hair is a sign of freedom and wildness. Tied hair is the symbol of bondage as well as culture. In the *Mahabharata*, the untied hair of Draupadi indicates the end of civilized conduct.
- Jatayu befriends Ram and Sita when they arrive in Panchavati and promises to watch over their hut. He is the first friendly creature that we encounter in the *Ramayana*. In

some versions, he goes on a pilgrimage and returns just as Ravana is abducting Sita.

- Jatayu is a vulture, but is often visualized as an eagle.
- In many performances, Jatayu and Ravana are presented as being equally matched. Finally the two decide to reveal each other's strengths. Jatayu reveals his strength is locked in his wings. Ravana lies and says it is locked in his toe, not his navel. So during the fight, Jatayu tries to peck Ravana's toe in vain, giving Ravana an opportunity to slice off Jatayu's wings.
- Jatayu plays a crucial role in the story as he points Ram to the direction in which Sita is taken. As Ravana travels on a flying chariot, there are no footprints to follow.
- The spot where Ram finds Jatayu is identified as Nashik in Maharashtra, as well as Lepakshi (from pakshi or bird, in Sanskrit) in Andhra Pradesh.

Across the Sea to Lanka!

Soon they were over the sea. Sita saw fishes and sea snakes pursuing the shadow of the Pushpak. Then, amidst the waves, she saw Ravana's shadow on the gleaming ocean. She realized he had ten heads and twenty arms. He kept talking to her, but she did not hear a word. She felt numb. She heard nothing but the drone of the flying chariot as it tore through the clouds on its way to Lanka.

Hidden by mists and clouds, Lanka was indeed a jewel, a golden citadel with tall towers and red fluttering flags atop a green mountain, ringed by a beach of silver sand and around it the vast blue sea.

A horde of cheering men and women gathered to receive their triumphant king and his trophy. They shouted and sang as he carried Sita over his shoulders to his palace gates. There stood Mandodari, his chief queen.

'Stop,' she said. 'Do not bring a woman into this house against her will. All the women, even those married to other men, who stay here come here of their own free will. This is a house of joy. Do not bring in a weeping woman. She brings bad luck.'

'She will come around eventually,' said Ravana, trying to get in. But Mandodari stretched out her arm and blocked his path.

'Is the great Ravana not capable of charming her, seducing her, enticing her to enter of her own free will? Is that why he wants to drag her in while she whimpers in protest?'

Ravana knew his wife had cornered him. 'I will keep her in the garden outside this palace until she willingly comes inside. Then she will get the bed that you occupy now, Mandodari, and you will serve her as a slave.'

'Challenge accepted,' said Mandodari with a smile.

Only Sita understood what Mandodari had done; she had protected her own station in the palace while ensuring another woman's freedom.

- The *Ramayana* narrated by shadow puppeteers of Odisha is called Ravanachhaya, or the shadow of Ravana, because according to one story it was inspired by Sita who saw Ravana's shadow cast on the sea when she was being taken to Lanka. Sailors, it is popularly believed, invented shadow puppetry using lamps behind the sail to create the shadows for their stories. These stories entertained them on their long journey up and down the Indian coast and to and from Suvarnabhumi, the golden land, as South-East Asia was called.
- Many scholars have challenged the identification of the island nation of Sri Lanka with the island of Lanka. One reason is that the island nation has traditionally been known as Sinhala, the country of lions (referring most probably to heroic men, as lions are not native to the island), and the name Lanka is traced to around the twelfth century. Another reason is that details of Lanka in the Valmiki *Ramayana* suggest an area in the

Deccan. Still others believe that the southern island is a metaphor, like 'going south' in modern language, referring to something negative. But tourist guides in Sri Lanka do take people to sites associated with the *Ramayana* like the place where Sita was held captive and where Ravana parked Pushpak, his flying chariot.

- A document called *Lankavatara Sutra* (circa fourth century CE) refers to a conversation in Lanka between the Buddha and Mahamati (the learned one) who scholars have identified as Ravana, indicating the popularity of the character and the story of Ram across all denominations of India. This text plays an important role in the development of Tibetan, Chinese and Japanese Mahayana Buddhism and speaks about the role of consciousness in constructing the mental world that we assume to be real.

The Garden of Ashoka Trees

Ravana carried Sita into the garden next to his palace and dropped her under a tree. 'Here she will stay,' said Ravana to the women of his palace. 'Take care of her needs. Let not jealousy get the better of you. I will ensure you have no reason to complain. I will satisfy all of you and she will satisfy me.' The women laughed when he said so, for Ravana always kept his promises.

Dressed in red, bereft of jewels except the hairpin binding her hair, Sita turned her face towards the tree, hugging it, as if expecting it to turn into Ram who would fight and liberate her from this prison. No fate is worse than that where one is deprived of one's freedom.

The garden she had been put in was full of Ashoka trees, short trees with mango-like leaves and bright bunches of red-orange flowers. Sita had seen this plant in her father's house and in Ayodhya. They were dedicated to Kama, the god of love. When the winter was waning, women were asked to embrace this tree. The gardeners believed it made the trees burst into bloom faster thereby heralding spring. What a cruel place to be held hostage, worse than any cage, for it reminded her of her Ram, of the possibilities of love denied first by Kaikeyi's cruelty and now by Ravana's rage.

Sita found herself surrounded by the women of Ravana's household: his wife, Mandodari; his mother, Kaikesi; his sister, Surpanakha; his sister-in-law Sarama, wife of his brother Vibhishana; his niece Trijata, Vibhishana's daughter; and his daughter-in-law Sulochana, Indrajit's wife. They had been instructed to take care of her needs.

They brought her food and water, clothes and dolls. But Sita was not interested. She was anxious about Ram and Lakshman. Who was feeding them? Who was taking care of them? She felt miserable at the thought of their anguish. They would surely be scouring the forest frantically. Would they have found Jatayu with his broken wing? Would they have found the jewels she had cast on the way? Would they find her, rescue her?

Women were posted to watch over Sita. Some spoke to her kindly. Some spoke to her rudely. Some tried to encourage her to submit to Ravana. Some warned her of the dire consequences if she annoyed Ravana. 'Do you think you are better than us? That he is not good enough for you?'

Sita did not reply to these taunts. She just looked at the blades of grass around her, and placed one blade to her left and another to her right. 'This is my Ram,' she said looking at the grass on the right. 'And that is my Lakshman,' she said looking at the grass on the left. She was convinced they would protect her.

'He has no army. How will he defeat Ravana who has an army of a thousand rakshasas?'

Sita did not reply. She knew that her Ram was king even without his kingdom. He would create armies out of nothingness if that was required to rescue her.

When Surpanakha came to the garden to gloat over Sita and to curse her, Mandodari shouted at her, 'Wasn't your brother supposed to simply kill her so that her husband would seek comfort in your arms? Why then has she been brought here? Do you realize, silly girl, in avenging your mutilation, this brother of yours has paved the way for his own satisfaction.'

'Ravana loves me,' said Surpanakha.

'Ravana loves no one but himself,' said Mandodari. 'Let us not pretend otherwise. We are his pets.'

- The idea of a brother as protector of the sister's honour, which is equated with family honour, is found in many cultures. In the Hebrew Bible, a Canaanite prince seduces Dinah, daughter of Jacob. Later, he asks his father to formalize the union and even agrees to get circumcised in keeping with the custom of his bride's household. However, Dinah's brothers view the seduction and marriage as rape. During the wedding party, they massacre the groom and all his male relatives.
- In the Valmiki *Ramayana*, while enlisting Ravana's help, Surpanakha feels the need to describe Sita's beauty. It is as if she instinctively knows that Ravana would not bother with avenging her insult unless there was something in it for him.
- Ashoka trees are evergreen and are sacred in classical Sanskrit literature. Its leaves were strung on doorways to invite the goddess of wealth. (Today, Ashoka leaves have been replaced by mango leaves.) People often confuse the Ashoka tree that has bright red-orange flowers with another tree, also called the Ashoka, a tall willowy tree that has green flowers.
- Valmiki's *Ramayana* describes Sita in Lanka as a sunken boat, a broken branch and a lotus covered with mud.
- The Valmiki *Ramayana* refers to an old rakshasa woman called Trijata, a daughter of Vibhishana called Kala and another rakshasa woman called Sarama who are Sita's friends. In later *Ramayanas*, Sarama is identified as Vibhishana's wife, and Trijata becomes the embodiment of the friendly rakshasa woman, sometimes called Vibhishana's daughter.
- In the tenth-century Indonesian *Ramayana Kakawin* (which means kavya or song in Old Javanese), and the thirteenth-century Sanskrit play *Prasanna-Raghav* by Jayadeva, Sita contemplates suicide by burning herself to death but is made to change her mind by Trijata.
- Family plays an important role in the *Ramayana*. Ram, Sita and even Ravana exist in a family ecosystem.

A House and Wife for Ravana

The women of Lanka told Sita that Ravana was the greatest devotee of Shiva.

As Shiva was a hermit he did not know how to build a house. So Parvati asked him to commission an architect. Ravana was summoned as he was skilled in Vastu-shastra, the science of space. Ravana built a great palace atop Mount Kailas for Parvati, much to her delight. Pleased with the happiness Ravana had given his wife, Shiva offered him anything he desired. Ravana asked for the house itself, for it had turned out to be so beautiful that he just could not bear to part with it. So, much to Parvati's annoyance, Ravana took away the palace he had built and placed it atop Mount Trikuta, right in the centre of Lanka.

Ravana once created a lute for Shiva using one of his heads as the gourd, one of his arms as the beam and the nerves of his arm as the strings. Pleased with this

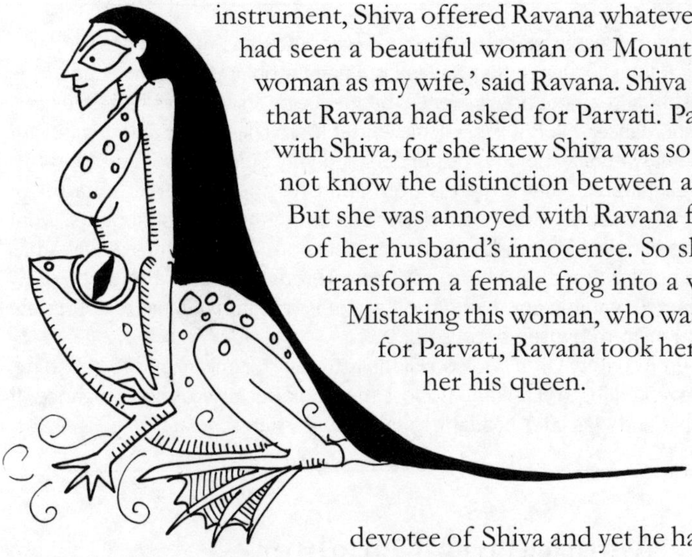

instrument, Shiva offered Ravana whatever he desired. Ravana had seen a beautiful woman on Mount Kailas. 'I want that woman as my wife,' said Ravana. Shiva agreed, not realizing that Ravana had asked for Parvati. Parvati was not angry with Shiva, for she knew Shiva was so innocent that he did not know the distinction between a woman and a wife. But she was annoyed with Ravana for taking advantage of her husband's innocence. So she asked Brahma to transform a female frog into a woman, her double. Mistaking this woman, who was named Mandodari, for Parvati, Ravana took her to Lanka and made her his queen.

These tales did not impress Sita. 'You call him the devotee of Shiva and yet he has no shame stealing the hermit's house and even desiring his wife. Ravana, whose hunger seems insatiable, clearly has learned nothing from Shiva, who has outgrown all hunger!'

'He is an expert in astrology. He has written the *Ravana-samhita*, which reveals how to predict the future by observing the movements of stars and planets and how to change the future using gemstones,' said Trijata.

'He who seeks to predict the future is insecure. He who seeks to control the future is insecure. Ah, your Ravana is so unlike my Ram,' said Sita.

When she learned how Lanka had been built by Kubera for the yakshas and how Ravana had driven him out and made this the home of rakshasas, Sita smiled, for she came from a household where brothers were eager to give each other the kingdom, not drive others away from it. Ravana-kula was no Raghu-kula. Ravana behaved like the territorial dominant beast who drives away rivals. Such behaviour was unbecoming of humans. It was certainly not dharma.

- Folk storytellers of Maharashtra narrate the story of Ravana craving Shiva's house.
- The story of the frog (manduka, in Sanskrit) being turned into a woman (Mandodari) comes from *Manduka Shabda*, a dance composed for the thirteenth-century court dancer Lakumadevi by Jayapa Nayak, author of the *Nritya Ratnavali*. It was performed in the Kuchipudi style before the great Andhra emperor Krishnadevaraya in the seventeenth century.

- Mandor, near Jodhpur, Rajasthan, marks the spot where Ravana married Mandodari.
- All retellings of the *Ramayana* agree that Ravana is a great scholar with knowledge of the Vedas, Tantra, shastras and various occult sciences besides being an accomplished astrologer, doctor, musician and dancer. He is a super-achiever, far more charismatic and flamboyant than the serene Ram. Naturally, he does not understand why Sita prefers Ram to him.
- Indian philosophy separates what a man is from what he possesses. We are a set of thoughts and we have a set of things. Ram derives his strength from his thoughts, what he is, while Ravana derives his strength from his possessions, what he has. Ravana has knowledge; he may be learned, but he is not wise. Through Ravana, the bards draw attention to the learned brahmin priest who spouts hymns verbatim but fails to appreciate their meaning or transform himself because of them.
- *Lal Kitab*, a nineteenth-century Urdu book on Hindu astrology, palmistry and face-reading, is attributed to Ravana, king of Lanka, who lost the book because of his arrogance. It resurfaced in Arabia and was later brought to India by Persian scholars.

Mandodari's Daughter

It was rumoured that long ago, before she became mother of Indrajit, Mandodari had borne a daughter. She had accidentally consumed a pot of blood thinking it was a pot of water. The blood was that of rishis, collected as tax by Ravana for a ritual meant to appease the Goddess and secure boons from her.

When the girl was born, the astrologers foretold that she would cause the death of Ravana. So the child was put in a box and the box cast into the sea. 'Did the sea-god give my daughter to the earth-goddess and did the earth-goddess give her to Janaka and did Janaka give her to Ram?' wondered Mandodari, each time she saw Sita. And that is why she did everything in her power to make Ravana give up Sita.

'A woman, it is foretold, will be the cause of your death,' she told Ravana.

Mandodari reminded him of the woman Vedavati, who had burned herself to death rather than submit to the passionate embraces of Ravana. Had she not sworn that she would kill Ravana in her next life?

Mandodari reminded him of Rambha, the nymph who was the wife of Nalkubera, Kubera's son. Ravana had forced himself on her and Nalkubera had cursed him that if he forced himself on a woman again his head would burst into a thousand pieces.

Every night Mandodari and the women of the city sang for Ravana and danced for him and pleasured him in every way, hoping to make him get over his obsession with Sita. But the more she said no, the more he desired her.

'When bad times come,' Mandodari remembered the wise men saying, 'we are unable to stop ourselves from doing stupid things.'

- The story of Sita being Mandodari's daughter hence Ravana's can be traced to the ninth-century Jain text *Uttarpurana* by Gunabhadra.
- The Tibetan *Ramayana* and Khotan *Ramayana* speak of peasants and sages finding the abandoned girl. In the Kashmiri *Ramayana*, the abandoned girl is found and raised by Janaka.
- In the Javanese *Serat Khanda*, Mandodari is asked to abandon the child which is destined to kill her husband and Vibhishana replaces the child by creating an infant from the clouds. This child is called Meghnad, born of the clouds and so sounding like the clouds.
- In the *Dashavatara-charita* of Kshemendra, Ravana finds a baby girl inside a lotus and gives her to Mandodari. But Narada warns Mandodari that Ravana will fall in love with the girl when she grows up, so Mandodari discards the girl in a box which is found by Janaka who adopts her as his daughter.
- In the Sanskrit *Adbhut Ramayana*, Ravana collects the blood of sages as tribute since they have nothing else to give him. Mandodari accidentally drinks this blood and becomes pregnant with Sita who she aborts and buries under the ground at Kurukshetra. Janaka eventually finds Sita and takes her home.
- In the Sanskrit *Ananda Ramayana*, a princess called Lakshmi enters the fire after disgruntled suitors who want to marry her kill her father, King Padmaksha. Years later, she steps out of the fire, but is seen by Ravana, so she retreats back into the flames. Ravana extinguishes the fire and keeps the glowing stones he finds in the fire pit in a box. When Mandodari opens the box, she finds a girl inside. Sensing trouble, she buries the box with the girl under the ground; it is found by Janaka in Mithila.
- The story of Sita being Ravana's daughter probably emerged to further the case that Ravana kept Sita at arm's length while she was in captivity. But alongside these stories are others of Ravana, the lovelorn, passionate lover.

Seduction Attempts

What is the greatest battlefield? The heart of a woman who is in love with someone else. To make her leave her beloved and come to your bed of her own free will, that is the greatest challenge. And so Ravana did everything in his power to make Sita fall in love with him.

He sang for her. All the women in Lanka swooned over his voice. But not Sita.

He danced for her. All the women in Lanka drooled over the rhythm of his body. But not Sita.

He told her stories. All the women in Lanka stayed awake all night enchanted by the plot. But not Sita.

He made himself vulnerable telling stories of how his father always compared him to Kubera and how he always felt inadequate before Vali and Kartavirya. All the women in Lanka wanted to comfort him. But not Sita.

He showered her with gifts – the finest flowers, the finest jewellery, the finest fabrics, the finest food. All the women in Lanka thought she was extremely lucky. But not Sita.

'He loves you so much,' said Trijata.

'Then why does he care for his happiness over mine?' asked Sita. 'Why does he not let me go?'

'What more can a woman ask of a man? He gives you all that you want. He makes you feel important, wanted, desired and powerful. He guards you jealously and protects you from harm.'

'That is not love. He does not see me. He just wants to possess me, and finds it frustrating that I do not submit to him. Love is not about power; it is about giving up power, a voluntary submission before one's beloved. Love is about seeing: I see Ram, and Ram sees me. I want to be seen by Ram and Ram wants to be seen by me. I have shown Ram my vulnerabilities without trepidation and so has he. Ravana cannot love another because he sees no one, not even himself.'

'He can take you by force.'

'And that is supposed to frighten me? You give too much value to this body, much more than I do. I am not my body. I will never ever be violated.'

- In the Jain *Ramchandra-charitra Purana* written in Kannada by Nagachandra, Ravana is described as a great sage until he sees Sita and is then overwhelmed by love and lust.
- The many stories that explain why Ravana could not possibly force himself on Sita are created to reassure audiences of Sita's purity. One must not forget that ritual pollution and purity creates a hierarchy in the Hindu scheme of things. Based on this scheme of hierarchy, members of various communities were kept away from the well and the temple and stripped of human dignity. So mere touching, not just sexual violation, can result in loss of reputation and status.
- Sita is not Renuka who desires Kartavirya or Ahilya who succumbs to Indra. She is confident of her love for Ram. Her fidelity has nothing to do with Ram or with the rules of marriage; it is an expression of who she is. This is often described as pativrata, or a wife's vow of chastity. But with Sita it seems less about the expectations of a wife, and more about the emotional choice of an individual.
- The *Ramayana* asks, what is love? Is it attachment? Is it control? Is it freedom? Is love transformative? Should love be exclusive? Is it physical, emotional or intellectual? Is Ram's gentle silence an indicator of love or Ravana's vocal pining?
- The *Ramayana*'s villain, Ravana, has many wives. In his next life, Ram becomes Krishna who also has many wives. Yet, Krishna's love for his wives is described very differently from Ravana's love for his wives. Ravana's love is full of lust, domination and control. Krishna's love is full of affection, understanding and freedom.
- Many who hear the story of the *Ramayana*, unlike Sita, fall prey to what psychologists call the Stockholm syndrome (falling in love with one's captors like hostages who start siding with the hijackers) and start appreciating the qualities of Ravana even though he uses force to drag a woman into his house and keep her captive by force.

The Board Games of Sita

Sita's words were strange. Trijata repeated everything she heard to the women of Lanka. 'She does not consider herself inferior to men, even though she willingly walks behind her husband. Those are social rules, she says, artificial, contextual, functional, necessary.'

'I would rather the men followed me,' said Sulochana one day, almost embarrassed at revealing the desire of her heart.

'That would be just another kind of pecking order,' said Sita. 'Where there is a pecking order, there is no love.'

They flocked to see her, to hear her speak, this strange woman from the far north, who had won the heart of Ravana and thought nothing of it. They came bearing her gifts – flowers and food and clothes and perfumes. 'But I have nothing to give you in exchange,' she said.

'Tell us about your world,' they said.

So she shared with them the stories of her life, the ways of her father's house and her husband's house: how they dressed and how they cooked and how they lived. She spoke of the rituals she followed every day, the gods she worshipped and the powers she invoked. 'We are the matriarchs of the household, priestesses of our homes. Every morning we worship the house, wipe the floor with water, decorate the walls with paintings and put strings of leaves and flowers on the doors. Every evening we light lamps in the courtyard and serve the evening meal.'

'What gives you this confidence?' they asked.

'Faith and patience,' said Sita. She told them the story of how long ago a demon took the earth under the sea. Vishnu took the form of a boar, plunged into the waters, gored the demon to death and, placing the earth-goddess on his snout, carried her to the surface. As they rose, they made love. His embraces caused the earth to fold, thus the mountains and valleys came into being. He plunged his resplendent trunks into the ground thus impregnating the earth which bore all plants. Now, satisfied, she reclines on the hood of the serpent Adi Sesha, gazing upon the blue-black sky adorned with clouds and stars that is Vishnu, her beloved and her guardian. He rescues her whenever she is in trouble. 'I am the earth. Ravana is the demon who has hidden me from the world. Ram will come as Vishnu did and rescue me, of that I am sure. He never disappoints.'

Sita knew herbs that could heal, cure skin rashes and unblock noses and aid the movement of bowels. And most exciting of all, she showed them board games that they could play.

Soon in every house in Lanka people were playing board games designed by Sita. Games that husbands could play with their wives, grandparents with grandchildren, groups of men and groups of women among themselves. This is how they passed the time, enjoying each other's company, not arguing, not fighting, not trying to prove who was the dominant one. By her sheer presence, Sita turned Lanka into a playground where everyone laughed and smiled.

At night, hearing the joyful sounds coming from every courtyard in Lanka, Mandodari said, 'You set out to conquer her heart. And she has ended up conquering all our hearts. Let this wonderful girl go.'

'Never,' said Ravana. He would not be defeated in his own land.

- Ramanuja, the Vedanta scholar, repeatedly identifies Sita as Lakshmi and Ram as Vishnu. Vishnu descends on earth primarily to protect Lakshmi. Vishnu took the form of a boar to rescue the earth from the asura Hiranyaksha. He takes the form of Ram to descend on earth to rescue Sita from the rakshasa Ravana. In Sri Vaishnavism, the bhakti school based on Ramanuja's teachings, devotees can reach Vishnu only through Sita, or Lakshmi, who he identifies as Sri, the embodiment of auspiciousness and affluence.
- Sitaipandi, or the game of Sita, is a form of solitaire. A single row of seven pits is created in the ground. One tamarind seed is kept in the first pit, two in the second, three in the third, and so on. Thus twenty-eight seeds are distributed. One collects all seven seeds of the seventh pit and sows one each in the remaining pits so that six becomes seven, five becomes six, four becomes five, and so on. The last remaining seed is put in the seventh pit. Now one takes the seeds from the sixth pit and redistributes them. This continues till one reaches the initial position with one seed in the first pit and seven in

the seventh. It is a repetitive game that occupies time intelligently and is said to be the first game designed by Sita during captivity.

- Board games like vimanam (flying chariot) and vagh-bakri (tigers and goats, or predators and prey) are said to be inspired from Sita's plight.
- *Rig Samhita*, the oldest collection of Vedic hymns, refers to the game of dice. One is not sure if the dice was accompanied by a board game. In popular imagery, gods and goddesses are often shown playing board games. Shiva plays games with Parvati, Vishnu with his devotees. In the *Mahabharata*, the gambling match with dice results in Draupadi being wagered by her husband Yudhisthira.
- Board games are now part of sacred rituals performed during Lakshmi Puja and Diwali.
- According to astrological data found in the Valmiki *Ramayana*, the abduction took place in 5077 BCE, the thirteenth year of exile.
- 'Cutting off the nose' is a metaphor for shame. When his sister's nose is cut off, Ravana feels he has been shamed, stripped of honour by the sons of the Raghu clan. And so he wishes to 'cut the nose' of Ram by abusing the symbol of his family honour – his wife, Sita. This notion of locating 'honour' in the women of the household has led to women in India being objectified and denied their freedom and choices. Whether Sita is physically abused or not, Ram's 'honour' has been stained. Modern notions of justice mock these deep-rooted traditional notions of shame that have been used to justify the violent oppression of women.

BOOK FIVE

Anticipation

'From her faith came her patience.'

The Monkey in the Tree

Her father had once said that she would never be lonely, even when alone. But he was wrong. Sita was lonely. The Ashoka tree bursting with flowers that heralded love seemed to mock her. The women around pitied her. She stood there firm as a rock with but two blades of grass between her and her tormentor, but her heart was growing restless: when would Ram come?

She curled herself to sleep like a baby and remembered her father and her mother and all the wise words they spoke. She remembered the kindness of the sages. No one had told her the world would be so cruel, that she would be forced to leave one house and dragged out of another. 'There is pain only when there is attachment,' Yagnavalkya had said. She felt pain. She was attached. Was that bad? She yearned for liberation: when would Ram come?

'He has forgotten you,' said Surpanakha. 'Soon he will be ready to accept me as you will be ready to accept my brother.' Sita did not reply. She watched the rains come and go. No one travels in the rain but she knew her Ram would seek her through flood and sludge: but when would Ram come?

Then suddenly, at night, when the autumn moon was high in the sky, she heard something, very distinct from the sound of insects and the rustling of the wind.

'Ram, Ram.'

Yes, that is exactly what she heard. Was she dreaming? Was it her imagination conjuring up what she wanted to hear?

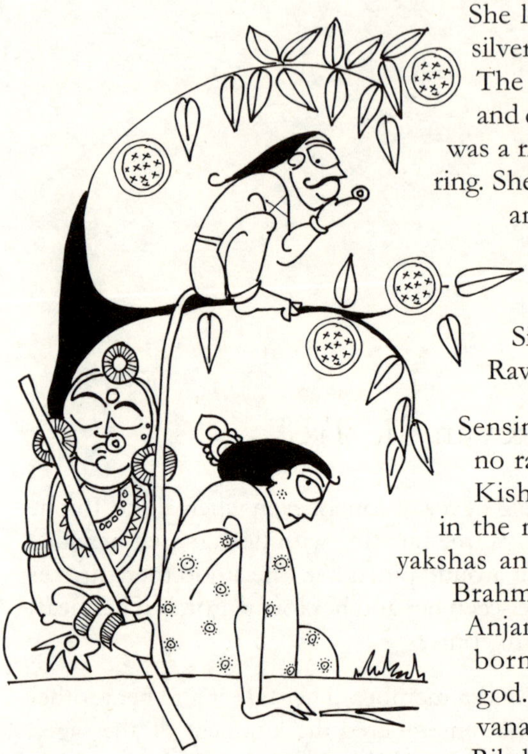

She looked up and saw a strange sight: a silver monkey chanting the name of Ram. The monkey opened the palm of his hand and dropped something on the ground. It was a ring. Sita's eyes widened: it was Ram's ring. She looked up; the monkey came down and spoke, in a human voice: 'I am Ram's messenger, Hanuman. I have been sent to find you.'

Sita withdrew, suspicious: another of Ravana's tricks?

Sensing her fears, Hanuman said, 'I am no rakshasa. I am a vanara. We reside in Kishkindha located between Dandaka in the north and Lanka in the south. Like yakshas and rakshasas, we too descend from Brahma through Pulastya. My mother is Anjana, daughter of Ahilya. And I was born by the grace of Vayu, the wind-god. My father is Kesari, who served the vanara-king Riksha. I serve the son of Riksha, Sugriva. Surya, the sun-god, is my teacher. And Ram, the noble prince of the Raghu clan, who wanders in the forest as a hermit to keep the word of his father, is my inspiration. We found the jewels you discarded from Ravana's flying chariot on the forest floor and have traced you to this garden on an island in the middle of the sea.'

The words, the tone of the voice, the sheer audacity of such an intervention, replaced doubt with trust. Through this monkey her Ram had reached out to her. Sita finally smiled, a flood of relief rising up in her heart.

- The gap between Sita's abduction and her meeting with Hanuman is at least one rainy season. She is abducted in summer before the rains and Ram fights Ravana in autumn, marked by the festival of Dussehra, after the rains.
- The meeting of Hanuman and Sita is described in many ways. In Valmiki's *Ramayana*, Hanuman comes to Sita after Ravana comes and threatens to kill her if she does not submit to him. In a Telugu *Ramayana*, Hanuman finds her about to commit suicide. In a

Marathi *Ramayana*, she hears a monkey chant the name of Ram. In an Odia *Ramayana*, he drops the ring and gets her attention while her guards are sleeping, tired after spending the day alternately terrifying and cajoling her.

- In the Valmiki *Ramayana*, Hanuman wonders if he should speak to Sita in deva-vacham, or language of the gods, meaning Sanskrit, or manushya-vacham, or language of humans, meaning Prakrit (or, some say, Tamil). Either way, she will wonder how a monkey can speak.
- The dialogue shows Sita's doubt and how Hanuman gradually gains her trust using his diplomatic skills.
- Divinity is on the sidelines of Valmiki's retelling. Ram can sense his divinity but it remains in the background. As the centuries passed, the divinity of Ram came to the foreground. His name became a mantra.
- As Ram starts being increasingly associated with Vishnu, Hanuman starts becoming increasingly associated with Shiva, either as his avatar (Rudra-avatar) or as his son, and Sita starts getting associated with the Goddess. Thus through the *Ramayana*, the three major sects of Hinduism devoted to Shiva, Vishnu and Shakti express themselves.
- The Sanskrit *Hanuman-nataka* informs us how there are eleven forms of Rudra. Ten of these protect the ten heads of Ravana but the eleventh one takes the form of Hanuman.
- Ram's signet ring given to Sita is said to have his name inscribed on it. The use of Devanagari script currently used for Sanskrit, Hindi, Marathi and Gujarati came into use in India about a thousand years ago while the *Ramayana* is over two thousand years old, leading scholars to conclude that the use of the written word comes into the Ram narrative much later.

The Story of the Vanaras

The vanaras of Kishkindha had turned north when they heard a vulture screech. They had watched Ravana's sword hack through Jatayu's wing causing him to tumble to the ground. The flying chariot had then made its way south. The sound of a woman's wail had filled the air. She had dropped her jewels from above leaving a trail. The vanaras had collected these jewels from the forest floor and given them to Sugriva, who wondered what the commotion was all about.

'Sugriva is the king of Kishkindha, and I serve him. When Ram met him, he too was an exile because of problems with his brother,' explained Hanuman.

Hanuman then proceeded to tell Sita all about the vanaras and their quarrels.

Brahma's son Kashyapa had a wife called Vinata, who was the mother of birds. Once she laid two eggs. But the eggs took a long time to hatch. Impatient, she

broke open one of the eggs. The child thus born became Aruni, the dawn-god, he of unknowable gender as his lower half remains unfinished.

Aruni served as charioteer of Surya, the sun-god, whose greatest rival was Indra, the flamboyant king of the sky, whose thunderbolts caused clouds to release rain. The reason for this rivalry was simple: people on earth prayed to Indra for wetness when the sun was the brightest and they prayed to Surya for dryness when Indra was most powerful.

One day, without informing Surya, Aruni entered the court of Indra to see the secret sensual dance of the apsaras. To do this he had to take a female form. Aruni's unfamiliar face intrigued Indra, who knew all his apsaras well. He approached her, enjoyed her company and eventually made love to her. As a result Aruni gave birth to a son called Vali. This childbirth happened instantly as happens with the devas. Aruni left the child in the care of the sage Gautama and his wife Ahilya.

This tryst with Indra delayed Aruni but when he told Surya the reason for the delay Surya was most curious. He demanded Aruni show him his female form, on seeing which he too was smitten. He also made love to Aruni, and Aruni instantly gave birth to a son called Sugriva, who too he left in the care of Gautama and Ahilya.

Gautama and Ahilya already had a daughter called Anjana. Anjana told her father about Indra visiting Ahilya while he was away. So Ahilya cursed her to turn into a monkey. Gautama cursed the two boys to turn into monkeys as well as they had failed to inform him of the same. Later, after cursing Ahilya to turn into a rock, Gautama felt sorry for the motherless monkeys. He could not retract the curse and so he gave all three monkeys to Riksha, the childless monkey-king of Kishkindha.

When the children grew up, Riksha got them all married: Anjana married Kesari, Vali married Tara, and Sugriva married Ruma. Before he died, Riksha told Vali and Sugriva to share the kingdom equally.

All was well in Kishkindha, until Vali killed a demon called Dundhubi.

Dundhubi's son, Mayavi, entered Kishkindha and challenged Vali to a duel to avenge his father's death. In the forest, a duel is a challenge to authority and so one can never say no to it. Sugriva watched as Vali and Mayavi began their fierce fight. It was a great fight with each hurling rocks and trees at each other at first, and then showering each other with blows and kicks. It lasted for days. Finally, Mayavi gave up and ran into a cave.

Vali wanted a decisive victory. Determined to kill Mayavi, he followed the demon into the cave while Sugriva watched the mouth of the cave. 'If he gives me the slip or succeeds in killing me, make sure you kill him as he leaves the cave,' Vali instructed Sugriva. Days passed. Thunderous roars of their fight kept coming out from the mouth of the cave. Sugriva waited patiently for the duel to end. Then came an eerie silence and no hoot of victory.

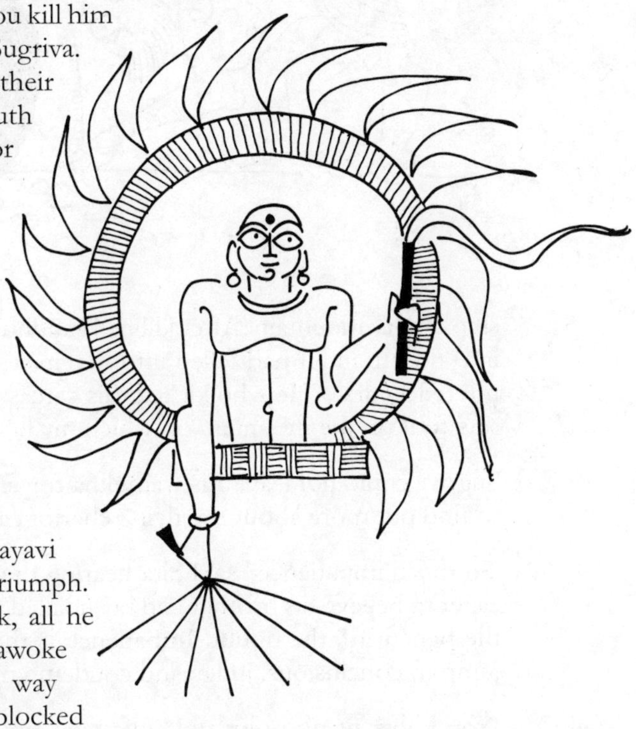

Was Vali dead? It was very unlike Vali not to loudly announce his triumph. Fearing that Vali may have been killed, Sugriva decided to seal the mouth of the cave and thus kill his brother's killer.

That was his undoing.

For Vali was alive. He had killed Mayavi but was too exhausted to declare his triumph. In fact, after breaking Mayavi's neck, all he wanted to do was sleep. When he awoke from a deep slumber and made his way out of the cave, he found its mouth blocked by a boulder.

With great difficulty, he pushed the rock aside and returned to Kishkindha, only to find Sugriva on the throne, enjoying the fruits of Kishkindha with both Ruma and Tara. 'Traitor! Backstabber!' Vali yelled and rushed towards Sugriva with bloodshot eyes, baring his fangs, determined to kill him.

Sugriva ran to save his life. For years, Vali chased him. Finally Sugriva took refuge atop Mount Rishyamukha where Matanga's hermitage was located. Vali dared not

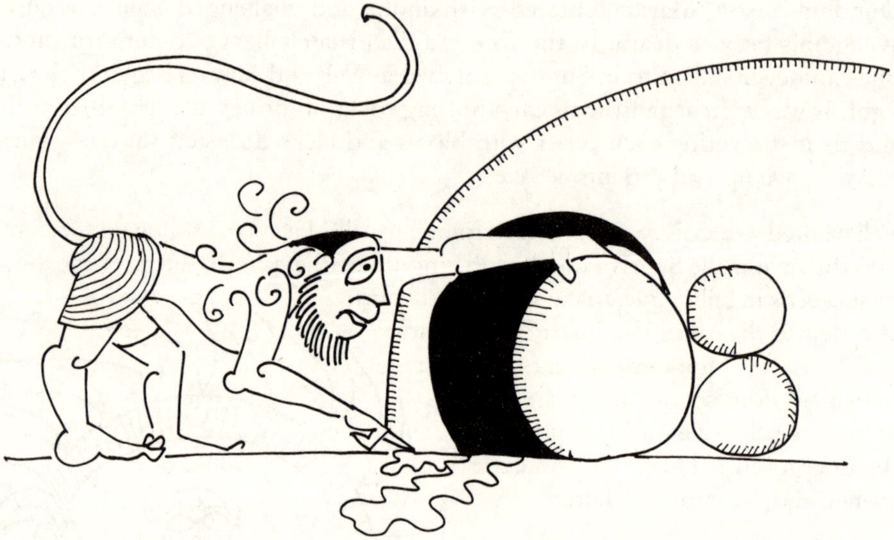

step on this mountain. After killing Dundhubi, Vali had kicked the demon's carcass into the air and it had fallen into Matanga's hermitage. The angry sage had then uttered a curse: 'He who kicked this carcass into my hermitage will die if he ever sets foot on the mountain on which my hermitage is located.'

Sugriva could not leave Rishyamukha for fear of Vali. So he had asked Hanuman to find out more about the flying chariot carrying the wailing woman.

'So much impatience,' said Sita hearing the tale of the vanaras. 'Sugriva was too eager to believe his brother had been killed. Vali was too angry to give his brother the benefit of the doubt. Impatience is the enemy of wisdom; it propels us to jump to conclusions, judge and condemn, rather than understand.'

'You know, at no point did your husband assume you had run away when he found you missing from your hut. He had faith in you. So he investigated patiently to find out how you had disappeared so mysteriously from the hut,' said Hanuman.

'How do you know that?' asked Sita.

Hanuman then told Sita how he met Ram.

- Vanara can be read as va-nara, less than human, or as vana-nara, forest people. Valmiki also describes them as kapi, monkeys. From a rational point of view they are perhaps forest tribes with monkey totems. But this does not explain their tails.
- Jain *Ramayanas* were the earliest *Ramayanas* that rejected the idea of talking monkeys. Vimalasuri describes Hanuman as a vidyadhara, a special class of being, probably inspired by tribes who had monkey images on their flags.
- In the Puranas, all living creatures descend from Brahma. Brahma himself is not associated with a wife, but his mind-born sons have wives. Each son fathers various species of beings. This can be seen objectively as the creation of various species like fishes, birds, reptiles, celestial beings, subterranean beings and humans. Or this can be seen as the birth of humans with different ways of thinking – people who feel entitled (devas), people who feel tricked (asuras), people who grab (rakshasas), people who hoard (yakshas) and people of artistic temperament (gandharvas).
- Brahma does not create the earth or plants; he creates only mobile creatures such as birds, fishes, animals and humans who populate the earth.
- The story of the incomplete, sexually ambiguous first son of Vinata comes from the Puranas. Aruni is a god and Usha is a goddess. Both embody dawn. Both are charioteers of the sun-god, often identified with Garuda, the eagle, the complete and perfect son of Vinata.
- In literature, the day is masculine, the night feminine and the twilight hour ambiguous, defying categorization.
- In the *Adhyatma Ramayana* and some regional retellings, the monkey-king Riksha himself turns into a woman when he falls into a magical pond and both Surya and Indra fall in love with him. Thus are born Sugriva and Vali.
- Vanaras are located in Kishkindha, situated between Aryavarta where the humans reside and Lanka where the demons reside. This location is as much psychological as it is geographical.
- Kishkindha is identified with parts of the present-day states of Karnataka and Andhra Pradesh in the Deccan region.

Ram's Anguish

Following Sugriva's orders, Hanuman took the form of a bee, and travelled rapidly north until he reached the spot where Jatayu lay. From the highest branches of a tree, he saw an ascetic – whom he later identified as Ram – circling his camp like a heartbroken lover, talking to the rocks, the trees, the birds and the animals.

'Have you seen my Sita?' he asked. 'Have you seen that gentle maiden who sat here and hummed songs as she watched the sunset?'

The rocks were silent.

'Where is the golden deer you went to fetch for our sister?' the trees demanded to know.

'It was no deer. It was a shape-shifting demon called Maricha. He could imitate my voice and he drew Lakshman away. He was a decoy. I fear something horrible has happened to Sita.'

'If you so cared for her, you should not have left our sister alone. The jungle is full of predators,' said the unforgiving trees.

'Maybe,' the rocks finally spoke, 'she created the distraction so that she could run away, tired of living like an exile in the forest.'

'No, I know my Sita,' said Ram.

Then a bird said, 'I know who she is with but I will not tell you.' Ram grabbed the bird's neck so fiercely that it got elongated. When Ram released his grip, the frightened bird flew away.

Another bird said, 'No animal begrudges a predator its prey, so why do you?' Ram was so angry with this bird that he cursed that bird to forever be separated from its mate at night. When the bird apologized, Ram amended his curse and said its mate, separated at dusk, would rejoin it at dawn.

Ram then began to cry. His tears fell on the grass, which wondered aloud, 'Does the prince weep for his wife or for himself?'

'Is there a difference? This pain of incompleteness is as much hers as it is mine. I am nothing without her. And she is no one without me,' Ram replied.

'You presume too much,' the bushes shouted. 'Sita does not need you. You need her. She is free. You once claimed her as yours. Now another claims her as his.'

'No one can claim Sita. Like the earth, my Sita, she allows herself to be claimed. She let me claim her. She found me worthy and I will not disappoint her. And I will find her. We will be reunited.'

'Only fools are so certain,' said a chorus of trees.

'I am Sita's fool then. She made me smile and laugh. She told me how thoughts can transform even a tragedy into a comedy.' Ram then shuddered in sorrow.

The trees swayed in joy as they felt his love.

Hanuman then heard another ascetic – whom he later identified as Ram's younger brother Lakshman – rebuke Ram: 'This does not befit you. Do not forget you are king of Ayodhya, scion of the Raghu clan.'

Ram stopped moaning immediately. With a deep breath he resumed the posture of a regal warrior, free of all self-pity. 'My pain can wait. What matters most is finding Sita.'

Many sages and their wives, having heard the commotion in the sky, had travelled to the banks of the Godavari to investigate. Learning what had happened to Ram, they tried to comfort him. But Hanuman watched Ram withdraw. 'I do not wish to be touched. None but Sita shall comfort me,' he said. Then seeing their unhappy faces, he said, 'You can hug me in affection, and I will reciprocate, in my next life for sure, when I descend on earth as Krishna. But for now, as Ram, I will be intimate only with my Sita. Where is she?'

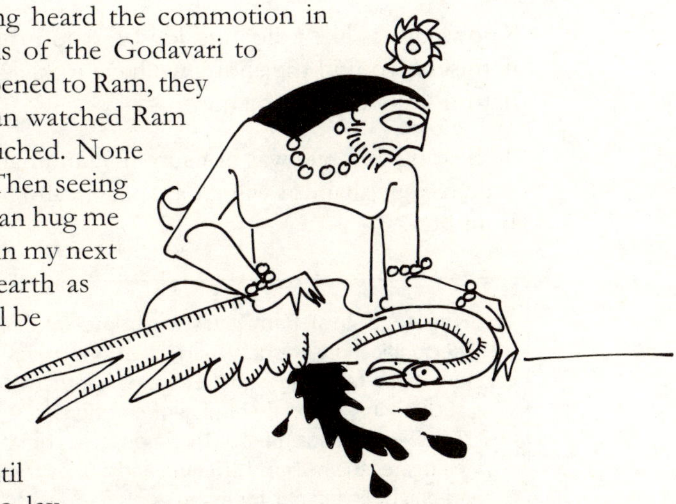

Ram kept going around Sita's hut in wider and wider circles until he finally came upon Jatayu, who lay wingless on the forest floor, bleeding profusely. With his dying breath, the old bird told Ram what had happened. 'She was taken away in the southern direction on a flying chariot by the rakshasa-king Ravana. That coward said this was your punishment for mutilating his sister. I tried stopping them but the demon chopped off my wing with his sword.'

Hanuman watched Ram comfort the bird until it breathed no more. He then saw Ram prepare to cremate the bird.

'It's just a bird,' said Lakshman.

'That may be so but he sacrificed himself trying to protect my Sita,' said Ram. 'What animal does that? No, Lakshman, he is no less than a human. He has displayed more humanity than most humans. We, the unfortunate sons who could not cremate our own father, let us find satisfaction in cremating this creature, who tried protecting us as our father would.'

When the fire claiming Jatayu's body rose to the sky, Ram became thoughtful. 'Every action has a reaction, Lakshman. Sita is being punished because I allowed you to mutilate a woman whose only crime was that she desired me and did not appreciate the rules of marriage. The laws of karma do not follow human logic. Simply by association, an innocent pays for the crimes of the guilty.'

Hearing this, Sita told Hanuman, 'He always told me that knowledge is no antidote to pain.'

'Knowledge is like a floating log of wood that helps us stay afloat in the ocean of misery. To find the shore, we have to kick our legs and swim. No one can do that for us,' said Hanuman.

On hearing this, Sita was not sure if Hanuman was a vanara or a siddha, one who could change shape at will, or a tapasvi, who had an acute sense of understanding about life.

- The anguish of Ram gives a glimpse into his private world. Until then he is the personification of social perfection and royal stoicism. Now, intellect crumbles and emotions take over, until Lakshman, otherwise very passionate, reprimands him for such an inappropriate display of emotions.
- Assamese ballads refer to the insensitive comments of birds that make Ram angry. He elongates the neck of the crane and causes the mythical chakravaka (goose) to wander the night crying out for its mate.
- The chakravaka is sometimes equated with the chakora (partridge) that is in love with the moonlight and weeps all day as its beloved only comes at night. It is a common motif for depicting the emotion of viraha, yearning and separation.
- The story of Ram rejecting the touch of the trees and the sages but promising to do so when he returns as Krishna is also part of folklore.
- It is said that Shakti, much against Shiva's wishes, took the form of Sita and met Ram in order to calm him down. But she did not fool Ram. He recognized her as the Goddess. He bowed to her. This story is part of the Tulja Bhavani legend in Maharashtra. Tulsidas also narrates this story. In his version, the failure of Shakti to recognize Ram's divinity and her desire to test him leads to her immolating herself as Sati.
- Stories that speak of Ram returning as Krishna in his next life connect the two avatars.

This is a recurring motif in the later retellings of Ram's story. It reinforces the image of Ram as the one who has only one wife who is also his beloved, as opposed to Krishna who has many wives and lovers.

Stomach Kabandha

Hanuman then told Sita how he discovered Ram's great skill as a warrior.

Armed with the information given by Jatayu, Ram moved straight south, looking neither this way nor that, not eating, not drinking, not sleeping, determined to find his Sita. Lakshman followed him. Ram was indifferent to the roars of hungry lions and the thunderous feet of wild elephant herds and the thick forest covers that refused to let even a sliver of sunlight reach the ground. He just kept walking.

Further south, the path was blocked by a demon called Kabandha. All the vanaras knew about this terrible beast. It had no head: the head had merged with its stomach; it had two long arms with which it grabbed prey. Its hunger was insatiable and all vanaras kept away from its reach.

Ram and Lakshman suddenly found themselves in its grasp: Ram in one hand and Lakshman in the other. Kabandha's nails were long and sharp, and covered with the blood and entrails of earlier prey, but the two brothers did not show any fear. They simply raised their swords and sliced off its arms in a single swoop, Ram the right arm and Lakshman the left, and made good their escape.

To their surprise, and Hanuman's, the monster thanked the brothers profusely instead of cursing them. 'Without arms to put food into my mouth, I am finally

able to shift my attention from finding food to understanding my hunger, at least in the moments before I die. Thank you. I am Vishwavasu, a gandharva. I was always hungry, for food, for wine, for music, for entertainment, for the company of women. I was too busy indulging my appetite to reflect on my hunger. Worse, I mocked tapasvis who tried to understand and outgrow hunger. One of the rishis I made fun of cursed me that since the head was wasted on me, I would turn into a monster whose stomach was his head, who did nothing all day but eat. One day, a man would come and make it possible for me to think. You have done that, by cutting off my arms, by compelling me to stop eating and reflect on my hunger. I am grateful to you for that. I realize how useless my life has been. Let me make my life worthwhile. Let me help you. Tell me how.'

Ram said, 'We are looking for my wife Sita who has been abducted by the rakshasa-king Ravana. Do you know where he could have taken her?'

'He must have taken her to the city of Lanka, located far to the south. No one has seen this city; it is too far south. But there are rumours that it is splendid, made of gold. You may need the help of the monkeys known as vanaras who live in Kishkindha around Mount Rishyamukha near Lake Pampa. These vanaras are great scouts. They know the whole world well and can find anything you want, for they scour the earth foraging for food.' After speaking these words, Kabandha died.

Hanuman then watched Ram and Lakshman cremate Kabandha. 'They cremate even their enemies. My husband says everyone must be given the option to be reborn,' said Sita to Hanuman.

From the flames arose a celestial being. It was Vishwavasu as he should have been. Ram saw Indra invite the gandharva to his paradise, Amravati, where all hungers are satisfied. But instead of going east where Indra resided, Vishwavasu chose to go north to Mount Kailas, where Shiva teaches all creatures how to outgrow hunger.

Hearing this, Sita asked Hanuman, 'Did my Ram eat after that? Or drink?'

Hanuman replied, 'No. He immediately set out for Kishkindha, refusing to eat or drink.'

'What about Lakshman?'

'He just followed his brother.'

- In the Valmiki *Ramayana*, Lakshman encounters another rakshasa woman called Ayomukhi who tries to seduce him and like Surpanakha gets her nose chopped off.
- Like Viradha, Kabandha is also a rakshasa as the result of a curse. Contact with Ram transforms him, liberates him. And so the story can be seen as one of mind expansion, outgrowing the instinct to feed and focus on hunger alone.
- Because of Kaikeyi, Ram, Lakshman and Sita are exposed to the primal fear related to survival, the end of social certainty and being enveloped by wilderness. In Tantra, this is represented by the Muladhara chakra or the base node located at the anus (the first thing a deer does when scared is clear its bowels and bladder to lighten itself and prepare for the chase and the tiger does the same to mark its territory). Then they are exposed to Viradha and Surpanakha and Ayomukhi who embody sexual desires marked by the Swadishtana chakra or the genital node. Kabandha embodies hunger marked by the Manipura chakra or the stomach node. With Ravana comes the emotional need to control and dominate marked by the Anahata or heart chakra. With Hanuman comes communication, the Vishuddha chakra located at the throat node, which leads to Vibhishana and the rise of insight and conscience, indicated by the Agna or forehead chakra. All this leads to the flowering of the final crown node, the Saharshapadma chakra, of wisdom.
- Ram's meeting Kabandha is key to the *Ramayana* plot as he points the way to the kingdom of monkeys, which transforms the narrative dramatically.

The Berries of Shabari

Hanuman then told Sita how he discovered Ram's sensitivity and compassion.

Ram walked for days and nights, weeping occasionally on thinking about Sita's condition, his body covered with sweat and grime, his unwashed face covered with unkempt hair, his eyes bloodshot.

Lakshman followed his brother silently, feeling guilty at times and ashamed at others. He knew his brother would not tolerate a pitying look or a comforting hug. He just followed him deeper and deeper into the forest, over rocks and streams that no rishi from the north had as yet crossed.

'I get the feeling we are being watched,' said Lakshman, looking above at the trees, noticing a bee.

'Don't get distracted. Let's just keep walking. We need to find the vanaras.'

Then a woman cried out, 'Stop!' Ram stopped. The woman was a resident of the forest, wearing animal skin, feathers and strings of rocks and beads.

'Sit!' she said. Ram sat. 'You look hungry,' she said. 'Perhaps you need to eat. I have berries with me. You can eat them.' Ram looked at the berries in the hand of the strange tribal woman and waited to be served.

The woman bit into a berry and then gave it to Ram. Ram ate it; it was sweet and succulent. She bit into another berry and threw that berry away. She then bit into the third berry and gave it to Lakshman.

Lakshman recoiled in disgust. 'How dare you feed me a fruit that you have bitten into? I am no servant to eat such soiled food. I am Lakshman, prince of Ayodhya, and this is Ram, its king. Don't you have any manners?'

The woman was surprised by Lakshman's outburst. She apologized profusely but Ram comforted her and spoke sternly to his brother: 'Clearly, what I saw is not what you saw. We are two men walking in the forest carrying weapons. We make a fearsome sight yet this woman comes to us. She is surely a brave woman. She stops us for our sake, to feed us; she is under no obligation to do so. She is clearly a caring, generous woman. And she bites into the berries to ensure they are sweet enough. She is a good host. This is what I saw, but what did you see? A woman without manners, manners you learned at the palace. Look at her, Lakshman, she is a forest woman, what does she know of palaces and its manners, its princes and its kings? You judge her by your standards. You don't even look at her. You have eyes, but you are blind.'

Ram ate the berries the woman offered with relish. He did not know her name but he called her Shabari, a woman of the savara tribe. Energized, he resumed his search for Sita.

Hearing this, Sita told Hanuman, 'I am like Shabari's berry. I belong to Ram but Ravana wants to taste me. Will Ram still accept me when I am thus contaminated?'

'In nature, nothing is contaminated,' said Hanuman.

'Ah, but Ram is a king, not a sage. He does not care for nature as much as he cares for culture. In culture, the polluted are cast out.'

- In the Valmiki *Ramayana* Shabari is described as a lowly caretaker of a hermitage whose residents have long died. She waits for the prophesied arrival of Ram and when he does she is so happy that after serving him she seeks liberation. She immolates herself. The story of the berries is not found either in Kamban's Tamil work or in the later Sanskrit *Adhyatma Ramayana*. In the Assamese *Ramayana*, Indra sends a vimana and takes Shabari to his paradise. The story of the berries comes much later in oral folklore, and appears in devotional literature as late as the eighteenth century in writings such as *Bhaktirasbodhini* of Priyadas.
- The feeding of pre-tasted berries (jhoothe ber, in Hindi) comes from the time in Indian history that saw a significant rise in the notion of pollution following contact with bodily fluids. To be untouched by contaminants placed one higher in the purity hierarchy. So people like butchers who dealt with carcasses of animals were considered inferior to vegetarian priests. Ram, the one to free Ahilya on Vishwamitra's instructions, comes into his own when he does not reject Shabari's offering. It shows Ram rising above common social taboos and looking at the humanity of a person. This is the Ram of the people, not the Ram of a priest.
- The *Ramayana* needs to be seen as an organic tradition, created by people who pour into it all that they consider best. The desire to fix and fossilize it is typically seen amongst politicians and academicians who wish to impose their views and dominate all discourse.
- In folk retellings in Odisha, Shabari offers Ram a mango. In other versions, the ber is identified as Indian blackberry or jamun.

Hanuman Reveals Himself

Hanuman then told Sita how he finally revealed himself to Ram.

As Dashratha's sons approached Lake Pampa near Mount Rishyamukha, they were approached by a young hermit. He offered them a mango and said, in chaste Sanskrit, 'Who are you? Your presence frightens every living creature in this forest. You carry weapons like warriors but are dressed like hermits. You walk stridently towards the south, confident in your every move. Are you devas? Are you asuras? Identify yourselves, strangers.'

Lakshman's hand reached for his sword. He was anxious.

Ram said, 'You see us as a threat and my brother sees you as a threat. Like rival beasts we can measure each other wondering who is stronger and smarter. But we are not beasts. We are humans. I see you and you see me. I see you speak in a polished tongue, indicating you know the meaning of being cultured. And you see me as an armed hermit, indicating I am confused, perhaps like Parashurama or Vishwamitra, neither completely warrior nor completely sage. Let me tell you who I am and then you tell me who you are.'

Ram proceeded to introduce himself, telling the hermit his tragic tale, how he had to live in the forest to keep his father's word to Kaikeyi, how his wife had been abducted by a demon in the forest and how he was looking for her. 'I have been told in these mountains dwell vanaras who can help me.'

The hermit replied, 'Long have I watched you, ever since the whole forest saw Ravana tear our Jatayu's wing in the sky. I watched you cremate the poor bird, kill Kabandha, and accept Shabari's berries. You are not an ordinary man. Now you tell me you let your brother be king of the kingdom that is rightfully yours. This is extraordinary. All living creatures I know chase food, grab food and hoard food. No one gives anyone anything; at best the parent, until the children can fend for themselves. Never have I heard of a creature who gives up his own pleasure to please someone else. You reveal a possibility that I never knew existed in humanity. I bow to you. I am Hanuman, son of Anjana and Kesari, servant of Sugriva, leader of the vanaras.'

The hermit then changed form and turned into a monkey.

'See, he is not what he appeared to be,' said Lakshman, grabbing an arrow.

'How do you expect him to show us the truth about him until we gain his trust? He trusts us now. It is time you trusted him too,' said Ram.

'Come sit on my shoulders,' said Hanuman, 'and I will

carry you to Mount Rishyamukha where Sugriva resides. On the way I will tell you our tale.'

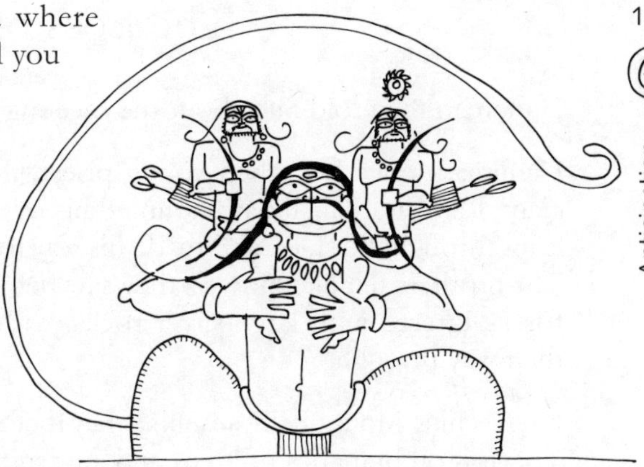

Sita looked at the small monkey and wondered how he had managed to carry Ram and Lakshman on his shoulders and fly.

With a twinkle in his eye, Hanuman said, 'Looks can be deceptive, as you well know. A golden deer can be a shape-shifting demon and a small monkey can be a shape-shifting god.'

- Pampa is sometimes identified not as a lake but as the Tungabhadra river. Some scholars trace the name Hampi in Karnataka, seat of the sixteenth-century Vijayanagara empire, to Pampa.
- Hanuman is known in literature for his command over Sanskrit. As a language, Sanskrit is considered a highly designed, structured and ornamental language as opposed to Prakrit which is more organic. Sanskrit is called deva-bhasha, language of the gods, while Prakrit is called manushya-bhasha, language of humans. In ancient India, the masses and all women spoke Prakrit. Sanskrit was restricted to priests and kings. That Hanuman knows the language, even though he is a monkey, makes him special.
- Hanuman is always called a monkey while Ravana, besides being called a demon, is constantly identified as the son of a brahmin, hence a member of the brahmin jati. Thus, in the forest, Ram hears of two creatures, one of the highest caste and one of the lowest (or no) caste, both of whom speak the language of the gods, both of whom are very different in nature. In Ravana, the animal instinct to dominate and be territorial is amplified, while in Hanuman it is outgrown.
- Mewati Jogis of Rajasthan who are Muslims as well as devotees of Shiva are bards who sing a song called '*Lanka Chadhai*' or the assault on Lanka. They say how a hungry Ram sends Lakshman in search of fruit. Lakshman encounters a monkey in an orchard who accuses him of theft and swallows him up. Ram fights Hanuman and sounds of the fight reach Shiva. Shiva comes to the rescue of Hanuman and fights Ram. Ram's touch cures Shiva of a skin ailment. Pleased, Shiva offers two boons to Ram. Ram asks for Lakshman, and Lakshman – who has realized Hanuman's strength while being locked in his stomach – asks for the support of Hanuman. That is how Hanuman comes to follow Ram.

The Loss of Wives

Hanuman then told Sita about the meeting between Ram and Sugriva.

Hanuman, once bee, then young priest, then tiny monkey, transformed into a giant. Ram and Lakshman mounted his mighty shoulders and were amazed as he leapt through the skies, and made his way to Sugriva's hideout atop Rishyamukha. The brothers felt like birds as they saw below them the carpet of the dense green forest, littered with large silver rocks, with glistening blue-green rivers snaking their way through.

On reaching Mount Rishyamukha, they met Sugriva. Introductions were exchanged. They sat on branches of trees and ate fruit and refreshed themselves with water from mountain springs as Hanuman narrated the tale of the sons of Dashratha to Sugriva.

'Tell me, scion of the Raghu clan, do you recognize these?' said Sugriva, presenting to Ram something wrapped in cloth.

Ram opened the cloth and found within exquisitely carved gold jewellery: rings of Sita's toes, fingers and nose, her anklets, her bracelets, her armlets, her waistband. Ram could not breathe. Lakshman said, 'I recognize those anklets. They are those that adorned the feet of my elder brother's wife. These must belong to Sita.'

Sugriva explained, 'I saw Ravana on a flying chariot carrying a woman with him. She was writhing and resisting, screaming out for someone called Ram, casting away these jewels on the forest floor as if to leave a trail. I got my monkeys to pick them up. I sent Hanuman north to investigate.'

'Do you know where Lanka is?' asked Ram, running his fingers delicately over Sita's jewellery.

'No vanara has laid eyes on it. It is much further south,' said Sugriva.

'Enough about my sorrows,' said Ram. 'Tell me why you live like a refugee in your own kingdom. Hanuman says you dare not leave this mountain.'

Sugriva then proceeded to tell Ram his tragic tale of the misunderstanding between his brother Vali and him. 'You lost your wife to Ravana; I lost my wife to my own brother. Help me and I will surely help you.'

Sita wondered what hurt Sugriva more: loss of kingdom or loss of wife. Kishkindha he was obliged to share with his brother, not Ruma. Now the brother had both, kingdom and wife.

'Do you always think so much?' Hanuman asked Sita.

'Is that bad?' asked Sita.

'The vanaras say it is the undoing of naras.'

'The difference between vanaras and naras is thought. Thought allows nara to discover Narayana.'

'Who is Narayana?'

'The sleeping Vishnu: our human potential that awaits blossoming.'

'What is this human potential?'

'To see the world from another's point of view, and make sense of it.'

'I think it has blossomed in Ram.'

'I agree.'

'I think it has blossomed in Sita too,' said Hanuman.

- Flying captures the imagination of Valmiki. Ravana flies on Pushpak Vimana. Hanuman flies to Kishkindha and later to Lanka.
- Long before Indians became familiar with the European fairy tale of Hansel and Gretel leaving a trail of breadcrumbs, they had heard about the trail of Sita's jewels.
- The narrative repeatedly stresses how Lakshman never saw Sita's face and how Sita never saw Ravana's face and how Ram never saw Tadaka's face. Thus looking upon the face has an intimacy that is traditionally associated with eroticism. In the animal kingdom, to look into another animal's eye evokes a threat response; lowering the eyes or looking away is an indicator of submission.
- Gold is an auspicious metal in India. Ram adorns his Sita with gold jewellery. Ravana lives in a city of gold. For Ram, gold must be placed on the body, while Ravana has gold at his feet. It is a golden deer that enchants Sita. The *Ramayana* thus reveals the dark side of gold, its ability to lure and entrap. Sita gives up her gold jewellery for what really matters in life.
- Unlike the brothers of the Raghu clan, the vanara brothers have to share their throne but a misunderstanding separates them. No one gives the other the benefit of the doubt.
- In Kerala's Theyyam tradition, Vali is visualized and worshipped as a deity and is often called the 'long-tailed', an indicator of both his physical and sexual prowess.
- In the monkey world, the alpha is the strongest monkey who claims all the females and foraging lands for himself and who keeps bachelor monkeys away from his harem and kills all rivals. Probably Vali and Sugriva followed monkey-like practices and so Valmiki identified them as monkeys. That they were sharing the kingdom shows that they are a step away from animal nature. But the animal nature returns when Vali kicks Sugriva out and claims his wife, Ruma.

Lessons from the Sun

'Why did you not help Sugriva yourself?' asked Sita. 'You are so strong and smart. Surely you could defeat Vali.'

Hanuman then explained to Sita his relationship with the sun and the son of the sun.

Hanuman wanted to study everything that there was to study. So he approached the sun who saw everything that there is to see on earth. But Surya was reluctant to teach him as he was busy all day riding across the sky and too tired to do anything at night. A persistent Hanuman had flown in front of Surya's chariot as the sun moved east to west, facing the sun-god, withstanding his glare, determined to learn one way or another. Pleased with this display of determination, Surya taught

Hanuman the Vedas, the Vedangas, the Upavedas, the Tantras and the Shastras. Surya's teachings helped Hanuman master every siddha and transform into a tapasvi. That is why Hanuman could, at will, expand his body, contract his body, change shape, fly like a bird, become heavy or weightless, attract and dominate. In exchange for this knowledge, Surya had only one request, 'Take care of my son, Sugriva, who is not as strong as Indra's son, Vali. Be his friend always.'

'And so I am always by Sugriva's side, protecting him. But that does not mean I have to oppose Vali, son of Indra. I see Sugriva's point of view and I see Vali's point of view. For Sugriva, Vali is being unreasonable. For Vali, Sugriva has done something that is unpardonable. Both are right from their point of view,' said Hanuman to Sita.

'That is so true,' said Sita.

Lakshman, however, did not think so. When he had heard the same story, he had said, 'You are like Shiva, who supports the rakshasas and the yakshas, the devas and the asuras. Don't you think you have to take sides, like Vishnu? You must side with the right and fight for the powerless.'

Hanuman had replied, 'But who decides who is right? Both Sugriva and Vali are convinced they are right. And who decides who is powerless? Is Ram powerless because he is in exile? Is Sita powerless because Ravana has abducted her? Does power come from within or is it granted from outside?'

Hanuman then told Lakshman a story he had heard from Surya.

Once Indra's Swarga was threatened by an asura who attacked them in the form of a buffalo. So the devas went to Shiva for help. He told the gods to release their inner strengths and merge it into one entity. From within came their Shaktis. The many Shaktis of the devas merged into a blinding light to become Durga. Durga, a goddess with many arms, entered the battlefield riding a lion, attacked the buffalo-demon Mahisha-asura and impaled him with her trident. Hanuman asked Lakshman, 'Tell me, brother of Ram, who would you protect: the devas from the buffalo or the buffalo from the armed, lion-riding goddess?'

'The devas are the victims and Durga is their saviour,' Lakshman said.

Hanuman then told Lakshman another story that Surya had told him.

'Long ago, the devas and the asuras churned the ocean of milk and out came many treasures. Amongst them the wish-fulfilling tree Kalpataru, the wish-fulfilling cow Kamadhenu, the wish-fulfilling gem Chintamani and Amrita, the nectar of immortality. Vishnu took the form of Mohini, enchanted everyone and promised to distribute these treasures freely but gave Amrita only to the devas. This made the devas so powerful that they claimed all the treasures for themselves and turned their abode Amravati into Swarga, paradise of pleasures. The asuras thus cheated never forgave the devas, attacking them repeatedly in various forms, like the buffalo-demon. So who are the real victims? Devas or asuras?'

This is when Ram spoke up. 'Why do you assume that Vishnu sides with the devas? Is it because he grants them the nectar of immortality? Yes, after drinking Amrita no longer do the devas fear death. Why then are they still so insecure? What are they afraid of losing? Why do they cling to their treasures? Yes, Vishnu gave the devas prosperity, but did he give them peace, for they still grant themselves an identity through things? And yes, Shiva gives everything to the asuras and to the rakshasas and the yakshas, everything they ask him for. But what do they ask him for? They ask him for wealth and power – things once again. They never ask him to help them outgrow their hunger. They never ask him to expand their mind with thoughts. And so hunger gnaws at their being as fear gnaws at the being of the devas. The fight continues endlessly, with victory following defeat with unfailing regularity, led by those who believe they are right and those who believe they are powerless.'

Every vanara had then looked at Ram as students gaze upon a teacher. Ram said, 'Know this: Durga is strength that we get from the outside. Shakti is strength that is inside. Nature gives us Shakti. Human society is designed to grant Durga through tools, rules and property. But having lived in the forest this long, for over thirteen years, both Sita and I have learned to value Shakti, not Durga. For strength from within is always there; strength from without may or may not be there. Ravana, however, seeks strength from outside. He seeks to punish the man whose brother mutilated his sister. He sees my wife as my property; by stealing her he wants me to feel deprived. He does not see Sita as a person, who did him no harm. I do not blame him. I am not angry with him. I see his point of view. I do think he is wrong. I do not begrudge him his power. I just seek to rescue my Sita, restore her freedom to her.'

'You do not judge Ravana?' Sugriva asked.

'No, I understand where he is coming from, just as I understood where Kaikeyi came from,' Ram replied. 'Ravana is capable of so much more. But he refuses to be what he can be. So he imagines me as his enemy, and refuses to see me for who I am. Like Kaikeyi, he is consumed by his own notion of what is reality.'

'Hearing Ram speak thus,' said Hanuman to Sita, 'I realized Ram was a true brahmin, he who expands his mind and of those around him, a householder with the mind of a hermit. He does not need a kingdom to be king.'

'He does not need control over a wife to be a husband,' said Sita.

- Indra and Surya are major deities in Vedic hymns. In Puranic stories, they take a subordinate position to Vishnu. When Vishnu descends as Ram, the old gods join him as vanaras: Indra through Vali and Surya through Sugriva.
- In the Upanishads, Yagnavalkya gets wisdom from the sun. In the Puranas, Hanuman gets wisdom from the sun. The sun is the source of all light and energy and hence the symbol of divinity. The famous Gayatri mantra from the *Rig Veda* is an invocation to this sun that dispels the darkness of ignorance.
- In temple art, the sun is often visualized seated on a chariot pulled by seven horses.
- Hanuman is at once the great sage, the mighty warrior and the curious monkey. Though he serves Sugriva and never seeks the limelight, he slowly emerges like the rising sun and becomes a dominant character in the epic. His role becomes increasingly central in medieval times with the rise of devotional texts.
- In folklore, Vali is annoyed that Sugriva has outwitted him by taking refuge on Mount Rishyamukha where he cannot step into because of a curse. So just to rile Sugriva, he leaps over the mountain several times a day and kicks Sugriva on the head. Finally, one day, Hanuman catches Vali by the ankle and threatens to pull him down to the mountain. Vali knows that if he so much as touches the mountain, his head will burst into a thousand pieces. Terrified, he tries in vain to escape Hanuman's grasp. Finally, they both agree that Vali will leave Sugriva alone as long as he stays in Rishyamukha.
- Hanuman serves Ram unconditionally. Unlike Sugriva, he has nothing to gain materially but he does gain a lot emotionally. Ram becomes a guru and Hanuman the perfect student, content to bask in the guru's glory even though he can easily outshine him.
- Exchanging stories is a key part of living in the forest. Stories are the tool through which wisdom spread in India. From Shiva comes the Brihad-katha, the ocean of stories, passed on to humanity through bards and storytellers. Scholars see India as the home of many of the folktales that reached Europe through Arab traders.
- Storytelling plays a key role in Hinduism, less explicitly in old ritualistic Vedic Hinduism than in later temple-based Puranic Hinduism. Divinity manifests in three forms: the hermit Shiva, the householder Vishnu and the Goddess who is the earth. Wisdom manifests in

how Shiva and Vishnu engage with the Goddess. Ingnorance is expressed through the relationship of Brahma and his sons with the Goddess. The Goddess is invoked by many names but the most common name is Shakti, power. Those who appreciate Hinduism through Shiva are called Shaivas, those who do so through Vishnu are called Vaishnavas and those who do so through Shakti are called Shaktas.

- It is very easy to see Ram as a classical Greek hero, wronged by the villain. But the *Ramayana* is a vehicle for Indic thought and notions of wisdom. At the heart of it is the human quest for validation through property. Ram is God because he understands the futility of property. Identity must come despite property, not because of it, something the learned Ravana fails to appreciate.
- All Indic religions – Hinduism, Buddhism and Jainism – explore the relationship of man's quest for power through things. Unlike Greek narratives, where achievement is celebrated, and biblical narratives, where submission and discipline are celebrated, in Indic thought understanding is celebrated.

The Death of Vali

Hanuman then told Sita how Sugriva finally became king of Kishkindha.

'He is all philosophical like a sage. That is fine. But I really need a warrior who can kill Vali,' said Sugriva. In response, Ram took an arrow out of his quiver, mounted it on his bow, pulled the string, chanted a mantra and released the arrow. Everyone watched in amazement as the arrow pierced seven palm trees and then turned to return to Ram's quiver.

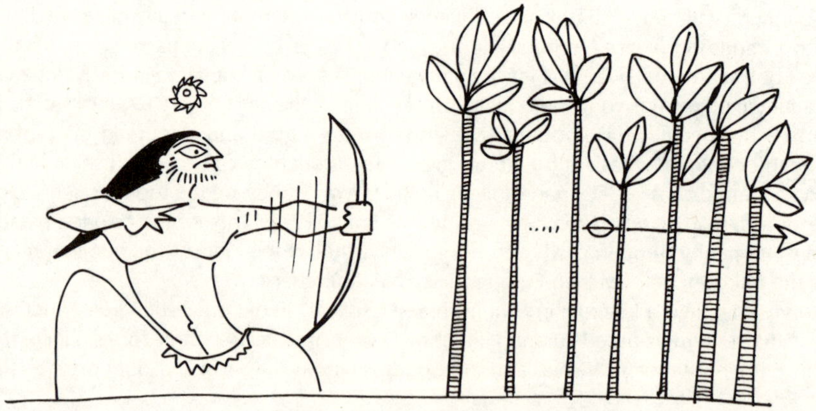

'You are skilled. But are you strong?' asked Sugriva.

In response, Ram kicked the carcass of Dundhubi, now reduced to bones, so hard that it flew off the slopes of Rishyamukha and landed right in the middle of Kishkindha.

'This is wonderful. You can shoot him with your arrow while I engage him in a duel. You help me become king of Kishkindha and I will get my vanaras to find your Sita and help you rescue her.'

'Why don't I invite him to a duel and defeat him in a fair fight?' asked Ram.

'Then you, not I, will become master of Kishkindha. You will be my saviour and not my assistant. The vanaras will follow you, not me. Unless I engage him in a duel and he dies in that duel, no one will respect me. And fairness: that is a concept for cities, not the jungle.'

To seal this agreement and their friendship, Hanuman lit a fire and, holding each other's hands, Ram and Sugriva walked around it seven times. Thus bound by ritual, the two were now obliged to be faithful to each other.

Sita realized that the Sugriva being described by Hanuman was vaishya-varna, a monkey with the calculating mind of a trader, while his rival Vali was kshatriya-varna, a monkey with the dominating mind of a master. Perhaps only Hanuman was a monkey with the empathizing and curious mind of a seer, so strong yet not seeking to be powerful, so wise and yet never flaunting his wisdom.

Hanuman then described the duel between the two monkey brothers.

Mace in hand, Sugriva roared out his challenge to Vali. Vali, with a sneer, left the company of Tara, who tried in vain to stop the brothers from fighting, and came to fight his cowardly brother in a clearing of the woods. Bow in hand, Ram hid behind some bushes.

Sugriva was no match for Vali. A few punches and kicks later, Sugriva was running for cover.

'Why did you not shoot your arrow?' he asked Ram angrily.

'You both look so alike. Challenge him again at dawn tomorrow. But wear a garland of forest flowers around your neck so that I can distinguish you. By dusk tomorrow, Vali will be dead and you will be king,' said Ram.

And so, the next day, Sugriva, with a garland around his neck and a mace in his

hand, once again challenged Vali to a duel in the clearing of the woods. 'This time, I will kill you, so that you do not trouble me again,' snarled Vali as he stomped out of Kishkindha.

The fight was fierce. Everyone watched Vali strike Sugriva mercilessly with his mace, biting his cheek in rage and tearing his skin with his nails. Sugriva looked like a helpless prey and Vali a fierce predator. No one would believe they were brothers.

That is when Ram shot his arrow from behind the trees and it hit its mark, ripping through Vali's back and tearing into his heart. Vali gave out a yelp and fell to the ground.

The vanaras who watched this fight from afar hooted angrily at this foul play. Tara ran to her husband and wailed when she realized there was no hope: the great Vali would die. 'Who did this?' she demanded to know.

'I did it,' said Ram. 'I am Ram, scion of the Raghu clan, representative of Bharata, king of Ayodhya, and friend to Sugriva who will help me find my Sita who has been abducted by the rakshasa-king Ravana.'

'This coward will help you?' Vali wanted to laugh despite the unbearable pain. 'He who defeats me through foul play? If you wanted to save Sita why did you not just come to me? I am stronger than Ravana. I had once bound him by my tail and kept him as a pet in Kishkindha. Why did you side with this weakling who uses cunning to defeat the strong? Is that fair? Is that right?'

Sita interjected, 'Vali grabs the kingdom he is supposed to share and now demands rules of civilized conduct be followed in war. Is it not strange that the most unfair people in the world often demand fairness?'

Hanuman, student of the sun-god, who knew the nature of Vali and his father, Indra, explained, 'Fairness is a human concept. It does not exist in the jungle. All that matters is survival, one way or another. Sugriva had found his way. To be outsmarted by his weaker brother, that was too much for Vali to handle. So he argued by appealing to humanity and civilization.'

Hanuman then proceeded to tell Sita how Ram had responded to Vali's accusation.

'You lived by one code of animals: you used force to get your way. Your brother has used another code of animals: he used cunning to get his way. Why do you then cry foul? Why do you speak of human values? You who lived like an animal all your life should accept being killed like an animal. I am the hunter and you are my trophy. And Sugriva is the beneficiary of this sport of kings.'

Holding the dying Vali in her arms, Tara cursed Ram, 'You killed my husband so that you can get your wife. May you never find peace when she is by your side.' Only then, with vengeful satisfaction, did Vali breathe his last.

Fair or not, a new pecking order had been established in Kishkindha. The vanaras, who until then had followed Vali, simply turned to Sugriva and accepted his leadership. Even Tara accepted Sugriva as her new lord. For such is the way of animals.

- Sugriva needs evidence to trust Ram; Lakshman needs evidence to trust Hanuman; neither Ram nor Hanuman need it to trust each other.
- The Valmiki *Ramayana* narrates the peculiar practice of Ram and Sugriva going around a fire to seal their friendship. This practice is not referred to anywhere else and is seen only in marriages. Perhaps it was an old Vedic practice of publicly acknowledging a relationship, something akin to the modern contract.
- In the *Ram-Sita-ni-varta*, the *Ramayana* of the Bhil tribes, the identities of Hanuman and Sugriva are merged. Lakshman drinks water from a pond and finds it is actually a pool of tears shed by a monkey who mourns for his wife. The monkey is identified with Hanuman/Sugriva whose wife has been abducted by Aria and Ram promises to secure his wife if he promises to help find Sita in exchange.
- People are divided on the tale of Ram killing Vali clandestinely. Most are convinced it is an act of cowardice and see any alternative explanation as forced justification. In the Sanskrit play *Mahavira-charita*, Bhavabhuti makes it a fair fight with Ram and Vali fighting face to face. Kamban does not try to explain it and assumes this is divine play at work that is

incomprehensible to mortals. Finally, there are stories narrated to explain why Ram does what he does: Vali has a boon that he will get, over and above his own strength, half the strength of all those who come before him and so the only way to kill him is by stealth.

- Dharma is often assumed to be a set of universal moral and ethical laws. Such universal laws do not exist but are imagined by all humans in every society because humans want them to exist. What exists is universal natural law, where the fit survive using strength and cunning. Social law with its notions of what is right and fair keeps changing with time, with place, with context and with the people involved. The beneficiaries of social law are convinced their laws are fair and right. But those who do not benefit from the same laws reject them and spark revolutions.
- Sugriva and Ram kill Vali by trickery. In nature, trickery is a valid tool of survival. In culture, trickery is often frowned upon but strength is respected, perhaps because trickery is too intangible for comfort.
- Ram is called maryada purushottam, the supreme upholder of rules. Whose rules does he uphold? Ayodhya's or Kishkindha's? Must he impose his rules on others?
- The scriptures wonder who decides what is fair: must the dominant Vali decide, must the deprived Sugriva decide or must the outsider Ram decide? Can the villain who treats everyone unfairly demand he be treated fairly by the victim? Does a hero impose fairness upon himself to feel good about himself and to create a fair society, and in doing so does he make himself vulnerable to villains who do not understand or respect or care for fairness? These subtle questions are provoked by the Vali story.
- The spot where Vali is killed, like other spots associated with various events in the *Ramayana*, has been located in different parts of India from Karnataka to Kerala to Assam.
- In the Tamil and Telugu *Ramayanas*, Tara is described as emerging from the ocean of milk and is given to both Sugriva and Vali who participated in the churning of the ocean.

A New King in Kishkindha

Hanuman then told Sita about the coronation of Sugriva.

In Swarga, Indras come and go, but Sachi stays the queen of paradise. She is married to the throne, not the person who sits on it. This is the code of the devas. This was also the code of the vanaras. Tara would be queen to whosoever was the leader of the vanaras. Once she was Vali's queen, now she was Sugriva's.

Ruma, Sugriva's first wife and now junior queen, said, 'Vali took me as wife to punish Sugriva. Sugriva takes Tara as wife to declare his right over the throne. Vali was driven by rage and Sugriva is driven by rules. Either way, it is I who suffers.' But no one heard her voice.

A dominant monkey kills all the children of the previous king as they are potential rivals. So Tara braced herself to watch Sugriva kill her son Angada without mercy.

'This must stop,' said Ram. 'For our friendship to thrive you must give up the way of animals and accept the way of humans. Tara must not be a trophy and Angada must not be seen as a rival. You must open your heart to see her as your wife and him as your son and heir. And you must find a way to make sure that Ruma does not feel she is less favoured, for I have personally seen the cost of such preferences. You must be king because you can care for all, not because you are stronger and smarter than the rest.'

Sugriva agreed to follow the path of the rishis when he was crowned king of Kishkindha. He swore he would change the ways of the vanaras. They would outgrow their animal instincts and be more human. They would submit to dharma not adharma.

Great celebrations were held to mark the occasion. The best of fruits and berries and nuts and tubers and flowers and pots of honey and bundles of sugar cane from every corner of Kishkindha were gathered so that everyone could feast and make the day memorable. Ram and Lakshman withdrew silently and watched the monkeys dance and sing and celebrate from a hill afar. 'Thus they would have danced and sung the day you would have been crowned king,' said Lakshman wistfully.

'Let us not allow our minds to wander to the past or to what could have happened. Let us focus on the future and what should happen,' said Ram.

Just as the celebrations came to an end, the rainy season arrived. A bit early, some might say; perhaps Indra was angry as his son Vali had been killed by Vishnu's avatar on earth. Clouds covered the sun and the sky. Wet mists covered the mountains. Thunder rumbled and roared. Lightning split the sky and the waters poured with a fury never seen before. The earth was covered with water. Rivers swelled and broke their banks. Mud slid from mountainsides, carrying rocks and trees and animals with it.

'The search for Sita may have to wait till the rains end,' said Sugriva. Ram nodded grimly in agreement.

For four months it rained. The vanaras hid in caves, eating what little they had hoarded or could find. Most of the time, they embraced their mates and made love, for there is little else to do at times like these. And the smell of wet earth and the sound of pouring rain is intoxicating. Kishkindha was filled with the sound of the monkeys' love sport.

'I stood outside the caves, watching Ram atop a hill, facing south, patiently yearning for you,' Hanuman told Sita.

'All these days in the garden of Ashoka trees I have sat facing north, in full faith,' said Sita to Hanuman.

- Angada who is Vali's son is declared Sugriva's heir and this is significant. The old king may be dead but an attempt is made to make peace with the past, not wipe it out. Revolutions often seek to wipe out all traces of the past – like the book burnings by Chinese emperors, or the denial of the pagan past by the Church in the Middle Ages, or of the mythical past by the scientific revolution. But this only festers rage and resentment that explodes into yet another revolution in the future.
- In the *Ramayana*, Vishnu as Ram supports Surya's son (Sugriva) against Indra's son (Vali). In the *Mahabharata*, Vishnu as Krishna supports Indra's son (Arjuna) against Surya's son (Karna). Thus balance is restored over two lifetimes.
- In ancient times, in some communities, a brave man acquired property by marrying a woman. Property was linked to the woman. She did not go to the husband's house; he came to hers. She was initially linked to the immovable asset, land, but gradually she came to be associated with movable assets like gold, popularly called stri-dhan or women's wealth. This is probably why women like Kaikeyi and Kaushalya in the *Ramayana* are given names linking them to the land they belong to. In Lanka, we find Lankini, identified with Lakshmi, who serves Kubera and then serves Ravana and finally Vibhishana.
- The idea of a woman serving more than one man disturbed the conservative section of India and so emerged the concept of Panchakanya, or five virgins, to indicate women who regained their virginity after intimacy with a man. These included three from the *Ramayana*: Ahilya, Tara and Mandodari. Only two are from the *Mahabharata*: Kunti and Draupadi. Sita is sometimes named instead of Kunti but this is unacceptable to most Hindus as Sita is seen as being only Ram's in mind and body.

Lakshman's Rage

Hanuman then told Sita about a delicate moment that could have led to war between Sugriva's vanaras and the sons of Dashratha.

Slowly the rains stopped. The land dried up. Green trees with yellow flowers covered the earth. The sky had no clouds and the moon shone brightly.

Ram waited for Sugriva to summon his monkeys and begin the search for Sita. But there was no sign of Sugriva. He was still busy with the song and dance and food and pleasure of his queens.

Ram waited and waited, and waited. Patience gradually wore away and was replaced by irritation, then rage. 'What is wrong? Why does he not keep his promise?'

'Because he is a liar and a cheat,' roared Lakshman. 'Let me teach that ungrateful monkey a lesson.' He picked up his bow and stormed towards the pleasure garden of Sugriva.

Watching him approach thus, full of rage, Hanuman became nervous. He rushed to Sugriva's side and warned him against upsetting the brothers. 'Ram killed Vali with a single arrow. He will hunt you down with less.' Sugriva snapped out of his happy drunken stupor, realizing his mistake. But who would calm Lakshman down? All the monkeys were afraid.

'I will,' said Tara. 'He will not harm a woman.'

'Don't be too sure,' said her son Angada. 'Remember how Ram dealt with Tadaka and Lakshman with Surpanakha?'

Fearlessly, Tara went to Lakshman, her palms joined, her face gentle and friendly. She found him facing, bow in hand. 'Where is the cheat who does not keep his word? Where is the good-for-nothing who forgets his promise when he gets what he wants? Where is the coward who calls himself king of Kishkindha?' he kept shouting.

Tara had approached him without bothering to arrange her clothes. Her hair was dishevelled. Her body was exposed, covered with marks of lovemaking. Her walk was the unsteady gait of a person reeling from the effects of great pleasure. 'Calm down, prince. You are indeed right and he is indeed wrong. But is it necessary to shatter the peace of this pleasure garden?' she murmured.

Embarrassed, Lakshman looked away. He felt like an intruder. His righteous indignation waned.

Tara then said in a voice that was like gentle music, 'Do not utter such harsh words, son. For years, Sugriva lived in the jungles, deprived of food and all the pleasures of life. Now finally he has obtained these and it is but natural that he would overindulge and in doing so lose sense of time. In the arms of an apsara a hundred years seem like a single night to a tapasvi, so you can appreciate what it does to a mere vanara. Empathize and forgive.' As she spoke, the flames of anger slowly died down. Lakshman understood.

Lowering his bow, Lakshman said, 'I can forgive but cannot empathize. I have never known the pleasure you speak of. I am impatient to experience it, but for that another year has to pass. Next autumn, I shall be with my Urmila, but only if I am able to rescue Sita for my brother Ram. And that I cannot do unless I get the help of Sugriva and his monkeys. So please tell him to summon his monkeys without delay.'

Sita remembered Lakshman fondly: earnest, loyal, quick to anger and easy to please. She could picture his nostrils flaring as he gave the orders. So simple and so different from his stoic brother.

- The Kishkindha-kanda ends with the coronation of Sugriva and the Sundara-kanda begins with the search for Sita. These are the fourth and fifth chapters of the *Ramayana*.
- The incessant rains seem like the revenge of Indra, the rain-god, who is angry with Ram who killed his son Vali.
- In Kamban's *Ramayana*, Tara approaches Lakshman without any jewellery or cosmetics.

Draped in a single cloth, she looks like a widow and reminds Lakshman of his mother the last time he met her at Chitrakut. This calms him down.

- Tara comes across as a negotiator and peacemaker. She shows a capability that Sugriva lacks. Her beauty and intelligence put her in a class of her own, giving rise to folklore that she was churned out of the ocean of milk by the gods. She was no ordinary vanara.
- The *Ramayana* is sensitive to the human condition: how time moves differently depending on our emotional state. When you are indulging in pleasure, time moves fast. In sorrow, time moves slowly. What is but a blink of the eye for Sugriva is an excruciatingly long wait for Ram.

Search Parties

Hanuman then told Sita how Sugriva emerged sheepishly from the pleasure garden, ready to throw himself at Ram's feet. But Ram was not interested in dwelling on the past. Nor was he interested in seeking satisfaction in Sugriva's supplication. He was interested only in finding out where Sita was.

Soon Sugriva's hundreds of thousands of monkeys gathered in Kishkindha, much to Ram's delight. They would scour the earth and find Sita, assured Sugriva. It was clear that Lanka was in the south. But where in the south? South-east or south-west? Over the hills, in the valleys, or deep in the forest? Groups of monkeys were appointed to travel in different directions.

Ram suggested that Hanuman be sent in the group led by Angada. 'Surely Hanuman should be the leader of a group?' said Sugriva.

'This group is most likely to find Lanka. Angada is young and too inexperienced to be a leader. He needs the experience. This is a great opportunity for him. Hanuman has the wisdom to let him lead, while keeping an eye on him,' said Ram. So Angada prepared to leave with a band of monkeys, with Hanuman by his side.

'Before leaving, I went to Ram and asked him how you would know that I was your messenger. I asked him to give me something that would help me gain your trust. That is when he gave me his signet ring, the one jewel he was not allowed to remove from his body by his father when he set out for exile.'

Sita looked at Ram's ring, impressed by Hanuman's foresight.

- It is indeed curious that Hanuman is not made a leader of monkeys in the Valmiki *Ramayana* despite his great strength. It is the audiences who have transformed Hanuman from super-monkey to god. He is strong and smart, and also wise enough to withdraw and let others enjoy the limelight.
- In the Valmiki *Ramayana*, Sugriva gives an elaborate description of every corner of the world that his scouts have to scour. Sugriva explains to Ram that he had travelled to all corners of the world (except Lanka) trying to escape Vali, till he finally found refuge in Rishyamukha.
- Since Ram is a hermit who gave up royal robes and ornaments, how does he wear a ring of gold? Questions such as these are part of the *Shankhavali*, or the garland of doubts, popular Hindi books written in the nineteenth and twentieth centuries to address doubts emerging from reading Tulsidas's Avadhi *Ram-charit-manas*. One answer states that the ring was actually Sita's. She had given it to Ram to repay Guha, the boatman, for his kindness. Guha had not accepted the ring and it had stayed in Ram's possession.

Scouring the South

Hanuman then told Sita of his adventures until he reached the shores of the sea.

The troops travelled south first through familiar forests and then through unfamiliar ones. They found new rivers and new mountains, new animals and new birds. The only thing that did not change was the sky with its stars and its constellations and its comets.

The monkeys told everyone they encountered the tale of Sita's Ram. Many joined the quest to find the wife of the unfathomable man who quite serenely gave up his kingdom to his brother, who did not see his wife's abductor as a villain and who had inspired monkeys to outgrow their natural animal instincts. He had to be special. Until then, the denizens of the forest had only encountered creatures who saw everything in the world either as threats to their life or as opportunities for food. Only Ram seemed to see the world as full of potential, with the ability to look beyond oneself at the fear and hunger of others.

Amongst those who joined the search party was an old bear called Jambuvan, who was convinced this prince of Ayodhya was Vishnu on earth.

Somewhere in the south, Angada's group of monkeys saw cows going to a termite hill and voluntarily shedding their milk on it. Within, the monkeys saw a Shiva-linga. The serpents around the termite hill told them Ravana had placed it there.

In his many trips north to Mount Kailas, Ravana had asked Shiva to give him something that would represent him symbolically. 'I will enshrine it in Lanka and worship it with unboiled milk and fresh leaves of the bilva and flowers of the dhatura,' he had said. Ravana knew that this representation of Shiva placed in Lanka would render his city eternally invincible.

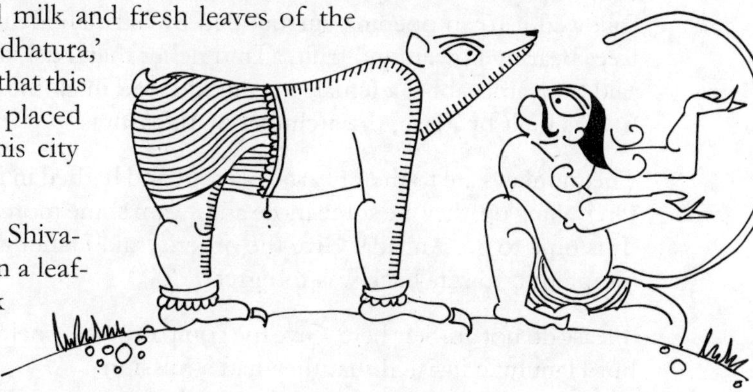

So Shiva gave Ravana a Shiva-linga, a rock held firmly in a leaf-shaped trough. 'The rock would roll aimlessly had the trough not held it. I am the rock and Shakti is the trough. Always worship us together. Do not place this on the ground, for it will get rooted to the earth wherever you place it,' Shiva said.

As Ravana went southwards with the Shiva-linga in his hand, Indra was disturbed, for if Ravana's city became invincible, he would become a greater threat to the world. He begged Ganesha to help him.

Ganesha used his power over water to induce in Ravana the urge to urinate. Ravana controlled this urge using siddha but it became so unbearable that no amount of tapa was enough to quell it. So he looked around and found a cowherd standing nearby. Ravana begged the cowherd to hold the Shiva-linga, pleading with him not to place it on the ground, while he urinated.

But there was so much urine to pass that hours went by. Ravana could not stop and watched in utter helplessness, from behind the bushes, as the cowherd grew tired and, despite the screams and pleas of Ravana, placed the Shiva-linga on the ground. Only then did Ravana's bladder empty. A furious Ravana tried to forcefully uproot the Shiva-linga but all he managed to do was twist the trough with great force until it looked like a cow's ear. Thus the Shiva-linga from Kailas did not reach Lanka. It rooted itself midway.

Jambuvan, Angada and Hanuman worshipped the Shiva-linga with river water, dhatura flowers and bilva leaves and made their way further south.

The land suddenly turned dry and there was not a drop of water to drink. The sun above burned their skin and the hot earth seared their soles. Then Hanuman saw birds leaving a cave. Their wings were wet. 'There is water in that cave. I am sure of it,' he said.

Sure enough, they found water in the cave. It was an underground river. They followed it to an opening surrounded by hills. Hidden here was an oasis full of trees bearing flowers and fruit, a land richer than Kishkindha. 'This is my garden,' said Swayamprabha, a female hermit, dressed in clothes of bark and animal hide. 'It was built by Maya, the architect of the asuras.'

The monkeys ate to their hearts' content and bathed in the water. Then they slept. On waking up, they ate some more and swam some more. This was monkey heaven. 'It is time to go, Angada. Give the orders,' said Hanuman. Angada hesitated. The temptation to stay back was too great.

'Please do not go. Stay here. Give me company. It is lonely here,' said Swayamprabha, but Hanuman insisted that they had a mission.

'The only mission for animals is to eat and mate, keep rivals away and keep away from predators. How can you have a mission?'

When Hanuman told them what the mission was, Swayamprabha said that no one had seen Lanka. 'You will surely fail. Why ruin your life for someone else? Stay here. Enjoy.'

'There is great joy in satisfying oneself,' said Hanuman. 'But there is greater joy when we satisfy ourselves by satisfying others. Still greater joy when we do not need satisfaction. And even more joy, when despite not needing satisfaction, we provide satisfaction to others.'

Hearing these words, Swayamprabha realized why despite years of being a hermit and living in a garden that provided all satisfaction she felt inadequate and incomplete. She had focused only on her satisfaction, not that of others. She decided to help the monkeys even though she was not obliged to. She simply wanted to experience what it felt like to bring joy unconditionally. By the powers of her siddha she transported Hanuman and all the other monkeys to the southern shore of the land. Beyond was the sea. Somewhere in the sea was Lanka.

By the grace of Swayamprabha, they had reached the ends of the earth. Beyond was the sea stretching to the horizon, joining the sky at a distance. Somewhere out there was Lanka.

'We can search the land but we can never search the sea. How will we ever find Lanka?' wailed Angada. He was angry that they had left the gardens of Swayamprabha. 'I cannot go back without news of Sita. My uncle is looking for an excuse to kill me. I would rather stay here and die.'

Hanuman and Jambuvan sat next to the young prince silently empathizing with his frustration and fear. They stared at the sea and wondered what could be done.

A vulture called Sampati overheard Angada speak thus and was very happy, for the dead monkeys would provide him nourishment for several days. He sauntered towards them, for he could not fly.

'Look, a vulture comes and waits for us to die. At least in death we will make someone happy, we who made no one happy when we were alive,' ranted Angada. Then he said, 'What if Jatayu got it wrong? What if Sita was not taken in the southern direction?'

Hearing Jatayu's name, Sampati perked up, for Jatayu was his younger brother. Long ago, the two of them had decided to race towards the sun. Being older and stronger, Sampati soared higher till he realized that the glare of the sun was too strong to bear. So he spread his wings to shield Jatayu from the searing rays. Jatayu was saved but Sampati's wings got singed. He would never be able to fly again. He made the southern shore his home. While all other vultures could fly in search for food, he had to learn patience and wait for food to come to him.

'Are you friends of Jatayu? I am his brother. Tell me all that you know of him,' Sampati said. So the monkeys told the old vulture the story of Ram, and how Ravana abducted Sita and how Jatayu lost his wing, and his life, trying to stop him, and how Ram helped Sugriva and how Sugriva, in return, was trying to help Ram find, and rescue, his beloved wife.

Sampati wept for his dear brother. 'His death shall not be in vain. I will help you find the man who killed my brother. I may not fly but I have keen eyesight. I can see even beyond the horizon and beyond the sea mists. I will locate Lanka for you.'

Sampati stood on a rock that overlooked the sea and stared south for a long time. Then he said, 'I see an island. I see a city on that island. And in that city, I see a woman. She is the only woman in this city who looks unhappy. All the others have a smile on their faces, like beloveds satisfied by lovers. She is the only woman who wears no gold in that city of gold. That lovelorn woman under the Ashoka tree must be Ram's Sita.'

'Is that how he described me?' asked Sita.

'Yes,' said Hanuman.

- Jambuvan, the wise bear, is part of the monkey search party. His role is not critical but he embodies the wisdom and patience that is associated with age.
- Bears (bhalukas) are seen by some modern commentators as tribes whose totem (favoured or emblematic object) was the bear.
- In the Puranas, Jambuvan is described as being so old that he had witnessed Vishnu overpowering the asura-king Bali in the form of Vamana. When Vamana the dwarf turned into Trivikrama the giant who traced the three worlds in two steps, Jambuvan went around him. He was very strong but Trivikrama accidentally bumped into him and the resulting injury made him weak. Hence, he cannot do what Hanuman can do.
- The inclusion of bears and monkeys in the narrative has been attributed to the use of hands by these animals. Both can grab and hug, making them closer to humans than birds and four-legged animals with claws and hooves. This is often seen as an early understanding of the theory of evolution. Some even propose the theory that vanaras and bhalukas are the missing link.
- The story of Ravana wanting to urinate is found in the Kashmiri *Ramayana*. Here, Narada ensures the Shiva-linga does not reach Lanka.
- Swayamprabha, like Sulabha and Gargi, is a female mendicant.

- South-East Asian versions of the *Ramayana* depict Swayamprabha as one of the many women who are smitten by Hanuman.
- In the Valmiki *Ramayana*, no one who enters the cave can escape. The vanaras are trapped but Hanuman convinces Swayamprabha to use her magical powers and let them go. A temple of Hanuman in Krishnapuram, which stands in Tamil Nadu's Tirunelveli district, marks the cave of Swayamprabha. On the way back to Ayodhya, after killing Ravana, Ram greets her and thanks her for her support.
- Sampati plays a key role in pointing to the exact direction of Lanka; otherwise the vanaras would be all at sea. Jatayu and Sampati are the ones who point to Ram, and later to Hanuman, the direction where Ravana had taken Sita. Birds are seen as the perfect scouts as they can travel fast over vast distances across land and water.
- The story of Sampati's wings getting singed because he flies too close to the sun echoes the Greek story of Icarus, the boy who flew too close to the sun with wings made of wax.
- After losing his wings, Sampati could not fly and hunt for fresh meat. And so, according to folklore, impressed by Sampati's sacrifice the gods blessed him with the ability to digest rotting flesh. Thus vultures became scavengers of the dead yet were never considered inauspicious.
- Both Sampati and Jatayu are described in various versions of the *Ramayana* as friends of Ram's father, Dashratha.
- Greeks venerated the vulture as the only creature that does not harm the living for its survival. The Zoroastrians venerate the vulture and invite it to eat the bodies of their dead in specially built towers of silence.
- In the Gosani festival of the Goddess in the temple city of Puri, Odisha, images of Sampati carrying monkeys on his wide wings are shown. It seems strange, as Sampati is not associated with wings. But according to folklore, Sampati gets his wings back for helping the monkeys and takes them back to Kishkindha on his wings. Perhaps in some earlier lost version the monkeys travelled to Lanka on the wings of birds. But this is pure speculation.

Hanuman's Story

'The fastest way to reach Lanka was to leap across the sea. Every monkey can leap: from one tree to another, across rivers, over chasms and gorges, but none had ever tried to leap across the sea. Jambuvan, the old bear, was sure I would be able to make the leap, but I was not sure,' said Hanuman to Sita.

'Leap across the sea? Did you really do that? How?' asked Sita.

'It happened after Jambuvan told me the story of my birth, which I had long forgotten.'

The gods wanted Shiva, the supreme tapasvi, to create a warrior who would support Ram and stand up to Ravana. So Vishnu took the form of the damsel Mohini and enchanted Shiva, until Shiva let his seed slip out of his body. Vayu, the wind-god, took this seed and slipped it into the ear of Anjana. From this seed was born Hanuman who came to be known as Maruti because his birth was mediated by Vayu, also known as Marutta, god of storms.

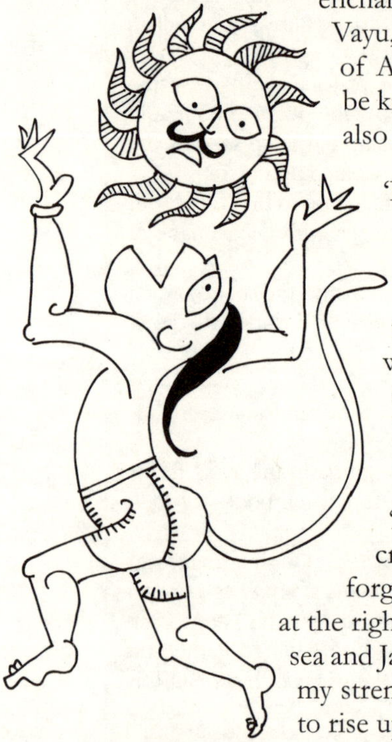

'I was a strong child, so strong that I did not know my strength. Once, I leapt up into the sky to eat the rising sun, assuming it to be a fruit. I began tossing the planets around like stars. To stop me, Indra struck me with a thunderbolt, the Vajra. This made Vayu so angry that he withdrew air from all the worlds. To appease him, Indra said that I would get a body that would be as swift as lightning and as strong as thunder. That is why I am also called Vajranga, or Bajrang,' said Hanuman to Sita.

'Another time, I kept hurling boulders and mountains and creating such a racket that the rishis cursed me that I would forget my strength until someone reminded me of the same at the right time. That time came when I stood at the edge of the sea and Jambuvan said only I could leap across the sea. He praised my strength, reminded me of my capabilities and motivated me to rise up to the sky and make my way to Lanka.'

- In the Valmiki *Ramayana* and early retellings, Hanuman is just a mighty monkey, and a son of the wind-god. Since medieval times, Hanuman has been identified as both Shiva's son and as Shiva's avatar. In Balaram Das's Odia *Dandi Ramayana*, Hanuman is clearly identified as a form of Shiva.
- In Eknath's Marathi *Bhavarth Ramayana*, Hanuman is born wearing a loincloth that is indicative of his celibacy.
- While Hanuman is always known as the son of Anjana, his fatherhood is shared between a monkey (Kesari), a god (Vayu) and God (Shiva).
- In the *Ramayana* from Malaysia one hears of Ram and Sita taking the form of monkeys and producing a child that turns into Hanuman who later comes to help Ram rescue

Sita from Ravana. A similar story is found in some Indian retellings, only here it is Shiva and Parvati who take the form of monkeys and give birth to Hanuman who they give to the childless monkey couple Anjana and Kesari.

- In North India, Hanuman is offered calotropis leaves that are wild and poisonous, thus reinforcing his association with Shiva, the hermit. In South India, Hanuman, popularly known as Anjaneya, son of Anjana, is offered betel leaves and butter.
- Jambuvan gives the earliest motivational speech, a song of praise reminding Hanuman of his origins and prowess, giving him the strength to do what has never been attempted before.
- Hanuman is worshipped as the remover of problems. He has control over celestial bodies like the sun and the stars and so can remove bad astrological influences. Across India, offerings are made to Hanuman on Tuesdays and Saturdays, days that are associated with two malefic planets, Mangal (the planet Mars) who creates conflict and Shani (the planet Saturn) who delays things.

Crossing the Sea

Hanuman then told Sita of his journey across the vast sea.

He first increased the size of his body. The branches of trees with leaves, fruit and flowers clung to his limbs as he grew in size. His head stretched beyond the sky and the planets wondered whether they had to go around his head or around the sun. Under his weight the mountains by the seaside started oozing liquid metal like the juice of crushed sugar cane. Then with a thunderous roar, he leapt into the sky and made his way south towards Lanka.

The flowers that clung to Hanuman's body as he gained size were swept away by the force of the wind, and they fell into the sea, arousing the curiosity of fishes that rose from the waters to see this incredible sight: a monkey flying like a bird towards Lanka. No bird had made this journey. No fish had swum that far. There was great excitement in the three worlds at this occurrence of the impossible.

Then, a few hours into his journey, a mountain rose from under the sea. Hanuman saw this as an obstacle perhaps created by demons. But it was Mainaka, the son of Himavan, king of the mountains. 'Stop, son of the wind. Rest on my peaks. Refresh yourself,' he said. No, said Hanuman, thanking the mountain. There was a mission to complete. No rest until then.

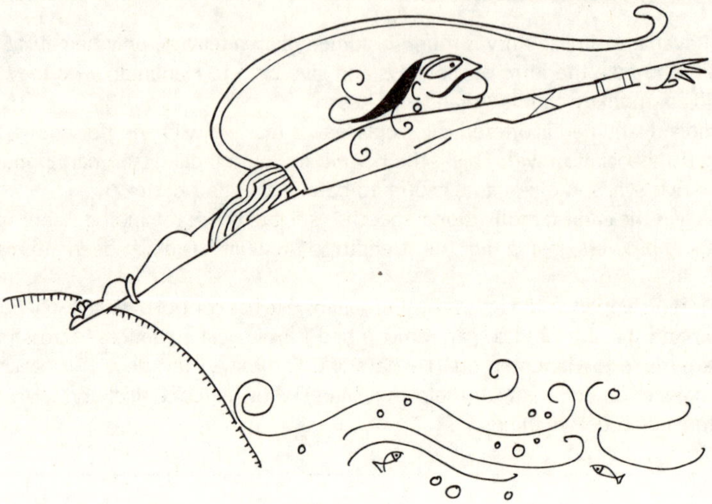

Then Hanuman found his path blocked by Surasa, mother of the sea creatures. 'Make way for me. I am Hanuman, on a mission for Ram,' he shouted.

Surasa responded, 'Who is Ram? Who is Hanuman? What is a mission? All I know is that I am hungry and you are my food. Surely feeding the hungry is more important than going on a mission. You must satisfy my hunger. Give me food or become my food. Only then will I let you pass.'

'I have no food to give and if I become food to satisfy your hunger, how then will you let me pass?' asked Hanuman.

Surasa smiled at the cleverness of this monkey and said, 'If you, who can be food or provide food, pass without entering my hungry mouth, you will earn so much demerit that you will never succeed in your mission.'

'It may be my dharma to feed you but it is your dharma to catch food given to you. Don't blame me if you can't catch me,' said Hanuman expanding the size of his body, forcing Surasa to widen her jaws that were lined with vast rows of venomous teeth. Then, very quickly, Hanuman reduced himself to the size of a bee and entered Surasa's mouth and left it just as quickly. Before Surasa could understand what was happening and was able to snap shut her jaws so greatly widened, Hanuman was gone, on his way to Lanka.

Hanuman heard Surasa chuckle in delight. 'A creature as smart, strong and sincere as you will surely succeed.'

Then a sea monster called Simhika caught Hanuman by pinning down his shadow with magic. Resistance seemed futile as her magic was very strong. So Hanuman allowed himself to be swallowed by the monster, but once inside, he expanded himself in size, tearing her insides apart and ripping out of her body. The sea, until then blue, turned purple as the red blood spread in every direction.

Finally, covered with the blood of Simhika and the sweat of his long journey, Hanuman saw the shores of Lanka, lined with coconut palms that waved in the wind as if welcoming him like the wives of warriors returning home after years in battle.

It was night when Hanuman landed on the beach and walked towards Lanka. His path was blocked by a fierce being, a woman with eight arms. She had a torch in one hand and a bell in another, a trident in one hand on which an elephant had been impaled, and a sword wet with the blood of a lion in another, a snake spitting venom in one hand and

a club fitted with a human skull in another, a pot of fire in one hand and an axe in another. Her hair was unbound and her forehead was smeared with vermilion. All she wore was a string of human heads, warriors she had killed in battle.

'I am Lankini, guardian of the city,' she said. 'I serve its master. First it was Kubera, king of yakshas, who built the city. Now it is Ravana, king of rakshasas, who drove Kubera and his yakshas out and declared himself overlord of this city.'

Hanuman swung his tail and knocked Lankini down. When Lankini tried getting up, he swung his tail once more and knocked her down again. Lankini then simply lay on the ground, spreadeagled, refusing to get up. The guardian of the city was not upset. Long had she protected the city. Now, finally, she had an opportunity to let go. 'You are no monkey. You are the herald of doom. Ravana's days are numbered,' Lankini said.

Hearing this exciting tale of the monkey who crossed the sea, who was as strong as he was smart and committed, Sita's heart was filled with hope and joy.

- The fifth chapter of the Ramayana, Sundara-kanda, which describes the monkeys' search for Sita, is the most popular and most auspicious chapter of the epic. It is symbolic of hope, of seeking and finding what one misses dearly.
- Hanuman displays perseverance with Mainaka, cleverness with Surasa, brute strength with Simhika.
- According to rationalists, Hanuman did not fly, he swam. In the Valmiki *Ramayana*, words for swimming and flying are used interchangeably.
- Every village in India is associated with a goddess. She is Gramadevi, the lady of the settlement, the domesticated earth who sustains the village. Lanka is no exception.
- Cities and villages across India are associated with Gramadevis, such as Mumbadevi of Mumbai, Kali of Kolkata and Chandika of Chandigarh.
- Images of reclining goddesses are found in many parts of South India. They represent the earth who receives seed and bears children, the plants.
- Most forts in India are called durg as they are guarded by Durga, the goddess who rides a lion and bears weapons and is the patron of kings.
- Contrary to popular belief that all fertility deities are female and guardian deities are male, this story reveals that even the mighty Ravana's city is protected by a goddess. Like Tadaka, Lankini is strong and fearsome.
- Lankini can be equated with the Amazons of Greek mythology, warrior women who are part of Indian folklore. Chandragupta Maurya is said to have been guarded by a contingent of female warriors.

Finding Sita

'The city of Lanka is vast, full of women. How did you know I was Sita?' asked Sita.

Hanuman admitted it was not easy. He flew from one house to another, sometimes in the form of a bee, sometimes in the form of a parrot, peeping through windows and hovering over courtyards. Most people were asleep. He saw mothers sleeping next to their children, children sleeping with their dolls, lovers embracing each other after having made love, old men and women who tossed and turned in their sleep.

How does Sita look, he wondered. In Ravana's palace he found Ravana sleeping surrounded by many women, all of them satisfied. They were dressed in the finest clothes, wearing the finest ornaments. Hanuman found the room full of perfume and music everywhere. If ever there was paradise on earth, Hanuman thought, it had to be here.

Amongst the women on Ravana's bed, he saw a particularly beautiful and serene woman. Could that be Sita? But something told him that she could not be Ram's wife. He decided to look elsewhere.

Finally, just as dawn was breaking, he found his way to the garden of Ashoka trees next to the palace. He saw there a woman under a tree, no jewels on her body except her hairpin, surrounded by many rakshasa women, clearly there to guard her, but who had dozed off.

'I remembered how Ram had remarked on seeing the jewellery collected by the monkeys of Kishkindha that the only piece of jewellery missing in the bundle was the hairpin. The only ornament you have on your body is your hairpin. So you had to be Sita. Thus it was that I found you,' said Hanuman to Sita.

Hanuman then asked Sita for something to prove to Ram that she had been found. Sita gave Hanuman her hairpin. 'When a woman's hair is unbound it means she is free. When it is neatly bound, it means she is committed. This hairpin, the only piece of jewellery I did not drop on the forest floor, reveals I am committed to

Ram in mind and spirit, but Ravana seeks to unbind my hair. Tell him to hurry. Ravana must be stopped or the consequences will be terrible.'

Then Hanuman had a doubt. 'What if Ram thinks I picked this up from the forest floor too? Is there something you can tell me that will prove beyond all doubt that I met you alive, none but you? Maybe a secret you shared?'

'You think of all possibilities,' said an impressed Sita. She then told a secret tale to Hanuman: 'One day, while he slept, a crow pecked me, it kept troubling me, biting my ear. It was no ordinary crow; it was Jayanta, son of Indra. I wept and I bled but I did not shout because I did not want to wake up Ram from the sleep he so richly deserved. But he sensed my pain and woke up and was so angry with the crow that he pierced one of his eyes and drove it back to the sky.'

Hanuman realized Sita was sharing a very intimate personal detail with him. It indicated how much Sita trusted him, and how much she yearned for Ram to rescue her.

Then Hanuman had an idea. 'Why don't you climb on my back? I will carry you back safely to him.'

'Did he ask you to carry me back?'

'No. I don't think he knows I am capable of this. It will be a surprise, a pleasant surprise.'

'Let my husband liberate me. His honour is at stake.'

- Valmiki uses Hanuman's search for Sita through the streets of Lanka as a clever device to give the audience a voyeuristic journey through the houses of the rakshasas. They appear human at times and demonic at others, at times barbaric and at times domestic. They are sensual on the one hand and fearsome on the other.
- Valmiki's description of Ravana in bed with many women is highly erotic. The women are shown in various stages of longing and satiation. Their clothes are a mess. Many have left their husbands to enjoy the pleasure that only Ravana can give them. Many women kiss each other to savour the aftertaste of Ravana in each other's mouths. It is an unabashed orgy, indicative of Ravana's virility. That Hanuman turns away from the sight reinforces Hanuman's hermit nature.

- In Krittivasa's *Ramayana*, Hanuman finds a house where a man is chanting Ram's name. He learns he is Vibhishana, Ravana's brother.
- In Marathi, the term Lanke-chi-Parvati means a woman in a rich household who wears no jewels. To be adorned is the sign of being happy. An unadorned woman indicates an unhappy household. Sita wears no jewels even though she is sitting in the city of gold, indicating the unhappy state of her mind and thus helping Hanuman identify her.
- The chudamani or the crest jewel, sometimes described as a tiara, was an elaborate head jewel for women in ancient India, usually pinned to the bun or placed in the parting of the hair. It is still worn by women of the northern hill tribes of India.
- According to folklore, the crow has only one eye as Ram pierced its other eye as punishment for troubling his wife.

Destroying the Garden

It was finally time to leave. The rakshasa guards and attendants were slowly getting up. 'Before I leave,' said Hanuman to Sita, 'I must eat something. I have not eaten for days and the journey back is long.'

'If this was my kitchen, I would have fed you the choicest of delicacies,' Sita said. 'But all I have to offer you is the fruit of these trees. These trees are my sisters, born of the earth. Eat their fruit, drink their nectar, and enjoy their fragrances until you are refreshed enough to make your journey back to my Ram.'

So Hanuman jumped up the tree and leapt from branch to branch, swinging and jumping, tearing leaves, ripping out flowers, eating the flesh of fruits and dropping the seeds on the ground, creating a commotion that made all the guards of the garden look up at him. He threw the skins of bananas at them, and the shells of coconuts and the pits of mangoes. Angry, the guards tried to catch him. But he was too fast for them.

They hurled sticks at him, threw rocks at him and spread out nets to catch him, but Hanuman proved too smart for them and dodged these easily, hiding behind trunks of trees, slipping down and swinging up vines with ease.

The beautiful royal pleasure garden of Lanka was a mess. Branches were broken, and trees had been stripped of leaves. Sita realized Hanuman was not just hungry for food, he was hungry for a fight, itching to annoy those who held her captive. She could not help but smile at the comedy of the situation.

The commotion in the garden disturbed Ravana's sleep and he roared in anger. Soldiers were sent to catch the audacious monkey. But even their axes, spears and clubs failed to come anywhere near Hanuman.

Finally, Ravana's son Akshaya came into the garden bearing a mighty bow. Hanuman realized his importance observing how all the rakshasas deferred to him. Akshaya shot an arrow at him; Hanuman caught it in his hand and hurled it back. It ripped through Akshaya's heart, killing him instantly.

The guards were stunned. A silence descended on the garden. This was no mischievous monkey. This was an act of war.

- The decision to meet Ravana, tell him about Ram's mission and terrify his people is Hanuman's alone, indicating an independent spirit. He does not wait for orders.
- In many folk retellings, Ram does not appreciate the havoc caused by Hanuman in Lanka. It is not clarified if it is the act that is not appreciated or the fact that it was done without permission.
- In the *Ranganatha Ramayana*, Sita offers Hanuman an armlet so that he could buy fruits from the markets of Lanka but Hanuman says he does not eat fruits plucked by others.
- For the first time Ravana faces defeat in his own city. He loses a son. The son, Akshaya, is no villain; he becomes a martyr, who dies protecting his father's property. The narrative starts getting complex as the lines between heroes and villains are blurred.

The Burning of Lanka

'Bring this monkey to me, Indrajit,' roared Ravana, holding the lifeless body of his son in his arms. Ravana's eldest son, Indrajit, immediately entered the garden blowing a conch shell, the sound of which revealed his strength and his rage.

Hanuman saw the confusion and fear on the faces of the rakshasas who accompanied Indrajit. All security that Lanka offered its residents had for the first time been breached. Now it was time to surrender, Hanuman realized.

Hanuman let Indrajit's arrow stun him. He let Indrajit bind him with a noose. He let Indrajit drag him to Ravana's pillared court by his tail. The rakshasa-king sat sprawled on his throne, Akshaya's body in his arms, surrounded by rakshasas who were growling and clamouring for Hanuman's blood.

Hanuman jumped up and sat right in front of Ravana, staring him in the eye. No one dared look at Ravana so. 'Don't you rakshasas know the rules of hospitality?' asked Hanuman. 'Get me a seat. Quick!' The rakshasas did not know how to respond to this. They had never seen a monkey talk. They had never seen anyone talk so in front of Ravana. 'Is this the way to treat a guest?' Hanuman's mocking tone did not escape Ravana. 'Very well, then I shall make a seat for myself.'

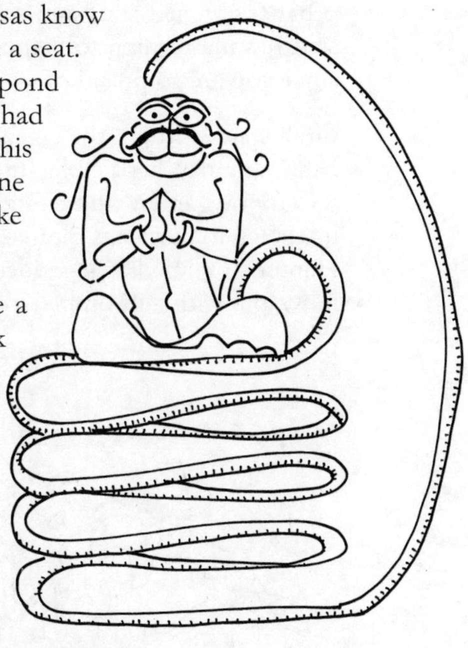

Hanuman extended his tail and coiled it to create a tower. He then sat on it. Ravana had to strain his neck up to look at him. He was not amused. 'Who are you? Who sent you? You are no ordinary vanara; you speak Sanskrit but don't look like a brahmin,' said Ravana.

'Speaking Sanskrit does not make anyone a brahmin. Expanding the mind does. I thought you with all your legendary knowledge of the Vedas would know that. Clearly, Ram knows more than you.' At the mention of Ram's name, there was an uncomfortable silence in the room. Ravana realized the monkey was here in Lanka on a mission, not by accident. 'Yes, I have been sent by the Ram whose wife you abducted like a thief. Unbecoming of one who calls himself brahmin, unbecoming of someone who calls himself king. Return her to her husband. Respect dharma.'

'A monkey teaches me dharma,' Ravana scoffed. On cue, his brothers laughed.

'Brother, don't you see this is no ordinary monkey and Ram whose wife you abducted is no ordinary man? Let Sita go. Even if you don't think there is anything morally wrong in keeping her here against her will, at least let her go for the sake of the city's security,' cried a rakshasa.

'What kind of a brother are you, Vibhishana? What kind of a rakshasa are you, Vibhishana? Frightened of a monkey! Wanting to make peace with Ram who mutilated our sister! This man goes hunting leaving his wife all alone. He is not worthy of Sita. Get out of Lanka if you prefer Ram. Those who are not with me are against me!' shouted Ravana.

Hanuman looked at the lone voice of reason in Lanka. Vibhishana! So unlike the other frightened sons and warriors who dared not speak against Ravana. 'You,' said Ravana turning to Hanuman, 'I shall roast and eat for dinner tonight. And since you are so proud of your tail, we shall begin by burning your tail.'

On Ravana's orders, the rakshasas tried to grab hold of the end of Hanuman's tail. But Hanuman kept elongating his tail, much to their irritation. So Ravana said, 'Go to the garden where Sita sits, rip off the cloth that covers her body and use it as a rag to burn this monkey's tail.' Realizing that he would get Sita into trouble, Hanuman immediately reduced the size of his tail, allowing the rakshasas to grab it, wrap it with rags dipped in oil and set it aflame. Hanuman realized that the fire

was not hot. It felt cool and comforting. He knew that a woman who is chaste has magical powers, like tapasvis with siddha, that give her control over the elements. Sita's chastity was protecting him from the heat of fire. She who needed help was helping him who needed no help. Hanuman's heart was filled with affection. How different Sita and Ram were from all the vanaras and rakshasas he had met!

As the fire blazed on the tip of his tail, Hanuman broke the bonds around his arms and leapt up to the ceiling and lashed his burning tail against the pillars of the palace. As Ravana watched, the tapestries adorning his palace and the columns of the courtyard began to burn. The flames spread across the walls and roofs, from the palace to the roofs of houses nearby. Before long the whole city was ablaze. The gold on the walls started melting. Roofs crumbled and collapsed. People rushed out of their homes screaming. Black soot covered their faces. The rakshasas ran to fetch water and douse the flames but the fire spread through the avenues, setting aflame everything in its path. Elephants and horses rushing out of the stables added to the commotion.

'This was but a warning of the fate in store for you if you do not release Sita,' said Hanuman. Indrajit raised his bow to shoot Hanuman down but Hanuman had leapt up into the sky far from the reach of any arrow.

The only place in Lanka that the fire did not spread to was the garden where Sita sat, surrounded by the women and children of Lanka. She was teaching them songs she had heard as a child from Gargi. Here it was cool and fragrant, an oasis of peace in a city once peaceful and prosperous, now struck by an unimaginable terror.

Now, thought Sita, they will blame Hanuman, hence Ram, hence me. Not once will they hold Ravana responsible for his obstinacy. Not once will they blame Surpanakha for her unbridled passion. When the mind is knotted in fear, the problem is always outside, never inside.

- Indrajit is unable to subdue Hanuman until he uses a weapon obtained from Brahma. Hanuman, out of respect for Brahma, lets the weapon stun and bind him.
- The throne created by coiling the monkey tail is variously attributed either to Hanuman when he is caught, as in Telugu retellings, or to Angada when he arrives as a formal messenger of Ram, as in Avadhi retellings.
- In temple art, especially in the south, when Hanuman is shown with his tail below, as in front of Ram, it indicates he is calm and gentle. To show Hanuman as an aggressive warrior and guardian, the tail is held aloft and forms a corona over his head.
- In some temples, Hanuman has an upraised palm. Some identify this as the gesture of

blessing and others as the gesture of a slap (tamacha Hanuman). Hanuman, in folklore, slaps the great Ravana and knocks his crowns away before setting Lanka aflame.

- A touch of humour is introduced into the story of Hanuman's tail being set aflame when Hanuman elongates it. No amount of fabric is enough to wrap it until Ravana threatens to get Sita's sari, suggesting he will disrobe her.
- In the Telugu retelling, rakshasas are unable to stoke the flames as they try to burn Hanuman's tail. Ravana is enlisted for help and he blows on it using his ten heads; the flames leap up and singe his beard and his hair.
- Fire, over which chaste women have control according to tradition, does not hurt either Hanuman or Sita.
- In the *Mahabharata*, Vishnu as Krishna encourages the burning of a forest to build a city. In the *Ramayana*, Shiva as Hanuman resides in a forest and burns down a city.
- Lankapodi is a festival commemorating the burning of Lanka. It has been celebrated around Ram Navami, in spring, in Sonepur district in western Odisha since the eighteenth century. Clay images are purchased by children, who play with them all day and set them afire on the streets at night, recreating the burning of Lanka. This region was known as Paschimi-Lanka or western Lanka in the eleventh century.
- By burning Lanka to punish the acts of a king, Hanuman ends up hurting its innocent residents. Does this turn the entire rakshasa clan against Ram and his monkey army? Suddenly they are as much victims as their king was a victimizer.
- When Shiva destroys the three cities or Tripura, its residents' cries make Shiva shed tears from which is born the rudraksha fruit. It is a reminder of the cost of yagna: when fire burns in the altar something is claimed as fuel. The human mind focuses on who benefits from the fire, rarely on who is consumed by the fire.
- To put out the flames, Hanuman puts his tail in his mouth and the soot makes his face black, which is why, according to folklore, vanaras, once red-faced monkeys, later became black-faced monkeys.

BOOK SIX

Rescue

'Lanka desired her submission. Ayodhya demanded her innocence.'

A Triumphant Return

Honey, the sweetest honey, could be found in Madhuvana, a garden just outside Kishkindha. The hives there were reserved for the monkey-kings. But the scout-monkeys, on their return from the south, raided this royal sanctuary and drank all the honey there, ignoring the warnings of the guards.

When this was reported to Sugriva, he smiled indulgently, saying, 'Such audacity can only spring from success.'

Indeed it had. After the excited chatter of the monkeys about their numerous adventures had died down, Hanuman opened his palm and showed Sita's hairpin to Ram. He then told Ram the secret story of the crow who long ago, in the forest, had attacked Sita while Ram was asleep. 'Like a proud tree in the vicious grip of venomous vines, she sits in Ravana's garden, awaiting your arrival.'

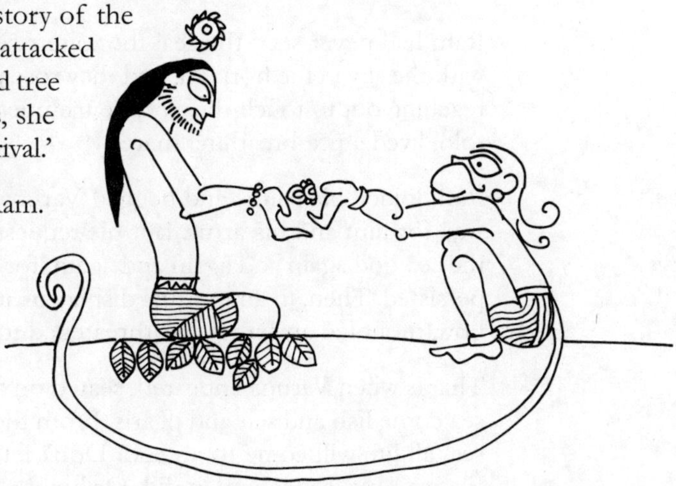

'Is she frightened, Hanuman?' asked Ram.

'No. She knows you will come.'

'Then there is not a moment to lose. Let us go south, to the shores of the sea, and find a way to that island city of the rakshasas.'

- Valmiki describes the boisterous return of the vanaras and the havoc they create to celebrate their success.
- The return of Hanuman marks the start of the Yuddha-kanda, the sixth and final chapter of the Purva-Ramayana.
- Ram is eternally indebted to Hanuman, who finds Sita. He hugs him as a brother. In a hierarchical and feudal society this is hugely significant: it indicates the debt of the master and the gratitude of those in authority.
- Hanuman has nothing to gain from the entire exercise. At first he is simply obeying Sugriva but later it is an act of unconditional affection. This elevates Hanuman to the level of a god in the eyes of the people. No temple of Vishnu is complete without a shrine to Hanuman. In North India people say, *'Pehle Hanuman, phir bhagavan,'* meaning 'First Hanuman and only then God'.
- The thirteenth-century Vedanta scholar Madhwa, based in Udupi, Karnataka, was identified as an incarnation of Hanuman. Madhwa is known for his doctrine of duality (Dvaita) where he saw a devotee as separate from the deity, in contrast to the foremost ninth-century Vedanta scholar, Shankara, who said such divisions were delusions. The name Madhwa alludes to the notion of a 'medium'. Just as Hanuman connects Sita to Ram, Madhwa's doctrine hopes to connect devotee to deity.

A Bridge across the Sea

The great army of monkeys and bears and vultures and other forest creatures led by Ram followed Hanuman. It was easy to cross the jungles, but not the sea.

Ram had never seen the sea: the waters seemed to stretch into infinity, blending with the sky in the horizon, and they rose up in waves and roared like angry lions, reaching out to touch the sky like trumpeting elephants. Under the waters, it was told, lived a fire-breathing mare.

Ram joined his palms and begged Varuna, the god of the sea, to part and make way for him and his army. But his request was greeted with silence. He invoked the sea-god again and again and again, for several days and nights. But the silence persisted. Then, in an unusual display of impatience and rage, Ram picked up his bow, mounted an arrow and threatened to destroy the sea.

That is when Varuna appeared, seated on a gigantic fish, and told Ram, 'From the sea come fish and salt and pearls. From the sea comes the rain. If you destroy the sea, all life will come to an end. Don't let your rage get the better of you, Ram. Fly over me, as Hanuman did. Or build a bridge over me. But do not expect me

to change my nature and make way
for you or your army.'

Varuna then saw the animals behind Ram, the great army of beasts, behaving so uncharacteristically in the presence of Ram. If they could be inspired to transform, so could he. So Varuna revealed a secret: 'Amongst the vanaras who have followed you are the brothers Nala and Nila, children of Agni, the fire-god. Rocks dropped by them into the sea cannot sink. Use them to build a bridge. I will keep it afloat. No more.'

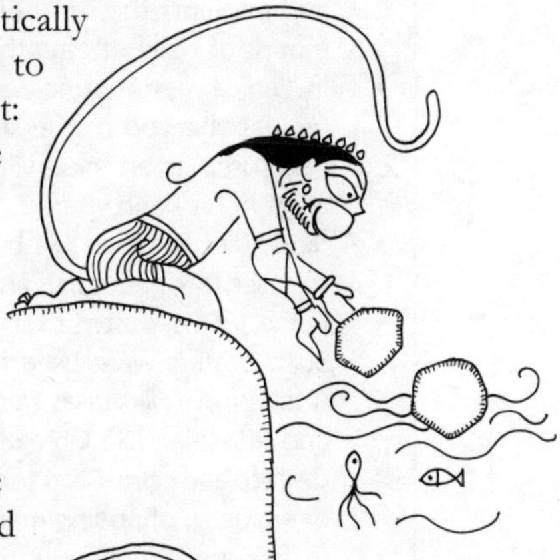

The monkeys let out a whoop of joy and Ram smiled. That was good enough.

The vultures scouted from the air, the bears made the plans and the monkeys executed them. They carried huge boulders and passed them on to the brothers Nala and Nila, who hurled them into the sea. These stayed afloat as Varuna had said, but they did not stay together: they drifted in different directions. 'What do we do now?' screamed the vanaras.

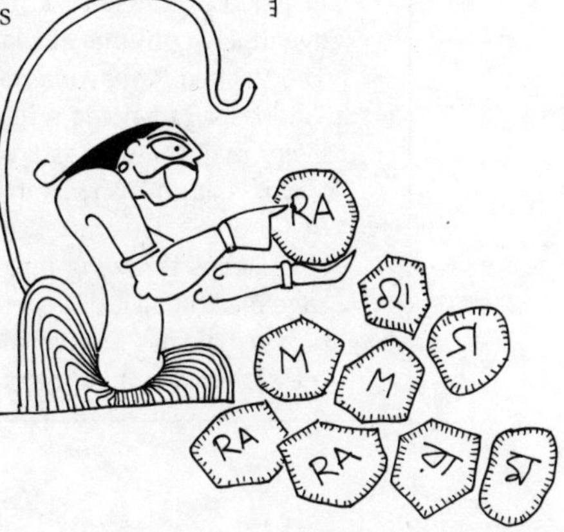

Hanuman then etched the name of Ram on the boulders that were being handed over to Nala and Nila. Now these rocks stuck to each other like a garland and extended southwards, towards Sita.

- It is said that under the sea is a fire-breathing mare whose heat turns seawater into mist and prevents the sea from overflowing into land. This fire-breathing mare will be the mount of Kalki, the tenth incarnation of Vishnu.
- In Vedic times, Varuna was the god associated with ethics and morality. In Puranic times, he was the god of the sea and father of Lakshmi, goddess of wealth, associated with generosity. In art, he is visualized riding a fish or a whale or a dolphin, holding a noose or a net in his hand.
- Since Ram mounts his bow with an arrow, he is bound to release it somewhere. He releases it to the north and the land struck by it turns into the Thar desert of Rajasthan.
- In the 1990s, poster art showing Ram raising his bow against the sea became very popular. Such posters were used to transform Ram into a political icon who would rescue Sita (India) from rakshasas (anti-Hindu forces). The imagery showed Ram as being aggressive and muscular, like Greek heroes, in contrast to traditional imagery where Ram is poised, delicate and calm. Ram's serenity was interpreted by Western art historians as sensuality and effeminacy, offending many Indians, who then reimagined Ram in this Western template.
- In folklore, the sea-god is so angry with Ram for raising a bow at him that the sea eventually consumes Dwarka, the city of Krishna, who is Ram reborn.
- The Valmiki *Ramayana* refers only to Nala, who is considered a form of Vishwakarma. Tulsidas's *Ramayana* refers to Nala and Nila, the sons of Agni.
- Every major vanara is linked to a deva: Vali to Indra, Sugriva to Surya, Hanuman to Vayu, Nala to Vishwakarma, Nila to Agni.
- In Giridhar's Gujarati *Ramayana*, written in the nineteenth century, a monkey called Nala keeps throwing into the sea the stone on which a sage washes his clothes. The sage has to pull it out every day. Fed up one day, he curses Nala that stones touched by him will always float in the sea, never sink. That is why the vanaras get Nala to touch the stones they hurl into the sea.

- Giridhar's *Ramayana* rejects the idea that Ram's name was written on the stones cast in the sea because then walking on those rocks would be like walking on Ram's name, which would be rather disrespectful.
- In Krittivasa's *Ramayana*, Hanuman gets angry with Nala because Nala uses his left hand to receive rocks from the monkeys. Ram pacifies Hanuman by informing him that that is what workers do: they take the rock with the left hand and place the rock using the right hand.
- The land from where the stones are taken is traditionally identified as parts of Karnataka and Andhra Pradesh known for their large rocks.
- That Hanuman carves the name of Ram on the stones makes him literate and so further raises his esteem in the eyes of the unlettered masses. Though a monkey, he speaks Sanskrit. Though a monkey, he can write. Though a monkey, he can help God.
- What script did Hanuman use to write the name Ram? Writing was probably not known in Valmiki's time. His narration was in all probability oral. Kharoshti and Brahmi scripts came much later. Later the Sharada script, once popular in Kashmir, and Siddham script, still used in Tibet, became popular. From the twelfth century onwards, the use of the Devanagari script became widespread. Popular calendar art shows Hanuman writing in the Devanagari script.
- The Ram Setu is a stretch of limestone shoals connecting the island of Rameswaram to the island of Mannar in Sri Lanka. Hindus believe this to be the bridge built by the monkeys. Sri Lankan historians do not accept this claim. Today many seek to break this natural barrier to facilitate maritime activity. The plan has as many proponents as it has opponents: while some see it as a historical monument, others see it as a natural, ecologically sensitive site and still others as a sacred structure that must be protected at all costs.
- European cartographers named Ram Setu Adam's Bridge.

The Squirrel's Contribution

Many helped Ram build his bridge, monkeys mostly, but also elephants and deer and crows. One of those who helped was a squirrel. He would jump into the water and then roll on the sand so that the grains stuck to his fur. He would then run up the bridge and shake off the sand grains, thus contributing to the bridge-building effort.

The monkeys found the squirrel's enthusiasm rather annoying. He kept coming in their way, so they shoved him aside. Ram, however, picked him up and comforted him. As a sign of encouragement and appreciation, Ram ran his fingers on the squirrel's back, thus creating its stripes.

'You give the little pest too much value,' chuckled Sugriva.

'From your point of view, his contribution may not be much. But from his point of view, his contribution is immense. In your grand scheme of things, he may not matter. But in his grand scheme of things, he surely does. He is also Brahma, creator of his own brahmanda, like you and me. I see the world from his point of view and see how unconditional his love for me is. Unless we do this, how can our mind expand?'

Sugriva realized then what it takes to be a Ram.

- The story of the squirrel's stripes occurs in the Telugu *Ranganatha Ramayana* and the Odia *Dandi Ramayana*.
- Balaram Das wrote the *Jagamohan* [world-delighting] *Ramayana*, which also came to be known as the *Dandi Ramayana* because the song was sung on *dandas* (streets) – to the horror of priests who preferred Sanskrit but to the delight of the common man. Dandi is also the meter in which the Valmiki *Ramayana* was composed.

The Head of Ram and the Body of Sita

Ravana stormed into the Ashoka garden with two heads in his hand. He threw them in Sita's direction. 'There, I have killed your husband and brother-in-law,' he said. 'No one will save you now.'

Sita wanted to cry, but tears would not flow from her eyes. She wanted to scream but no sound escaped her mouth. She did not feel the pain she knew she would feel if ever Ram left her. Instead, she felt his reassuring presence in her heart. No, Ram was not dead. Lakshman was not dead. This was a sorcerer's trick. 'You do not fool me with your magic, Ravana,' she said.

Sita did not smile, nor was her tone mocking. Nevertheless, Ravana felt like a fool.

'He tried doing this to Ram too, you know, to demotivate him,' said Trijata, when Ravana left. She then told Sita how the sorceress Benjkaya was dispatched to make Ram give up his search for Sita.

As they were working on the bridge, the monkeys saw something floating in the waters, drifting from Lanka towards Jambudvipa. It was a body and they fished it

out. It was a beautiful woman with no jewels on her body. Lakshman saw the feet and said in alarmed voice, 'It is Sita. The rakshasa-king has killed her and dumped her body into the sea.'

When news of this reached Ram, he could not believe it. Was Sita really dead? Had he failed to protect the daughter of Janaka? He felt a deep laceration in the innermost recesses of his being. He rushed to the beach to see the body and found Hanuman already preparing to cremate it. The corpse had been placed on logs of wood and he was about to light the flame. 'No, she deserves all the rituals due to a royal princess and a royal wife,' said Ram.

Ignoring Ram, Hanuman set alight the pyre. A furious Ram ran to stop the flames from consuming his beloved, when suddenly he heard a blood-curdling scream and the 'corpse' suddenly came to life and leapt out of the pyre. It was Benjkaya, the sorceress.

Ravana had underestimated the sharp gaze of Hanuman.

- The story of Benjkaya, sometimes identified as Vibhishana's daughter, comes from the Thai *Ramayana*. An image of her jumping off the pyre which Hanuman lit is found on Bangkok's Wat Po temple wall. This story is unique to South-East Asia.
- That Ravana uses sorcery to dishearten Ram and Sita is a repeated motif in the various retellings of the *Ramayana*.
- Stories related to sorcery and black magic increasingly appear in regional *Ramayanas*, especially those from Bengal, Assam and Odisha, and from South-East Asia. It indicates the rise of Tantric practices. Hanuman is seen as an antidote to these practices.

The Arrival of Vibhishana

To the great wonder of all the vanaras, a rakshasa came flying from the south. The monkeys growled and screeched in fear, determined to kill him, but Hanuman recognized him from Ravana's court: he was the lone rakshasa who had fearlessly given sensible advice to Ravana. Hanuman got the monkeys to calm down and brought the rakshasa before Ram.

'I am Vibhishana,' said the rakshasa, introducing himself, 'Ravana's brother. I tried to make him see the senselessness of his actions. So he has kicked me out of his house. Let me fight on your side. He must be destroyed before his madness destroys Lanka.'

Ram welcomed Vibhishana. 'So there are good rakshasas in this world,' said a beaming Lakshman.

'Will you fight me if I do something wrong?' Ram asked Lakshman.

'You can do no wrong,' said Lakshman.

'I am sure the other brothers of Ravana feel Ravana can do no wrong. So who is better: the good rakshasa who sides with me or the loyal rakshasas who side with Ravana?'

Ram's words made both Lakshman and Vibhishana uncomfortable. What was better: to be right or to be loyal? Both have consequences.

- Vibhishana is a devotee of Ram even though he is a rakshasa, just as Prahalada is a devotee of Vishnu even though he is an asura. Thus being a rakshasa or an asura does not automatically make one a 'demon'. In fact the English word 'demon' is full of a value judgement that is wrongly attributed to the words rakshasa and asura.
- In Puri, Odisha, it is said that Vibhishana comes every night to pray to Vishnu who is enshrined there as Jagannatha.
- On an island on the river Kaveri is located Srirangam with its famous image of Ranganathaswami, the reclining Vishnu. The deity faces south, rather than the traditional east, so that Vibhishana can offer prayers facing him from Lanka.
- That Ravana worships Shiva and Vibhishana worships Vishnu has led to speculation that this is indicative of Shaiva and Vaishnava rivalry that was rife amongst priests in medieval times.

Spies of Lanka

As Vibhishana mingled with the monkeys, assisting them in any way he could, he noticed that amongst the monkeys were a few shape-shifting rakshasas: spies of Ravana. He recognized Shuka, Shardula and Sarana.

Vibhishana pointed them out to the monkeys who grabbed them and showered them with kicks and punches until Ram stopped them.

'Let them go. They are doing their duty. Let them go back and tell Ravana what they have seen. This army and its plans is no rumour; it is reality.'

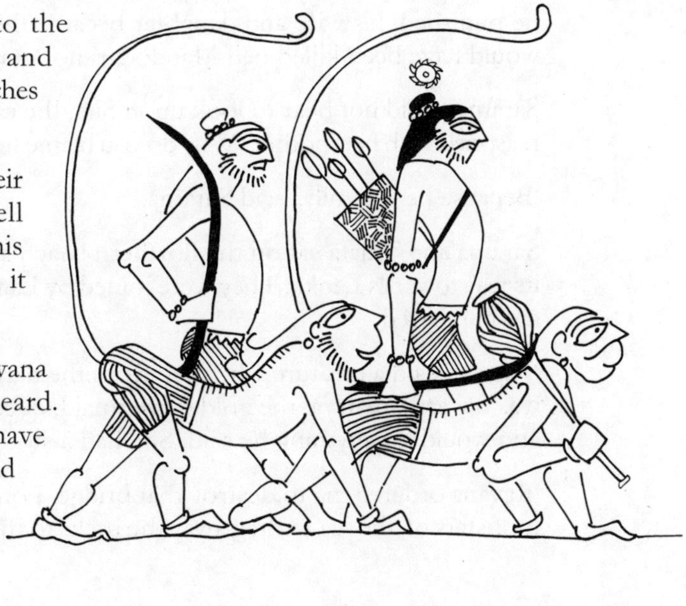

The spies ran back and told Ravana everything they had seen and heard. 'They have no weapons. They have sharp nails and pointed fangs. And they fight with sticks and stones. But what they lack in tools they make up in confidence. They want to fight for Ram. He makes everyone around him want to follow him and do their best.'

The information angered Ravana who kicked them aside, for the truth frightened him.

Shuka said, 'Our enemy treats us with dignity. Our master treats us with disdain.'

Sarana retorted with a voice that conveyed experience, 'Only because the message we carry benefits our enemy, not our master.'

- Valmiki was clearly familiar with the practice of engaging spies by kings of his time. Chandragupta Maurya had an entire department of spies, according to Kautilya's treatise on administration, the *Arthashastra*.
- At one level, the rakshasas have supernatural powers to change shape. At another level, they have mundane needs like spies.

The Golden Mermaid

The women of Lanka dragged Sarama and Trijata out of their house and began thrashing them. They were angry at Vibhishana's betrayal and, since he could not be punished, his wife and daughter became the victims of rakshasa wrath. They would have been killed had Mandodari not granted them refuge.

Sarama could not bear to look upon Sita, the cause of all this trouble. But Trijata reasoned with her mother, 'Why do you blame her? Why do you not blame Ravana?'

'Because he is family,' said Sarama.

Sarama and Trijata sat on the northern beach and saw the bridge steadily making its way towards Lanka. They were joined by Lankini who said, 'The days of Lanka are numbered.'

'I agree,' said a creature who rose from the dark sea waters, gleaming like gold. It was Suvarna-matsya, the golden mermaid, queen of the sea, who adored Ravana and would do anything he said. She had a story to tell.

'Ravana ordered me to destroy that bridge. I ordered all the fish and serpents and monsters of the sea to drag away the rocks to the bottom of the sea. The monkeys were helpless but none dared enter the water, none but a monkey called Hanuman. I wanted to lash him with my tail, sting him with my venomous scales, but when I saw him, I just froze. He was the most beautiful and serene creature I have ever seen in my life: silver and gold, with large eyes, wide nostrils and an upraised tail, the body of a warrior and the aura of a sage. We fought. No, we wrestled. I just wanted to feel his toughness. But he withdrew, sensing my desire. He said he would serve only Ram, no other. Why, I asked. And he said, because he liberated me by having no expectations of me. And I realized how trapped we are by expectations: those that others have of us and those we have of others. I expected something from Ravana, Ravana expected something from me. I expected something from Hanuman, but he expected nothing from me. I suddenly felt this great urge to be liberated. I wanted to break free from everything. I stopped fighting. I decided I would let the bridge be built, encourage all sea creatures to help in building the bridge, and risk Ravana's wrath.'

Trijata told the women on the beach, 'Sita keeps saying something she heard during the Upanishad long ago: I am the creator of my world and so are you. We can widen our world by breaking free from the maze of expectations. We can shrink our world by entrapping ourselves with expectations.'

'If I was just a fish,' said the golden mermaid, 'I would have no expectations of the sea. I would have been resigned to fend for myself. But since I am only half a fish, I expect the sea to provide for me and get frustrated when that does not happen. My human side keeps berating the sea, cajoling the sea and seeking control over the sea.'

Sarama observed, 'Ravana expects his brothers to behave in a particular way. When they don't, he rejects them. Vibhishana also expects Ravana to behave in a particular way. When he does not, he rejects Ravana. This Ram, does he have expectations of his father, mother, brother and wife? Does he reject them if they do not behave as he wants them to?'

Trijata replied, 'If Sita is any indicator, then I think not.'

- The story of the golden mermaid is unique to South-East Asia and finds no reference in Indian retellings. In most versions she is Ravana's daughter.
- This story is amongst the few surviving pieces of Cambodia's *Ramayana* dance heritage.
- In India, there is a close link between Hanuman's celibacy and his great strength. But this is not so in South-East Asia, where Hanuman is a noble rake who has numerous amorous encounters.
- The idea of Hanuman being a romantic rake is also reflected in Jain retellings where he is a form of the love-god Kama.
- The South-East Asian Hanuman is like a guardian knight who helps Prince Ram find Sita. The relationship of deity and devotee so critical in Indian retellings is missing.
- In the *Vinaya Patrika* of Tulsidas written in Avadhi in the sixteenth century, Hanuman is described as being 'manmatha-manthana' (he who churns desires in the mind) as well as 'urdhava-retas' (he who through meditation draws his semen upwards towards the mind rather than towards the womb). Thus he is at once sexual and celibate; all erotic energies are transformed into wisdom in his being. This is why Hanuman was much adored by Tantric yogis, sadhus, sanyasis and vairagis, who gave up worldly life and smeared themselves with ash and became ascetics.
- The story is significant as in the *Adbhut Ramayana* we are informed of Hanuman's son born as a result of a sea creature, probably the golden mermaid, drinking the sweat of Hanuman as he passed over the sea (according to Indian retellings) or while he fought the golden mermaid (according to South-East Asian retellings).

Hanuman's Tail

The bridge was finally complete, in just five days, and the monkey army marched across it carrying Ram and Lakshman on their shoulders. It was a spectacular sight. The sky was covered with celestial beings who could not believe their eyes. Ram had done the impossible: raised an army of monkeys and got them to create a bridge of sticks and stones across the sea. Birds showered flowers on the marching armies. Fishes cheered them along the way.

But just when the army was about to reach the shores of Lanka, an explosion was heard. Rocks from either side of the bridge were cast asunder. Ravana had hurled two missiles with his mighty bow, breaking the two ends of the bridge, entrapping the monkeys in the middle of the sea. Suddenly there were sea monsters circling around, ready to devour Ram and his army. It seemed like all was over.

Once again, Hanuman came to the rescue. He expanded his size, jumped to the shores of Lanka and stretched his tail across to the broken end of the bridge,

making a bridge to the shore of Lanka. Ram and his monkey army walked over his tail and crossed over, thanking him for his quick thinking.

As Ram was about to place his foot on the island, Vibhishana noticed a rakshasa approaching the army; he was blindfolded. 'That is Bhasmalochan,' he informed Ram. 'If he removes his blindfold, all that he will see will burst into flames and be reduced to ashes.'

Ram immediately shot an arrow that transformed into a mirror. That was the first thing Bhasmalochan saw when he removed his blindfold. He who was sent to set aflame Ram's army saw his own reflection and was himself reduced to ashes.

- The story of Hanuman making a bridge of himself seems influenced by the Jataka tale of the Bodhisattva (Buddha in a previous life) as a leader of a troop of monkeys enabling them to escape across a chasm by stretching himself across it. In the process, his back is broken and he dies.
- Rationalists believe that the bridge was built across a river, not the sea.
- There is much speculation on the 'real' location of Lanka. Scholars have speculated that it must be located somewhere in Madhya Pradesh or in Karnataka or Andhra Pradesh, based on information in the Valmiki *Ramayana*. But such rational speculations have no impact on the faithful who are convinced the bridge was built from Rameswaram in Tamil Nadu to Sri Lanka. In the island nation there are many places identified with where Sita was imprisoned (Sita-eliya) and the battle against Ravana was fought (Ravana-goda, Sita-waka).
- The episode of the bridge breaking and Ram's army crossing over to Lanka on Hanuman's tail (in some retellings, on his back) is purely South-East Asian.
- Ram travels across the bridge on Hanuman's shoulders and Lakshman on Angada's.
- The story of Bhasmalochan comes from Krittivasa's Bengali *Ramayana* and is based on similar stories found in the Puranas.

Facing Ravana

Now the island was swarming with monkeys. They circled the land, like a noose determined to choke Lanka.

Ravana climbed up to the tallest tower of Lanka to see the monkey army that had gathered on the shores of Lanka. For the first time, the monkeys and Ram had a view of the man who had abducted Sita. There he stood tall and arrogant, arms crossed, his crowns flashing diamonds. Ravana remembered the words of Nandi, Shiva's bull, 'One day, you arrogant fool, you will face defeat at the hands of monkeys.' Was that curse coming true?

Hundreds of monkeys started scrambling up the towers, determined to bring the rakshasa-king down like a coconut. Their screaming and swift movements took the rakshasas by surprise. Before they knew it, or could do anything, many monkeys tore down the banners that fluttered proudly over the palaces, and Sugriva was dancing on top of Ravana's heads, knocking off the crowns.

The monkeys who were on the beach saw this and roared in approval. Sugriva ran back, beaming with joy. The enemy who sought to intimidate was thus intimidated.

Ram, however, did not smile. He did not approve of such an attack; it was against the rules of war.

Angry at how the monkeys had insulted his father, Indrajit raised his bow and shot arrows at Ram and Lakshman. These were not ordinary arrows. They were naga-pashas, the noose of serpents that coiled around their limbs and immobilized them with deadly venom. Try as they might, the monkeys could not break their bonds. Neither Ram nor Lakshman could move a muscle.

Suddenly from the horizon came a bird, followed by hundreds of other birds, eagles and vultures and crows and geese. They crossed the sea and landed on Lanka and with their sharp beaks and talons ripped away the serpents. Garuda, king of the eagles, led them.

'We heard someone call out to us,' said Garuda.

'Who was it?' asked Ram.

'Sita, from within the walls of this golden city. She knows you have come and rescue is not far away.'

- In most retellings, Sugriva dances on Ravana's heads and knocks his crowns down. In some, it is Angada. Occasionally one hears of Hanuman doing it.
- Ram's displeasure at the attack indicates his discomfort with brute force and barbaric displays of courage. He wants a civilized war, one that follows after appropriate warnings are given and peace efforts made. In that, he is similar to Krishna in the *Mahabharata* who insists on peace negotiations before war is finally declared between the Kauravas and the Pandavas.
- Western scholars see the *Ramayana* in social terms. Thus they see the rakshasas and vanaras divided along religious, social, sectarian and racial lines. Indian scholars prefer seeing the two groups in psychological terms: those whom we don't like are always rakshasas, while those who serve us unquestioningly are vanaras.
- In Bali, the famous Kecak dance or monkey chant tells the story of how the monkeys help Ram defeat Ravana. Kecak was originally a trance ritual that was turned into a theatre form based on the *Ramayana* by the German artist Walter Spies in the 1930s.
- The arrival of Garuda to save Ram from the naga-pasha is the earliest indicator of Ram being seen as an avatar of Vishnu. The episode is found in the Valmiki *Ramayana*. In it, Garuda does not identify Ram as Vishnu but says cryptically that Ram should wait for a time later to know why Garuda came to his rescue. Ram is thus unaware of his own divinity in the Valmiki *Ramayana*.
- In the Gobind *Ramayana*, Sita prays to the snake-gods to save Ram from the snake-bonds.
- Nagas (snakes) and Garuda (the eagle) have an ancient rivalry, akin to the rivalry between asuras and devas, rakshasas and yakshas. All these creatures descend from Kashyapa, son of Brahma.
- South Indian temple lore has it that Garuda enfolds Ram in his wings and begs him to prove that he is indeed Vishnu by taking the form of Krishna. Hanuman does not like this and so, when Ram is reborn as Krishna, he travels to Dwarka and demands Krishna present himself as Ram for his benefit, in the presence of Garuda. These tales speak of rivalry within Vaishnava sects between Ram-worshippers and Krishna-worshippers. Ram-worshippers kept the image of Hanuman before the Vishnu shrine while Krishna-worshippers kept the image of Garuda.

- The lost text of the Bhusundi *Ramayana*, which Tulsidas refers to, was the story of Ram narrated by the crow Kakabhusandi to the eagle Garuda who is confused whether Ram is really Vishnu as he is subjugated by Indrajit's snake-arrows. These medieval *Ramayanas* gradually established the idea that Ram was no hero of Vedic kavyas but God as described in the Puranas.

Angada, the Messenger

On recovering from the snake-arrows, Ram said, 'Let us not fight like barbarians raiding a village. Let us send a messenger to the rakshasas offering to withdraw if they let my Sita go.'

Angada was chosen to serve as Ram's messenger. When he entered Ravana's palace, jeering rakshasas surrounded him. But young Angada was not intimidated. He entered Ravana's hall and made note of the many warriors there, and the fabulous weapons they carried.

First Angada identified himself: 'Long ago, Ravana, king of Lanka, mistook Vali for an ordinary monkey and tried to catch his tail. Vali coiled his tail around Ravana and dragged him around Kishkindha, where the monkeys mistook him for the royal pet. I am Angada, son of that Vali.'

Then Angada clarified his role: 'Long ago, Kartavirya of the Haiheya clan stretched his thousand arms to block the flow of a river, causing a flood that washed away all the flowers and leaves Ravana had gathered for his worship of Shiva. Kartavirya thus humiliated Ravana. Kartavirya was killed by Parashurama, and Parashurama was defeated by Ram of the Raghu clan. I am the messenger of that Ram.'

Finally, Angada communicated the message: 'Ram stands outside the gates ready to attack this city with his army of monkeys. But there can be peace if you return to Ram his wife. A king should care for the welfare of his subjects first, not his own pride, or lust.'

'Monkeys do not make armies,' scoffed Ravana. 'They are captured, and trained to perform. Ram is your master and you are his servants. Join me, and you will be free, unbound by such rules. But if you persist, I will treat you like the animals you are, hunt you down and feast on your flesh.'

'You overestimate your strength. Let me see if there is one rakshasa here who can move this left leg of mine that I have firmly planted on the ground,' challenged Angada.

The rakshasas laughed and came one by one to yank the leg of the audacious monkey and hurl him into the sea. All of them failed.

Still Ravana said, 'I do not fear you. I will kill you and your band of monkeys and your king and that Ram and that Lakshman and that traitor who calls himself my brother.'

Ravana's father, Vishrava, did not like this and advised his son to make peace. So did Ravana's mother, Kaikesi. As did Kaikesi's brother, Malyavan. But Ravana was adamant. No monkey would make a fool of him.

- Angada is chosen as the messenger, not Hanuman, as he is young, royal and perhaps because he does not have a history of burning Lanka.
- In the *Mahabharata*, when Krishna tries to make peace, Duryodhana tries to arrest him and Krishna escapes by spellbinding all with a vision of his cosmic form. In the *Ramayana*, when Ravana tries to catch Angada, he displays his phenomenal strength.
- In the Valmiki *Ramayana*, Angada simply kicks away the rakshasas who try to catch him. In Ram-leela performances of North India, Angada challenges the rakshasas to move his feet from the ground; even Ravana fails.

- Many of Ravana's family members appeal to his good sense. They want him to think of his subjects first. But unlike Ram, who always thinks of Ayodhya, Ravana is consumed by his own self-image, risking the welfare of Lanka.

The Attack

At dawn, the rakshasa army marched out to protect Lanka. They were so different from the band of monkeys who held sticks and stones in their hands They came riding on chariots drawn by donkeys, carts pulled by oxen, and on horses and elephants. They carried bright flags, which fluttered magnificently against the sky, and numerous weapons: clubs, maces, axes, lances, swords, bows and arrows. Every soldier had an armour and a helmet and wore protective magical talismans. And leading them was Ravana himself – a sight to behold, a great parasol over his head, deadly weapons in each of his twenty hands, on a chariot pulled by magnificent horses, surrounded by musicians and trumpeting elephants who announced his arrival.

But the monkeys were not afraid. They moved like a swarm of bees towards the rakshasa horde. They hurled trees and boulders that shattered the chariots and frightened the elephants. Their screams and snarls so terrified the horses that they started retracing their steps. For none who lived in Lanka had ever seen a monkey.

Ravana raised his bow and showered arrows on the monkeys, killing them by the dozens. Cheered by this sight, the rakshasas raised their weapons and began fighting the monkeys, swinging swords to chop off their heads and arms and tails, thrusting spears to puncture their hearts and guts and eyes, pounding their clubs to crush skulls and break bones. Their eyes were filled with rage and their hearts knew no mercy. Those on chariots shot a steady stream of arrows, pinning hundreds of monkeys to the ground. The screams of dying monkeys filled the air, pleasing Ravana. His fears had been unfounded.

The massacre had to stop. They were dying to save his wife. Ram raised his bow, and chanting the hymns that Vishwamitra had taught him, released missile after missile that wiped out column after column of the rakshasa army. He broke their bows, shattered their wheels, their swords, their spears. His arrows caused many to raise their shields and take refuge behind dead soldiers. They forced the advancing army to stop in its tracks, even retreat in some places.

Many fell in the battle, vanaras and rakshasas, sons and brothers, friends and servants – by the hundreds. Many more were maimed, losing hand or foot or ear or eye. But the fighting continued despite their groans and pleas for help.

The battle continued through the day, and stretched into the night. The rakshasas fought holding flaming torches in one hand and weapons in the other. The monkeys grabbed the torches and hurled them into the city, setting towers aflame.

The sounds of war outside the city filled the streets and frightened the women and children, who started to wail.

The only place that was silent and peaceful was the bower of Ashoka trees where Sita sat. She watched the men and women of Lanka run this way and that looking for a place where they would be safe. They had never ever felt so unsafe.

Finally, Ram started shattering the arrows of Ravana as soon as he released them from his bow. So intense was the torrent of arrows released by Ram that it became impossible for Ravana to strike anyone. Exasperated, he decided to turn around, but Ram's arrows would not let him. He felt confined. He could not fight, he could not move. Finally, he dropped his bow in helplessness. Only then did Ram pause and allow the great king's chariot to turn around and return to the city.

Word spread through the city: Ravana had withdrawn his forces. The sound of cheering monkeys could be heard outside. They had not been thrown back into the sea. The rakshasas had been locked in.

- The siege of Lanka has reminded many European and American academicians of the siege of Troy in Greek mythology. In both, husbands are trying to free their wives from within the walls, but that is where the similarity ends. The Greek Helen had eloped with the Trojan prince Paris, while Ravana had abducted Sita. Helen's husband is aided by his elder brother, Agamemnon, who rallies Greek warlords with the promise of plunder. Ram is aided by his younger brother, Lakshman, and they rally monkeys but there is no talk of plunder. This is a battle for all that is good and decent in human society. In the end, Troy is sacked, its women raped and taken into captivity. Not so in the *Ramayana* where the residents of Lanka are treated with the utmost dignity.
- That the war, according to the Valmiki *Ramayana*, stretches into the night is interesting as civilized warfare according to the shastras ends at dusk and resumes at dawn allowing warriors to rest and recover.
- Indian *Ramayanas* value the emotions evoked by war while Thai *Ramayanas* give greater attention to the technicalities of warfare, perhaps because Thai society was witness to long periods of war.
- In the Sri Vaishnava temple tradition, where Ram is viewed as the embodiment of God, it is said that as long as Ravana held the bow in his hand, Ram would not let him leave the battlefield. Ravana had to learn to surrender to the divine but doubt made him cling to weapons.
- Some of the sons of Ravana killed during the war include Akshaya, Atikaya, Indrajit or Meghnad, Trishira, Virabahu, Narantaka, Devantaka and Mantha. The list of names of Ravana's sons varies in different retellings. Conventionally, he is said to have had seven sons. The two most popular ones are Akshaya, killed by Hanuman, and Indrajit, killed by Lakshman.

Recipes of Sita

People have to be fed during a war. And so the kitchens of Lanka were busy. Those who were going to the war had to be fed; those who were returning from the war had to be fed. Food had to inspire, comfort and stir passions.

The smell of rice boiling, vegetables frying and fish roasting filled the city streets, mingling with the smell of blood, rotting flesh and burning towers.

The aromas reached Sita's grove.

'Don't you like that smell?' asked Trijata noticing Sita's expression as she inhaled the vapours. Trijata, Vibhishana's daughter, had become a friend.

'If I was cooking, I would change the proportion of the spices,' Sita said. She gave her suggestions to Trijata, who promptly conveyed them to the royal kitchen.

Mandodari followed these instructions and soon a different aroma wafted out of the kitchen.

So enticing was the resulting aroma that other rakshasa cooks came to the Ashoka grove and asked Sita for cooking tips. Without tasting the food, just by smelling what had been prepared, like a skilled cook, Sita gave her suggestions. 'Add more salt.' 'Replace mustard with pepper.' 'Mix ginger with tamarind.' 'Less cloves, more coconut milk.' These suggestions were promptly executed, and before long Lanka was full of the most delightful aromas and flavours, so delightful that sons and brothers and husbands and fathers wanted to stay back and relish more food. They wanted to burp, then sleep, then wake up and eat again. They wanted to chew areca nuts wrapped in betel leaves and enjoy the company of their wives on swings. No war, no fighting, just conversations over food.

Ravana noticed the lethargy in his men, their reluctance to fight. They were not afraid. They were not drunk. They were just too happy to go to war. Furious, he ordered the kitchens to be closed. 'Starve the soldiers. Hungry men are angry men. In anger they will kill the monkeys. The only food they can eat is monkey flesh.'

- Sita's kitchen is a common theme in folklore and at pilgrim spots. She was a great cook. Traditionally, the belief is that people who are well fed are less angry and not prone to violence.
- The Valmiki *Ramayana* is clear in pointing out the consumption of non-vegetarian food, especially game, in Lanka, but is shy of the same when it comes to Kishkindha and Ayodhya. Traditionally, Indians associate non-vegetarian food and alcohol with sensuality and violence.

Lakshman Struck Down

As the war resumed, Ravana sent out his sons to fight. Bravely they rode out bearing weapons. Lifeless they returned, their bones broken by monkeys, their limbs torn by the arrows of Ram, or Lakshman. As the number of widows and orphans increased in the palace, Ravana's eldest son, Indrajit, decided it was time for him to lead the troops, enter the battlefield and boost the sagging morale of his people.

Indrajit was named Meghnad as at the time of his birth, instead of crying, he had roared like a storm cloud. He had earned the title Indrajit after defeating Indra in battle. Everyone feared Indrajit. It was he who had captured Hanuman and immobilized Ram and Lakshman with his dreaded snake arrows. Though he did not approve of his father's action, Indrajit felt as a son it was his duty to fight his father's enemies.

'He is a good son,' Ravana said proudly as Indrajit rode out.

'He is a fool,' thought Mandodari, not liking the idea of her son fighting to help his father secure a new wife.

Indrajit's wife, Sulochana, watched the rakshasas cheering her husband. She belonged to the Naga clan and in her dowry she had brought with her the many naga-pashas that Indrajit used in battle. But with the eagles on Ram's side, she wondered if her arrows could save her husband.

It was a fierce battle, made complicated by the magical powers of Indrajit. He could make his chariot invisible and create illusions that would distract Ram and Lakshman. Once he created the illusion of Sita being carried on his flying chariot and being slaughtered above the monkey army, a vision that had even Ram confused for a moment. Ram realized Indrajit was faster and smarter than any warrior he had encountered before. Indrajit realized that Ram was not an easy warrior to defeat. Cunning was needed to overpower him.

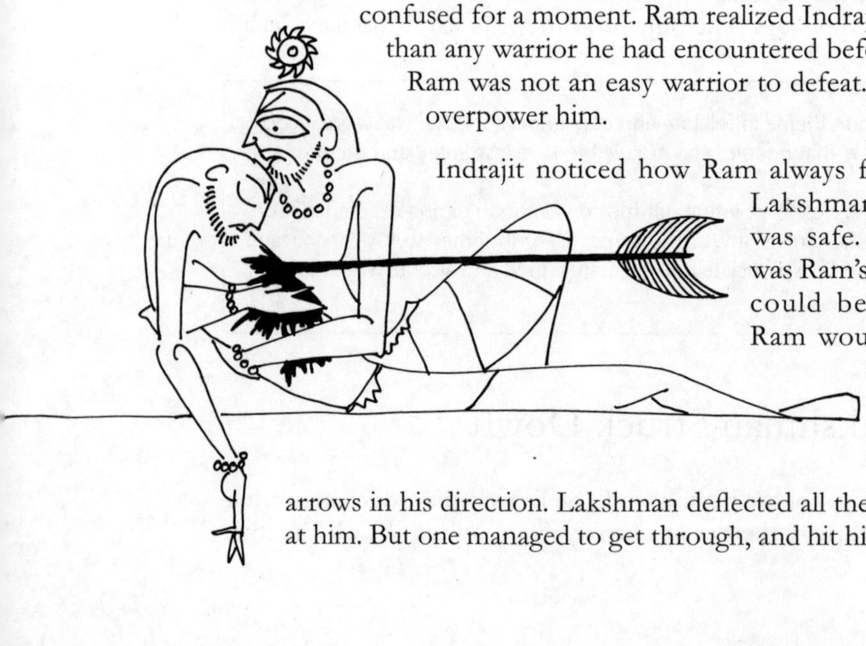

Indrajit noticed how Ram always fought with one eye on Lakshman, making sure that he was safe. He realized Lakshman was Ram's weak spot; if Lakshman could be brought down, then Ram would be too demotivated to continue the war. So he focused all his energies on Lakshman – shooting a volley of arrows in his direction. Lakshman deflected all the arrows Indrajit directed at him. But one managed to get through, and hit him right next to his heart.

It felt like a sharp scorpion sting. As he fell, he felt as if a python had grabbed him and was squeezing the life out of him. Fire seemed to course through his blood. The pain was excruciating. He screamed and that scream brought the battle to a halt. Indrajit tried to grab the fallen body and drag it into the city, but Hanuman rushed to the spot, pushed Indrajit away and took custody of Lakshman's limp body.

Ram rushed to the spot as the rakshasas withdrew, singing songs of triumph, pleased that Indrajit had finally turned the war in their favour. Ram was inconsolable in his grief. 'I failed to protect Sita. I failed to protect Lakshman. What will I tell his mother when I return to Ayodhya? Will I return to Ayodhya alone? Must I even return so to Ayodhya?'

- Dashratha's relationship with Ram needs to be contrasted with Ravana's relationship with Indrajit. Dashratha is a protective father while Ravana is an exploitative father. Dashratha is forced by royal rules to send his son to exile while Ravana's rage and lust prevent him from letting Sita go, thus compelling Indrajit to fight Ram.
- Ram may be God but he displays human emotions like grief when Sita is abducted and Lakshman is hurt. Some scholars call it leela, or playacting. Everyone agrees it is a unique feature of Hindu tradition where God is also subject to all human experiences and emotions.

Hanuman to the Rescue

As the venom spread through Lakshman's veins, the old bear Jambuvan said that the only thing that could save him was a herb called Sanjivani found on the hill of herbs, Gandhamadan, far to the north of the Vindhyas on the slopes of the Himalayas. 'It has to reach here before sunrise. If anyone can do it, it is Hanuman.'

Hanuman immediately leapt into the air and made his way north.

Ravana saw this from his tower, and dispatched the rakshasa Kalanemi, time-traveller and shape-shifter, to thwart Hanuman's mission.

Hanuman reached Gandhamadan very quickly and was greeted by a sage who said he would point out the magical herb provided Hanuman took a bath in the lake. The plant was sacred and was not to be touched by unwashed hands!

But in the waters was a great crocodile ready to eat Hanuman. As Hanuman battled the crocodile, the crocodile spoke in a woman's voice, 'I am an apsara cursed to live as a crocodile until a monkey overpowers me. If you do succeed in overpowering me and liberating me, know this: the sage you met at the foot of the mountain is no sage; he is Kalanemi sent by Ravana to destroy you.'

Hanuman managed to overpower the crocodile. He then crushed Kalanemi underfoot and went in search of the magical herb. Time was running out; the sun would soon rise and it would all be over.

To make matters worse, Ravana, who controlled the celestial bodies in the sky, compelled Surya to rise before time, despite his protests. When Hanuman realized this, he caught the sun and trapped him in his underarm.

Hanuman then scoured the mountain for the herb. In the moonlight it was difficult to distinguish one plant from another. So he decided to carry the entire mountain to Lanka and let Jambuvan find the herb. The devas watched in amazement as Hanuman increased his size and then proceeded to uproot the entire mountain, balance it in the palm of one hand and leap up into the sky making his way southwards, the sun trapped in his armpit.

- The most popular image of Hanuman in temples is of him carrying the mountain in one hand and crushing Kalanemi under his foot.
- The mountain of herbs is identified as the Valley of Flowers near Badri in Uttarakhand on the slopes of the Himalayas. It is sometimes called Gandhamadan, and at other times Dronagiri.
- Hanuman, though a great warrior, is not viewed as a god in the Valmiki *Ramayana*. This transformation starts around the eighth century CE, with naga-babas (naked ascetics) identifying him with Shiva, and later with him being seen as the perfect bhakta of Ram by scholars and sages such as Ramanuja of Tamil Nadu (twelfth century), Madhwa of Karnataka (thirteenth century), Ramanand (fourteenth century) whose influence was great in North India, and Ramdas (seventeenth century) who was popular in Maharashtra.
- In the Gangetic plains are akharas, local gymnasiums, where men hope to be like Hanuman, strong and celibate warriors who serves Ram unconditionally. Here they spend their free time bodybuilding.
- Hanuman is the patron god of physical training across India.

Hanuman Encounters Bharata

To go south, Hanuman had to cross Ayodhya and the strange sight of a flying hill frightened the residents of the city. What was even more intriguing was that the monkey carrying the hill kept chanting the name of Ram.

Bharata, caretaker of the Kosala kingdom, immediately mounted his bow and, also chanting the name of Ram, shot at the beast carrying the hill. The arrow struck Hanuman and he fell down near Nandigram where Bharata had taken residence. 'Who are you,' asked Bharata, 'and why are you chanting the name of my brother Ram?'

Hanuman fell at Bharata's feet. 'Are you the brother of Ram who gave up the kingdom that his mother had secured for him through guile? Blessed am I to meet you.' Bharata was surprised that the monkey knew so much about him. Hanuman then introduced himself and told him the situation Ram was in. Bharata had had no news of Ram ever since they parted ways at Chitrakut. He felt miserable for his brother and for Sita and for Lakshman and thanked Hanuman for coming to the aid of his brother.

'Sugriva owes my brother a favour. But you, why do you help Ram?' asked Bharata.

'He inspires me to be a better man,' said Hanuman. Bharata smiled on hearing this from a monkey. 'But soon it will be time for the sun to rise. I am afraid by interrupting my journey you have delayed me and I may not be able to make it in time to give the life-saving herb to Lakshman.'

'Don't say that,' said Bharata. 'Climb on my arrow and I will ensure it carries you to Lanka in time.' Trusting Bharata's abilities completely, Hanuman, mountain in hand, sun in armpit, jumped on Bharata's arrow that he shot southwards. Charged with the power of hymns and the name of Ram, it managed to transport Hanuman to Lanka in no time.

Jambuvan found the magical herb on the mountain and it was given to Lakshman early enough to counter the effects of Indrajit's poisonous dart. His breathing became normal, his eyes cleared, energy flowed through his limbs and he jumped up ready to do combat.

'I think it is time for you to let the sun go,' said Ram to Hanuman in a voice full of gratitude. Hanuman had quite forgotten about the sun. He raised his arm and Surya made his way to the sky. In the glory of the morning light, Ravana saw the monkeys march towards Lanka once more, chanting the name of Ram, led by an invigorated and determined Lakshman.

- The story of Bharata's intervention comes from regional retellings of the *Ramayana* written after the tenth century.
- The story reveals the tension between establishing the greatness of Hanuman, the monkey-servant, and the greatness of Bharata, the royal brother. Hanuman flies carrying the mountain while Bharata's arrow carries Hanuman carrying the mountain. Bharata is seen almost as a twin of Ram.
- In the Valmiki *Ramayana*, Hanuman brings the mountain of herbs to Lanka twice.
- In Rameswaram is a hill identified as the remains of the mountain brought to the south by Hanuman.

Sulochana

Indrajit was furious that Lakshman had been revived. Then a piece of information reached him that turned his rage into fear. He learned that Lakshman had not slept for over twelve years and through that period had been a celibate ascetic. It had been foretold that Indrajit would die only at the hands of such a man.

A nervous Indrajit withdrew to a cave and began worshipping Kali. If anyone could save him from Lakshman it was the Goddess.

Not finding Indrajit on the battlefield, Lakshman growled like a frustrated lion. Vibhishana said, 'I am sure he has gone to the cave inside the Nikumbila Hill to appease the Goddess with sacrifices and gain powers from her. If he does succeed, he will be invincible.'

'Show me the way to that cave. Let us interrupt this sacrifice. Let us kill Indrajit,' said Lakshman.

'Do you realize, Lakshman,' said Ram, 'when Tadaka interrupted Vishwamitra's yagna, we called her a demon. Now we plan to interrupt Indrajit's worship. Are we demons too?'

Lakshman was too angry to think about the irony of the situation. He followed Vibhishana along with a group of monkeys to the cave where they found Indrajit in the midst of a ritual, offering sacrifices to the Goddess, determined to satisfy her.

While the monkeys kicked away the sacred utensils, pulled away the mat on which Indrajit sat and screamed loudly to drown all sounds of chanting, Lakshman raised his bow and challenged Indrajit to a duel.

Cursing his uncle for revealing his secret temple, Indrajit picked up his bow and shot arrows to counter the arrows shot by Lakshman. It was a fierce fight that lasted for hours. No one interfered, as it was between Lakshman and Indrajit. The flesh of both warriors was pierced with hundreds of arrows

but they continued fighting. Finally, Lakshman released an arrow with a crescent blade and it cut off Indrajit's head.

The arrow carried Indrajit's head through the air right into Ravana's hall in Lanka. 'I am sorry I failed you,' said Indrajit's head before shutting its eyes.

Ravana broke down on seeing his son's severed head. Mandodari beat her chest in sorrow. Gloom descended on the city. The greatest and noblest warrior of Lanka was dead.

Indrajit's wife, Sulochana, said, 'My husband must be cremated in full. We must get back the rest of his body so that it can be joined to the head before the funeral takes place.' The body lay unattended in the battlefield and no rakshasa was willing to go there and fight the vanaras to claim the body. 'Then I will go myself,' said Sulochana.

'No, don't go,' said Mandodari to her daughter-in-law. 'They may capture you and hold you hostage and ask for Sita as ransom. They may do unspeakable things to you.'

'I must take my chances,' said Sulochana bravely. She marched to the battlefield with a group of women and found the headless body of Indrajit surrounded by monkeys. She walked straight up to Ram and said, 'My husband was a dutiful son just like you. And I have been his devoted wife, as Sita has been yours. Allow me to claim his body. Let him be complete when he makes his journey across the Vaitarni to the land of Yama.'

Impressed by the nobility and the courage of this lady, Ram let her claim Indrajit's body. She took it away, speaking not a word. If she was angry with Lakshman, or Ram, or the monkeys, she did not show it. She had tried stopping her husband but knew that he would not be able to say no to his father. This was an eventuality she had been prepared for. She accepted her fate with grace.

- In one Bhil version of the tale, Kubera sends a magic potion to Lakshman to wash his eyes with, after using which he can see, and kill, the invisible Indrajit. Thus Kubera takes revenge on Ravana through Lakshman.
- Sulochana, known as Prameela in some retellings, emerges as a character in medieval literature. That Indrajit is associated with snake-arrows may have inspired the idea that he had a snake-wife.
- Indrajit's wife performs sati: she burns herself on Indrajit's funeral pyre. This practice, now illegal, was long considered the sign of a noble woman. Women across Maharashtra, Andhra Pradesh and Karnataka sing praises of Sati Sulochana.
- The story of Sati Sulochana has been made into many films, the first of which was a silent film in 1921. In 1934 it was the theme of the first Kannada talkie.
- Michael Madhusudan Dutt in the nineteenth century wrote the ballad *Meghnad Badh Kavya* in Bengali in the Homeric style, projecting Meghnad as an Indian version of the Greek hero Hector, who fights for the wrong side out of a sense of duty. Hector was the elder brother of the Trojan prince Paris who eloped with Helen, wife of Menelaus, and incurred the wrath of the Greeks. Hector did not like what his brother had done but still fought for him. Hector's relationship with his wife, Andromache, is a loving one, just like the relationship between Indrajit and his wife, called Pramila in Madhusudan Dutt's work. Hector was killed and his body desecrated by the Greek hero Achilles, until the king of Troy, Priam, came to him at night in disguise and begged him to release the body so that it could be cremated with dignity.

Kumbhakarna

'He has a brother who does not ever go to sleep. And I have a brother who sleeps all the time,' yelled Ravana, remembering Kumbhakarna, his younger brother, who woke up just one day a year.

Kumbhakarna's tapasya had earned him a boon. He wanted to ask for the throne of Indra, but instead he asked for the throne of Nidra, the goddess of sleep, a slip of the tongue that led to him being asleep all year round. It was foretold that he would be invincible on the day he awoke but if his sleep was interrupted, he would be killed that very day.

'My city is overrun by monkeys. My sons are dead. I cannot wait for Kumbhakarna to wake up at his leisure. He must be woken now,' said Ravana.

And so musicians with drums and blaring conch shells were sent to his chambers to create a cacophony that would force him to wake up. Servants poked and prodded Kumbhakarna with sharp implements in the hope that he would open his eyes. Nothing worked. Finally the most aromatic of foods were brought into his room, at the smell of which he stirred and finally woke up. 'I guess my brother would rather I die than sleep,' he said as he yawned and stretched himself.

When he heard what had transpired while he was asleep, he knew what was expected of him – unquestioning obedience. So armed with weapons he entered the battlefield.

The sight of this giant rakshasa frightened all the monkeys. Never had anyone seen anything as big as this creature. They hurled boulders at him. Kumbhakarna felt as if grains of sand were hitting him. They hurled trees at him. Kumbhakarna felt twigs and leaves were tickling him. When he roared, it sounded like a thunderclap. When he walked, it felt like an earthquake.

Watching every monkey quiver in fear, Sugriva rushed towards Kumbhakarna but Kumbhakarna caught him by his tail and mocked his efforts. Not one to give up, Sugriva swung his body until he could grab Kumbhakarna's ear. Then he bit it with such force that he tore the lobe. Kumbhakarna screamed in agony and let him go.

Suddenly, the demon did not seem as invincible as before. With their faith renewed, the monkeys resumed their fight with vigour. And Ram mounted his bow to face this giant.

No single arrow would kill Kumbhakarna. And so Ram shot arrows to break the demon down part by part. With one arrow he sliced off the left arm, with another the right arm, with the third his left leg, with the fourth his right leg, and with the fifth his head. The great giant, as foretold, was killed on the day his sleep was interrupted.

The rakshasas wanted to blame Ram for his death but knew in their hearts it was the impatience of Ravana that had caused it.

- In the Valmiki *Ramayana*, Kumbhakarna is killed before Indrajit. But different retellings follow different sequences. In the Kashmiri *Ramayana*, Indrajit is killed first.
- Kumbhakarna has become a colloquial metaphor for a person who is forever sleeping.
- Before dying, Kumbhakarna begs that his head be thrown into the sea so that rakshasas cannot see his ears ripped to shreds by monkeys.
- A satellite peak on Mount Kanchenjunga in Nepal is named Kumbhakarna. It was here that Kumbhakarna's head was supposed to have fallen after he was killed in battle.
- If Indrajit represents skill then Kumbhakarna represents brute force. In the *Mahabharata*, Arjuna is to Yudhisthira what Indrajit is to Ravana and Bhima is to Yudhisthira what Kumbhakarna is to Ravana. A king needs both, the skilled warrior and the strong warrior.
- At the culmination of the Ram-leela performance in North India, the actor playing the role of Ram sets aflame the effigies of Ravana, Indrajit and Kumbhakarna. According to one theory, this practice was started in the Gangetic plains during medieval times as a symbolic act of rejecting Muslim rule.

Taranisen

Then a warrior entered the battlefield, the kind no monkey or Ram had seen before. He called himself Taranisen and every inch of his body was tattooed with the name of Ram. He led the rakshasas into the battlefield and under his leadership they fought like a pack of wolves determined to catch their prey.

'How can I kill him? He worships me,' said Ram. 'Can I breach the fortress built using my name?'

Vibhishana said, 'Strike him in his mouth. Knock out his teeth and slice off his

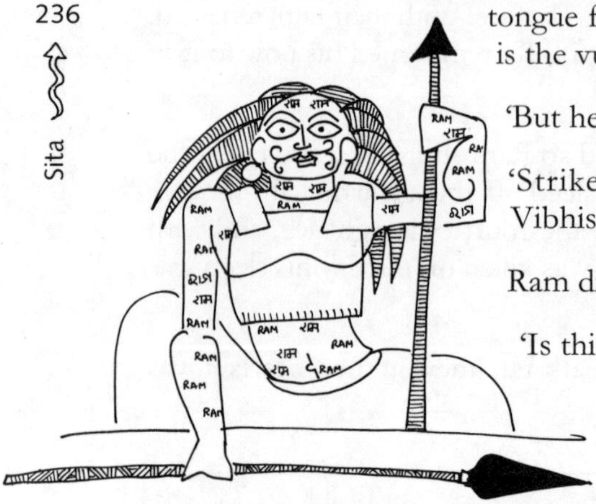

tongue for they are not marked with your name. That is the vulnerable spot.'

'But he chants my name with great devotion.'

'Strike in the pause between two chants,' said Vibhishana.

Ram did as he was told. And Taranisen was killed.

'Is this Ravana's son too?' asked Ram.

'No,' said Vibhishana, tears streaming down his cheeks, 'that is my son. Too loyal to leave his uncle, too angry to call me father.'

- The character Taranisen is found only in Krittivasa's *Ramayana*.
- The *Dandi Ramayana* refers to Virabahu, son of Ravana, who is a great warrior as well as a great devotee of Ram. He fights Ram, defeats Ram, and then falls at Ram's feet and wants Ram to cut off his head so that he can go to Vaikuntha, the abode of Vishnu, where one is liberated from the cycle of rebirths. Ram refuses. So he abuses Ram until Ram cuts his head off. This is an example of viparit-bhakti, reverse devotion, displaying devotion by mocking and taunting God.
- The power of Ram's name became popular in the fourteenth century after Ramanand popularized devotion to Ram especially in North India. Chanting the name of Ram became the greatest of prayers to invoke the power of God.

Mahiravana

Ravana then turned to his friend Mahiravana, king of Patala, the subterranean realm. He was a great devotee of Kali and a sorcerer. He would offer the Goddess human sacrifices and in exchange acquire siddha. 'Kill Ram who killed Kumbhakarna. Kill Lakshman who killed Indrajit. I am sure their sacrifice will secure you more powers,' Ravana told Mahiravana. The idea appealed to the great sorcerer, who had initially hesitated attacking a man who had done him no harm.

Vibhishana meanwhile told Hanuman, 'With Kumbhakarna and Indrajit gone, Ravana will surely turn to Mahiravana. Only you can protect Ram and Lakshman for you are also blessed with siddha.'

Hanuman therefore extended his tail and coiled it around to create a fortress in which Ram and Lakshman were told to rest whenever they were not in battle. No one would be able to cross the ring without Hanuman's permission.

Mahiravana made many attempts to enter this fortress: he came disguised as Jambuvan, then Kaushalya, then Janaka. Each time Vibhishana recognized him. Finally, he took the form of Vibhishana himself, duped Hanuman and managed to enter the fortress. He cast a spell on Ram and Lakshman, and carried them off to Patala through a tunnel he bore into the ground.

When the abduction was discovered Hanuman leapt into the tunnel and followed Mahiravana to Patala, determined to rescue the brothers.

At the entrance of Patala, Hanuman met a fierce warrior, who was equal in strength to him. They fought for a long time and Hanuman found it impossible to overpower him. 'Who are you?' he asked.

'I am Makaradvaja, son of Hanuman,' he said.

'That is impossible. I am Hanuman and I have no wife. I have been celibate all my life.'

Makaradvaja demanded proof that Hanuman was indeed who he claimed to be. 'There are five lamps burning in the five different directions of Patala. If you can blow them all out simultaneously, I will believe you are indeed Hanuman.'

Hanuman sprouted four extra heads: of a boar, an eagle, a horse and a lion. He then exhaled vigorously from all five mouths and extinguished the five lamps of Patala, convincing Makaradvaja that he was indeed who he claimed to be.

Makaradvaja then revealed that when Hanuman was flying over the sea to Lanka a drop of his sweat fell into the waters and was consumed by Makaradvaja's mother, a fish. Thus was he born. He had been told by sages to guard the gates of Patala, for here he would meet his father.

Makaradvaja bowed to his father and said, 'No one in Patala will stop you now, for I have let you pass.'

True enough, no one in Patala stopped Hanuman. He found his way to the corner where Ram and Lakshman had been kept chained, ready to be sacrificed. They were anointed with turmeric, decked with red hibiscus flowers and fed savoury dishes. 'You are lucky. You are going to be offered to the Goddess,' said the residents of Patala.

Hanuman took the form of a bee, flew close to Ram and told him how he could get out of this messy situation. When Ram was taken to the sacrificial altar and told to bend so that his head could be severed from his body, Ram said what Hanuman had told him to say, 'I am the eldest son of the Raghu-kula, prince of Ayodhya. I have never bowed my head in my life. I would like the great sorcerer to show me how.'

Since all wishes of the creature being sacrificed have to be fulfilled, Mahiravana went down on his knees and demonstrated how to place the neck on the sacrificial altar. As soon as he did this, Hanuman moved like lightning. He picked up the sacrificial sword and beheaded Mahiravana in one stroke.

The sacrifice was thus completed. Pleased with the sacrifice, the Goddess blessed Hanuman and said, 'When Ram is gone from this earth, serve as my guardian.'

'But Ram will never leave the earth,' said Hanuman. The Goddess smiled on hearing this, as did Ram.

When Hanuman placed Ram and Lakshman on his shoulders and prepared to leave Patala, Chandrasena, Mahiravana's wife, blocked his path. Hanuman kicked her aside.

Chandrasena was pregnant with Mahiravana's child. The unborn child, Ahiravana, was so furious at his mother being treated like this that he emerged out of his mother's womb, a full-grown warrior, and challenged Hanuman to a duel.

Hanuman trampled Ahiravana underfoot, leapt out of Patala and returned to earth.

- The story of Ram's abduction and Hanuman's journey to the subterranean regions comes from the Sanskrit *Adbhut Ramayana*. It has fantasy elements that make it more entertainment than sacred story.
- Ram had admonished Hanuman for taking the decision to burn Lanka. After that Hanuman decided never to be proactive and only to obey Ram. To make Hanuman change his ways, and become proactive once again, the gods devised the whole adventure to Patala where Hanuman had to take decisions on his own, as Ram was not around.
- According to the *Hanuman Chalisa*, the hymn of forty verses in praise of Hanuman, composed by Tulsidas in the sixteenth century in Avadhi, Hanuman has eight siddha powers: the power to expand, the power to shrink, the power to change shape, the power to overpower, the power to become extremely heavy, the power to become extremely light, the power to travel anywhere and the power to grant any wish.
- The idea of Hanuman having children is awkward as Hanuman is renowned for his chastity.
- Across India one has temples of Patal-Hanuman (the Hanuman who went to the netherworld), Dakshin-mukhi Hanuman (the Hanuman who faces south, the direction of death) and Pancha-mukhi or Dasa-mukhi Hanuman (the Hanuman with five or ten heads). In this form, he is not Ramdas (servant of Ram); he is the very autonomous Mahavir or Mahabali (the great hero).
- The image of Hanuman sprouting heads of a lion, a horse, an eagle and a boar is popular amongst Madhwa sampradaya in Karnataka. It transforms Hanuman from servant of God to God himself as this form is visually similar to Krishna's cosmic form found in the Mahabharata.
- In some stories, Mahiravana is addressed as Ahiravana; in others Mahiravana is the father of Ahiravana.
- In the Krittivasa *Ramayana*, Ahiravana, the newly-born child of Mahiravana, is a full-grown warrior. He is covered with afterbirth and naked; still he fights his father's killer.
- In the Gujarati Giridhar *Ramayana*, Mahiravana's wife, Chandrasena, turns against her husband on the promise that Ram will be her husband. Ram refuses to marry her but promises her that when he takes birth as Krishna, she will be reborn as Satyabhama and will be his wife.

- In art, Hanuman is sometimes shown trampling a woman, variously identified as Surpanakha, Chandrasena, or Panvati, a malefic astrological influence that can be overcome by the grace of Hanuman. This rather misogynistic side of Hanuman is not very popular amongst devotees.
- With the Goddess being the ishta-devata, or chief deity, of Indrajit and Mahiravana, the Shakti cult of the Goddess makes its presence felt in the *Ramayana*.

Ravana's Wives

On rising to earth, Hanuman learned that Ravana was invoking Kali: he had heard of Mahiravana's defeat and was filled with dread. If Ravana succeeded, he would become invincible in battle.

Hanuman immediately rushed into Lanka along with Angada and found this was indeed true. He created a racket, and kicked away the utensils and the baskets of fruits and flowers being offered to the Goddess. He shouted and screamed, hoping to distract Ravana; but Ravana was lost in meditation and refused to stop his ritual.

Finally, Angada grabbed Mandodari's clothes and started to yank them off, and she screamed, 'What is this, Ravana? Will you let a monkey treat me, your wife, like this?'

Ravana could not ignore her piteous cries. He stopped his ritual and came to her rescue. Angada immediately let Mandodari go and returned to the battlefield with Hanuman, their mission successful.

- In different versions, Ravana either invokes Shiva or Kali. These narrations gain prominence in regional *Ramayanas*, especially those from Bengal, indicating the rise of the Shakta or Goddess cult, alongside Shaivism and Vaishnavism.
- In Krittivasa's *Ramayana*, Hanuman wipes clean the document containing hymns to Kali and so Ravana is unable to invoke the Goddess.
- This episode of Mandodari being treated with disrespect by Angada is found in the *Adhyatma Ramayana* and a few regional narrations. The idea of laying claim over the wives of the enemy, however, does not find great favour in Indian epics; in contrast Greek epics such as the *Iliad* are replete with instances of Trojan women being raped and turned into slaves.
- In South-East Asian versions, many rakshasa women fall in love with Hanuman. This did not find favour in the Indian subcontinent.
- That Hanuman disrupts the yagnas and rituals of Indrajit and Ravana is in line with his association with Shiva, who destroyed the yagna of Dakṣha.
- Stories of disruption of yagnas and pujas resulting in the failure of an enterprise draws attention to ritualism and sorcery that is practised by people. This practice was frowned upon by those who favoured bhakti, affectionate devotion, over magic.

The Blue Lotus

Ram said, 'Indrajit worships Kali. Mahiravana worships Kali. Ravana worships Kali. Perhaps I should also worship Kali. But while they make offerings of fear, through human sacrifices, I shall offer her only love, through 108 lotuses.'

These were gathered and Ram began worshipping the Goddess. He chanted her many names and with each name offered a lotus flower. To test Ram's devotion to her, Kali caused one of the lotus flowers to disappear. And so when Ram was chanting the 108th name, he found he was one lotus short.

Ram did not want to stop the ritual so he decided to offer one of his eyes instead, for did his mother not describe him as lotus-eyed? He picked up an arrow and was about to carve out his eye, when the Goddess appeared before him as Durga, who is as wild as Kali and as demure as Gauri, who looks like a bride but is a warrior ready to jump into battle astride a lion. 'Stop,' she said and blessed Ram, assuring him of victory in battle.

Thus Ram entered the battle with the blessings of Durga who is Shakti. Ravana entered the battle chanting the name of Shiva.

- The story of Ram offering his eye to Durga is popular in Bengal. In many households, during Dussehra, 108 lamps are lit to commemorate his offering of 108 lotuses to the Goddess.
- The Goddess is worshipped for nine nights in spring. Ram is responsible for also shifting Goddess-worship to autumn. Hence the worship of Durga in autumn is called Akal Bodhon (untimely invocation).
- Suryakant Tripathi 'Nirala', the great Hindi poet, wrote the iconic 'Ram ki Shakti Puja' (the Shakti worship of Ram) based on this episode from the Bengali *Ramayana*.
- The episode draws attention to the personal sacrifices that must be made in order to reach one's goal.
- Durga is a less wild form of Kali. She is less domesticated than Gauri. She stands in between, bride and warrior. Kali is more associated with the rakshasas and Durga with Ram, indicating Ram embodies civilization, not Ravana.

Ravana Falls

Ravana's sons were dead. His brothers were dead. His friends were dead. His soldiers were dead, or dying. The city was filled with the maimed: those who had lost an eye, an ear, a hand, a foot. Many had been scarred both physically and mentally, the screams of monkeys keeping them awake all night. The towers were burning, the walls crumbling. The moat was filled with rotting corpses. The smell was unbearable. Children kept crying, asking for their fathers who would not return. Lanka, once a pleasure garden, had become a city of ghosts and widows. Their unhappy faces lined the streets as Ravana finally decided to face the enemy.

'Just give her up,' begged Mandodari.

'No,' said Ravana, stubborn as ever.

His march was grand, as it always was: his chariot pulled by magnificent horses, flanked by elephants and soldiers and musicians. But the soldiers dragged their feet and the music did not inspire confidence. Still it was a splendid sight, with the rakshasa-king holding bows and arrows in his twenty arms, flags fluttering on either side, his ten heads gazing upon the enemy defiantly.

'You have trained your monkeys well,' Ravana taunted Ram, who had no chariot and rode on Hanuman's shoulders.

'They fight because they want to. Your rakshasas fight because they have no choice,' said Ram.

'Lanka will never be yours.'

'This is not an invasion. This is a rescue. I don't want Lanka, just Sita. Let her go and all will be well.'

'No,' said Ravana, raising his bow.

As Ram and Ravana invoked Shiva for blessings, Shakti asked Shiva, 'Who do you really support?'

'Both, of course. Ram will win because he will make Ravana see. Ravana will win because he will finally open his eyes,' said Shiva.

Magnificent arrows were released from either side of the battlefield. Ravana used his arrows to deflect Ram's arrows and Ram used his arrows to deflect Ravana's arrows.

Ravana remembered Surpanakha with her bleeding nose, the mocking tail of Hanuman, the burning towers of Lanka, Vibhishana's betrayal, Sulochana on Indrajit's funeral pyre, the dismembered body of Kumbhakarna, the ripped mouth of Taranisen and the lamentations of Mandodari. And this made him grow angrier and angrier. Ram kept thinking of Sita, quietly awaiting him somewhere behind the walls, and he became calmer and calmer.

Ram finally shot an arrow that severed one of Ravana's heads from his body. To his surprise, another head replaced it. He shot another arrow that severed even this head. But once again, another head replaced it. The fallen heads laughed contemptuously.

'There is a pot of the nectar of immortality hidden in his navel,' whispered Vibhishana, 'a gift he obtained from Brahma.'

Ravana watched Vibhishana whisper, and roared in rage, 'We reveal our vulnerabilities to those we love and trust. And you take advantage of this, share it with this killer, all because you want to be king!'

'I am not like you,' Vibhishana cried out, hoping his brother could hear him. But nothing was heard. The time for talking and listening was over. Ravana mouthed profanities at his brother and kept shooting arrows at Ram.

Ram hesitated to aim the arrow at Ravana's navel. He remembered his father telling him that during war the leader of one army should only direct his arrows at the head or heart of the leader of the other army, nowhere else. It was the right thing to do. Sensing what was going through his brother's mind, Lakshman came between Ram and Ravana, raised his bow, and shot an arrow that struck Ravana's navel, broke the pot of nectar and left Ravana vulnerable.

'Why did you do that?' said Ram, turning to his brother.

'Because you would not, and someone had to,' said Lakshman. 'Now, don't think, don't wonder, just get done with the deed.'

Ram decided to shoot the greatest arrow in the world, the Brahmastra, charged with the power of Brahma, to kill the grandson of Brahma, who claimed to be a brahmin but never sought the brahman.

Chanting the right mantra, Ram mounted his bow and from Hanuman's shoulders shot the arrow that ripped through Ravana's heart; he fell to the ground, chanting, to everyone's surprise, the name of Ram.

A stunned silence followed. The vanaras could not believe that Ravana had finally been struck. The rakshasas could not believe that their great, invincible leader had actually been defeated. The sun stopped in its tracks. The clouds became still. The wind paused. Ravana had fallen. Yes, the great son of Vishrava, descendant of Pulastya and Brahma, would never rise again.

- In the Valmiki *Ramayana*, Indra sends his chariot and charioteer for Ram as Ravana refuses to fight a warrior who does not stand on a chariot.
- In many South-East Asian and folk retellings, it is Lakshman, not Ram, who kills Ravana.
- In Jain scriptures there is the concept of sixty-three salaka purushas or worthy beings: nine sets of heroes, twelve kings and twenty-four enlightened sages. The set of heroes always includes a violent hero (Vasudeva), a pacifist victim (Baladeva) and a villain (Prati-Vasudeva). The *Ramayana* is the story of one such set of heroes: Ram is the Baladeva, Ravana is the Prati-Vasudeva and Lakshman is the Vasudeva, which means Lakshman has to kill Ravana, not Ram.
- In the Bhil *Ramayana*, Lakshman kills the bee that contains the life of Ravana.
- The Puranas speak of Ravana seeking from Brahma protection from all creatures except humans, whom he did not fear. This is the loophole that Vishnu takes advantage of when he takes the form of Ram to kill Ravana.
- In Kamban's Tamil *Ramayana*, Ram's single arrow pierces Ravana's body several times seeking the love he has for Sita or the space in his heart where he has held Sita captive.
- In the *Ramayana* from Laos, Phra Lam (Ram) is seen as the Buddha in his earlier life and Ravana is visualized as the demon of desire, Mara.
- The sage Agastya teaches Ram the Adityahridayam, a chant invoking the sun-god who gives courage and strength to the warrior.
- In one Telugu retelling, Ram refuses to shoot the arrow at Ravana's navel as appropriate conduct demands that arrows be shot only at the enemy's face. So Hanuman gets his father, Vayu, the wind-god, to change the direction of Ram's arrow and force it on a downward trajectory towards Ravana's navel.
- On Dussehra day, a community of Dave brahmins of the Mudgal gotra in Rajasthan

performs funeral ceremonies (shradh) for Ravana. On the same day, the doors of the temple of Ravana in Kanpur are opened. The temple was built in the nineteenth century and Ravana is seen as the guardian of the Shiva and Shakti shrines.

- Ravana is the feared and revered doorkeeper and guardian of many shrines in Thailand.
- Both Ram and Ravana are devotees of Shiva. There are Shiva temples at all sites associated with Ram including Ayodhya (Uttar Pradesh), Chitrakoot (Uttar Pradesh), Panchavati (Maharashtra), Kishkindha (Karnataka) and Rameswaram (Tamil Nadu). Ravana is believed to have established Shiva temples at Gokarna (Karnataka), Murudeshwar (Karnataka), Kakinada (Andhra Pradesh) and Baidyanath (Jharkhand).
- In household conversations, Vibhishana is often looked down upon as the traitor who gave away family secrets, though he is also recognized as a much-adored devotee of Ram.

Learning from Ravana

Ravana lay on the ground, breathing heavily, waiting for death to come. 'Quickly,' said Ram to Lakshman, 'go to him and seek out his knowledge. He knew a lot.'

So Lakshman went to Ravana and towering over him said, 'I am Lakshman, brother of Ram, who has punished you for the crime of abducting his wife. As victor, he has a right to all that you possess, your knowledge included. If you have any honour, pass it on to him before you die.'

Ravana simply turned his face away, angering Lakshman, who reported the scene to Ram.

Ram said, 'Here is a man who grabbed his brother's house and another man's wife and you expected him to just give you what you so rudely and authoritatively demanded as your right. You clearly never saw Ravana.'

Ram then discarded his weapons, walked up to Ravana, sat at his feet, joined his palms and spoke to Ravana in a gentle voice. 'Noble one, son of Vishrava and Kaikesi, devotee of Shiva, brother of Surpanakha, Vibhishana and Kumbhakarna, father of Indrajit, uncle of Taranisen, friend of Mahiravana, husband of Mandodari, I salute you. I am Ram, who was responsible for mutilating your sister's body, for which I have been duly punished. I am Ram, whose wife you abducted, for which you have been duly punished. We owe each other no debts. But I seek from you knowledge that you wish to leave behind as your legacy.'

Like a dying lamp restored to life with a fresh offering of oil, Ravana's eyes lit up. 'I realize I never saw you, Ram. I just saw the man who my sister hated, my brothers respected, my queens admired and Sita loved. In seeking knowledge from me, you are hoping that I will finally expand my mind and discover the essence of the Vedas, which has eluded me, even though I know all the hymns and all the rituals. You are the ideal student whose curiosity makes the teacher wiser. I bow to you. Brahma tells us that to receive we have to give but most of us, like Indra, seek to receive without giving. Shiva seeks nothing, so he does not bother with the accounts of giving or receiving, but only Ram, who is Vishnu, receives by simply giving. That is why Sita follows him, not me.'

Ravana then breathed his last.

- The story of Ram at Ravana's feet is part of regional retellings such as Krittivasa's Bengali *Ramayana*; it is not in the Valmiki *Ramayana*.
- Both the *Ramayana* and the *Mahabharata* end not with victory of the heroes but knowledge transmission, a reminder that the war is less about things and more about thoughts.
- To look at a person is to do 'darshan'. This does not mean simply gauging the objective and measurable, it also means getting an insight into the other's character so deep that

it reflects one's own character. Ram, throughout the *Ramayana*, admonishes Lakshman for not seeing things as they are as he is too quick to judge and too fettered by his emotions.

- The war of the monkeys and the rakshasas lasts eight days traditionally, some say ten, marked by the festival of nine nights or Navaratri culminating in Vijaya-dashami, the victorious tenth day (Dussehra).

Vibhishana Becomes King

Vibhishana, despite all his righteous rage against his brother, felt a great loss when Ravana died. He wept on the battlefield while Mandodari burst into tears inside the palace. Hearing Mandodari cry, all the women of Lanka beat their chests and rolled on the ground, inconsolable in their grief. And the men, who had never shed a tear in their life, bawled like orphaned babies. Sita hugged Trijata and comforted her friend.

'It is a happy day for you. You have finally been liberated,' said Trijata.

'Can joy really spring from such a sea of sorrow?' was the question that came into the mind of Janaka's daughter.

The whole city gathered outside the citadel of Lanka to pay homage to their great king as the last rites were being performed. Ram had insisted that everyone who had been killed, vanara or rakshasa, be given a decent cremation. 'The dead are no one's enemies,' he said. The bodies of Indrajit and Kumbhakarna, stored in oil, were placed beside Ravana's, as well as the bodies of the other soldiers who had died in defence of Lanka. A great fire consumed Ravana and his entourage. The ashes were scattered in the sea and food was offered to crows, who cawed happily, informing all that Ravana had finally made his way across the river Vaitarni to the land of the dead.

When the mourning ended, the men took a bath and

washed off the blood that covered their bodies; the women wiped their tears, washed their faces, tied their hair up with flowers, wore fresh clothes and anointed their bodies with perfumes and bedecked themselves with gold. 'The old king has gone. Time to welcome the new king. The troop must always have a leader.'

Turmeric water was poured on Vibhishana. He was anointed with vermilion, offered a garland of lotus flowers, made to hold a bow. Mandodari replaced his silver anklets with the gold anklets of Ravana. With that act, the queen of Lanka accepted Vibhishana as the new king of Lanka. She sat beside him as Tara had sat beside Sugriva after the death of Vali.

'May you accept the wife of the previous king out of love, not as a trophy. May neither the kingdom nor its women be seen as your property. May you not derive your worth from your dominion. May you expand your mind with tapasya and yagna, and encourage others to do so. May you thus lead the rakshasas away from the ways of the jungle towards the way of dharma,' said Ram.

- Ravana is killed on the ninth night of the Navaratri festivities and cremated on the tenth day.
- According to Assamese folklore, if one cups one's hand over one's ears the sound one hears is that of Ravana's funeral pyre still burning.
- It can always be argued that Sugriva and Vibhishana helped Ram so that they could overthrow their respective brothers. But such ambition is not the underlying theme of the *Ramayana*; it is found in the *Mahabharata*.
- Later, Vibhishana attends the coronation of the Pandava Yudhisthira, but refuses to touch his feet saying he will only bow to Ram. Krishna then bows to Yudhisthira saying all kings are like Ram, until they act otherwise. Vibhishana follows suit.
- Vibhishana and Hanuman are chiranjivi, meaning 'those who live forever'.

Trial by Fire

Patiently Sita heard the mourning end and being replaced by celebration. Patiently she watched the city being cleaned and decorated for the new king. Patiently she watched the streets being watered, the flags being unfurled. Patiently she heard the war drums being replaced by flutes of joy. Patiently she waited for Ram to send for her.

But something told her there was agitation in his heart. She remembered how

Renuka had been beheaded because she was unchaste in thought. She remembered how Ahilya had been turned to stone because she was unchaste in deed. She had been unchaste in neither thought nor body, but how does one prove purity? Those who trust need no proof; those who do not trust reject all proof. And whether she liked it or not, she was a blot on Ram's reputation. Ravana had seized her while she was in Ram's protection; she symbolized Ram's failure. Would the world be as forgiving as him? Would he speak his own mind or give voice to the world he ruled?

The women came to her carrying news that Ram had sent for her. Vibhishana would hand her over as the brother who hands over the bride. Hanuman had been sent by the groom to accompany her; he carried with him her jewellery that the vanaras had found cast away on the forest floor. Besides this, every woman in Lanka had sent a piece of jewellery for the woman they had come to love. They wanted her to be more resplendent than the starry sky when she finally met Ram.

But then there was an argument. Some women said, 'Should her husband not see what she has become in his absence – dull and lifeless? Let him know how much she missed him.' Others disagreed: 'No. He is seeing her after many moons. Let him be dazzled by her beauty.' There were those who argued, 'If she looks radiant and beautiful, he might assume she was happy in captivity. Let us take her as she is right now, unwashed, unkempt, like a tree bereft of flowers and leaves.' 'Let the world not say that Lanka does not treat its guests well,' said Sarama. 'She was no guest, she was a captive,' snapped Trijata.

Finally, bathed, perfumed, bejewelled and wrapped in fine robes, to the singing of bridal songs, with a canopy over her head, Sita left the garden of Ashoka trees, emerged from Lanka and made her way towards Ram.

Everyone rushed to see the woman over whom this vast war had been fought. They had heard so much about her. Rakshasas and vanaras climbed on top of each other just to catch a glimpse of Sita. Soldiers had to be called in to control the crowds. This display of impatience and impropriety by the men annoyed both Sugriva and Vibhishana. But Ram said, 'Let it be. Let them see what this fight was all about.'

'She is a person, your wife, not a trophy to be displayed,' said Lakshman.

Ram did not reply.

When Sita finally came before Ram, she saw a very different man, not the youth with sparkling eyes who had set out to fetch the golden deer. This was a tired, unsure warrior covered with battle scars. She sensed he was like a boat struggling against the current. He lacked the excitement and enthusiasm she saw on Lakshman's face. This was a king taking a decision, not a lover awaiting his beloved.

Ram finally spoke. 'I, scion of the Raghu clan, have killed Ravana, the man who abducted you. Thus have I restored the honour of my family name. Let it be known this was the reason this war was fought, not to save you. Let it be known that your presence before me does not bring me any joy; you are like grit in my eye, a blot on my family name, for you have chosen to live under the roof of another man through the rainy seasons instead of killing yourself. I would like you to go freely wherever you wish, to Vibhishana, to Sugriva, to Lakshman. Let it be known I stake no claim on you.'

Everyone was shocked to hear Ram say this. This was not the man with whom they had fought the war. This was not the man who wept every night thinking of his wife, staring at her hairpin. Who was this cold, unfeeling creature?

Very calmly Sita asked that logs of wood and bundles of straw be brought and a bonfire be lit. Everyone thought she wanted to burn herself alive after being insulted so. But when she entered the fire, the flames withdrew from her person and Agni, the fire-god, said, 'I burn only impure things. This one

I cannot burn, for she is pure of thought and body.'

'What about reputation?' asked Ram.

'That,' said Agni, 'is a human measuring scale that makes no sense to nature. Take this woman as your wife, Ram, for she will take no other as her husband but you.'

Ram beamed like a child on hearing this, but only for a moment. Then the stoic expression returned. 'So it shall be,' he said, stretching out his hand, inviting Sita to be by his side.

- Ram is lovelorn before Sita's arrival but cruel when she actually appears before him. Before her arrival, he is her husband but on her arrival he transforms into the scion of the Raghu clan.
- Ram describes the sight of Sita as hurtful as 'a lamp to the diseased eye' in the Valmiki *Ramayana*.
- From the Tamil Sri Vaishnava tradition comes the story of Ram instructing Sita via Vibhishana that she bathe and bedeck herself before coming to see him. Sita obeys, angering Ram who had expected her to understand that what he said was not what he meant. She should have sensed his real wish and insisted on seeing him unbathed and unbedecked.
- That Ram values his family more than his wife is a cause of deep resentment to women across India, for traditional society typically gives the young wife a lower status until she becomes the matriarch of the household. The fear is that the wife will make the husband dance to her tune and the grip of the family over the son will go away. Thus the husband becomes the territory over whom the family and the wife feud.
- In the Kashmiri *Ramayana*, Sita burns for fourteen days and emerges resplendent as gold.
- A common theme in medieval retellings of the *Ramayana* such as the *Adbhut Ramayana* and Ezhutachan's Malayalam *Ramayana* is that the Sita abducted by Ravana is Chhaya-Sita or Maya-Sita, a duplicate and not the real person. It is actually Vedavati and the reason for the trial by fire is to restore the real Sita. This narrative stems from the concept of pollution. With Ram being increasingly seen as God, devotees cannot bear the idea of his consort being rendered impure by a demon.
- The idea of a duplicate being abducted, and the original remaining pure, is found in Greek mythology too. Herodotus argued that the Helen abducted by Paris and taken to Troy was a lookalike and that the real Helen languished in Egypt while the Greeks and Trojans fought their war over her. Thus Helen, we are told by playwrights such as Euripides, was chaste and not the shameless woman portrayed by Homer. Women's chastity and fidelity become a currency for male honour in cultures around the world, perhaps because it indulges the male self-image.
- The fire trial is seen as a purification rite. In the *Mahabharata*, when Draupadi moves from one husband to another, she passes through fire to purify herself.

- Ritual purity, and the resulting hierarchy, has played a critical role in shaping Indian society where members of certain professions such as butchers and cobblers and sweepers, and people who eat non-vegetarian food, are sidelined.
- In the *Mahabharata* retelling of the *Ramayana*, Ramopakhyan, Sita simply faints after being accused of infidelity and then is revived by Brahma who testifies to her chastity.

The Thousand-headed Demon

Just as Sita took her place beside Ram, a roar was heard from the horizon and a creature with a thousand heads rose from beyond the hills. 'That is Ravana's twin, who lives in the Pushkara Island,' said Vibhishana, quivering with fear. 'Even Ravana feared him.'

Before Ram could reach for his bow, everyone saw an incredible sight. Sita suddenly transformed. Her eyes widened, her skin turned red, her hair came unbound, and she sprouted many arms with which she grabbed the sticks and stones of the

vanaras and the swords and spears of the rakshasas. Thus armed, she leapt on to a lion that appeared out of nowhere and rushed to do battle with the demon. It was a fierce battle, the Goddess with her many arms pounding the demon who dared interrupt her union with her husband. She ripped out his entrails, chopped away his limbs, crushed his heads, broke his knees and drank his blood. Thus satiated, she returned to sit beside Ram as the demure Sita, a gentle smile on her lips.

No words were spoken. Everyone was stunned by the realization that Sita was Gauri who was also Kali. She had allowed herself to be abducted. She had allowed herself to be rescued. She was the independent Goddess who had made Ram the dependable God.

- The story of a rakshasa who has a hundred or a thousand heads and so is greater than Ravana and is killed by Sita, not Ram, is part of the *Adbhut Ramayana*. The story emerges in the fifteenth century as part of Shakta Hinduism.
- The Odia *Bilanka Ramayana* of Sarala Das also tells the story of Sita the Goddess.
- While Vedic schools of Hinduism visualized the supreme being as male, the Tantric schools visualized the supreme being as female. Both these schools came under the umbrella term of 'saguna' – those who seek divinity in form. Many chose the 'nirguna' approach – seeing divinity as formless. But the masses sought the tangible as it was more accessible, hence the need to see God embodied in gendered forms.
- The *Adbhut Ramayana* repeatedly shifts between the fearsome (Chandi-rupa) and the gentle (Mangal-rupa) forms of the Goddess. The latter form is the result of domestication. In temples, the Goddess is offered cloth and jewellery, and prayers are offered so that she voluntarily domesticates herself to benefit humanity. Forcible domestication leads to problems later on.
- Yuddha-kanda is called Lanka-kanda in some retellings.
- In the Telugu *Ranganatha Ramayana*, Ravana's father learned that while he was meditating his wife had missed ten periods. He felt sad and so gave the son she finally bore ten heads, one for each of the missed periods.
- From a psychoanalytical point of view, both Dashratha and Ravana are father figures. Both deny Ram pleasure, one by exiling him from Ayodhya and the other by kidnapping Sita. In one, Ram cannot express his rage as anger is seen as a base instinct unbecoming of an evolved being. In the other, he can, through monkeys.
- In Sri Vaishnava literature, Sita is described as having the capability of killing Ravana on her own but not doing so as Ram had not instructed her to kill him.

BOOK SEVEN

Freedom

'He remained trapped in culture, but nature set her free.'

Pushpak

The war was over, Ravana was dead, Sita was liberated, Lanka had a new king, Sugriva had repaid his debt and the fourteen years of exile were over. It was time to return home. 'Let us hurry,' said Ram. 'It is a long walk.'

'Why walk when you can fly?' said Vibhishana. 'This flying chariot, Pushpak, desires to return to its true master, Kubera. It needs to fly north, to Alaka. But on the way, it can surely take you home, for did you not liberate it from Ravana's clutches?'

Sita hesitated, for she had unpleasant memories of the chariot. 'But now you are with Ram and Lakshman,' said Vibhishana, 'what is there to fear? Besides we will accompany you, myself and Sarama and Mandodari, and your friend Trijata.'

'We will come too,' said Sugriva, Hanuman, Angada, Nala, Nila and Jambuvan.

And so everyone stepped on Kubera's magnificent aerial chariot. It flapped its wings like a swan and rose to the sky and made its way north out of Lanka to Ayodhya.

- According to the Padma Purana, Ram and the others flew back home because the bridge across the sea had been destroyed. Vibhishana had asked Ram to destroy the bridge built by the monkeys to prevent others from invading Lanka.
- Artists visualize the vimana, or flying chariot, in different ways. At times it is a cart or chariot pulled by donkeys, horses or swans, and sometimes the structure itself has wings.
- A traditional Hindu or Jain temple is also called a vimana and is seen as a flying chariot used by divine beings to travel between heaven and earth.
- In Greek mythology, one hears of gods and heroes flying: Zeus has his eagle, Bellerophon his flying horse, Hermes has shoes with wings and Medea has a chariot of flying serpents. But descriptions of earth from the sky are more frequently seen in Sanskrit poetry, starting with Valmiki.

Ram's Atonement

The entourage stopped many times along the way.

First at the tip of Jambudvipa, from which sprang the bridge to Lanka, where Ram and Sita offered prayers to Shiva, to Sampati and to Varuna, thanking them for their support during the war. After a brief halt at the caves of Swayamprabha, they passed over Kishkindha and Ram pointed to the clearing in the woods where he had killed Vali and the boulder by which he had met Hanuman. Sita recognized the trees and the riverbanks over which she had strewn her jewels. She thanked them for passing on her message to her Ram.

Then they stopped at the ashramas of the rishis they had visited earlier: Agastya, Atri, Sharabhanga, Sutikshna and Bharadwaja. The birds and snakes had informed the tapasvis of Sita's plight and the rishis were glad she was safe again. Lopamudra told Sita to think of the future. Anasuya warned her against dwelling on the past.

Later Ram asked the Pushpak to travel beyond Ayodhya to the Himalayas. 'I killed a man who knew the hymns of the Vedas and was a master of many sciences and the arts.

By killing its transmitter, I have committed the crime of brahmahatya. I need to atone for this disservice to humanity.'

'But he abducted your wife,' said Lakshman.

'Ravana had ten heads. Nine were filled with delusion, which made him impatient, lustful, greedy, arrogant, insecure, angry, envious, rude and dominating. But he had one head filled with wisdom and faith. The cacophony of nine heads overpowered the music of that head. I regret killing that head.'

So on the slopes of the Himalayas, the vanaras and the rakshasas and Lakshman and Sita watched Ram seek Ravana's forgiveness. He sat on the ground, shut his eyes and, contemplating on the events of the war, invoked the memory of that enemy of his with ten heads and twenty arms.

Two celestial beings appeared before Ram and said, 'Know this. We are Jaya and Vijaya, doorkeepers of Vaikuntha. Once we had stopped four sages from entering the abode of Vishnu because Vishnu was asleep. We stopped them three times. And for this reason they cursed us to be born on earth three times. Vishnu promised us that he would liberate us from our mortal lives. The first time we were born as the asuras Hiranyaksha and Hiranyakashipu. Vishnu liberated us, taking the form of the boar Varaha and the man-lion Narasimha. Then we took the form of two rakshasas, Ravana and Kumbhakarna. Vishnu liberated us, taking the form of Ram. Now we shall be reborn as two humans, Shishupala and Dantavakra. Vishnu will liberate us taking the form of Krishna. Go to Ayodhya in peace, Ram. Know that you have done what you were destined to do.'

Only after this did Ram make his way to Ayodhya.

- At Rameswaram, people make Shiva-lingas using sand, imitating Ram and Sita who did the same to invoke Shiva and thank him for his support.
- At the temple of Rameswaram, there are two lingas of Shiva, not one. The story goes

that Ram had sent Hanuman to Kashi to fetch a linga but it took him so long to return that he asked Sita to make one of sand instead. By the time the rituals started, Hanuman arrived with his linga and was angry that no one had waited for him. He tried uprooting Sita's sand linga with his tail but failed. Thus he realized he was not indispensable. To pacify him and please him, Ram worshipped Hanuman's Shiva-linga beside Sita's Shiva-linga.

- The idea of Ram atoning for brahma-hatya-paap, the crime of killing a priest, became a popular pilgrims' tale in medieval times. Both Rameswaram in the south and Rishikesh in the north are identified as spots where Ram performed penance and ritual in memory of Ravana.
- In the bhakti marga or devotional path, there is reference to viparit-bhakti or reverse devotion. By constantly abusing God, the enemy of God remembers God so many times that he forges for himself a path to divine grace. So it is with Ravana.
- In both Jain and Buddhist traditions, Ravana is a wise man with a flaw. In the Jain tradition, he will be reborn as a sage. In the Buddhist tradition, he converses with the Buddha.

Testing Bharata

As Ram approached the borders of Kosala, he dispatched Hanuman to inform Bharata of his imminent arrival. 'Tell him there is still time to claim what his mother secured for him. Tell him Ram will not think less of him if he chooses to be king.'

When Hanuman said this to Bharata, he said, 'Like Ram, even I do not hunger for a kingdom. I do not need the crown of Ayodhya to feel validated. But the kingdom certainly hungers for a good king.'

'And who is a good king?' asked the ever-curious Hanuman.

Bharata replied, 'A good king is one who does not see the kingdom as a measure of his worth. Such a king does not fight his brothers for the crown, nor does he demand the loyalty of his subjects. Such a king encourages people to take responsibility for their lives, and enables them to be dependable rather than dependent. Thus a happy kingdom comes into existence.'

'Such a kingdom does not exist,' argued Hanuman, remembering Kishkindha, where brothers were killed for a crown, and Lanka, where people were totally dependent on their great king.

'It will,' said Bharata, 'when Ram sits on the throne, for it is a throne that he neither seeks nor claims as his right, but occupies only because he has been invited to do so by his people, his father and his brothers.'

Just as Bharata uttered these wonderful words, Ram emerged through the dark clouds on the horizon like the sun on his aerial chariot. Beside him sat Sita; behind him stood Lakshman. He was surrounded by vanaras and rakshasas. Bharata's eyes widened in delight. The exile was over. His brother the king had finally returned.

- In the Valmiki *Ramayana*, Hanuman simply goes to check if Bharata is comfortable with Ram's return. He finds Bharata living like an ascetic in the village of Nandigram, ruling the kingdom in the name of Ram, whose sandals are placed on the throne. To make the return more melodramatic, Kamban in his Tamil *Ramayana* describes how Bharata plans to immolate himself if Ram does not arrive on time, disregarding the entreaties of his family, including Kaushalya's.
- The *Ramayana* is essentially the story of three sets of royal brothers: those of Ayodhya (humans) who are eager to give away the throne to the other brother; those of Kishkindha (monkeys) who cannot share the throne as their father had wanted them to; and those of Lanka (demons) where one brother claims the throne that rightfully belongs to the other. The relationship of Bharata and Ram is an indicator of brotherly love rising above all territorial desires and sibling rivalry.
- Both the *Ramayana* and the *Mahabharata* raise the question of whether kingdoms are the properties of kings. Both agree that they are not.

Waking Up Urmila

The mothers did not recognize them at first: the boys who had left home fourteen years ago had returned as men. Their hair was long and thick and bleached by the sun. Their skin was dark and coarse. They had beards, and their bodies were emaciated, their features gaunt.

And the daughter-in-law who had left as a girl had returned a fully bloomed woman, dressed in bridal finery. And the jewels, which had once made her beautiful, now took their beauty from her.

Their eyes were calmer, like those of hermits who have solved the mystery of life and are surprised by nothing. The forest had not turned them into savages. Instead, in their presence even monkeys and bears had turned civilized.

When they stepped on earth at the gates of Ayodhya, everyone wept with joy. There was Guha, the fisherman, and Sumantra, the old king's charioteer.

The mothers had changed so much: the regal bearing was gone. They were bent and grey, with wrinkled skin, even Kaikeyi, she of spellbinding beauty. The sight made Sita cry.

Sumitra told Lakshman, 'Go and wake up Urmila. Too long has she slept.' Lakshman rushed to his mother's courtyard and found a beautiful woman asleep on a mat. Was this his Urmila? He touched her. She awoke with a start. She looked at him and screamed, until the palace women assured her that the dark, bearded hermit was indeed Lakshman, and no one else. As she got up, she was trembling with excitement and was unable to tie her hair. Lakshman did it for her, and she blushed.

They were bathed, the men in the royal veranda, Sita and Urmila in the women's courtyard. Vast quantities of water, milk, turmeric, oil and fragrant pastes made of herbs and flowers were poured on to their bodies to remove the sweat and grime.

The men saw the cuts and bruises on Ram's and Lakshman's arms and chests and realized how hard a life it had been in the forest. The soles of their feet were full of calluses, and the heels were cracked. On Lakshman's chest was a dark wound,

where he had been struck by Indrajit's arrow. Their beards were shaved off, their moustaches oiled and curled.

On Sita's body, the women found jewels of many kinds: those from Ayodhya, those gifted by the wives of rishis and those from her many friends in Lanka. They found a dark bruise on Sita's arm, the mark of the only man who had touched her in the fourteen years in the forest – Ravana. Sita saw their eyes: yes, they had heard of what she had undergone. What was going through their minds? Sympathy? Indifference? Disgust?

When the mothers had finished feeding the exiles with their own hands, Ram was led into a new courtyard, built for Sita, the next queen of Ayodhya. He was made to recline on the vast swing. Sita was then asked to slice an areca nut, wrap it in a betel leaf and put it in Ram's mouth, while the swing swayed gently.

The eldest daughter of the Raghu clan, Shanta, joined the festivities and said, 'Too long have the young men and women of this household lived like sullen hermits. It is time there was joy in the palace, sounds of lovemaking and eventually the laughter of children,' she said as only she could. Everyone enjoyed the acute embarrassment of the young couples.

Finally the people of Ayodhya asked Ram, 'And have you brought anything for us from the forest?'

'Yes, Shabari's berries,' he said.

- The return of Ram to Ayodhya is celebrated across India as the festival of lights or Diwali.
- Songs sung by Telugu women focus less on the adventure of the *Ramayana* and more on the relationships and the corresponding intimate emotions, often witnessed only in the privacy of the home. Thus, there are songs describing Urmila's fear when she finds herself being woken up by a man she cannot recognize and how Lakshman combs Urmila's hair after his return.
- In modern poster art, Ram is always clean-shaven, with no trace of facial hair, a common feature of most gods. But in traditional paintings like Chitrakathi of Maharashtra and Kalamkari of Andhra Pradesh, and even a few miniatures, one does find Ram with a moustache, but no beard, indicating they shaved in the forest. The curled and oiled moustache has long been a symbol of masculinity in Indian society; to cut off a man's moustache is a metaphor of insult to his male pride.
- The transgendered community of hijras have an oral tale where on his return to Ayodhya Ram finds a group of hijras waiting for him outside the gate. He realizes that they have

been waiting there for fourteen years and asks them why. 'When you set out for exile and the people followed you, you begged the men and women of Ayodhya to return. We also followed you, but since we are neither men nor women, we had nowhere to go and so we stood where we were,' they say. With this story this marginalized sexual minority grants itself validation through the *Ramayana* tradition.

Lakshman Laughs

Vishwamitra and Vasishtha arrived along with the rishis of the forest to perform the coronation ritual, long overdue. But just when the ceremonies were about to start, Lakshman started to laugh.

Everyone wondered who Lakshman was laughing at. Was he laughing at Ayodhya, victim of palace politics which had bowed before a pair of sandals for fourteen years? Was he laughing at Kaushalya, who had always wanted to see her son crowned king? Was he laughing at Kaikeyi, for all her plans to become queen mother had failed? Was he laughing at Bharata for letting go of an opportunity to be king? Was he laughing at his mother, Sumitra, and his brother, Shatrughna, who would always be servants no matter who was king? Was he laughing at Sugriva, who got Ram to kill his brother so he could be king, or at Vibhishana, who became king because he sided with his brother's enemy? Was he laughing at Jambuvan because the bear was too old and so was overshadowed by Hanuman? Was he laughing at Hanuman, who set his own tail aflame to save Ram's wife and got nothing in exchange? Was he laughing at Sita, who had to prove through a trial by fire that she was chaste after she was liberated from Lanka? Was he laughing at Ram for ending up with a wife of soiled reputation?

But actually Lakshman was laughing at no one. He was laughing at a tragedy that he knew was about to unfold. He could see Nidra, the goddess of sleep, approaching him. He had requested her to return to him after fourteen years. The fourteen years were up and he had to keep his word, fall into deep slumber exactly when he was about to see the one thing he desired most in life – his beloved brother, Ram, being crowned king.

- The story of Lakshman laughing comes from the Telugu *Ramayana* of Buddha Reddy and is popular in Telugu folklore and folk songs.
- In the *Adbhut Ramayana,* Ram bans laughter in his kingdom because it reminds him of Ravana's mocking laugh. But then Brahma himself comes to Ayodhya and tells Ram how laughter indicates happiness and without happiness no ritual is successful and no society can thrive.
- Though the epic *Ramayana* is generally projected as rather ponderous and lacking in humour, comic relief is typically provided by vanaras and rakshasas. Ram is shown joking in Valmiki's retelling of the Surpanakha episode but what could be jest seems rather perverse and dark when one considers how the episode ends.

The Coronation of Ram

Finally, fourteen years after Dashratha's declaration, Ram sat on the throne of the Ikshavakus as the head of the Raghu clan and caretaker of Ayodhya. Sita sat on his lap, completing him. Bharata held aloft the royal umbrella. Lakshman and Shatrughna waved chowries, the yak-tail fly whisks reserved for kings. Hanuman sat at Ram's feet. The people of Ayodhya enjoyed gazing upon this much-anticipated sight. Tears of joy gave way to robust cheers and a shower of flowers.

During the coronation, Anjana asked her son, Hanuman, 'You are so strong. You leapt over the sea, defeated Surasa and Simhika, set Lanka aflame, carried a mountain from the north to the south, overpowered Mahiravana. Surely you could have defeated Ravana on your own. There was no real need to build the bridge to Lanka and make all the vanaras fight the rakshasas. So why didn't you?'

Hanuman replied, 'Because Ram did not ask me to. This is his story, not mine.'

Sita, seated on Ram's lap, smiled on hearing this, for she clearly saw how Hanuman saw the world. Most people seek to be the sun around which the world revolves. Very few are willing to be the moon, allowing others to be the sun, despite having full knowledge that they can outshine everyone else. Ram's brothers served him to uphold the integrity of the royal clan. She too was bound by wifely obligations. But only Hanuman did so out of pure love. That is why Ram held him closest.

- 'Ram-patta-abhishekam' or the coronation of Ram with his wife by his side and his brothers around him marks the end of the Yuddha-kanda, the sixth chapter of the Valmiki *Ramayana*. This image is very auspicious to the devout Hindu as the episode marks the final chapter of the Tamil Kamban *Ramayana* and the Tulsidas's Avadhi *Ramayana*. Many reject the episodes that follow this ending.
- Ram is the only avatar of Vishnu to be visualized as king. People often assume Krishna is a king, as he is called Dwarkadhish, lord of Dwarka. But as descendant of the accursed Yadu, Krishna could never wear the crown. He was at best a nobleman and defender of his people, never king.
- The chowrie, or yak-tail fly whisk, is a mark of royalty. Traditionally, only images of Ram are adorned with it. Krishna's images are adorned with a morcha, a fan of peacock feathers, meant for noblemen who served royalty.
- Ram Rajya or the rule of Ram is described as the age of perfection when rains come on time, women never become widows, sons outlive their fathers, there is no hunger or disease, and the arts flourish.
- Nalambalam yatra is a unique religious journey popular in Kerala connected with the visit to four temples dedicated to the four sons of Dashratha: the Ram temple at Triprayar,

the Bharata temple at Irinjalakuda, the Lakshman temple at Moozhikulam and the Shatrughna temple at Payammel near Irinjalakuda.
- From the tenth century onwards, Hanuman became a deity in his own right. Unlike the regal and distant Ram, Hanuman was more accessible and identifiable. His images could be seen on streets and at marketplaces. He was not associated with lofty philosophies. He solved problems and gave courage.
- Hanuman embodies devotion that gets the individual soul or jivatma (Sita) to meet the cosmic soul or paramatma (Ram) by overpowering the ego (Ravana), according to the *Adhyatma Ramayana*.
- Many hymns to Ram are found in the *Ananda Ramayana* including the Ramashatanamastotra (the 108 names of Rama), the Ramastotram (the hymn to Ram), the Ramaraksha Mahamantra (the great hymn of Ram that grants protection) and the Ramkavacha (the armour of Ram's grace).
- Some Rajput families, especially royal ones, trace their ancestry to Ram and the Raghu-kula.

Hanuman's Heart

Sita gave a necklace of pearls to Hanuman in gratitude for all that he had done for her. Hanuman started biting each pearl as if it was a fruit, and throwing it away in distaste on finding its contents wanting. Taking this to be an act of disrespect against their king, the people said, 'What is that stupid monkey doing?'

Hanuman said, 'The stupid monkey is checking to see if Sita and Ram are in them. If they are not, these pearls are useless.' When people started to laugh saying that even the blind knew that Ram and Sita were seated on the throne and were not inside pearls, Hanuman tore open his chest and said, 'I am not lying. Sita and Ram are in my heart. Are they not in your heart yet?' Everyone was dumbstruck on seeing this incredible sight. They did not know how to react. They wondered what was in their heart. They dared not tear it open.

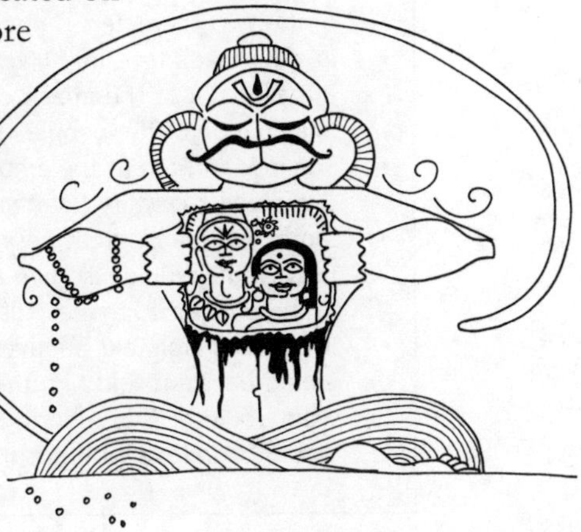

In the fullness of Hanuman's heart, Vibhishana remembered the emptiness of Ravana's.

Ravana wanted Shiva to be with him all the time, because the presence of Shiva energized him,

made him happy. So with his twenty hands he uprooted Mount Kailas, intent on taking Shiva with him to Lanka. This upset Shiva's wife and children. They begged Ravana to stop. When Ravana refused to heed their cries, Shiva pressed his big toe against the mountain slope, creating so much pressure that Ravana's knee buckled and he fell flat on the ground, the mountain crushing his back. In apology, Ravana composed a wonderful song in praise of Shiva called the Rudra-stotra. Pleased, Shiva pulled him out from underneath Mount Kailas and Ravana returned home to Lanka shamefaced. 'Shiva is much stronger than me,' he said on returning home. He had failed to hear what Shiva was trying to tell him: God is not an external trophy to be possessed; God is internal human potential to be realized. Ravana refused to see the world as Shiva could, but Hanuman had learned to appreciate the world as Ram did.

- Ravana is born to a learned priest and functions as a king, but fails to gain wisdom despite great knowledge and great power and great wealth. Hanuman is born a monkey and studies from the sun, has no social status or wealth, but by serving Ram finds purpose for his knowledge and power, and thus becomes the embodiment of wisdom. The contrast of the two characters is not accidental but clearly designed to provoke thought.
- In a Kannada retelling, Hanuman reveals the name of Ram written across his bones. But the idea of the image of Sita and Ram etched on Hanuman's heart captured the imagination of the people.
- The idea of Ram as the embodiment of the purusha and Sita as prakriti is found in the seventeenth-century Ramtapaniya Upanishad.
- Jambuvan had a great desire to wrestle with Ram. So Ram promised him that in his next life he would visit him as Krishna and wrestle with him following a disagreement. In the Bhagavat Purana, Krishna marries Jambuvan's daughter, Jambavati.
- In one Odia folktale, Sugriva saw Sita's feet and wondered how beautiful the rest of her would be. Ram told him that in his next life he would marry a woman called Radha, who would be Sita reborn, but the relationship would never be consummated for she would be in love with Krishna.

Ram's Name

Hanuman took care of all the guests who visited Ayodhya. These included rajas, rishis, rakshasas, yakshas, devas, asuras, gandharvas, bhalukas, vanaras and garudas. Amongst them was Narada, the sage who loves to create trouble.

He told Hanuman, 'The vermilion dot on Sita's forehead is a mark of her unconditional love for Ram. How do you express your selfless love for Ram?' In response Hanuman covered his entire body with vermilion powder, as he felt that for a monkey a simple dot, or even multiple dots, would not be enough.

Narada then told Hanuman, 'It is good manners to touch the feet of all rishis. But there is no need to fall at the feet of Vishwamitra; he is not a real seer – he is just a king who pretends to be a sage.'

Hanuman did as told and touched the feet of all the rishis, except Vishwamitra. This upset Vishwamitra so much that he demanded that Ram teach Hanuman a lesson: 'Raise your bow and pin this arrogant monkey's tail to the ground.'

Hanuman saw the amusement on Narada's face, as the situation got tense: Ram would have to listen to his teacher however unreasonable his demands were. Hanuman wondered how he could protect himself from Ram. He then remembered Taranisen, Vibhishana's son, and got an idea.

He sat on the ground and began chanting Ram's name. Ram shot his arrows and they were unable to penetrate the shield created by the chanting of his name.

Vishwamitra smiled in realization: greater than a person is the idea that person embodies; greater than Ram is the idea that Ram embodies; greater than Vishwamitra's name is the idea that Vishwamitra embodies. 'Lower your bow, Ram,' said the old teacher who had just learned a new lesson, 'you cannot defeat Hanuman as long as he chants Ram's name.'

- Hanuman is often shown covered in red colour, which is associated with the Goddess. Some art historians hold that old tribal deities known as yakshas were bathed in blood, which was later substituted with red dye. Nowadays there is a preference to visualize Hanuman in saffron, the colour associated with celibacy.
- The battle between the deity and the devotee is a common theme in late devotional literature. The devotee protects himself by chanting the deity's name. The idea these stories try to convey is that the thought (the name of the deity) is more important than the thing (the image of the deity). Thus Ram nam is greater than Ram rup. It is the supreme mantra and is greater than visiting temples. It indicates the rise of nirguna-bhakti (worship of the formless divine) over saguna-bhakti (worship of the forms of the divine).
- Ramnamis are people for whom chanting the name of Ram is the greatest means to wisdom and realization. They usually belong to the lower castes of the Gangetic plains. When they read Tulsidas's retelling of the *Ramayana*, they often replace all references that favour upper castes with the phrase 'Ram Ram nam'.
- For Kabir and Nanak of the Sant tradition, which thrived between the fifteenth and eighteenth centuries, Ram is not so much a person as the idea of divinity.
- In many parts of India people greet each other with the phrase 'Ram Ram'.
- During funeral processions it is common amongst many Hindus to chant 'Ram Ram' or 'Ram nam satya hai' (the name of Ram is the truth). The Ram being referred to might be the divine hero of the *Ramayana* (saguna Ram) or the formless divinity (nirguna Ram).

United at Last

All through that day, the people of Ayodhya gazed upon their king and queen seated like a god and a goddess on the golden throne of the Ikshavakus.

That night, when everyone had left, and when the clouds parted to let the moonlight stream into the courtyard of the new queen, Ram finally saw Sita as only a husband can and Sita finally saw Ram as only a wife can.

The exile was finally over.

- Ram-rasiks are devotees of Ram who through meditation seek to discover in their mind the heaven called Saket, with its bowers and the Kanak-bhavan palace, where, if worthy, they are allowed to witness the intimacy of Ram and Sita and thus find peace.
- Many Ram-rasiks believe that the exile of Ram and the abduction of Sita did not take place. These are delusions created by Sita and Ram to amuse those who seek the thrill of adventure and are not content simply with their bliss.
- One Ram-rasik visualized himself as the brother of Janaka, hence Sita's uncle, and in keeping with common custom never ate food in Ayodhya, the land of his son-in-law. Another Ram-rasik saw himself as Sita's younger brother and travelled to Ayodhya hoping she would feed him sweets. Still another bought toys for Sita whom he considered his daughter. Thus was intimacy with the divine couple expressed.
- Unlike Krishna, Ram is rarely associated with eroticism. But this has not stopped poets like Upendra Bhanja who wrote the rather sensual *Baidehi-bilasa* (pleasures of Sita's husband) in Odia in the seventeenth century.
- For many, the *Ramayana* is Ramveda, great wisdom, and the relationship between Ram and Sita is of word (mantra) and meaning (artha): one cannot exist without the other.

Ravana's Drawing

It was the royal cat that first sensed that Sita was with child. Then it was the royal dog. Then the parrots. Finally the rooster, who could not contain himself; he crowed out the news so loudly that the fishes could hear it in the river and they took the news downstream all the way to Mithila. Janaka smiled on hearing the news, and then went about his royal chores.

The vultures flew over the sea and the news reached Lanka. Vibhishana was pleased. But not Surpanakha. She travelled to the city of Ayodhya and made her way to the women's quarters, identifying herself as a hairstylist from beyond the Vindhyas. This got everyone excited. All the women were curious. 'Do you know of this place called Lanka?'

'Of course. The city of gold in the middle of the sapphire blue sea where once lived the most handsome king, Ravana,' she said.

'How handsome was he?' they asked.

'None would know him better and more intimately than your own queen,' she chuckled, making the women even more curious.

When the women asked Sita, she smiled and said, 'Ravana was for me but a dancing shadow on the surface of the sea. I heard his voice. I felt his footsteps. But I never saw his face.'

The women, with a little encouragement from Surpanakha, begged Sita to draw the outline of Ravana's shadow. Sita indulged them: she drew the image on the floor using rice flour.

The ten heads, the twenty arms: it was so perfect that Surpanakha wept in memory of her beloved brother. Her tears fixed the drawing to the floor. No matter how hard they tried, they could not wipe out Ravana's image from the floor of Ram's palace.

That is how the gossip began.

'She has drawn the virile Ravana's image under her bed.'

'She did live under his roof through the rainy season.'

'She lived with her husband in the forest for fourteen years, and only now, after a sojourn in Lanka, is she with child. Something to think about, no?'

A washerman was heard shouting at his wife who had taken refuge in the house of the boatman during a storm, 'Get out. Ram may keep a wife who has spent many a night in another man's house, but I will not.'

- In the Kashmiri *Ramayana*, the two parts of the *Ramayana* are called *Sri-Ram-avatar-charitam* and *Luv-kush-yuddha-charitam*.
- It is said that the Chola king commissioned two poets, Kamban and Ottakoothar, to write the *Ramayana* in the twelfth century. Impressed and overwhelmed by Kamban's inspired retelling, Ottakoothar decided to destroy his retelling. But Kamban managed to save the last book. So in Tamil literature, the Purva-Ramayana is written by Kamban while the Uttara-Ramayana is written by Ottakoothar, both accomplished storytellers.
- In the Valmiki *Ramayana*, there is a reference to street gossip only.
- In the Sanskrit *Kathasaritsagar* (eleventh century) and the Bengali Krittivasa *Ramayana* (fifteenth century), there is a reference to the quarrel of the washerman and his wife.

- The story of Sita being made to draw Ravana's shadow is found in the Telugu, Kannada and Odia retellings.
- A story of Sita being made to draw Ravana's big toe only comes from Telugu folklore.
- In various retellings, the one who goads Sita to draw the image of Ravana ranges from Surpanakha, Surpanakha's daughter, Manthara, Kaikeyi, to one of the many palace women.

Ram's Decision

The gossip was at first a trickle. Then it was a flood. Ram could not ignore it. The queen of the Raghu clan had to be above blemish. Sita was not.

'Take her to the forest on some pretext and leave her there. Let her not know of my decision until she is far away in the forest, far away from me, too far to protest,' said Ram to Lakshman.

'That is so unfair. You must tell the people how she proved her chastity with fire,' insisted Lakshman.

'This has nothing to do with chastity or fidelity,' said Ram. 'This gossip provides people an opportunity to feel superior to the king. My exacting standards of conduct perhaps make them feel inadequate, inferior. So they strike back by mocking my choice of queen. She is not pure enough for me, they say.'

'She is pure. She walked through fire.'

'Pure in body and pure in mind, for sure. But pure in reputation? That stain can never be removed. Never forget the human yearning to dominate. The rich dominate with wealth. The educated dominate with knowledge. The beautiful with their beauty. Those who have nothing use the idea of purity to dominate. Thus the sweeper who cleans dirty streets is declared impure, the washerman who cleans soiled clothes is declared inferior, the woman who is menstruating is declared polluted. By that measuring scale, Sita is not pure enough for Ram, they say. If I resist, forever will I be the object of ridicule. I have no choice.'

'You do have a choice. You are king. Do not indulge this vile desire of the people.'

'A good king must listen to his people, and respect the rules of his family, howsoever distasteful they may be.'

'Surely a king can change rules, impose his will on people?'

'Yes, in Kishkindha. Yes, in Lanka. But not in Ayodhya, not as long as a scion of Raghu-kula sits on the throne. I will not be a tyrant. This is the verdict of the people. It must be respected.'

'People are fools. People are cruel. Do not submit to them, Ram.'

'How will my subjects see their own cruelty? How will they learn that they operate from aham, not atma? They are too busy being self-righteous. They must witness how powerful they are, how they can dehumanize Sita and get Ram to submit to their will.'

'Why must Sita suffer for this?'

'Because she is Janaka's daughter. She alone will not see herself as a victim, as I did not when Kaikeyi forced me into exile. I can rely on her.'

'Tell Hanuman to do it. I don't want to do it.'

'But I want you to. You, only you. Must the king make an order? Will the brother not obey?'

'I hate being younger than you. I have to obey.'

'In our next life, when I am Krishna, you will be my elder brother, Balaram, but you will still agree with me for you know what I do is necessary.'

Shoulders drooping, Lakshman asked, 'The least you can do is tell her all this clearly and openly. Why reject her in so clandestine a manner?'

'She never listens,' snapped Ram. 'When I told her to stay in the palace, she insisted on accompanying me to the forest. When you told her to stay inside the hut in the forest, she insisted on stepping out. When I was rude and tried to set her free from the obligations of marriage after I killed Ravana, she insisted on walking through fire, displaying her chastity, and returning to this city with me. If I tell her that she is the subject of gossip and so cannot be associated with me in any way, she will ask complex questions that I will not be able to answer. It is best this way. She will understand. She *has to* understand.'

- In the Valmiki *Ramayana*, a spy named Bhadra reports to Ram what his people are saying on the streets. Only when Ram rebukes him for saying only positive things does Bhadra reveal the vulgar gossip.
- Lakshman is the voice of the common man who is outraged by Ram's cruelty.
- Following gossip, Ram refuses to see Sita, let alone talk to her. He simply turns away. This cold reaction from one who is supposed to be God comes across as cruel and extremely distressing, especially when storytellers justify it as the 'right' thing to do. Actions in Hindu mythology are never 'right', though they are often necessary or obligatory, and they always come at a price.
- Ram is called purushottam, which means ideal man. So it is only natural to wonder how an ideal man can treat a woman so. But Ram is not just purushottam; he is maryada purushottam, who follows rules and respects boundaries, as one ideally should. Rules and boundaries are human constructions, inherently cruel, as they create artificial hierarchies and notions of appropriate conduct. Krishna is also purushottam, leela purushottam, who plays the game of life, as one ideally should, appreciating its necessity but not taking it too seriously.
- In Telugu folk songs, the sisters of Sita stand by her and demand that they too be thrown out of the palace as they too think of Ravana.

Return to the Forest

'I crave for tiger's milk,' Sita had said when she had her first pregnancy cravings. Lakshman was sent to fetch it.

Then she had said, 'In the middle of the sea, as we returned from Lanka, I saw an island full of sandalwood trees. Hanging from each one was a honeycomb. I dream of sipping that special honey, flavoured with the scent of sandal and sea breeze.' Hanuman was sent to fetch it.

'My, my, the girl who went to the forest has returned a queen indeed,' the women of the palace had remarked in private.

Sita had other cravings too: for the tamarind she had seen grow in the gardens of Anasuya; for the bananas that grew around the house of Agastya; for the berries offered by Shabari that Ram had described to her in detail.

She was therefore pleasantly surprised when she was told that the royal chariot was ready to take her to the forest where the berries of Shabari could be found; she could pluck them herself.

The previous night Sita had dreamt of the forest. She missed the freedom of the wild. She missed the tigers and the snakes. She missed the trees and the grass, the taste of roots and shoots, the dips in mountain streams. Only this time, she wanted to enjoy it all holding Ram's hand, her head on his chest, as he rested on the rocks warmed by the rays of the rising sun, feeling him caress her hair.

Sita packed lightly, her clothes, his clothes, just enough for the day. She knew he would want to return quickly the following day: there were duties to perform, rituals to preside over, cows to be distributed, petitions to be heard.

The chariot was ready early, before anyone in the palace had woken up. She did not expect to find Lakshman as the charioteer, no attendant in sight, no sign of Ram. Lakshman's face did not display the excitement of an excursion. In fact, he busied himself by checking the horses' hooves and the chariot wheels, repeatedly.

That is when Sita knew Ram's worst fears had come true. The people had gossiped. Ayodhya had mocked its king and queen.

'Wait for me,' she told Lakshman, 'I have forgotten something.'

She went back to the palace and instructed the cook, 'Pour ghee generously on his rice, even if he protests. He will not admit it but he likes it.'

She said to the lady who cleaned his room, 'Make sure you mop the room after you sweep. He will not complain but dust bothers him.'

She said to the man who arranged his clothes, 'Make sure you sprinkle the scent of jasmine on his upper garments. He will never demand it, but he likes the perfume.'

She said to the gardener, 'Every morning prepare a garland of white lotus flowers and deep-green tulsi leaves for him. He is too shy to ask you for it.'

She said to his masseur, 'He prefers the oil slightly warmed, and be gentle when you massage his feet. He has not got used to the royal footwear yet.'

She then boarded the chariot and said, 'Let us go, Lakshman. All is well.'

Sita turned around. There was no one to bid her farewell. Her sisters were still asleep. Even the handmaidens slumbered. The streets were deserted. Was it that early? But the sky was red, ready to receive the rising sun. And she heard the conch shells announcing that Ram was seated on the throne, ready to receive the courtiers and his subjects. Against the dawn sky, the bright yellow flags of Ayodhya fluttered proudly.

- Marathi folk songs speak of Sita's pregnancy cravings and of the last-minute instructions she gives while leaving for the forest.
- Folk songs often speak of how women are jealous of Sita's happiness and want her to suffer. Thus they project their own life into the *Ramayana*.
- Sita had promised to make offerings to the river Ganga when she was leaving for the exile. This is one more excuse often made to take Sita out of the palace back into the forest.
- The Padma Purana states that Sita heard the *Ramayana* from two parrots when she was a child. The parrots did not know the whole story. Sita felt they were lying and in trying to force out the rest of the tale she accidentally killed one of the pair. The surviving parrot cursed Sita that in her life she would also be separated from her mate. Tales such as these make Sita's exile an inevitable consequence of her own actions.

Lakshman Conveys Ram's Decision

Lakshman was silent as the chariot rolled into the forest. This was a different route, a narrow route, not the great royal highway that cut through Kosala's rich farms and orchards. She would not see Guha. There would be no river to cross, just a desolate mountain pass. 'Never seen this part of the forest before,' she said. It was rocky and barren. A lizard ran before the chariot. Sita chuckled. Lakshman remain unmoved.

The chariot finally stopped. Sita alighted, eager to walk amongst the trees. Lakshman remained seated. Sensing he had something to say, Sita paused.

Lakshman finally spoke, eyes to the ground: 'Your husband, my elder brother, Ram, king of Ayodhya, wants you to know that the streets are full of gossip. Your reputation is in question. The rules are clear on this: a king's wife should be above all doubt. The scion of the Raghu clan has therefore ordered you to stay away from his person, his palace and his city. You are free to go wherever else you please. But you may not reveal to anyone you were once Ram's queen.'

Sita watched Lakshman's nostrils flare. She felt his embarrassment and his rage. She wanted to reach out and reassure him, but she restrained herself. 'You feel Ram has abandoned his Sita, don't you?' she asked gently. 'But he has not,' she stated confidently. 'He cannot. He is God; he abandons no one. And I am Goddess; I cannot be abandoned by anyone.'

'I don't understand your strange words.'

'Ram is dependable, hence God. I am independent, hence Goddess. He needs to do his duty, follow rules, and safeguard reputation. I am under no such obligation. I am free to do as I please: love him when he brings me home, love him when he goes to the forest, love him when I am separated from him, love him when I am rescued by him, love him when he clings to me, love him even when he lets me go.'

'But you are innocent,' said Lakshman, tears streaming down his face.

'And if I was not? Would it then be socially appropriate and legally justified for a husband to throw his woman out of his house? A jungle is preferable to such an intolerant society.'

The words of Sita were like a slap in Lakshman's face. Ram was not like Jamadagni who beheaded his Renuka. Ram was not like Gautama who cursed his Ahilya. Ram accepted even the soiled berries of Shabari with love.

'You were not even given the dignity of being told. You were tricked into leaving the palace,' said Lakshman.

'You judge him, Lakshman, but I love him. You see your brother as an ideal and are angry because he has not lived up to your expectations. I see my husband for what he is, and understand his motivations; at every moment he strives to be what he thinks is best. I will not burden him with my expectations. That is how I make him feel loved. And he sees me, knows that I will support him no matter what, even when he resorts to such a devious route like an errant child,' Sita said with a smile. 'Go back home; observe Ram well. Know that the man who calls himself the husband of Sita will never remarry. Of the king of Ayodhya, I do not know.'

'This is not right. I can't stand this nobility,' shouted Lakshman.

'Imagine what would have happened if Ram had refused to obey his father. Imagine what would happen if Ram refused to banish his wife. People would forever pass snide remarks about him, even if his actions could be justified. It is not about being right. It is about being a king who is above all doubt. To be such a king, he needs our support.'

'What will you do now? Where will you go? I was told to leave you near the hermitage of sages so that you will find refuge,' said Lakshman.

Sita looked at her brother-in-law, older than her, taller than her, battle-scarred and weary, looking down at the ground, looking like a child consumed by shame.

With a smile, she said, 'I know the forest well, Lakshman. I remember more years here than in the palace. Do not worry about me. I am not happy with this situation, but I accept it and will make the most of it. Thus I submit to karma without letting go of dharma.'

A mystified Lakshman returned to Ayodhya. Sita stayed back in the forest, smiled and unbound her hair, for when the farmer abandons the field, the field is finally free to return to being a forest.

- In the folk songs of the Gangetic plains, Sita asks Lakshman to fetch water. He says there is no waterbody nearby. So she asks him to pierce the earth with an arrow and cause water to spring out as he always did in the forest. He tells her to do it herself as he does not want to stop the chariot. Sita uses the power of her chastity to create a well. This proves to Lakshman that she is indeed chaste and has not thought of Ravana since the fire trial.
- In regional *Ramayanas*, in keeping with a motif found in many folktales, Ram asks Lakshman to kill Sita and bring proof of her death, either her eyes or her blood. Lakshman, however, spares Sita and takes the eyes of a deer to Ram instead.
- In a Bhil song, Ram wants Lakshman to kill Sita but Lakshman does not, realizing she is pregnant. In Telugu songs, Ram even conducts funeral rituals for Sita assuming she is dead.

- Public readings of the Uttara-Ramayana are forbidden because the tragedy may upset the earth, Sita's mother, and result in earthquakes.
- When Lakshman returns to the palace, he has a philosophical conversation with Ram on the nature of reality. This is the Ram Gita found in the *Adhyatma Ramayana*.

Sita Weeps as Surpanakha Gloats

When Sita wept finally, she wept for Ayodhya, the imagined powerlessness that makes people snatch power through gossip.

As she walked into the forest, she observed the absence of boundaries. There was nothing to distinguish the crop from the weed. Everything had value. In nature, nothing is pure or polluted. Culture excludes what it does not value. Nature includes all.

Sita heard a flute. The sound led her to a patch in the forest that was as dark as night. Here she saw glowing figures: a man in the centre and many women around him. He made the music; they danced around him. Neither was bound to the other by law or custom. There were neither expectations nor obligations, only immense affection and understanding. So many possibilities, Sita thought.

'One day, in another lifetime, Ram will be Krishna and Sita will be Radha. They will dance together in joy,' shouted the hopeful trees.

'But duty will call. He will leave the village to go to the city. Her heart will be broken once more,' said the blades of grass, stretching themselves to comfort Sita.

The darkness gave way to a harsh sunlight. The trees were weeping. The birds were howling. The serpents were wailing. 'Ram has banished Sita,' they cried. 'Ayodhya does not think she is good enough for it.'

Sita calmed the trees and the birds and the serpents: 'Weep for my Ram who is locked by rules, unable to breathe free in the palace. I am back in the forest, where I can do whatever I please, whenever I please. I am no longer anyone's wife; I am now a woman with child. Gauri is not bound to bow her head and watch her step any more; I am now Kali. Come, let us swim in the river and eat Shabari's berries.'

Under the berry tree, Sita found Surpanakha, full of hate and rage, gloating. 'They rejected you as they rejected me. Now you suffer as I do, stripped of status as I was stripped of beauty.'

Sita smiled, and offered Surpanakha a berry. 'These are really sweet, as sweet as the berries in Mandodari's garden.' Surpanakha was surprised. She had expected to derive pleasure from Sita's pain. But Sita was not in pain. 'Surpanakha, how long will you expect those around you to love you as you love them? Find the Shakti within yourself to love the other even when the other does not love you. Outgrow your hunger by unconditionally feeding the other.'

'But I want justice,' said Surpanakha.

'How much punishment will be enough? Ever since the sons of Dashratha disfigured you, they have known no peace. Yet you rave and rant relentlessly. Humans are never satisfied with justice. Animals never ask for justice.'

'I am not an animal, Sita. I will not be treated as one.'

'Then be human. Let go and move on. They who hurt you cannot expand their mind. But surely you can.'

'I refuse to submit.'

'You trap yourself in your own victimhood. Then be like Ravana. Stand upright while your brothers die, your sons die and your kingdom burns, imagining your own nobility. Who loses, but you? Cultures come and go. Ram and Ravana come and go. Nature continues. I would rather enjoy nature.'

Surpanakha picked up the berry offered by Sita. It was indeed sweet, sweeter than any lover's impatient, lustful gaze. She ate another berry and smiled. 'Now I will race you to the river,' shouted Sita as she ran for the stream. Surpanakha giggled as she jumped into the waters. Once again she felt beautiful.

- Many authors wonder about what happens to Surpanakha. Many retellings make her responsible for Sita's rejection by Ram. So while some authors see Sita's fate as an outcome of patriarchy, many also see it as an outcome of women's jealousy.

- Reference to repairs of damaged noses by surgery (rhinoplasty) in the Sushrut Samhita has led people to conclude that Ravana's surgeons repaired Surpanakha's nose.
- In Rajasthan, bards narrate the story of Surpanakha's rebirth. She is born as Phulvanti and Lakshman is reborn as Pabuji, a great folk hero. They are destined to marry but Pabuji uses every excuse not to consummate the relationship. Like Lakshman, he remains the celibate ascetic-warrior. Surpanakha's love remains unrequited.

The Thief Becomes a Poet

She was a queen after all, with every limb covered with exquisite jewellery. All alone in the forest, seated on a rock under a tree, contemplating her next move, she looked like a lonely nymph. She naturally caught the attention of a bandit called Ratnakar. He moved menacingly towards her with his sword. 'Give me your gold,' he growled.

With no trace of fear on her face, Sita removed a pair of bangles and handed them over with regal grace.

As the bandit examined the bangles, Sita asked, 'Why do you steal?'

'I was a farmer once, but the pain of burning forests to clear land for fields was unbearable. I was a hunter once but the pain of killing animals was unbearable. So now I steal. There is no pain in taking things from humans who have taken things from nature,' said Ratnakar.

'Why steal at all? Why not become a tapasvi like Shiva, outgrow all hunger?'

'I have a family to feed,' said Ratnakar, intrigued by the strange, bejewelled lady in the forest.

'That sounds like a good excuse. But tell me, will your family who enjoys your loot also suffer the punishment that will be meted out to you when you are caught by the king?' asked Sita.

'Of course they will,' said Ratnakar.

'Are you very sure?' asked Sita.

The bandit decided to check. And to his great disappointment, his wife said,

'Why should the children and I suffer for your crimes? You are the head of this household, responsible for feeding us. How you do so is your concern.'

'My family is no family at all,' said the bandit, when he returned, with drooping shoulders. 'I feel so alone.'

'Open your eyes, expand your mind and you will learn to stop blaming the world for your problems and you will accept your family with all its limitations,' said Sita.

'How?'

'Sit down and keep repeating the one word that very naturally springs from your mouth.'

The bandit sat down and the only word he could utter was 'mara', which means 'death'. He kept repeating the word for hours, and slowly as his mind calmed down, the world inverted itself on its own. 'Mara, Ma-Ra, Ma, Ra, Ma, Ra-Ma, Rama, Ram . . .'

'Who is this Ram who calms my mind so?' he asked Sita.

Sita told him the story of Ram, of his birth, his marriage, his exile, his war, his triumph, his return and his coronation. She did not disclose that she was the wife who accompanied him to the forest, the wife whom Ravana abducted and Ram rescued, the wife who was cast out following palace rumours. But the tone of her voice betrayed her identity: Ratnakar was in no doubt that this was the queen of Ayodhya, the wise daughter of Janaka that many travellers spoke of.

'This story calms my turbulent mind. Let me chant his name and think about him some more.'

'Who will take care of your family while you are busy meditating and finding answers to your life's problems?' asked Sita.

'Time they took responsibility for their lives as I have taken for mine. We are responsible for our own actions. We alone have to face the consequences of our choices,' said Ratnakar.

So Ratnakar sat in one place, calming his mind by thinking about Ram and his tale. Days passed. He did not budge from his position. Sita kept watch, eating fruit from nearby trees, drinking water from the river, sleeping on rocks. She saw termites make a hill around Ratnakar's body and realized he had gone deep into meditation; he felt no pain, heard no sound, smelt no fragrance. No apsara of Indra could seduce him. The bandit was transforming. The inner fire of tapa was turning him into a sage.

Then one day, a pair of lovebirds sat on the branches of the tree above. An arrow struck the female of the pair and she dropped to the ground. The male circled around its mate, wailing piteously. The sound disturbed the bandit's meditation. He opened his eyes, emerged angrily from the termite hill and cursed the hunter, 'May you who separated the lovers never find happiness.'

The curse came out in verse. From pain was born poetry.

The bandit decided he would spend the rest of his life composing the story of Ram in verse. 'I shall call it *Ramayana*,' he said, 'the story of Ram.'

'It will be known as Valmiki's *Ramayana*,' said Sita encouragingly.

'Who is this Valmiki?' asked Ratnakar.

'You,' said Sita, 'reborn out of the hill of valu or sand.'

'You are my guru, you made my rebirth possible.' Valmiki bowed down and touched Sita's feet with his forehead. 'I don't know who you are. But clearly you have been abandoned by your family as I have been abandoned by mine. Let me take care of you.'

'I can take care of myself,' said Sita.

'Then take care of me.'

'Only if you expand your mind, include your wife and children too. They may have abandoned you but you must not abandon them.'

Valmiki nodded his head and returned home. Sita followed him.

Ratnakar's wife, Gomti, screamed at him, demanding to know where he had been for so many weeks, and why he was dressed like a tapasvi, covered with ash and wrapped in clothes of bark. She wailed at the misery of her life, how she had had to fend for herself and her children, of the nights she had spent without food, comforting her starving children. She cursed her husband and her fate and the gods. She wept uncontrollably. Valmiki did not react. When she calmed down, he apologized and hugged her. She started to weep again.

Then her gaze drifted to Sita. 'Who is this?' Gomti asked, her gaze suspicious. 'Your mistress?' Then she looked at him: unkempt and dirty. 'Can't be,' she scoffed.

'My husband left me in the forest, banished me from his home. I have nowhere to go. Your husband invited me to your home. Will you accept me as your guest?' asked Sita.

'We have nothing,' said Ratnakar's wife, looking at Sita suspiciously. How could someone abandoned by her husband look so calm? 'But I guess we can share nothing.'

Sita smiled and gave her royal robes and jewellery to Valmiki's wife. As daughter-in-law she was expected to wear this bridal finery to uphold the reputation of her husband's house. Now she had been relieved of that burden. She could finally wear the clothes of leaf and bark of forest dwellers she had always longed to wear.

Valmiki's wife enjoyed wearing Sita's clothes for some time but then gradually lost interest, for Sita showed her what really matters in life: good food, decent shelter and a loving, supportive family.

What was once a thief's den gradually became a poet's hermitage. Valmiki busied himself turning the story of Ram into a song while Sita ate Shabari's berries to her full satisfaction.

- Ram asks for Sita to be abandoned in the forest in some retellings and near the hermitage of sages in other retellings. Typically, Sita is shown as forlorn and dependent on the sages who care for her, stripped of all her autonomy.

- The story of Ratnakar, the thief who turns into Valmiki, the poet, after chanting Ram's name is 500 years old, from the bhakti period. It is not found in the oldest 2000-year-old Sanskrit retelling, where Valmiki is a rishi of the Pracheta lineage. These are two different stories of two different people, popularly confused as one.
- Ratnakar turns into Valmiki through the intervention of Narada in some versions or that of the Saptarishis, the set of seven celestial sages. This tale first comes from the Skanda Purana and later from the *Ananda Ramayana* and *Adhyatma Ramayana*.
- In the Odia *Bilanka Ramayana* of Sarala Das, Valmiki is born when the sweat of Brahma falls on the sand (valu) of a riverbank.
- The community of subordinate castes which includes sweepers and cobblers in North India have accepted Valmiki as their patron saint.
- Ram is called 'patita-pavana', he who cleanses the unclean, rids the polluted of all pollution. This phrase can be traced to the hierarchy of pollution that led to denial of dignity and resources to castes in India associated with what were deemed unclean and menial tasks. Some reformers saw in Ram an icon for liberation from the caste hierarchy while others saw the *Ramayana* as the source of the caste hierarchy.
- In the seventh century, a temple to Valmiki was erected in Champa (modern Vietnam) where he is venerated as the poet-sage and an incarnation of Vishnu.
- Traditionally, Valmiki's hermitage is said to be located in the Banda district of Uttar Pradesh.
- Valmiki's first verse and later his entire *Ramayana* is composed in a metre known as Anustup.

Shambuka

Hearing how Ratnakar had turned into a rishi called Valmiki, many in Ayodhya decided to give up the householder's way and become hermits. Priests became hermits; warriors became hermits; farmers, herders, craftsmen and traders became hermits. Ayodhya was in a crisis. 'Our king left his wife in the jungle and his subjects are leaving their wives for the jungle,' the people wailed.

One day, a priest came to Ram's palace and cried, 'Look, my young son is dying. There is no doctor around to heal him. Everyone is too busy performing tapasya to do yagnas. Familiar structures and hierarchies and edifices of society are crumbling. In such a world, the predictable order of life is bound to collapse. The young are bound to die before the old. You, Ram, are responsible for this chaos. Restore it, before things get worse.'

So Ram went to the forest and found there the leader of the tapasvis. It was a man called Shambuka. 'Here I am no one's servant. I am equal to all other creatures in the forest. I prefer the forest to the city. There is wisdom here,' Shambuka said.

'Do not romanticize the forest,' said Ram. 'In the jungle, no one helps the helpless. You have to take care of yourself, live in constant fear of starvation or predators. You have to let the strongest have all the mates, and you have to migrate when the seasons change. But in the city there is enough food to feed the weak. And there are social structures that grant you meaning, purpose and validity.'

'I refuse to be inferior to anyone. In your city, Ram, I am inferior to the trader, the warrior and the priest. Why?'

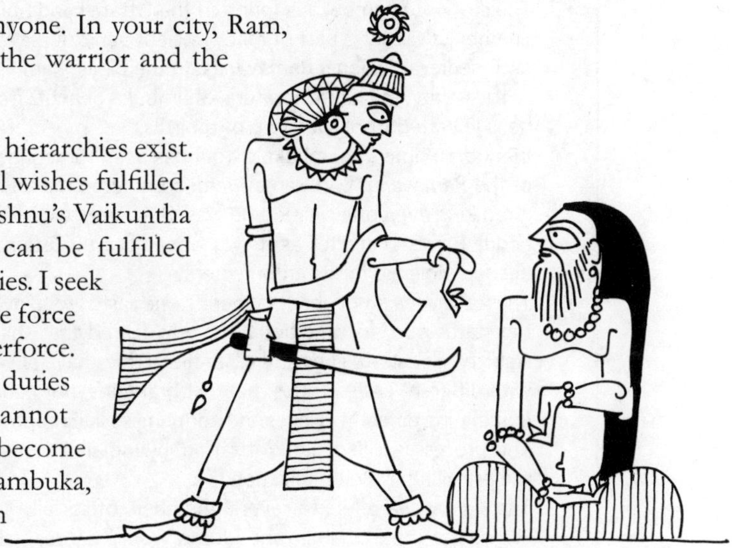

'Only in Shiva's Kailas do no hierarchies exist. Only in Indra's Swarga are all wishes fulfilled. I, Ram, struggle to create Vishnu's Vaikuntha in Ayodhya where wishes can be fulfilled without the need for hierarchies. I seek to churn life with reality as the force and imagination as the counterforce. But for Ayodhya to survive, duties have to be performed. I cannot allow every householder to become a hermit. Return home, Shambuka, do your duty. You may return to the forest only after you have passed on your skills to the next generation. Else I will kill you, to deter all those who seek to follow you.'

'You can kill me, Ram. But I will not return.'

So Ram raised his sword and beheaded Shambuka, just as Parashurama had beheaded Renuka and hacked away Kartavirya's limbs. Rules of society had to be upheld by the perfect king, whether he, or his subjects, agreed with them or not.

When Ram returned home, the priest whose son had died in the meantime rushed to Ram's side and said, 'My son has miraculously come back from the dead. The god of death let him return, saying he was satisfied by the sacrifice of Shambuka.'

Ram looked at the boy and told him, 'Be a brahmin like your father.'

'Not like my father, but like Shambuka,' said the son. 'My father transmits the hymns of the Vedas, but does not understand what they mean. He enjoys dominating and feeling superior. No, I will not be like him. I choose brahmin-varna over brahmin-jati. I want to be a tapasvi like Shambuka and turn Ayodhya into Vaikuntha on earth.'

Ram, his royal hands still stained by Shambuka's blood, felt reassured, for he knew Shambuka had been reborn.

- The story of Shambuka is found in the Uttara-kanda of the Valmiki *Ramayana*.
- Shambuka's story is part of many ancient Sanskrit plays such as the one by Bhavabhuti, and medieval regional *Ramayanas*. In the plays, Ram's actions are justified on the basis of royal duty. In bhakti literature, Shambuka benefits from the killing as the killer is God; he is liberated from the cycle of rebirths.
- In modern times, Shambuka's story has been turned into plays that show the caste bias of the *Ramayana*. E.V. Ramaswami considered it a tale that revealed Ram was not the good king everyone claimed he was. B.R. Ambedkar believed the tale was not so much about Ram's character as it was about the unsustainability of the caste system that needed violence for its enforcement.
- The *Ramayana* is not about favouring one caste group over another but about maintaining the status quo, for traditionally it was feared that shifts in caste would disrupt social stability. Yet, caste lines and caste hierarchies have always shifted across Indian history, with different caste groups, not just brahmins, but generally landowning communities, dominating different villages and adopting socially approved habits such as vegetarianism. This process is called 'Sanskritization' by Indian sociologists; a few Western sociologists prefer calling it 'Brahminization'.
- The *Ramayana* refers to several members of socially subordinate castes: the boatman Guha, the tribal Shabari and, some would argue, Valmiki, and the vanaras and the rakshasas. Ram's relationship with each is different, determined more by emotion than by rules, except in the case of Shambuka, an episode that takes place after Ram is king.

The Twins

Sita gave birth in the forest in solitude. Had she been in the palace this would have been a great event; she would have been surrounded by her sisters, mothers-in-law, midwives and servants. Music would have been played, banners would have been unfurled, and sweets would have been distributed.

But here she was all alone, lying behind a rock, on soft, green grass, watching the stars all night, bearing the pain until Aruni, goddess of dawn, appeared in the sky and encouraged her to give the final push.

The rules of purity and impurity, so important in a palace, do not apply in the jungle. She had to be up on her feet immediately to take care of herself, eat the fruits and the berries and the roots and shoots that would give her enough nourishment to feed her baby. Valmiki was busy writing his song and so his wife had to forage for food for her children. She could not be expected to feed Sita too, and her newborn.

Valmiki named the boy Luv and watched over him while he slept so that Sita could have some time to herself, to bathe and gather firewood, collect some water, tend to her little kitchen garden and collect some riverbank clay to make a few pots and pans.

Soon the boy was able to crawl. One day, when Sita was away, and Valmiki was lost in writing the perfect verse describing the eve of Ram's coronation, Luv simply wandered away. Valmiki suddenly felt an uneasy silence and realized the baby was gone. He searched his hut and Sita's hut and found no trace of the boy. He was not behind the baskets or the pots. Had he wandered off beyond the fence made of tall stones? Had a fox or an eagle snatched him away? Valmiki was filled with dread and terror. Then he heard Sita returning, singing her favourite lullaby. In panic, he collected some kusha grass, bundled it in the shape of a doll, and used the power of siddha collected through months of tapasya to create a child who was the very likeness of Luv.

Sita walked in with Luv in her arms. 'He just followed me to the river,' she said with a smile. Then she saw the twin child in Valmiki's lap. 'Who is that?'

'That,' said Valmiki, rather sheepishly, 'is your other son, Kush.'

Sita did not question or admonish Valmiki. She just picked Kush up and turning to Luv said, 'See, you have a brother. A twin brother.'

- While the Valmiki *Ramayana* talks of Sita giving birth to twins, *Kathasaritsagar* and Telugu folk songs speak of how Valmiki creates the second son from kusha grass.
- The idea of symmetry is very important in Hinduism. The gods have two wives, one on either side. The Goddess is flanked by two sons (Gauri with Ganesha and Kartikeya), two brothers (Subhadra with Jagannatha and Balabhadra in Puri) or two warriors (Bhairav and Langurvir or Hanuman in the Sheravali temples of North India). So too the two sons of Sita create a sense of symmetry. Ravana's ten heads create a visual asymmetry as there are four heads on one side of the main head and five on the other, indicating a lack of stability.

Mother Sita

The sons of Ram grew up in the shadow of the forest, under trees and atop rocks, bathing in rivers, and playing with deer. One could describe this as an idyllic life, as poets often do. But on days when the forest caught fire or the skies burst to pour relentless rain, or when the air was filled with the roars of hungry animals, or on days when neither Sita nor Gomti could find enough fruits or roots, it was hardly idyllic. So the children grew up tough, responsible, dependable, well versed with the rhythms of the forest and the tunes they heard Valmiki constantly hum.

The twins assumed that Valmiki was their father until Gomti's children got upset and yelled, 'He is ours. Get one of your own.'

So the twins went crying to Sita and asked her who their father was. Sita told them the story of Satyakama. He came to the Upanishad and wanted to be part of the conference. The rishis there asked him to name his father. He told the sages what his mother had told him: that she did not remember his father and so they should simply call him his mother's son, Jabali, son of Jabala. Pleased with this display of honesty and absence of awkwardness and embarrassment, the rishis named him Satyakama, and welcomed him to the Upanishad. 'I want you to be like Satyakama,' said Sita. 'Be satisfied being Sita's sons.' After that day, the boys did not miss their father.

With Sita, they learned the secrets of the forest, that all actions – good or bad – have consequences. 'Look,' she said, 'the deer eats every day but cannot ever eat to a full stomach because when the stomach is full you cannot run. And the tiger eats once in ten days but when he eats he eats to a full stomach. Thus, nature does not favour either prey or predator.' Luv and Kush learned to appreciate the hunger of the predator and the fear of the prey. They understood the nature of trees, why they brought forth leaves and flowers and fruit. At night, they heard their mother tell stories of devas and asuras and Valmiki sing of rishis.

The boys grew up watching every move of Sita's. Every morning she made her way to the river to bathe and fetch water. She spent all day repairing and cleaning the house, stocking it with food and keeping the fire burning. There were always fresh banana leaves in the house to serve food, and hollow gourds filled with sweet river water and garlands of fragrant flowers around everyone's neck. She never rested. She always smiled. Chores were never a burden.

Unlike Gomti, Sita never tied her hair, allowing it to fly in the wind. Unlike Gomti, who constantly complained and kept fighting with Valmiki, not once did Sita express resentment about her life. 'Being satisfied with life is but an option. You can demand more too if you wish. That is also the hallmark of humanity,' Gomti kept reminding Luv and Kush. Sita did not argue.

When they were old enough, Sita taught the boys how to make fire by striking rocks together, how to collect firewood from dry branches on the forest floor, how to make sharp tools for hunting, how to build traps, how to swing swords, hurl spears and, finally, how to make and use a bow. 'Hunt for food. Hunt to defend. But never hunt for sport,' she told her sons. 'And always check what you are hunting. Do not assume it is a deer you hear drinking water on the other side of the bush; it just might be a boy collecting water in a pot.'

The boys were very different from each other in character. Luv loved mathematical formulae, while Kush enjoyed the rules of grammar. Luv enjoyed the chase, while Kush enjoyed ambush. Luv loved conversation, while Kush preferred silence. Both were good archers; but while Luv excelled in striking moving targets, Kush excelled in striking distant ones. Sita never compared one to the other. 'All trees in the forest are unique and all trees are valid,' she would say. She would also remind them, 'Plants compete for sunlight and animals for mates. Blessed with humanity, only you and I have the power to abandon competition. To do so is dharma.'

Sita taught her sons the value of fire, how it could be contained in the kitchen hearth, which she called the first yagna-shala. She taught them to worship the pot that enables humans to drink water wherever and whenever they wished. She taught them hymns she had learned from rishis of the Upanishad. At night, she taught them how to read the stars. And whenever they were hungry, they knew, in Sita's hand would always be a fruit, or a nut, or a berry. No one went hungry when Sita was around.

- Sita functions as a single mother. Kunti in the *Mahabharata*, Jabala of the Upanishads, and Shakuntala, mother of Bharata, after whom India is called Bharat, are also single mothers.
- Most writers present Sita's life in the forest in a tragic mood as they equate life in the forest with poverty, not wisdom. They forget the wisdom of India that regards wealth only in functional terms and not as an indicator of self-worth. The sage is never poor even though he has nothing.
- The *Mahabharata* tells the story of how Ashtavakra mistakes his grandfather Uddalaka to be his father until his uncle Shvetaketu corrects him, much like Valmiki's sons correct Luv and Kush.
- The story of Satyakama Jabala comes from the Chandogya Upanishad, dated to the seventh century BCE.
- In Wayanad, Kerala, there is a temple of Sita with her two sons. The local *Ramayana* has many twists and turns not found in the Valmiki *Ramayana*. The locals are convinced the *Ramayana* took place in and around Wayanad.

Gandharva

One day, Sita heard a lute being played. It sounded like Ravana's Rudra-veena. Memories stirred. She let them rise; they made her smile. They were children of the past, now independent, who visited her from time to time. Leaving Luv and Kush with Valmiki, still busy writing his song, she went to find out the source of the music.

She found a handsome man playing it. A rakshasa? A gandharva? A rishi? He looked like Ravana might have looked in his younger days.

'Ah, you have finally come. Every bee and butterfly, every ant and termite, every migrating bird and deer speaks of your tranquil beauty. It inspired me to make this music and play it for you. I hoped it would bind your heart and draw you towards me.'

'Nice music, child. Who are you? Introduce yourself. You clearly know me.'

'Names do not matter. Just know that I am a man who offers you his music. My heart is yours. My life is yours. Make me yours.'

'I am Ram's and he is mine. We are complete with each other. I need no other.'

'But he has abandoned you. And you are free of the fetters of marriage. Do not cling to him. Come to me.'

'It is not whether he binds me or not. It is whether I want to or not. And I do not want to. I do not need to. With or without Ram, I am complete in myself. Ram reflects my completion as I reflect his. You, who are incomplete, should not assume my incompleteness, just because I am alone in the forest.'

The music stopped. The man frowned and snarled, like Surpanakha. But Sita was not afraid. These were memories, children of the past, who having grown up sometimes return to taunt the present.

- Fidelity is often seen in modern times as a burden imposed mostly on women by men. But for many women and men it is also an expression of love.
- Sita, daughter of Janaka, embodies wisdom. Wisdom is all about outgrowing hunger, be it physical, emotional, intellectual or social.
- Jain scriptures tell the story of Rajulmati, wife of the Tirthankara Neminath, who pines for her husband who has become an ascetic, and rejects the advances of youths who wish to seduce her with words of profound wisdom. A similar story is also told of Mallika, the princess who rejects all men who wish to marry her and becomes Tirthankara Mallinath.
- From the Brihadaranyaka Upanishad comes the hymn of completeness (purnamadah purnamidam). It describes the brahman as being complete, creating completeness, and remaining complete even when it gives birth to completeness.

Hanuman's *Ramayana*

Finally, Valmiki completed the *Ramayana*. He showed it to Sita and she loved it. He showed it to his wife and she praised it. Then he showed it to Narada, the sage who keeps travelling between heaven and earth, but he was not impressed. 'It is good, but Hanuman's is better,' he said.

'That monkey has written the *Ramayana* too!' Valmiki did not like this at all, and he wondered whose *Ramayana* was better. So he set out to find Hanuman.

Narada directed him to the kadali-vana, the grove of plantains, not far from Ayodhya, that Hanuman frequented. There, on seven broad leaves of the banana tree, Valmiki found inscribed Hanuman's *Ramayana*. He read it and found it to be perfect. The most exquisite choice of grammar and vocabulary, metre and melody. Valmiki could not help himself. He started to cry.

'Is it so bad?' asked Hanuman.

'No, it is so good,' said Valmiki.

'Why then are you crying?' asked Hanuman.

'Because,' replied Valmiki, 'after reading Hanuman's *Ramayana* no one will read Valmiki's *Ramayana*.' Hearing this, Hanuman simply tore up the seven banana leaves on which he had inscribed his telling of Ram's tale. 'What have you done?' screamed Valmiki, watching Hanuman cast the pieces into the wind. 'Now no one will ever read Hanuman's *Ramayana*.'

Hanuman said, 'You need your *Ramayana* more than I need mine. You wrote your *Ramayana* so that the world remembers Valmiki; I wrote my *Ramayana* so that I remember Ram.'

At that moment, Valmiki realized how he had been consumed by the desire for validation through his work. He had not used the work to liberate himself from the fear of invalidation. He had not appreciated the essence of Ram's tale to unknot his mind. His *Ramayana* was a product of ambition; Hanuman's *Ramayana* was a product of affection. That is why Hanuman's *Ramayana* sounded so much better.

Valmiki fell at Hanuman's feet and said, 'Just as the flesh distracts us from the mind, so do words distract us from the idea. Now I realize that greater than Ram is the idea of Ram.'

- Many retellings give Hanuman as the source of the *Ramayana*. Valmiki is said to have written only a part of what Hanuman had to say.
- The idea that all narratives are incomplete and so no one must be arrogant about their creation is a common theme in Indian stories.
- In some versions, Hanuman carves the *Ramayana* on rocks. In others he writes it on palm leaves that the wind carries to different parts of India.

Shatrughna Hears the *Ramayana*

Valmiki taught the idea that is Ram through the song that is the *Ramayana* to Luv and Kush. He also hoped that they would grow up admiring the man who was their father, understand why he did what he did. As they learned the song of Ram, Luv and Kush experienced wonder, and understood the difference between being learned and being wise.

Then one day, when Luv and Kush were approaching the fourteenth year of their life, a warrior with his soldiers bearing banners of the Suryavamsa and the Raghukula came to Sita's hermitage. Sita recognized the warrior as her brother-in-law Shatrughna. He looked just like Lakshman. Memories welled up inside her. She chose to withdraw into her hut.

'May I rest here for the night?' asked Shatrughna. He explained he was returning after defeating Lavana, the terrible king of Mathura, who had challenged the authority of Ram. Valmiki welcomed him and offered him fruit and water, and some fish that the twins had caught earlier that day. When Shatrughna had eaten, Valmiki asked the two boys to sing the song he had taught them.

The two boys picked up a stringed instrument and sang their song through the night. Shatrughna was spellbound by the verse and the voices. 'What is this musical instrument that you hold? It looks like a fiddle but is very different,' he said.

'It is like a lute, just like a veena, but instead of plucking its strings with our fingers we run the string of our bow on it to create sound,' said the boys. 'We call it Ravana-hatta, the hand of Ravana. The hand that stole Sita from Ram now makes music for our song that praises Ram.'

'Bows that we use to shoot arrows, you use to make music. You two are truly gifted.' Turning to Valmiki, Shatrughna said, 'You must bring these boys to Ayodhya and sing this song before the king. It describes his life so beautifully. This is the perfect time. He is conducting the Ashwamedha yagna and, as you know, between the rituals, bards and minstrels and dancers are invited to entertain the city.'

- In the Valmiki *Ramayana*, Ram encourages his brothers to establish independent kingdoms of their own. Lakshman and Bharata refuse to leave his side. Shatrughna ventures out and establishes a kingdom after defeating Lavana-asura. On the way back, he stops at Valmiki's ashrama and hears two young boys learning to sing the sage's composition, the *Ramayana*. He invites them to sing in Ayodhya. Does he recognize his nephews? Does he orchestrate the reunion? Is that the only role given to Shatrughna in the *Ramayana*?
- Shatrughna does not have much to do in the *Ramayana* except shadow Bharata and defeat Lavana-asura in the Uttara-Ramayana.
- Folk retellings speak of how Lakshman often visited Sita secretly. Once he brought Ram along to see the children, and Sita, noticing Ram, threw garbage at him, a folk expression of rage.
- Ravana-hatta is a folk musical instrument, a fiddle made using a coconut shell at one end, used by the musicians of Rajasthan. Rudra-veena is a classical lute, with two pumpkin gourds at either end. Stringed instruments are associated with Ravana; he is often described as their creator.

Entertainers in Ayodhya

When Shatrughna left, Valmiki sniggered, 'The great prince does not realize that he has just invited his own nephews to dance and sing on the streets of the city like common entertainers.'

'Is that bad?' asked Sita, realizing that Valmiki had known her identity all along, but had respected her silence on the matter. 'Do you think to be an entertainer is inferior to being a prince? As long as you think so, Brahma will never be a true brahmin, for hierarchy stems from the animal need to dominate, not the human ability to expand the mind in the quest for brahman.'

Duly chastised, Valmiki decided to take the sons of Sita to Ayodhya and make them perform the *Ramayana* before the king. 'Should I introduce them to their father?' wondered Valmiki.

'Do not impose the burden of fatherhood on Ram. It will create more turbulence in Ayodhya, for then these boys will become contenders to his throne,' said Sita.

'But is it not their right by birth?' asked Valmiki.

'The kingdom is not a king's property. Besides, property is a human delusion granted by man to man. The children belong to no one and nothing really belongs to Ram.'

The sons of Sita were excited at the prospect of visiting Ayodhya for the first time. They knew all the stories about this famed city: how it came into being following the wedding of the king of North Kosala and the princess of South Kosala, how its people followed Ram to the edge of the forest, for they loved him so much, and how the old king Dashratha died alone at the threshold of the palace without his sons or his subjects around him. As they prepared to leave, Sita gave her hairpin to Valmiki. 'Give this to Ram's new queen.'

'New queen? Ram does not have a new queen.'

'He is conducting a yagna. He cannot conduct the ritual without a wife by his side. Give this to that lady with my love. She will be a lonely woman, for I know while Ram will respect her he will never love her as he loved me,' she said. Valmiki wondered how Sita could stay so calm. Sensing his thoughts, Sita said, 'This was an eventuality. I accept it with grace. Sorrow only comes when we resist reality, for a dream.'

The children touched their mother's feet before following Valmiki through the forest to Ayodhya. The city had four gates: one for kings and warriors, one for priests and poets, one for farmers, herders, artisans and traders, and one for servants and entertainers. The sons of Sita entered by the fourth gate.

Right from the gate, Luv and Kush started singing and dancing. The bells on their feet tinkled. Everybody stopped to see the boys who had the Ravana-hatta in one hand and a bow in the other. They had the arms of archers but the mannerisms of entertainers. Their voice was beautiful and the words they sang were even more wonderful. The people clapped and cheered and followed the boys to the square in front of the palace where the king was performing his great yagna.

Valmiki saw Ram seated on a tiger skin, a firm moustache curled around his cheek, his eyes serene as he made offerings to the fire.

In the interval between the ceremonies, when the rishis declared that the gods were asleep and they needed to rest, Luv and Kush were called to present Valmiki's song to the king. He now sat on a golden throne. Bharata held the parasol behind him. Lakshman and Shatrughna fanned him with yak-tail fly whisks. The women of the household sat behind them, bedecked with gold and diamonds and the three old queen mothers sat at a distance in the attire of widows. At the feet of Ram was a monkey. 'That is Hanuman,' said Valmiki to the boys. 'Look how comfortable he is, seated at Ram's feet, this great creature who leapt across the ocean and set Lanka aflame.'

The boys sang the six chapters of Valmiki's *Ramayana* over six nights. At the end of each chapter, the king gave each of the boys a string of gold coins. When the sixth chapter was over, everyone praised the composition and the performance. And Ram said something that surprised everyone: 'Whose story was this? Who is this noble man whose life you describe so beautifully?'

The boys were surprised to hear this. 'It is your story, king of Ayodhya, as narrated by our mother to our teacher, Valmiki, composer of this song.'

'Is it? The Ram you describe is too noble to be me. And the Sita you describe is just not as wonderful as I remember her.' Everyone watched as the king shut his eyes, took a deep breath and smiled. They knew he was thinking of his wife. 'The gifts I have given you are not enough. You deserve more. What do you want?'

Luv said, 'May we see the queen? She has not stepped out of the palace even once in the six days and nights we have been here.'

'But she has always been beside me. Have you not seen her?' Ram turned left and the boys saw an image that until then they had assumed was a beautiful doll made of gold. 'That is my Sita, pure as gold. She never leaves my side.'

'That is a doll. We want to see the real Sita,' said Kush.

'This is the Sita that is my wife. The Sita who was the queen of Ayodhya has been cast out long ago.'

The boys could not believe what they heard. 'You abandoned Sita!' they cried out in horror. 'Why? Did she not survive the fire and prove her chastity?'

'Infidelity is never a reason to abandon anyone.'

'Then why?'

'Unwittingly, she had become a stain on the royal reputation, a reason for people to mock the king. She had to be washed away.'

The cruelty of Ram's statement made Luv and Kush so angry that they threw away the chain of gold coins they had received. They also threw away their fiddles. 'We shall never sing your song again,' they said, and stormed out with just the bows in hand. The king's brothers reached for their swords at this display of insolence.

Valmiki apologized to the king before things got out of hand: 'They are children and we are entertainers. We do not understand the ways of kings. Please forgive us.'

Gesturing to his brothers to calm down, Ram said, 'There is nothing to apologize for. I do not expect to be understood.'

The people had asked him to remarry, take more wives as his father had for the sake of an heir – or at least one for the ritual – but Ram had refused saying, 'Brahma may have two wives – Savitri and Gayatri. Vishnu may have two wives – Shridevi and Bhudevi. Shiva may have two wives – Gauri and Ganga. Kartikeya may take two wives – Valli and Sena. Ganesha may take two wives – Riddhi and Siddhi. Krishna will have Radha, Rukmini and Satyabhama. But for me, there will only be Sita.'

- Gold is the purest metal. That Ram makes the image of Sita using this metal is significant.
- The word 'kushilava' means travelling bards. The bards who narrated the *Ramayana* were the original 'sons of Ram' questioning his decision to abandon his wife. Was it because he doubted her? Was it to simply satisfy his people? Or was it to make society question its underlying assumptions?
- In traditional visual renderings of the *Ramayana*, Valmiki and the sons of Sita are visualized as hermits singing the song of Ram. They look like priests almost. But they are bards, members of the lowest strata of society, with no roots. In many parts of India, an entertainer (or nat) is a term of derision. By making Ram's sons members of this community, Valmiki dramatically demonstrates the personal tragedy of the royal couple and the cost of social propriety.
- In the Jain *Ramayana* written in Sanskrit by Hemachandra known as *Yogashastra*, Ram follows Sita to the forest to bring her back but finds no trace of her. He assumes she is dead, killed by wild animals and performs her funeral rites.
- In Telugu folk songs, the golden image of Sita has to be bathed by the women of the household. The women, led by Ram's elder sister, refuse to do so.

Ram's Horse

As part of the Ashwamedha yagna, the royal horse was let loose and the king's warriors followed it. All the lands the horse crossed unchallenged came under the king's control. Thus the empire and influence of the Raghu clan could expand without bloodshed.

When the horse entered the forest and came by the hermitage of Valmiki, Luv and Kush captured the horse and refused to part with it. 'We shall never be subjects of Ram,' they said. They raised their bows, determined to defend themselves against Ram's warriors.

'Give the horse back. Or let it pass. This is no game, children. If you do not do as we say, we will attack and drag you like chained calves to the king's prison,' said the warriors to Luv and Kush, but the boys refused to budge.

To the astonishment of the warriors, the boys were well versed in the martial arts and they knew the chants to turn arrows into missiles. Ayodhya's warriors were suddenly showered with arrows that contained within them the power of serpents, eagles, bears, rats, vultures and lions. The arrows caused the royal chariots to burst into flames, or caused the wind to sweep up the soldiers into the sky. Not used to being challenged, let alone being defeated, the warriors were at their wits' end.

Word was sent to Ayodhya. The king sent his brothers to capture the boys. But Shatrughna was defeated, and Lakshman and Bharata. Even Hanuman was caught by the boys and tied to a tree like a pet.

Surprised to learn this, Ram entered the forest. He came wearing his armour of gold, on a golden chariot bearing his royal flag, carrying his magnificent bow and a quiverful of splendid arrows. He raised his bow determined to teach the boys a lesson. The boys also raised their bows determined to kill the man who was no longer their hero.

'Stop!' said Sita coming between the boys and the king. 'You cannot defeat these boys. No one can. They are the children of Sita and Ram.'

- The episode of the horse is not found in the Valmiki *Ramayana*. This comes from later narratives such as in Bhavabhuti's eighth-century Sanskrit play *Uttara Ramcharitra* and the fourteenth-century Patal-khand of the Padma Purana.
- That Ram and his entire army are unable to defeat Sita's sons is an indicator of defiance, a rejection of unfair society.
- In a Kathakali dance performance, Hanuman is so depressed in the absence of Sita that he wanders in the forest looking for her. Sita's sons catch him, tie him up and keep him as a pet. Since they can so easily subdue him, Hanuman concludes they can only be Sita's children.
- In some Assamese and Bengali retellings, the children not just defeat Ram, but they kill him and carry his crown to their mother who is horrified at what they have done. She then invokes the gods to undo the damage. This episode seeks to right the wrong done to Sita. It is her revenge, in a way. But she forgives and restores everyone to life.
- The ritual of Ashwamedha enabled a king to claim overlordship over other kingdoms using minimum force. That Ram seeks to expand his dominion and is resisted by his own sons expresses the limitations of any human rule. No rule is entirely fair; someone is always suffering on account of it. And those who suffer will resist. Gauri will never be sovereign; only Kali will.
- The tenth-century Sanskrit play *Chalita Ram* (deceived Ram) is based on the later part of the *Ramayana*. The entire play is no longer available and the author remains untraced. Here, the demon Lavana sends his spies disguised as Kaikeyi and Manthara to cast aspersions on Sita's character. Luv and Kush capture Ram's horse in the forest but in the fight that follows Luv is captured and taken to Ayodhya where he sees the golden statue of Sita and identifies her as his mother.

- In the eleventh-century *Kathasaritsagar*, Lakshman seeks out a man with sacred marks on his body for Ram's sacrifice. He encounters Luv in the forest who has these marks and takes him captive. Kush immediately sets out to rescue his brother and in the fight that follows successfully defeats Ram's soldiers, Ram's brothers and even Ram. When asked who he is, he identifies himself as the son of Sita and Ram. Ram is so overjoyed on hearing this that the family unites and returns to Ayodhya to live happily ever after.

Sita Returns to Her Mother

Suddenly the might of the boys made sense. The invincible Ram finally had to accept defeat. Ram said, 'The boys have captured the royal horse of the Raghu clan. They can either kill it or ride back on it to Ayodhya to take their rightful place beside their father on their ancestral throne.'

The boys did not know whether to stay disappointed with Ram, or rejoice in the knowledge that he was their father. Should they hug him or stay by their mother's side? 'Go to your father and do as he says,' said Sita.

'Let the boys' mother also be accepted by Ram,' pleaded Valmiki.

Ram said, 'Tell the mother of these boys that Ram rejected the queen of Ayodhya, never his wife. Tell her that the past fourteen years in the palace have been worse than the fourteen years in the forest. She made the wilderness a wonderful place. In her company I enjoyed the heat of the summer, the cold of the winter, the wetness of the rains. In her company I did not mind the days without food and the nights without sleep. In her company I did not feel the sharp stones that split my heel, the thorns that tore my skin, the ants that gnawed at my flesh, the wind that chilled my bones. Without her, the palace with its silks and its perfumes was an unbearable prison, food had no taste and music had no rhythm. But I had to bear it, for I was the king and I would never let my people down. I performed the rites and rituals as the eldest of the clan, and I oversaw the welfare of my people. I ensured everyone followed their profession and retired to make way for the next generation. I tried to make life as orderly and as predictable as possible. Let her know that I strove to make the kingdom happy, but I myself was never happy. Tell her that I will be happy only if she returns to Ayodhya. But to return as queen she has to prove her chastity publicly before the people of Ayodhya so that they will never ever mock their king again.'

Ram did not look at Sita. Sita did not look up at Ram. Both knew the implications of what was being said.

The people of Ayodhya had rushed to Valmiki's hermitage on hearing what was happening there. The boys who had entertained them with song and dance, they now realized, were the sons of Ram.

When they arrived, they found Ram standing on his chariot and Sita on the ground below. In between were the twins. They heard Sita say, 'The earth accepts all seeds with love. She bears the judgement of her children with love. If I have been as true as the earth in my love for Ram then may the earth split open and take me within.'

And that was what happened in a moment, without warning. The mountains rumbled, the rivers stopped, the earth split open and Sita descended below the earth.

Ram, taken by surprise at what was happening, rushed to stop his wife, hold her hand and pull her out, but the earth had closed before he could reach her. All that he could clutch were the ends of her hair that turned into blades of grass.

Would the pain have been less had she chastised him before she left? Would the pain have been less had they at least spoken before she left? Would the pain have been less had she at least looked at him before she left? But then she was under no obligation. He had liberated her long ago from the burden of being Ram's wife. But he would always be Sita's husband.

There was nothing more Ram could do but return home to Ayodhya with his sons, and live the rest of his life with the doll of gold that was his Sita.

- By refusing to return to Ram, Sita turns away from sanskriti and the rules of society. She does not need social structures to give her status. She chooses the earth, where there are no boundaries and rules.
- Many modern renditions of the *Ramayana* focus on Sita's banishment by Ram, but do not even refer to Ram's refusal to remarry and even his refusal to live after Sita's descent. Such incomplete narratives, often qualified as a woman's perspective, strategically reveal a very different Ram. These have won many admirers in the West, perhaps because they reinforce a particular image of India and Indians.
- In the Gobind *Ramayana*, after the defeat of Ram by Luv and Kush, Ram returns to Ayodhya with Sita and rules for ten thousand years, but then the women of the palace get Sita to draw Ravana's image and a jealous and insecure Ram once again demands that Sita prove her chastity. It is then that she enters the earth.
- In another folk version, Sita refuses to return to Ayodhya even when called and so is told that Ram is dead. She rushes to the city but, on finding that he is alive, and that she has been tricked, asks the earth to open up to claim her.
- In one Assamese *Ramayana*, Hanuman goes to the netherworld in search of Sita and convinces her to come back to Ram.
- The Sitamai temple at Karnal in Haryana marks the spot where the ground split so that Sita could enter the earth.

Solitude for Ram

'I wish to be alone,' said Ram, after he had put Luv and Kush to bed.

That night, their first night in the palace, the twins had chosen to sleep on the floor on a mat of reeds. Ram had let them. It would be some time before they got used to beds and cushions.

All the palace women sat around all night watching the two boys sleep. In the lamplight, one looked like Ram and the other like Sita. In the moonlight, he who looked like Ram looked like Sita and he who looked like Sita looked like Ram.

The old mothers, who had never spoken to Ram since the departure of Sita, kept sobbing. These were their grandsons, gaunt like ascetics, hardly the next kings of the Raghu clan.

'I will guard the door. No one will disturb you. I will put to death anyone who dares open the door to your chamber,' said Lakshman, theatrical as ever. This time, however, Ram did not smile.

Sword in hand, Lakshman sat in front of the closed door and kept watch all night.

Then, just before dawn broke, he saw the sage Durvasa rush towards him. 'Let me pass. I wish to see Ram this very instant,' grunted the sage.

'He seeks solitude. Please wait for some time,' said Lakshman, bowing to the rishi known for his short temper.

'No. Now. I want to see him now. This very instant.'

'He needs some time. Just a little time. You know what happened yesterday, don't you?' Lakshman tried to reason with the sage.

'Now. Now. Now,' insisted the sage, 'I want to see Ram now. And if you don't open that door, I will curse the city of Ayodhya, set it aflame with my rage.'

A frightened Lakshman opened the door to Ram's chamber and fell at Ram's feet. 'I had to open the door. I had to disturb your solitude. I had to disobey you. For Ayodhya.' As he spoke, he turned around and found to his surprise no Durvasa, just an empty corridor. There never was a Durvasa. It was just an apparition. What was going on?

Ram pulled Lakshman up and said, 'You finally understand, little brother.' Lakshman was not sure he did. 'Ayodhya matters more than Ram. All my actions are for Ayodhya, not for my wife, not for my sons, not for my brother, not for my father, not for my mother, only for my people. But all your actions were out of love for me. You were loyal to me. You demanded loyalty for me. But I only demanded love for the people of Ayodhya, all their faults notwithstanding. That, my brother, is kingship.'

'So much sacrifice.'

'Is it sacrifice to give up sleep for your crying child, Lakshman?' asked Ram. He then added, 'I will miss you so much, Lakshman, when you are gone.'

'But I am going nowhere,' said Lakshman, puzzled at Ram's remark.

Ram then reminded him, 'Did you not say that you would behead anyone who opened the door to my chambers and disturbed my solitude? Keep your word, Lakshman, as scion of the Raghu clan. '

'Will that make you happy, brother?'

'Not for me, Lakshman. For family reputation. Let no one question the integrity of the Raghu clan.'

'But I am your brother.'

'And Sita was my wife, Shambuka was my subject. Rules are rules, Lakshman. I will always uphold the rules, however distasteful they may be. I expect you to do the same.'

Lakshman looked up at Ram and saw the same expression as when Sita was presented to him in Lanka. Lakshman did not like this expression, but finally he understood it. With understanding came peace. In peace, he turned around and walked into the forest, unafraid like Sita, ready to behead himself and walk into the arms of Yama.

As Ram sank into his throne, aware of his aloneness, he heard, from beyond the gates of Ayodhya, Yama shout, 'She is gone. He is gone. Now it is time for you to go. But that will not happen as long as Hanuman guards the gates of Ayodhya.'

He who breaks no rules would not break the law of nature. All things have to come to an end: exile in the forest, joy with Sita, as well as the reign of Ram. Yes, it was time to enter the river Sarayu and return to Vaikuntha.

So Ram dropped his ring into a crack in the palace floor, and called out, 'Hanuman!'

- Is loyalty a virtue? This story in the Valmiki *Ramayana* questions this popular notion. Lakshman's actions are based on his love for his brother. He does not care for the rules or for Ayodhya. For Ram, the latter is more important than the former. Through his rather cruel approach, Ram compels Lakshman to appreciate dharma and not be simply blinded by Ram.
- The dog is a loyal, lovable animal but Hindu scriptures do not treat it as an auspicious creature perhaps because loyalty feeds on fear and the purpose of Vedic scriptures is to outgrow fear by expanding the mind.
- Ram is dependable and Lakshman is dependent on Ram. Through this story, Ram seeks to make Lakshman outgrow his dependence and become more dependable. That his 'head is cut off' is, like always, a metaphor for expanding the mind.
- In Jain narratives, Ram weeps when Lakshman dies, until a Jain monk starts watering a rock to tell him that his tears will not awaken a corpse just as the water will not get the rock to bear fruit.
- In a way the *Ramayana* warns us about the dangers of excessive reliance on rules. It reveals the personality of a man who values rules above all else: he is predictable, dependable, but not very pleasant. This is balanced by Krishna who looks beyond rules at intent and, more importantly, affection. Ram seems cold and distant when compared to the lovable Krishna. Together they create Vishnu, the preserver of the world.
- Both the *Ramayana* and the *Mahabharata* end with death and the wisdom that follows death. That wisdom is sukhant, a true happy ending.

EPILOGUE

Ascent to Ayodhya

Hanuman stopped speaking, suddenly aware that he had been describing events he had not witnessed. The narration was as much for him as it was for the nagas who sat before him spellbound. In the glow of Vasuki's gems, Hanuman realized he was being told something he was not willing to accept.

'I have told you all that I know of Ram's Sita,' said Hanuman. 'Now please point me to the ring of Sita's Ram.'

'Why do you call him Sita's Ram? Why not just Ram? Why do you call her Ram's Sita? Why not just Sita?' asked Vasuki, ignoring Hanuman's impatience.

'Ravana's rage separated Sita from Ram. Ayodhya's gossip separated Ram from Sita. But Hanuman's tongue will never separate Sita from Ram or Ram from Sita.'

'Yet you seek to stop Yama who seeks to bring the two together?'

Silence ensued as realization dawned. Hanuman's shoulders fell, his heart sank as he felt Ram's yearning for Sita on the other shore. Taking a deep breath he said, 'Still, I must complete my mission. I have told you the story. Now where is the ring?'

'You will find it there,' said Vasuki, pointing to a vast mountain in the centre of Naga-loka.

Hanuman rushed to the mountain and found to his surprise it was no mountain but a gigantic pile of rings. Each ring looked like an exact copy of Ram's ring. 'What is this mystery?' he asked Vasuki.

The seven hoods of Vasuki sprouted a thousand hoods as he spoke. 'Did you think there was only the one? As many rings, so many Rams. Every time a ring falls into Naga-loka, a monkey follows it and Ram up there dies. This is not the first time it has happened. This is not the last time it will happen. Every time the world awakens and Treta yuga begins, Lakshmi rises from the earth as Sita and Vishnu descends from the sky as Ram. Every time the Treta yuga ends Sita returns to the earth and Ram to the sky. So it has happened before. So it will happen again.'

The enormity of the cosmos and of Ram's story suddenly unfolded before Hanuman's eyes. 'Why does the story repeat itself again and again?'

'So that every generation realizes the point of human existence.'

'Which is?'

'Fear is a constant, and faith is a choice. Fear comes from karma, from faith arises dharma. Fear creates Kaikeyis and Ravanas, streets full of gossip, families with rigid rules and fragile reputations. They will always be there. Faith creates a Sita and a Ram. They will come into being only if we have faith that the mind can expand until we do not abandon the world even when the world abandons us.'

Hanuman remembered how Sita and Ram were always at peace, whether in the palace or in the forest, whether together or apart. Committed to each other, they did not fear the forces that strove to break their commitment. Yes, there were doubts, uncertainties, anxieties, but these only served to unfold more wisdom. They understood the ways of the world and the nature of living creatures, and loved them unconditionally. Hanuman bowed to Vasuki for making explicit the implicit.

Leaving Ram's ring behind in Naga-loka, Hanuman rose back through the tunnel and found an Ayodhya desolate without its lord. He followed the footprints of Ram to the banks of the Sarayu and learned how his master had walked into the river, chanting Sita's name, while all of Ayodhya stood on the riverbank weeping. He would never rise again.

Luv and Kush sat on the throne. Would they share the throne? If anyone could, they would.

The waters that contained Ram seeped into the earth that contained Sita, and caused the seeds to germinate. Leaves rose, flowers bloomed, fruits formed. Luv and Kush ate the fruits with relish.

- Vedic thought, commonly known as Vedanta, always speaks in terms of relationships. There is never one, there are always two. This is Dvaita, the dualistic school of Vedanta. In wisdom, the one realizes he has no existence without the other and the other has no existence without the one. This is Advaita, the monistic school of Vedanta.
- The heartbreak of Ram after Sita's departure, his gradual loss of interest in worldly matters and his eventual departure into the river is described in vivid detail in the Uttara-kanda of the Valmiki *Ramayana*.
- The idea of a king killing himself is distasteful to modern sensibilities. Rationalists view it as suicide while devotees view it as samadhi, an act of voluntary rejection of the flesh by enlightened beings. This practice of voluntarily rejecting the body was observed by Jain monks as well as by many Hindu saints, like Dnyaneshwar.
- Ram emerges from the womb and so is destined to die. Thus nothing in the world is permanent. Yet, Hanuman is chiranjivi, immortal, perhaps because he is celibate. The householder Ram dies but the hermit Hanuman does not. All possibilities exist in Indian mythology.
- Every time the *Ramayana* is read out as a holy book, a seat in the audience is kept empty, for Hanuman.
- In many retellings, Luv and Kush inherit two different cities, Shravasti and Kushavati. Later, Luv returns to Ayodhya and finds it derelict and shorn of splendour. He restores it to its former glory. In Jain versions, Luv and Kush become ascetics. In some versions, Kush follows his mother and Luv inherits Ayodhya.
- The *Raghuvamsa* of Kalidasa tells the story of Ram's descendants. It ends with Agnivarna,

who is a spoiled, hedonistic king and spends all his time with his queens; when asked to grant an audience to the people, he shows his feet through the window, as he is too lazy to get off the bed. Finally he dies and his pregnant widow is installed on the throne.

- In the seventeenth century, Latin American fruits of the Annona family reached India. They were given Indian names to make them popular. Thus we have sita-phal or fruit of Sita (custard apple) and ram-phal or fruit of Ram (bull's heart). There is even a lakshman-phal and hanuman-phal.
- Hindus in Kerala observe the *Ramayana* month in monsoon when the entire *Ramayana* written in Malayalam by Ezhuthachan in the sixteenth century is read out to the household.
- That there are many Rams and many *Ramayana*s is a recurring theme in Indian mythology. It indicates that life is not linear; there is no full stop. Life is cyclical; what goes around comes around. Such a view of time will never respect history, for what is the past is also the future. That is why in many Indian languages the word for tomorrow and yesterday is the same, for example 'kal' in Hindi.
- Traditionally, Ram is always invoked after invoking Sita, hence the phrase 'Jai Siya Ram', meaning victory to Sita's Ram. However, increasingly, in many pockets, the feminine is being edited out as people prefer 'Jai Shri Ram' indicating the rise of a less inclusive culture. Some argue, however, Shri is not a mere honorific like mister, but the Vedic name of Lakshmi, goddess of wealth.
- The *Ramayana*, like the *Mahabharata*, is called itihasa, which can be translated in two ways: first, as history, a record of events of the past; second, as a story that is tense-neutral or timeless. Thus, it can be located in a particular period (5000 BCE or earlier) and place (the Gangetic plains) and ascribed to a single poet (Valmiki); or it can be seen in psychological terms with each character representing a different aspect of our personality.

Acknowledgements

- To the mothers and fathers, grandmothers and grandfathers, aunts and uncles, teachers and household help, whose *Ramayana* is in all probability the first *Ramayana* for most children in India, long before they are exposed to other retellings.
- To my teachers (Ms Pinto, Ms Pereira, Ms Lobo, Ms Rodricks, Ms Fernandes, Ms Coutino, Ms Gulvadi, Ms Gersape, Ms Qadri) of Our Lady of Perpetual Succour High School, Chembur, Mumbai, who encouraged us to stage those wonderful plays based on episodes of the epic with childlike innocence and wonderment. No one then even thought politics.
- Adishakti Laboratory for Theatre Arts Research, Pondicherry, for their vast *Ramayana* archive.
- Chinmayi Deodhar and Madhavi Narsalay of Department of Sanskrit, Mumbai University, for helping me write the name Ram in the Ashokan and Gupta Brahmi scripts.
- Rupa and Partho (my friends) for helping me with the manuscript, and Partho again along with Shami (my sister), Janardan and Aniket (my assistants) and Deepak (my driver) for helping me clean, shade and scan the illustrations.
- The talebearers who for the past 3000 years have been writing and narrating the *Ramayana* as song and stories.
- The artists who have made the *Ramayana* visible through their art and their performances.
- The translators of the various *Ramayana*s who made these accessible to people like me.

- The art historians and curators who made available the various paintings and images of Ram from different regions from different historical periods.
- The scholars whose essays on the *Ramayana* showed me how to think and how not to think about the nuances of the epic.
- The academicians whose work on various aspects of Hindu mythology enabled me to contextualize the *Ramayana*.
- The cultural experts who helped me appreciate what distinguishes Indian thought patterns from thought patterns of other parts of the world.
- The thinkers who wondered on the nature of mythology and how stories, symbols and rituals construct humanity's truths.

Bibliography

Bulke, Camille. *Ramkatha and Other Essays.* Delhi: Vani Prakashan, 2010.

Dodiya, Jaydipsinh K. (ed.). *Critical Perspective on the Ramayana.* Delhi: Sarup & Sons, 2001.

De Selliers, Diane (ed.). *Valmiki Ramayana: Illustrated with Indian Painting from the 16th to the 19th Century*. Paris: Editions Diane de Selliers, 2011 (French).

Hawley, J.S., and D.M. Wulff (eds.). *The Divine Consort.* Boston: Beacon Press, 1982.

Hiltebeitel, Alf (ed.). *Criminal Gods and Demon Devotees.* New York: State University of New York Press, 1989.

Hopkins, E. Washburn. *Epic Mythology.* Delhi: Motilal Banarsidass, 1986.

Jakimowicz-Shah, Marta. *Metamorphosis of Indian Gods.* Calcutta: Seagull Books, 1988.

Jayakar, Pupul. *The Earth Mother.* Delhi: Penguin, 1989.

Kinsley, David. *Hindu Goddesses.* Delhi: Motilal Banarsidass, 1987.

Knappert, Jan. *An Encyclopedia of Myth and Legend: Indian Mythology.* New Delhi: HarperCollins, 1992.

Kulkarni, V.M. *Story of Rama in Jain Literature.* Ahmedabad: Saraswati Pustak Bhandar, 1990.

Lutgendorf, Philip. *Hanuman's Tale: The Messages of a Divine Monkey.* Delhi: Oxford University Press, 2007.

Lal, Malashri and Namita Gokhale (eds.). *In Search of Sita.* Delhi: Penguin, 2009.

Lalye, P.G. *Curses and Boons in the Valmiki Ramayana.* Delhi: Bharatiya Kala Prakashan, 2008.

Macfie, J.M. *The Ramayana of Tulsidas.* Reprint, Varanasi: Pilgrims Publications, 2006.

Mani, Vettam. *Puranic Encyclopaedia.* Delhi: Motilal Banarsidass, 1996.

Meyer, Johann Jakob. *Sexual Life in Ancient India.* Delhi: Motilal Banarsidass, 1989.

Nagar, Shantilal (trans.). *Adbhut Ramayana.* Delhi: B.R. Publishing, 2001.

——— (trans.). *Ananda Ramayana.* Delhi: Parimal, 2006.

——— (trans.). *Jain Ramayana-Paumacaryu.* Delhi: B.R. Publishing, 2002.

——— (trans.). *Madhava Kandali Ramayana in Assamese.* Delhi: B.R. Publishing, 2000.

——— (trans.). *Miniature Paintings on the Holy Ramayana.* Delhi: B.R. Publishing, 2001.

——— (trans.). *Sri Ranganatha Ramayana in Telugu.* Delhi: B.R. Publishing, 2001.

——— (trans.). *Torvey Ramayana in Kannada.* Delhi: B.R. Publishing, 2004.

Nagar, Shantilal and Tripta Nagar (trans.). *Giradhara Ramayana in Gujarati.* Delhi: Munshiram Manoharlal, 2003.

Nath, Rai Bahadur Lala Baij (trans.) *The Adhyatma Ramayana.* Delhi: Cosmo, 2005.

O'Flaherty, Wendy Doniger (trans.). *Hindu Myths.* Delhi: Penguin, 1975.

Ohno Toru. *Burmese Ramayana.* Delhi: B.R. Publishing, 2000.

Phalgunadi, Gusti Putu. *Indonesian Ramayana: The Uttarakanda.* Delhi: Sundeep, 1999.

Richman, Paula (ed.). *Many Ramayanas: The Diversity of a Narrative Tradition in South Asia.* Berkeley: University of California Press, 1991.

Richman, Paula (ed.). *Questioning Ramayanas: A South Asian Tradition.* Delhi: Oxford University Press, 2003.

Sanyal, Sanjeev. *Land of the Seven Rivers: A Brief History of India's Geography.* Delhi: Penguin, 2012.

Saran, Malini and Vinod C. Khanna. *The Ramayana in Indonesia.* Delhi: Ravi Dayal Publisher, 2004.

Sattar, Arshia (trans.). *The Ramayana of Valmiki.* Delhi: Penguin, 1996.

Sen, Makhan Lal. *The Ramayana of Valmiki.* Delhi: Munshiram Manoharlal, 1978.

Singh, Avadhesh Kumar (ed.). *Ramayanas Through the Ages.* New Delhi: D.K. Printworld, 2007.

Singh, N.K. (ed.), Bolland, David (trans.). *The Ramayana in Kathakali Dance Drama.* New Delhi: Global Vision Publishing House, 2006.

Singh, Upinder. *A History of Ancient and Early Medieval India: From the Stone Age to the 12th Century.* Delhi: Pearson Longman, 2009.

Subramaniam, Kamala. *Ramayana.* Mumbai: Bharatiya Vidya Bhavan, 1992.

Sundaram, P.S. (trans.). *The Kamban Ramayana.* Delhi: Penguin, 2002.

Whaling, Frank. *The Rise of Religious Significance of Rama.* Delhi: Motilal Banarsidass, 1980.

Williams, Joanna. *The Two-Headed Deer: Illustrations of the Ramayana in Odisha.* Berkeley: University of California Press, 1996.

YOU MAY ALSO LIKE

DEVDUTT
PATTANAIK
INDIA'S BESTSELLING MYTHOLOGIST
SHIKHANDI
AND OTHER QUEER TALES THEY DON'T TELL YOU

DEVDUTT
PATTANAIK
INDIA'S BESTSELLING MYTHOLOGIST
THE BOOK
OF RAM

DEVDUTT
PATTANAIK
INDIA'S BESTSELLING MYTHOLOGIST
MYTH=MITHYA
DECODING HINDU MYTHOLOGY

DEVDUTT
PATTANAIK
INDIA'S BESTSELLING MYTHOLOGIST
THE
PREGNANT KING
A NOVEL

DEVDUTT PATTANAIK
JAYA
AN ILLUSTRATED RETELLING OF THE
MAHABHARATA

DEVDUTT PATTANAIK
OLYMPUS
AN INDIAN RETELLING OF THE
GREEK MYTHS

SHYAM
BHAGAVATA
DEVDUTT PATTANAIK
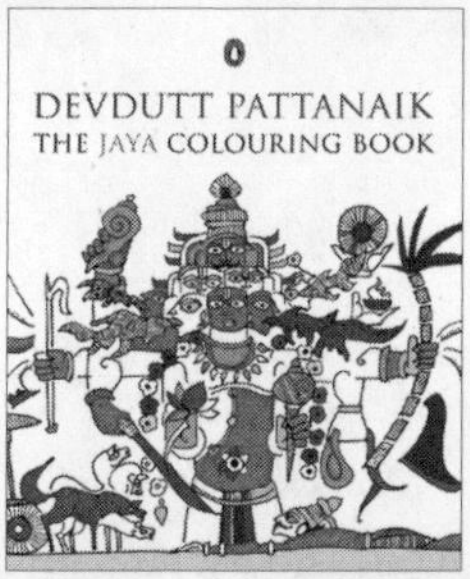
DEVDUTT PATTANAIK
THE JAYA COLOURING BOOK

DEVDUTT PATTANAIK
THE SITA COLOURING BOOK

DEVLOK
with Devdutt Pattanaik
Based on the first season of the popular television show

epic
DEVLOK
with Devdutt Pattanaik
2
Based on the second season of the popular
television show on the EPIC Channel

epic
DEVLOK
with Devdutt Pattanaik
3
Based on the third season of the popular
television show on the EPIC Channel

BY THE SAME AUTHOR

Myth=Mithya: Decoding Hindu Mythology
The Book of Ram
The Pregnant King
Jaya: An Illustrated Retelling of the Mahabharata
Shikhandi and Other Queer Tales They Don't Tell You
The Jaya Colouring Book
The Sita Colouring Book
Devlok with Devdutt Pattanaik
Olympus: An Indian Retelling of the Greek Myths
Devlok with Devdutt Pattanaik 2
Devlok with Devdutt Pattanaik 3
Shyam: An Illustrated Retelling of the Bhagavata
Devlok with Devdutt Pattanaik 3
Shyam: An Illustrated Retelling of the Bhagavata

SITA